## Praise for *New York Times* bestselling author Diana Palmer

"The popular Palmer has penned another winning novel, a perfect blend of romance and suspense."

—*Booklist* on *Lawman*

"Palmer knows how to make the sparks fly!"

—*Publishers Weekly*

"Diana Palmer is one of those authors whose books are always enjoyable. She throws in romance, suspense and a good story line."

—*The Romance Reader* on *Before Sunrise*

## Praise for *New York Times* bestselling author Brenda Jackson

"[Brenda] Jackson's characters are wonderful, strong, colorful and hot enough to burn the pages."

—*RT Book Reviews* on *Westmoreland's Way*

"Jackson is a master at writing."

—*Publishers Weekly* on *Sensual Confessions*

**Diana Palmer** is a multiple *New York Times* bestselling author of over one hundred books and one of the top ten romance writers in America. She has a gift for telling even the most sensual tales with charm and humor. Diana lives with her family in Cornelia, Georgia. Visit her website at dianapalmer.com.

**Brenda Jackson** is a *New York Times* bestselling author of more than one hundred romance titles. Brenda lives in Jacksonville, Florida, and divides her time between family, writing and traveling.

Email Brenda at authorbrendajackson@gmail.com or visit her on her website at brendajackson.net.

New York Times Bestselling Author

# DIANA PALMER

## WILL OF STEEL

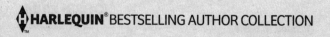

HARLEQUIN® BESTSELLING AUTHOR COLLECTION

ISBN-13: 978-0-373-28486-3

Will of Steel

Copyright © 2017 by Harlequin Books S.A.

The publisher acknowledges the copyright holders of the individual works as follows:

Will of Steel
Copyright © 2010 by Diana Palmer

Texas Wild
Copyright © 2012 by Brenda Streater Jackson

PLEASE RECYCLE
THIS PRODUCT IS RECYCLABLE

Recycling programs
for this product may
not exist in your area.

This edition published by arrangement with Harlequin Books S.A.

For questions and comments about the quality of this book, please contact us at CustomerService@Harlequin.com.

® and TM are trademarks of Harlequin Enterprises Limited or its corporate affiliates. Trademarks indicated with ® are registered in the United States Patent and Trademark Office, the Canadian Intellectual Property Office and in other countries.

Printed in U.S.A.

www.Harlequin.com

# CONTENTS

For a complete listing of books by Diana Palmer,
please visit dianapalmer.com.

# WILL OF STEEL

## Diana Palmer

To the readers, all of you,
many of whom are my friends on my Facebook
page. You make this job wonderful and worthwhile.
Thank you for your kindness and your support
and your affection through all the long years.
I am still your biggest fan.

# Chapter 1

He never liked coming here. The stupid calf followed him around, everywhere he went. He couldn't get the animal to leave him alone. Once, he'd whacked the calf with a soft fir tree branch, but that had led to repercussions. Its owner had a lot to say about animal cruelty and quoted the law to him. He didn't need her to quote the law. He was, after all, the chief of police in the small Montana town where they both lived.

Technically, of course, this wasn't town. It was about two miles outside the Medicine Ridge city limits. A small ranch in Hollister, Montana, that included two clear, cold trout streams and half a mountain. Her uncle and his uncle had owned it jointly during their lifetimes. The two of them, best friends forever, had recently died, his uncle from a heart attack and hers, about a month later, in an airplane crash en route to a cattleman's convention. The property was set to go up on the auction block, and a California real estate developer was skulking in the wings, waiting to put in the winning bid. He was going to build a rich man's resort here, banking on those pure trout streams to bring in the business.

If Hollister Police Chief Theodore Graves had his way, the man would never set foot on the property. She felt that way, too. But the wily old men had placed a clause in both their wills pertaining to ownership of the land in question. The clause in her uncle's will had been a source of shock to Graves and the girl when the amused attorney read it out to them. It had provoked a war of words every time he walked in the door.

"I'm not marrying you," Jillian Sanders told him firmly the minute he stepped on the porch. "I don't care if I have to live in the barn with Sammy."

Sammy was the calf.

He looked down at her from his far superior height with faint arrogance. "No problem. I don't think the grammar school would give you a hall pass to marry me anyway."

Her pert nose wrinkled. "Well, you'd have to get permission from the old folks' home, and I'll bet you wouldn't get it, either!"

It was a standing joke. He was thirty-one to her almost twenty-one. They were completely mismatched. She was small and blonde and blue-eyed, he was tall and dark and black-eyed. He liked guns and working on his old truck when he wasn't performing his duties as chief of police in the small Montana community where they lived. She liked making up recipes for new sweets and he couldn't stand anything sweet except pound cake. She also hated guns and noise.

"If you don't marry me, Sammy will be featured on

the menu in the local café, and you'll have to live in the woods in a cave," he pointed out.

That didn't help her disposition. She glared at him. It wasn't her fault that she had no family left alive. Her parents had died not long after she was born of an influenza outbreak. Her uncle had taken her in and raised her, but he was not in good health and had heart problems. Jillian had taken care of him as long as he was alive, fussing over his diet and trying to concoct special dishes to make him comfortable. But he'd died not of ill health, but in a light airplane crash on his way to a cattle convention. He didn't keep many cattle anymore, but he'd loved seeing friends at the conferences, and he loved to attend them. She missed him. It was lonely on the ranch. Of course, if she had to marry Rambo, here, it would be less lonely.

She glared at him, as if everything bad in her life could be laid at his door. "I'd almost rather live in the cave. I hate guns!" she added vehemently, noting the one he wore, old-fashioned style, on his hip in a holster. "You could blow a hole through a concrete wall with that thing!"

"Probably," he agreed.

"Why can't you carry something small, like your officers do?"

"I like to make an impression," he returned, tongue-in-cheek.

It took her a minute to get the insinuation. She glared at him even more.

He sighed. "I haven't had lunch," he said, and managed to look as if he were starving.

"There's a good café right downtown."

"Which will be closing soon because they can't get a

cook," he said with disgust. "Damnedest thing, we live in a town where every woman cooks, but nobody wants to do it for the public. I guess I'll starve. I burn water."

It was the truth. He lived on takeout from the local café and frozen dinners. He glowered at her. "I guess marrying you would save my life. At least you can cook."

She gave him a smug look. "Yes, I can. And the local café isn't closing. They hired a cook just this morning."

"They did?" he exclaimed. "Who did they get?"

She averted her eyes. "I didn't catch her name, but they say she's talented. So you won't starve, I guess."

"Yes, but that doesn't help our situation here," he pointed out. His sensual lips made a thin line. "I don't want to get married."

"Neither do I," she shot back. "I've hardly even dated anybody!"

His eyebrows went up. "You're twenty years old. Almost twenty-one."

"Yes, and my uncle was suspicious of every man who came near me," she returned. "He made it impossible for me to leave the house."

His black eyes twinkled. "As I recall, you did escape once."

She turned scarlet. Yes, she had, with an auditor who'd come to do the books for a local lawyer's office. The man, much older than her and more sophisticated, had charmed her. She'd trusted him, just as she'd trusted another man two years earlier. The auditor had taken her back to his motel room to get something he forgot. Or so he'd told her. Actually he'd locked the door and proceeded to try to remove her clothes. He was very nice about it, he was just insistent.

But he didn't know that Jillian had emotional scars already from a man trying to force her. She'd been so afraid. She'd really liked the man, trusted him. Uncle John hadn't. He always felt guilty about what she'd been through because of his hired man. She was underage, and he told her to stay away from the man.

But she'd had stars in her eyes because the man had flirted with her when she'd gone with Uncle John to see his attorney about a land deal. She'd thought he was different, nothing like Uncle John's hired man who had turned nasty.

He'd talked to her on the phone several times and persuaded her to go out with him. Infatuated, she sneaked out when Uncle John went to bed. But she landed herself in very hot water when the man got overly amorous. She'd managed to get her cell phone out and punched in 911. The result had been…unforgettable.

"They did get the door fixed, I believe…?" she said, letting her voice trail off.

He glared at her. "It was locked."

"There's such a thing as keys," she pointed out.

"While I was finding one, you'd have been…"

She flushed again. She moved uncomfortably. "Yes, well, I did thank you. At the time."

"And a traveling mathematician learned the dangers of trying to seduce teenagers in my town."

She couldn't really argue. She'd been sixteen at the time, and Theodore's quick reaction had saved her honor. The auditor hadn't known her real age. She knew he'd never have asked her out if he had any idea she was under legal age. He'd been the only man she had a real interest in, for her whole life. He'd quit the firm he worked for, so he never had to come back to Hollister. She felt bad about it. The whole fiasco was her own fault.

The sad thing was that it wasn't her first scary episode with an older man. The first, at fifteen, had scarred her. She'd thought that she could trust a man again because she was crazy about the auditor. But the auditor became the icing on the cake of her withdrawal from the world of dating for good. She'd really liked him, trusted him, had been infatuated with him. He wasn't even a bad man, not like that other one…

"The judge did let him go with a severe reprimand about making sure of a girl's age and not trying to persuade her into an illegal act. But he could have gone to prison, and it would have been my fault," she recalled. She didn't mention the man who had gone to prison for assaulting her. Ted didn't know about that and she wasn't going to tell him.

"Don't look to me to have any sympathy for him," he said tersely. "Even if you'd been of legal age, he had no right to try to coerce you."

"Point taken."

"Your uncle should have let you get out more," he said reluctantly.

"I never understood why he kept me so close to home," she replied thoughtfully. She knew it wasn't all because of her bad experience.

His black eyes twinkled. "Oh, that's easy. He was saving you for me."

She gaped at him.

He chuckled. "He didn't actually say so, but you must have realized from his will that he'd planned a future for us for some time."

A lot of things were just becoming clear. She was speechless, for once.

He grinned. "He grew you in a hothouse just for me, little orchid," he teased.

"Obviously your uncle never did the same for me," she said scathingly.

He shrugged, and his eyes twinkled even more. "One of us has to know what to do when the time comes," he pointed out.

She flushed. "I think we could work it out without diagrams."

He leaned closer. "Want me to look it up and see if I can find some for you?"

"I'm not marrying you!" she yelled.

He shrugged. "Suit yourself. Maybe you can put up some curtains and lay a few rugs and the cave will be more comfortable." He glanced out the window. "Poor Sammy," he added sadly. "His future is less, shall we say, palatable."

"For the last time, Sammy is not a bull, he's a cow. She's a cow," she faltered.

"Sammy is a bull's name."

"She looked like a Sammy," she said stubbornly. "When she's grown, she'll give milk."

"Only when she's calving."

"Like you know," she shot back.

"I belong to the cattleman's association," he reminded her. "They tell us stuff like that."

"I belong to it, too, and no, they don't, you learn it from raising cattle!"

He tugged his wide-brimmed hat over his eyes. "It's useless, arguing with a blond fence post. I'm going back to work."

"Don't shoot anybody."

"I've never shot anybody."

"Ha!" she burst out. "What about that bank robber?"

"Oh. Him. Well, he shot at me first."

"Stupid of him."

He grinned. "That's just what he said, when I visited him in the hospital. He missed. I didn't. And he got sentenced for assault on a police officer as well as the bank heist."

She frowned. "He swore he'd make you pay for that. What if he gets out?"

"Ten to twenty, and he's got priors," he told her. "I'll be in a nursing home for real by the time he gets out."

She glowered up at him. "People are always getting out of jail on technicalities. All he needs is a good lawyer."

"Good luck to him getting one on what he earns making license plates."

"The state provides attorneys for people who can't pay."

He gasped. "Thank you for telling me! I didn't know!"

"Why don't you go to work?" she asked, irritated.

"I've been trying to, but you won't stop flirting with me."

She gasped, but for real. "I am *not* flirting with you!"

He grinned. His black eyes were warm and sensuous as they met hers. "Yes, you are." He moved a step closer. "We could do an experiment. To see if we were chemically suited to each other."

She looked at him, puzzled, for a few seconds, until it dawned on her what he was suggesting. She moved back two steps, deliberately, and her high cheekbones flushed again. "I don't want to do any experiments with you!"

He sighed. "Okay. But it's going to be a very lonely marriage if you keep thinking that way, Jake."

"Don't call me Jake! My name is Jillian."

He shrugged. "You're a Jake." He gave her a long look, taking in her ragged jeans and bulky gray sweatshirt and boots with curled-up toes from use. Her long blond hair was pinned up firmly into a topknot, and she wore no makeup. "Tomboy," he added accusingly.

She averted her eyes. There were reasons she didn't accentuate her feminine attributes, and she didn't want to discuss the past with him. It wasn't the sort of thing she felt comfortable talking about with anyone. It made Uncle John look bad, and he was dead. He'd cried about his lack of judgment in hiring Davy Harris. But it was too late by then.

Ted was getting some sort of vibrations from her. She was keeping something from him. He didn't know what, but he was almost certain of it.

His teasing manner went into eclipse. He became a policeman again. "Is there something you want to talk to me about, Jake?" he asked in the soft tone he used with children.

She wouldn't meet his eyes. "It wouldn't help."

"It might."

She grimaced. "I don't know you well enough to tell you some things."

"If you marry me, you will."

"We've had this discussion," she pointed out.

"Poor Sammy."

"Stop that!" she muttered. "I'll find her a home. I could always ask John Callister if he and his wife, Sassy, would let her live with them."

"On their ranch where they raise purebred cattle."

"Sammy has purebred bloodlines on both sides," she muttered. "Her mother was a purebred Hereford cow and her father was a purebred Angus bull."

"And Sammy is a 'black baldy,'" he agreed, giving it the hybrid name. "But that doesn't make her a purebred cow."

"Semantics!" she shot back.

He grinned. "There you go, throwing those one-dollar words at me again."

"Don't pretend to be dumb, if you please. I happen to know that you got a degree in physics during your stint with the army."

He raised both thick black eyebrows. "Should I be flattered?"

"Why?"

"That you take an interest in my background."

"Everybody knows. It isn't just me."

He shrugged.

"Why are you a small-town police chief, with that sort of education?" she asked suddenly.

"Because I don't have the temperament for scientific research," he said simply. "Besides, you don't get to play with guns in a laboratory."

"I hate guns."

"You said."

"I really mean it." She shivered dramatically. "You could shoot somebody by accident. Didn't one of your patrolmen drop his pistol in a grocery store and it went off?"

He looked grim. "Yes, he did. He was off duty and carrying his little .32 wheel gun in his pants pocket. He reached for change and it fell out and discharged."

He pursed his lips. "A mistake I can guarantee he will never make again."

"So his wife said. You are one mean man when you lose your temper, do you know that?"

"The pistol discharged into a display of cans, fortunately for him, and we only had to pay damages to the store. But it could have discharged into a child, or a grown-up, with tragic results. There are reasons why they make holsters for guns."

She looked at his pointedly. "That one sure is fancy," she noted, indicating the scrollwork on the soft tan leather. It also sported silver conchos and fringe.

"My cousin made it for me."

"Tanika?" she asked, because she knew his cousin, a full-blooded Cheyenne who lived down near Hardin.

"Yes." He smiled. "She thinks practical gear should have beauty."

"She's very gifted." She smiled. "She makes some gorgeous *parfleche* bags. I've seen them at the trading post in Hardin, near the Little Bighorn Battlefield." They were rawhide bags with beaded trim and fringe, incredibly beautiful and useful for transporting items in the old days for native people.

"Thank you," he said abruptly.

She lifted her eyebrows. "For what?"

"For not calling it the Custer Battlefield."

A lot of people did. He had nothing against Custer, but his ancestry was Cheyenne. He had relatives who had died in the Little Bighorn Battle and, later, at Wounded Knee. Custer was a sore spot with him. Some tourists didn't seem to realize that Native Americans considered that people other than Custer's troops were killed in the battle.

She smiled. "I think I had a Sioux ancestor."

"You look like it," he drawled, noting her fair coloring.

"My cousin Rabby is half and half, and he has blond hair and gray eyes," she reminded him.

"I guess so." He checked the big watch on his wrist. "I've got to be in court for a preliminary hearing. Better go."

"I'm baking a pound cake."

He hesitated. "Is that an invitation?"

"You did say you were starving."

"Yes, but you can't live on cake."

"So I'll fry a steak and some potatoes to go with it."

His lips pulled up into a smile. "Sounds nice. What time?"

"About six? Barring bank robberies and insurgent attacks, of course."

"I'm sure we won't have one today." He considered her invitation. "The Callisters brought me a flute back from Cancún when they went on their honeymoon. I could bring it and serenade you."

She flushed a little. The flute and its connection with courting in the Native American world was quite well-known. "That would be nice."

"It would?"

"I thought you were leaving." She didn't quite trust that smile.

"I guess I am. About six?"

"Yes."

"I'll see you then." He paused with his hand on the doorknob. "Should I wear my tuxedo?"

"It's just steak."

"No dancing afterward?" he asked, disappointed.

"Not unless you want to build a bonfire outside and dance around it." She frowned. "I think I know one or two steps from the women's dances."

He glared at her. "Ballroom dancing isn't done around campfires."

"You can do ballroom dances?" she asked, impressed.

"Of course I can."

"Waltz, polka…?"

"Tango," he said stiffly.

Her eyes twinkled. "Tango? Really?"

"Really. One of my friends in the service learned it down in Argentina. He taught me."

"What an image that brings to mind—" she began, tongue-in-cheek.

"He didn't teach me by dancing with me!" he shot back. "He danced with a girl."

"Well, I should hope so," she agreed.

"I'm leaving."

"You already said."

"This time, I mean it." He walked out.

"Six!" she called after him.

He threw up a hand. He didn't look back.

Jillian closed the door and leaned back against it. She was a little apprehensive, but after all, she had to marry somebody. She knew Theodore Graves better than she knew any other men. And, despite their quarreling, they got along fairly well.

The alternative was to let some corporation build a holiday resort here in Hollister, and it would be a disaster for local ranching. Resorts brought in all sorts of amusement, plus hotels and gas stations and businesses. It would be a boon for the economy, but Hollister would lose its rural, small-town appeal. It wasn't something Jillian would enjoy and she was certain that other people would feel the same. She loved the forests with their tall lodgepole pines, and the shallow, diamond-bright trout streams where she loved to fish when she had free time. Occasionally Theodore would bring over his spinning reel and join her. Then they'd work side by side, scaling and filleting fish and frying them, along with hush puppies, in a vat of hot oil. Her mouth watered, just thinking about it.

She wandered into the kitchen. She'd learned to cook from one of her uncle's rare girlfriends. It had delighted her. She might be a tomboy, but she had a natural affinity for flour and she could make bread from scratch. It amazed her how few people could. The feel of the dough, soft and smooth, was a gift to her fingertips when she kneaded and punched and worked it. The smell of fresh bread in the kitchen was a delight for the senses. She always had fresh homemade butter to go on it, which she purchased from an elderly widow just down the road. Theodore loved fresh bread. She was making a batch for tonight, to go with the pound cake.

She pulled out her bin of flour and got down some yeast from the shelf. It took a long time to make bread from scratch, but it was worth it.

She hadn't changed into anything fancy, although she did have on a new pair of blue jeans and a pink checked shirt that buttoned up. She also tucked a pink ribbon into her long blond hair, which she tidied into a bun on top of her head. She wasn't elegant, or beautiful, but she could at least look like a girl when she tried.

And he noticed the minute he walked in the door. He cocked his head and stared down at her with amusement.

"You're a girl," he said with mock surprise.

She glared up at him. "I'm a woman."

He pursed his lips. "Not yet."

She flushed. She tried for a comeback but she couldn't fumble one out of her flustered mind.

"Sorry," he said gently, and became serious when he noted her reaction to the teasing. "That wasn't fair. Especially since you went to all the trouble to make me fresh rolls." He lifted his head and sniffed appreciably.

"How did you know that?"

He tapped his nose. "I have a superlative sense of smell. Did I ever tell you about the time I tracked a wanted murderer by the way he smelled?" he added. "He was wearing some gosh-awful cheap cologne. I just followed the scent and walked up to him with my gun out. He'd spent a whole day covering his trail and stumbling over rocks to throw me off the track. He was so shocked when I walked into his camp that he just gave up without a fight."

"Did you tell him that his smell gave him away?" she asked, chuckling.

"No. I didn't want him to mention it to anybody when he went to jail. No need to give criminals a heads-up about something like that."

"Native Americans are great trackers," she commented.

He glowered down at her. "Anybody can be a good tracker. It comes from training, not ancestry."

"Well, aren't you touchy," she exclaimed.

He averted his eyes. He shrugged. "Banes has been at it again."

"You should assign him to school crossings. He hates that," she advised.

"No, he doesn't. His new girlfriend is a widow. She's

got a little boy, and Banes has suddenly become his hero. He'd love to work the school crossing."

"Still, you could find some unpleasant duty to assign him. Didn't he say once that he hates being on traffic detail at ball games?"

He brightened. "You know, he did say that."

"See? An opportunity presents itself." She frowned. "Why are we looking for ways to punish him this time?"

"He brought in a new book on the Little Bighorn Battle and showed me where it said Crazy Horse wasn't in the fighting."

She gave him a droll look. "Oh, sure."

He grimaced. "Every so often, some writer who never saw a real Native American gets a bunch of hearsay evidence together and writes a book about how he's the only one who knows the true story of some famous battle. This guy also said that Custer was nuts and had a hand in the post trader scandal where traders were cheating the Sioux and Cheyenne."

"Nobody who reads extensively about Custer would believe he had a hand in something so dishonest," she scoffed. "He went to court and testified against President Ulysses S. Grant's own brother in that corruption trial, as I recall. Why would he take such a risk if he was personally involved in it?"

"My thoughts exactly," he said, "and I told Banes so."

"What did Banes say to that?"

"He quoted the author's extensive background in military history."

She gave him a suspicious look. "Yes? What sort of background?"

"He's an expert in the Napoleonic Wars."

"Great! What does that have to do with the campaign

on the Greasy Grass?" she asked, which referred to the Lakota name for the battle.

"Not a damned thing," he muttered. "You can be brilliant in your own field of study, but it's another thing to do your research from a standing start and come to all the wrong conclusions. Banes said the guy used period newspapers and magazines for part of his research."

"The Lakota and Cheyenne, as I recall, didn't write about current events," she mused.

He chuckled. "No, they didn't have newspaper reporters back then. So it was all from the cavalry's point of view, or that of politicians. History is the story of mankind written by the victors."

"Truly."

He smiled. "You're pretty good on local history."

"That's because I'm related to people who helped make it."

"Me, too." He cocked his head. "I ought to take you down to Hardin and walk the battlefield with you sometime," he said.

Her eyes lit up. "I'd love that."

"So would I."

"There's a trading post," she recalled.

"They have some beautiful things there."

"Made by local talent," she agreed. She sighed. "I get so tired of so-called Native American art made in China. Nothing against the Chinese. I mean, they have aboriginal peoples, too. But if you're going to sell things that are supposed to be made by tribes in this country, why import them?"

"Beats me. Ask somebody better informed."

"You're a police chief," she pointed out. "There isn't supposed to be anybody better informed."

He grinned. "Thanks."

She curtsied.

He frowned. "Don't you own a dress?"

"Sure. It's in my closet." She pursed her lips. "I wore it to graduation."

"Spare me!"

"I guess I could buy a new one."

"I guess you could. I mean, if we're courting, it will look funny if you don't wear a dress."

"Why?"

He blinked. "You going to get married in blue jeans?"

"For the last time, I am not going to marry you."

He took off his wide-brimmed hat and laid it on the hall table. "We can argue about that later. Right now, we need to eat some of that nice, warm, fresh bread before it gets cold and butter won't melt on it. Shouldn't we?" he added with a grin.

She laughed. "I guess we should."

## Chapter 2

The bread was as delicious as he'd imagined it would be. He closed his eyes, savoring the taste.

"You could cook, if you'd just try," she said.

"Not really. I can't measure stuff properly."

"I could teach you."

"Why do I need to learn how, when you do it so well already?" he asked reasonably.

"You live alone," she began.

He raised an eyebrow. "Not for long."

"For the tenth time today…"

"The California guy was in town today," he said grimly. "He came by the office to see me."

"He did?" She felt apprehensive.

He nodded as he bit into another slice of buttered bread with perfect white teeth. "He's already approached contractors for bids to build his housing project." He bit the words off as he was biting the bread.

"Oh."

Jet-black eyes pierced hers. "I told him about the clause in the will."

"What did he say?"

"That he'd heard you wouldn't marry me."

She grimaced.

"He was strutting around town like a tom turkey," he added. He finished the bread and sipped coffee. His eyes closed as he savored it. "You make great coffee, Jake!" he exclaimed. "Most people wave the coffee over water. You could stand up a spoon in this."

"I like it strong, too," she agreed. She studied his hard, lean face. "I guess you live on it when you have cases that keep you out all night tracking. There have been two or three of those this month alone."

He nodded. "Our winter festival brings in people from all over the country. Some of them see the mining company's bankroll as a prime target."

"Not to mention the skeet-and-trap-shooting regional championships," she said. "I've heard that thieves actually follow the shooters around and get license plate numbers of cars whose owners have the expensive guns."

"They're targets, all right."

"Why would somebody pay five figures for a gun?" she wondered out loud.

He laughed. "You don't shoot in competition, so it's no use trying to explain it to you."

"You compete," she pointed out. "You don't have a gun that expensive and you're a triple-A shooter."

He shrugged. "It isn't that I wouldn't like to have one. But unless I take up bank robbing, I'm not likely to be able to afford one, either. The best I can do is borrow one for the big competitions."

Her eyes popped. "You know somebody who'll loan you a fifty-thousand-dollar shotgun?"

He laughed. "Well, actually, yes, I do. He's police chief of a small town down in Texas. He used to do shotgun competitions when he was younger, and he still has the hardware."

"And he loans you the gun."

"He isn't attached to it, like some owners are. Although, you'd never get him to loan his sniper kit," he chuckled.

"Excuse me?"

He leaned toward her. "He was a covert assassin in his shady past."

"Really?" She was excited by the news.

He frowned. "What do women find so fascinating about men who shoot people?"

She blinked. "It's not that."

"Then what is it?"

She hesitated, trying to put it into words. "Men who have been in battles have tested themselves in a way most people never have to," she began slowly. "They learn their own natures. They… I can't exactly express it…"

"They learn what they're made of, right where they live and breathe," he commented. "Under fire, you're always afraid. But you harness the fear and use it, attack when you'd rather run. You learn the meaning of courage. It isn't the absence of fear. It's fear management, at its best. You do your duty."

"Nicely said, Chief Graves," she said admiringly, and grinned.

"Well, I know a thing or two about being shot at," he reminded her. "I was in the first wave in the second incursion in the Middle East. Then I became a police officer and then a police chief."

"You met the other police chief at one of those conventions, I'll bet," she commented.

"Actually I met him at the FBI academy during a training session on hostage negotiation," he corrected. "He was teaching it."

"My goodness. He can negotiate?"

"He did most of his negotiations with a gun before he was a Texas Ranger," he laughed.

"He was a Ranger, too?"

"Yes. And a cyber-crime expert for a Texas D.A., and a merc, and half a dozen other interesting things. He can also dance. He won a tango contest in Argentina, and that's saying something. Tango and Argentina go together like coffee and cream."

She propped her chin in her hands. "A man who can do the tango. It boggles the mind. I've only ever seen a couple of men do it in movies." She smiled. "Al Pacino in *Scent of a Woman* was my favorite."

He grinned. "Not the 'governator' in *True Lies?*"

She glared at him. "I'm sure he was doing his best."

He shook his head. "I watched Rudolph Valentino do it in an old silent film," he sighed. "Real style."

"It's a beautiful dance."

He gave her a long look. "There's a new Latin dance club in Billings."

"What?" she exclaimed with pure surprise.

"No kidding. A guy from New York moved out here to retire. He'd been in ballroom competition most of his life and he got bored. So he organized a dance band and opened up a dance club. People come up from Wyoming and across from the Dakotas just to hear the band and do the dances." He toyed with his coffee cup. "Suppose you and I go up there and try it out? I can teach you the tango."

Her heart skipped. It was the first time, despite all the banter, that he'd ever suggested taking her on a date.

He scowled when she hesitated.

"I'd love to," she blurted out.

His face relaxed. He smiled again. "Okay. Saturday?"

She nodded. Her heart was racing. She felt breathless.

She was so young, he thought, looking at her. He hesitated.

"They don't have grammar school on Saturdays," she quipped, "so I won't need an excuse from the principal to skip class."

He burst out laughing. "Is that how I looked? Sorry."

"I'm almost twenty-one," she pointed out. "I know that seems young to you, but I've had a lot of responsibility. Uncle John could be a handful, and I was the only person taking care of him for most of my life."

"That's true. Responsibility matures people pretty quick."

"You'd know," she said softly, because he'd taken wonderful care of his grandmother and then the uncle who'd owned half this ranch.

He shrugged. "I don't think there's a choice about looking after people you love."

"Neither do I."

He gave her an appraising look. "You going to the

club in blue jeans and a shirt?" he asked. "Because if you are, I plan to wear my uniform."

She raised both eyebrows.

"Or have you forgotten what happened the last time I wore my uniform to a social event?" he added.

She glowered at him.

"Is it my fault if people think of me as a target the minute they realize what I do for a living?" he asked.

"You didn't have to anoint him with punch."

"Sure I did. He was so hot under the collar about a speeding ticket my officer gave him that he needed instant cooling off."

She laughed. "Your patrolman is still telling that story."

"With some exaggerations he added to it," Theodore chuckled.

"It cured the guy of complaining to you."

"Yes, it did. But if I wear my uniform to a dance club where people drink, there's bound to be at least one guy who thinks I'm a target."

She sighed.

"And since you're with me, you'd be right in the thick of it." He pursed his lips. "You wouldn't like to be featured in a riot, would you?"

"Not in Billings, no," she agreed.

"Then you could wear a skirt, couldn't you?"

"I guess it wouldn't kill me," she said, but reluctantly.

He narrowed his eyes as he looked at her. There was some reason she didn't like dressing like a woman. He wished he could ask her about it, but she was obviously uncomfortable discussing personal issues with him. Maybe it was too soon. He did wonder if she still had scars from her encounter with the auditor.

He smiled gently. "Something demure," he added. "I won't expect you to look like a pole dancer, okay?"

She laughed. "Okay."

He loved the way she looked when she smiled. Her whole face took on a radiance that made her pretty. She didn't smile often. Well, neither did he. His job was a somber one, most of the time.

"I'll see you about six, then."

She nodded. She was wondering how she was going to afford something new to wear to a fancy nightclub, but she would never have admitted it to him.

She ran into Sassy Callister in town while she was trying to find something presentable on the bargain table at the single women's clothing store.

"You're looking for a dress?" Sassy exclaimed. She'd known Jillian all her life, and she'd never seen her in anything except jeans and shirts. She even wore a pant-suit to church when she went.

Jillian glared at her. "I do have legs."

"That wasn't what I meant." She chuckled. "I gather Ted's taking you out on a real date, huh?"

Jillian went scarlet. "I never said…!"

"Oh, we all know about the will," Sassy replied easily. "It's sensible, for the two of you to get married and keep the ranch in the family. Nobody wants to see some fancy resort being set up here," she added, "with outsiders meddling in our local politics and throwing money around to get things the way they think they should be."

Jillian's eyes twinkled. "Imagine you complaining about the rich, when you just married one of the richest men in Montana."

"You know what I mean," Sassy laughed. "And I'll

remind you that I didn't know he was rich when I accepted his proposal."

"A multimillionaire pretending to be a ranch foreman." Jillian shook her head. "It came as a shock to a lot of us when we found out who he really was."

"I assure you that it was more of a shock to me," came the amused reply. "I tried to back out of it, but he wouldn't let me. He said that money was an accessory, not a character trait. You should meet his brother and sister-in-law," she added with a grin. "Her parents were missionaries and her aunt is a nun. Oh, and her godfather is one of the most notorious ex-mercenaries who ever used a gun."

"My goodness!"

"But they're all very down-to-earth. They don't strut, is what I mean."

Jillian giggled. "I get it."

Sassy gave her a wise look. "You want something nice for that date, but you're strained to the gills trying to manage on what your uncle left you."

Jillian started to deny it, but she gave up. Sassy was too sweet to lie to. "Yes," she confessed. "I was working for old Mrs. Rogers at the florist shop. Then she died and the shop closed." She sighed. "Not many jobs going in a town this small. You'd know all about that," she added, because Sassy had worked for a feed store and was assaulted by her boss. Fortunately she was rescued by her soon-to-be husband and the perpetrator had been sent to jail. But it was the only job Sassy could get. Hollister was very small.

Sassy nodded. "I wouldn't want to live anyplace else, though. Even if I had to commute back and forth to Billings to get a job." She laughed. "I considered that, but

I didn't think my old truck would get me that far." Her eyes twinkled. "Chief Graves said that if he owned a piece of junk like I was driving, he'd be the first to agree to marry a man who could afford to replace it for me."

Jillian burst out laughing. "I can imagine what you said to that."

She laughed, too. "I just expressed the thought that he wouldn't marry John Callister for a truck." She cocked her head. "He really is a catch, you know. Theodore Graves is the stuff of legends around here. He's honest and kindhearted and a very mean man to make an enemy of. He'd take care of you."

"Well, he needs more taking care of than I do," came the droll reply. "At least I can cook."

"Didn't you apply for the cook's job at the restaurant?"

"I did. I got it, too, but you can't tell Theodore."

"I won't. But why can't I?"

Jillian sighed. "In case things don't work out, I want to have a means of supporting myself. He'll take it personally if he thinks I got a job before he even proposed."

"He's old-fashioned."

"Nothing wrong with that," Jillian replied with a smile.

"Of course not. It's just that some men have to be hit over the head so they'll accept that modern women can have outside interests without giving up family. Come over here."

She took Jillian's arm and pulled her to one side. "Everything in here is a three-hundred-percent markup," she said under her breath. "I love Jessie, but she's overpriced. You're coming home with me. We're the same size and I've got a closet full of stuff you can wear. You can borrow anything you like. Heck, you can have what you like. I'll never wear all of it anyway."

Jillian flushed red and stammered, "No, I couldn't...!"

"You could and you're going to. Now come on!"

Jillian was transported to the Callister ranch in a Jaguar. She was so fascinated with it that she didn't hear half of what her friend was saying.

"Look at all these gadgets!" she exclaimed. "And this is real wood on the dash!"

"Yes," Sassy laughed. "I acted the same as you, the first time I rode in it. My old battered truck seemed so pitiful afterward."

"I like my old car. But this is amazing," she replied, touching the silky wood.

"I know."

"It's so nice of you to do this," Jillian replied. "Theodore wanted me to wear a skirt. I don't even own one."

Sassy looked at her briefly. "You should tell him, Jilly."

She flushed and averted her eyes. "Nobody knows but you and your mother. And I know you won't say anything."

"Not unless you said I could," Sassy replied. "But it could cause you some problems later on. Especially after you're married."

Jillian clenched her teeth. "I'll cross that bridge if I come to it. I may not marry Theodore. We may be able to find a way to break the will."

"One, maybe. Two, never."

That was true. Both old men had left ironclad wills with clauses about the disposition of the property if Theodore and Jillian refused to get married.

"The old buzzards!" Jillian burst out. "Why did they have to complicate things like that? Theodore and I could have found a way to deal with the problem on our own!"

"I don't know. Neither of you is well-off, and that California developer has tons of money. I'll bet he's already trying to find a way to get to one of you about buying the ranch outright once you inherit."

"He'll never get it," she said stubbornly.

Sassy was going to comment that rich people with intent sometimes knew shady ways to make people do what they wanted them to. But the developer wasn't local and he didn't have any information he could use to blackmail either Theodore or Jillian, so he probably couldn't force them to sell to him. He'd just sit and wait and hope they couldn't afford to keep it. Fat chance, Sassy thought solemnly. She and John would bail them out if they had to. No way was some out-of-state fat cat taking over Jillian's land. Not after all she'd gone through in her young life.

Maybe it was a good thing Theodore didn't know everything about his future potential wife. But Jillian was setting herself up for some real heartbreak if she didn't level with him. After all, he was in law enforcement. He could dig into court records and find things that most people didn't have access to. He hadn't been in town when Jillian faced her problems, he'd been away at the FBI Academy on a training mission. And since only Sassy and her mother, Mrs. Peale, had been involved, nobody else except the prosecuting attorney and the judge and the public defender had knowledge about the case. Not that any of them would disclose it.

She was probably worrying unnecessarily. She smiled at Jillian. "You are right. He'll never get the ranch," she agreed.

They pulled up at the house. It had been given a makeover and it looked glorious.

"You've done a lot of work on this place," Jillian commented. "I remember what it looked like before."

"So do I. John wanted to go totally green here, so we have solar power and wind generators. And the electricity in the barn runs on methane from the cattle refuse."

"It's just fantastic," Jillian commented. "Expensive, too, I'll bet."

"That's true, but the initial capital outlay was the highest. It will pay for itself over the years."

"And you'll have lower utility bills than the rest of us," Jillian sighed, thinking about her upcoming one. It had been a colder than usual winter. Heating oil was expensive.

"Stop worrying," Sassy told her. "Things work out."

"You think?"

They walked down the hall toward the master bedroom. "How's your mother?" Jillian asked.

"Doing great. She got glowing reports from her last checkup," Sassy said. The cancer had been contained and her mother hadn't had a recurrence, thanks to John's interference at a critical time. "She always asks about you."

"Your mother is the nicest person I know, next to you. How about Selene?"

The little girl was one Mrs. Peale had adopted. She was in grammar school, very intelligent and with definite goals. "She's reading books about the Air Force," Sassy laughed. "She wants to be a fighter pilot."

"Wow!"

"That's what we said, but she's very focused. She's good at math and science, too. We think she may end up being an engineer."

"She's smart."

"Very."

Sassy opened the closet and started pulling out dresses and skirts and blouses in every color under the sun.

Jillian just stared at them, stunned. "I've never seen so many clothes outside a department store," she stammered.

Sassy chuckled. "Neither did I before I married John. He spoils me rotten. Every birthday and holiday I get presents from him. Pick something out."

"You must have favorites that you don't want to loan," Jillian began.

"I do. That's why they're still in the closet," she said with a grin.

"Oh."

Sassy was eyeing her and then the clothes on the bed. "How about this?" She picked up a patterned blue skirt, very long and silky, with a pale blue silk blouse that had puffy sleeves and a rounded neckline. It looked demure, but it was a witchy ensemble. "Try that on. Let's see how it looks."

Jillian's hands fumbled. She'd never put on something so expensive. It fit her like a glove, and it felt good to move in, as so many clothes didn't. She remarked on that.

"Most clothes on the rack aren't constructed to fit exactly, and the less expensive they are, the worse the fit," Sassy said. "I know, because I bought clothes off the sales rack all my life before I married. I was shocked to find that expensive clothes actually fit. And when they do, they make you look better. You can see for yourself."

Jillian did. Glancing in the mirror, she was shocked to find that the skirt put less emphasis on her full hips and more on her narrow waist. The blouse, on the other hand, made her small breasts look just a little bigger.

"Now, with your hair actually down and curled, instead of screwed up into that bun," Sassy continued, pulling out hairpins as she went and reaching for a brush, "you'll look so different that Ted may not even recognize you. What a difference!"

It was. With her long blond hair curling around her shoulders, she looked really pretty.

"Is that me?" she asked, shocked.

Sassy grinned. "Sure is."

She turned to her friend, fighting tears. "It's so nice of you," she began.

Sassy hugged her. "Friends look out for each other."

They hadn't been close friends, because Sassy's home problems had made that impossible before her marriage. But they were growing closer now. It was nice to have someone she could talk to.

She drew away and wiped at her eyes. "Sorry. Didn't mean to do that."

"You're a nice person, Jilly," Sassy told her gently. "You'd do the same for me in a heartbeat, if our situations were reversed, and you know it."

"I certainly would."

"I've got some curlers. Let's put up your hair in them and then we can snap beans."

"You've got beans in the middle of winter?" Jillian exclaimed.

"From the organic food market," she laughed. "I have them shipped in. You can take some home and plant up. Ted might like beans and ham hocks."

"Even if he didn't, I sure would. I'll bet it's your own pork."

"It is. We like organic all the way. Put your jeans back on and we'll wash your hair and set it. It's thin enough that it can dry while we work."

And it did. They took the curlers out a couple of hours later. Jillian was surprised at the difference a few curls made in her appearance.

"Makeup next," Sassy told her, grinning. "This is fun!"

"Fun and educational," Jillian said, still reeling. "How did you learn all this?"

"From my mother-in-law. She goes to spas and beauty parlors all the time. She's still gorgeous, even though she's gaining in years. Sit down."

Sassy put her in front of a fluorescent-lit mirror and proceeded to experiment with different shades of lipstick and eye shadow. Jillian felt as spoiled as if she'd been to an exclusive department store, and she said so.

"I'm still learning," Sassy assured her. "But it's fun, isn't it?"

"The most fun I've had in a long time, and thank you. Theodore is going to be shocked when he shows up Saturday!" she predicted.

Shocked was an understatement. Jillian in a blue ensemble, with her long hair soft and curling around her shoulders, with demure makeup, was a revelation to a man who'd only ever seen her without makeup in ragged jeans and sweatshirts or, worse, baggy T-shirts. Dressed up, in clothes that fit her perfectly, she was actually pretty.

"You can close your mouth, Theodore," she teased, delighted at his response.

He did. He shook his head. "You look nice," he said. It was an understatement, compared to what he was thinking. Jillian was a knockout. He frowned as he thought how her new look might go down in town. There were a couple of younger men, nice-looking ones with wealthy backgrounds, who might also find the new Jillian a hot item. He might have competition for her that he couldn't handle.

Jillian, watching his expressions change, was suddenly insecure. He was scowling as if he didn't actually approve of how she looked.

"It isn't too revealing, is it?" she worried.

He cleared his throat. "Jake, you're covered from stem to stern, except for the hollow of your throat, and your arms," he said. "What do you think is revealing?"

"You looked…well, you looked…"

"I looked like a man who's considering the fight ahead."

"Excuse me?"

He moved a step closer and looked down at her with pure appreciation. "You really don't know what a knockout you are, all dressed up?"

Her breath caught in her throat. "Me?"

His big hands framed her face and brought it up to his dancing black eyes. "You." He rubbed his nose against hers. "You know, I really wonder if you taste as good as you look. This is as good a time as any to find out."

He bent his head as he spoke and, for the first time in their relationship, he kissed her, right on the mouth. Hard.

Whatever he expected her reaction to be, the reality of it came as a shock

# *Chapter 3*

Jillian jerked back away from him as if he'd offended her, flushing to the roots of her hair. She stared at him with helpless misery, waiting for the explosion. The auditor had cursed a blue streak, called her names, swore that he'd tell every boy he knew that she was a hopeless little icicle.

But Theodore didn't do that. In fact, he smiled, very gently.

She bit her lower lip. She wanted to tell him. She couldn't. The pain was almost physical.

He took her flushed face in his big hands and bent and kissed her gently on the forehead, then on her eyelids, closing them.

"We all have our own secret pain, Jake," he whispered. "One day you'll want to tell me, and I'll listen." He lifted his head. "For the time being, we'll be best buddies, except that you're wearing a skirt," he added, tongue-in-cheek. "I have to confess that very few of my buddies have used a women's restroom."

It took her a minute, then she burst out laughing.

"That's better," he said, and grinned. He cocked his head and gave her a very male appraisal. "You really do look nice." He pursed his lips as he contemplated the ensemble and its probable cost.

"They're loaners," she blurted out.

His black eyes sparkled with unholy glee. "Loaners?"

She nodded. "Sassy Callister."

"I see."

She grinned. "She said that she had a whole closet of stuff she never wore. I didn't want to, but she sort of bulldozed me into it. She's a lot like her new husband."

"He wears petticoats?" he asked outrageously.

She glared at him. "Women don't wear petticoats or hoop skirts these days, Theodore."

"Sorry. Wrong era."

She grinned. "Talk about living in the dark ages!"

He shrugged. "I was raised by my grandmother and my uncle. They weren't forthcoming about women's intimate apparel."

"Well, I guess not!"

"Your uncle John was the same sort of throwback," he remarked.

"So we both come by it honestly, I suppose." She noted his immaculate dark suit and the spotless white shirt and blue patterned tie he was wearing with it. "You look nice, too."

"I bought the suit to wear to John Callister's wedding," he replied. "I don't often have the occasion to dress up."

"Me, neither," she sighed.

"I guess we could go to a few places together," he commented. "I like to hunt and fish."

"I do not like guns," she said flatly.

"Well, in my profession, they're sort of a necessity, Jake," he commented.

"I suppose so. Sorry."

"No problem. You used to like fishing."

"It's been a while since I dipped a poor, helpless worm into the water."

He chuckled. "Everything in life has a purpose. A worm's is to help people catch delicious fish."

"The worm might not share your point of view."

"I'll ask, the next time I see one."

She laughed, and her whole face changed. She felt better than she had in ages. Theodore didn't think she was a lost cause. He wasn't even angry that she'd gone cold at his kiss. Maybe, she thought, just maybe, there was still hope for her.

His black eyes were kind. "I'm glad you aren't wearing high heels," he commented.

"Why?"

He glanced down at his big feet in soft black leather boots. "Well, these aren't as tough as the boots I wear on the job. I'd hate to have holes in them from spiked heels, when you step on my feet on the dance floor."

"I will not step on your feet," she said with mock indignation. She grinned. "I might trip over them and land in a flowerpot, of course."

"I heard about that," he replied, chuckling. "Poor old Harris Twain. I'll bet he'll never stick his legs out into the walkway of a restaurant again. He said you were pretty liberally covered with potting soil. You went in headfirst, I believe…?"

She sighed. "Most people have talents. Mine is lack of coordination. I can trip over my own feet, much less someone else's."

He wondered about that clumsiness. She was very capable, in her own way, but she often fell. He frowned.

"Now, see, you're thinking that I'm a klutz, and you're absolutely right."

"I was wondering more about your balance," he said. "Do you have inner ear problems?"

She blinked. "What do my ears have to do with that?"

"A lot. If you have an inner ear disturbance, it can affect balance."

"And where did you get your medical training?" she queried.

"I spend some time in emergency rooms, with victims and perps alike. I learn a lot about medical problems that way."

"I forgot."

He shrugged. "It goes with the job."

"I don't have earaches," she said, and averted her eyes. "Shouldn't we get going?"

She was hiding something. A lot, maybe. He let it go. "I guess we should."

"A Latin dance club in Billings." She grinned. "How exotic!"

"The owner's even more exotic. You'll like him." He leaned closer. "He was a gun runner in his wild youth."

"Wow!"

"I thought you'd be impressed. So was I."

"You have an interesting collection of strange people in your life," she commented on the way to his truck.

"Goes with the—"

"Job. I guess." She grinned when she saw the truck. "Washed and waxed it, huh?" she teased.

"Well, you can't take a nice woman to a dance in a dirty truck," he stated.

"I wouldn't have minded."

He turned to her at the passenger side of the truck and looked down at her solemnly in the light from the security lamp on a pole nearby. His face was somber. "No, you wouldn't. You don't look at bank accounts to judge friendships. It's one of a lot of things I like about you. I dated a woman attorney once, who came here to try a case for a client in district court. When she saw the truck, the old one I had several years ago, she actually backed out of the date. She said she didn't want any important people in the community to see her riding around in a piece of junk."

She gasped. "No! How awful for you!"

His high cheekbones had a faint flush. Her indignation made him feel warm inside. "Something you'd never have said to me, as blunt as you are. It turned me off women for a while. Not that I even liked her. But it hurt my pride."

"As if a vehicle was any standard to base a character assessment on," she huffed.

He smiled tenderly. "Small-town police chiefs don't usually drive Jaguars. Although this guy I know in Texas does. But he made his money as a merc, not in law enforcement."

"I like you just the way you are," she told him quietly. "And it wouldn't matter to me if we had to walk to Billings to go dancing."

He ground his teeth together. She made him feel taller, more masculine, when she looked at him like that. He was struggling with more intense emotions than he'd felt in years. He wanted to grab her and eat her alive. But she needed careful handling. He couldn't be forward with her. Not until he could teach her to trust him. That would take time.

She felt uneasy when he scowled like that. "Sorry," she said. "I didn't mean to blurt that out and upset you..."

"You make me feel good, Jake," he interrupted. "I'm not upset. Well, not for the reasons you're thinking, anyway."

"What reasons upset you?"

He sighed. "To be blunt, I'd like to back you into the truck and kiss you half to death." He smiled wryly at her shocked expression. "Won't do it," he promised. "Just telling you what I really feel. Honesty is a sideline with most people. It's first on my list of necessities."

"Mine, too. It's okay. I like it when you're up-front."

"You're the same way," he pointed out.

"I guess so. Maybe I'm too blunt, sometimes."

He smiled. "I'd call it being forthright. I like it."

She beamed. "Thanks."

He checked his watch. "Got to go." He opened the door for her and waited until she jumped up into the cab and fastened her seat belt before he closed it.

"It impresses me that I didn't have to tell you to put that on," he said as he started the engine, nodding toward her seat belt. "I don't ride with people who refuse to wear them. I work wrecks. Some of them are horrific, and the worst fatalities are when people don't have on seat belts."

"I've heard that."

He pulled out onto the highway. "Here we go, Jake. Our first date." He grinned. "Our uncles are probably laughing their ghostly heads off."

"I wouldn't doubt it." She sighed. "Still, it wasn't nice of either of them to rig the wills like that."

"I guess they didn't expect to die for years and years," he commented. "Maybe it was a joke. They expected the lawyer to tell us long before they died. Except he died first and his partner had no sense of humor."

"I don't know. Our uncles did like to manipulate people."

"Too much," he murmured. "They browbeat poor old Dan Harper into marrying Daisy Kane, and he was miserable. They thought she was a sweet, kind girl who'd never want anything more than to go on living in Hollister for the rest of her life."

"Then she discovered a fascination for microscopes, got a science degree and moved to New York City to work in a research lab. Dan wouldn't leave Hollister, so they got a divorce. Good thing they didn't have kids, I guess."

"I guess. Especially with Dan living in a whiskey bottle these days."

She glanced at him. "Maybe some women mature late."

He glanced back. "You going to develop a fascination with microscopes and move to New York?" he asked suspiciously.

She laughed out loud. "I hope not. I hate cities."

He grinned again. "Me, too. Just checking."

"Besides, how could I leave Sammy? I'm sure there isn't an apartment in a big city that would let you keep a calf in it."

He laughed. "Well, they would. But only in the fridge. Or the freezer."

"You bite your tongue!" she exclaimed. "Nobody's eating my cow!"

He frowned thoughtfully. "Good point. I'm not exactly sure I know how to field dress a cow. A steer, sure. But cows are, well, different."

She glared at him. "You are not field dressing Sammy, so forget it."

He sighed. "There go my dreams of a nice steak."

"You can get one at the restaurant in town anytime you like. Sammy is for petting, not eating."

"If you say so."

"I do!"

He loved to wind her up and watch the explosion. She was so full of life, so enthusiastic about everything new. He enjoyed being with her. There were all sorts of places he could take her. He was thinking ahead. Far ahead.

"You're smirking," she accused. "What are you thinking about?"

"I was just remembering how excited you get about new things," he confessed. "I was thinking of places we could go together."

"You were?" she asked, surprised. And flattered.

He smiled at her. "I've never dated anybody regularly," he said. "I mean, I've had dates. But this is different." He searched for a way to put into words what he was thinking.

"You mean, because we're sort of being forced into it by the wills."

He frowned. "No. That's not what I mean." He stopped at an intersection and glanced her way. "I haven't had regular dates with a woman I've known well for years and years," he said after a minute. "Somebody I like."

She beamed. "Oh."

He chuckled as he pulled out onto the long highway that led to Billings. "We've had our verbal cut-and-thrust encounters, but despite that sharp tongue, I enjoy being with you."

She laughed. "It's not that sharp."

"Not to me. I understand there's a former customer of the florist shop where you worked who could write a testimonial for you about your use of words in a free-for-all."

She flushed and fiddled with her purse. "He was obnoxious."

"Actually they said he was just trying to ask you out."

"It was the way he went about it," she said curtly. "I don't think I've ever had a man talk to me like that in my whole life."

"I don't think he'll ever use the same language to any other woman, if it's a consolation." He teased. "So much for his inflated ego."

"He thought he was irresistible," she muttered. "Bragging about his fast new car and his dad's bank balance, and how he could get any woman he wanted." Her lips set. "Well, he couldn't get this one."

"Teenage boys have insecurities," he said. "I can speak with confidence on that issue, because I used to be one myself." He glanced at her with twinkling black eyes. "They're puff adders."

She blinked. "Excuse me?"

"I've never seen one myself, but I had a buddy in the service who was from Georgia. He told me about them. They're these snakes with insecurities."

She burst out laughing. "Snakes with insecurities?"

He nodded. "They're terrified of people. So if humans come too close to them, they rise up on their tails and weave back and forth and blow out their throats and start hissing. You know, imitating a cobra. Most of the time, people take them at face value and run away."

"What if people stand their ground and don't run?"

He laughed. "They faint."

*"They faint?"*

He nodded. "Dead away, my buddy said. He took a friend home with him. They were walking through the fields when a puff adder rose up and did his act for the friend. The guy was about to run for it when my buddy walked right up to the snake and it fainted dead away. I hear his family is still telling the story with accompanying sound effects and hilarity."

"A fainting snake." She sighed. "What I've missed, by spending my whole life in Montana. I wouldn't have known any better, either, though. I've never seen a cobra."

"They have them in zoos," he pointed out.

"I've never been to a zoo."

"What?"

"Well, Billings is a long way from Hollister and I've never had a vehicle I felt comfortable about getting there in." She grimaced. "This is a very deserted road, most of the time. If I broke down, I'd worry about who might stop to help me."

He gave her a covert appraisal. She was such a private person. She kept things to herself. Remembering her uncle and his weak heart, he wasn't surprised that she'd learned to do that.

"You couldn't talk to your uncle about most things, could you, Jake?" he wondered out loud.

"Not really," she agreed. "I was afraid of upsetting him, especially after his first heart attack."

"So you learned to keep things to yourself."

"I pretty much had to. I've never had close girlfriends, either."

"Most of the girls your age are married and have kids, except the ones who went into the military or moved to cities."

She nodded. "I'm a throwback to another era, when women lived at home until they married. Gosh, the world has changed," she commented.

"It sure has," he agreed. "When I was a boy, television sets were big and bulky and in cabinets. Now they're so thin and light that people can hang them on walls. And my iPod does everything a television can do, right down to playing movies and giving me news and weather."

She frowned. "That wasn't what I meant, exactly."

He raised his eyebrows.

"I mean, that women seem to want careers and men in volume."

He cleared his throat.

"That didn't come out right." She laughed self-consciously. "It just seems to me that women are more like the way men used to be. They don't want commitment. They have careers and they live with men. I heard a newscaster say that marriage is too retro a concept for modern people."

"There have always been people who lived out of the mainstream, Jake," he said easily. "It's a choice."

"It wouldn't be mine," she said curtly. "I think people should get married and stay married and raise children together."

"Now that's a point of view I like."

She studied him curiously. "Do you want kids?"

He smiled. "Of course. Don't you?"

She averted her eyes. "Well, yes. Someday."

He sighed. "I keep forgetting how young you are. You haven't really had time to live yet."

"You mean, get fascinated with microscopes and move to New York City," she said with a grin.

He laughed. "Something like that, maybe."

"I could never see stuff in microscopes in high school," she recalled. "I was so excited when I finally found what I thought was an organism and the teacher said it was an air bubble. That's all I ever managed to find." She grimaced. "I came within two grade points of failing biology. As it was, I had the lowest passing grade in my whole class."

"But you can cook like an angel," he pointed out.

She frowned. "What does that have to do with microscopes?"

"I'm making an observation," he replied. "We all have skills. Yours is cooking. Somebody else's might be science. It would be a pretty boring world if we all were good at the same things."

"I see."

He smiled. "You can crochet, too. My grandmother

loved her crafts, like you do. She could make quilts and knit sweaters and crochet afghans. A woman of many talents."

"They don't seem to count for much in the modern world," she replied.

"Have you ever really looked at the magazine rack, Jake?" he asked, surprised. "There are more magazines on handicrafts than there are on rock stars, and that's saying something."

"I hadn't noticed." She looked around. They were just coming into Billings. Ahead, she could see the awesome outline of the Rimrocks, where the airport was located, in the distance. "We're here?" she exclaimed.

"It's not so far from home," he said lazily.

"Not at the speed you go, no," she said impudently.

He laughed. "There wasn't any traffic and we aren't overly blessed with highway patrols at this hour of the night."

"You catch speeders, and you're local law enforcement," she pointed out.

"I don't catch them on the interstate unless they're driving on it through my town," he replied. "And it's not so much the speed that gets them caught, either. It's the way they're driving. You can be safe at high speeds and dangerous at low ones. Weaving in and out of traffic, riding people's bumpers, running stop signs, that sort of thing."

"I saw this television program where an experienced traffic officer said that what scared him most was to see a driver with both hands white-knuckled and close together on the steering wheel."

He nodded. "There are exceptions, but it usually

means someone who's insecure and afraid of the vehicle."

"You aren't."

He shrugged. "I've been driving since I was twelve. Kids grow up early when they live on ranches. Have to learn how to operate machinery, like tractors and harvesters."

"Our ranch doesn't have a harvester."

"That's because our ranch can't afford one," he said, smiling. "But we can always borrow one from neighbors."

"Small towns are such nice places," she said dreamily. "I love it that people will loan you a piece of equipment that expensive just because they like you."

"I imagine there are people in cities who would do the same, Jake, but there's not much use for them there."

She laughed. "No, I guess not."

He turned the corner and pulled into a parking lot next to a long, low building. There was a neon sign that said Red's Tavern.

"It's a bar?" she asked.

"It's a dance club. They do serve alcohol, but not on the dance floor."

"Theodore, I don't think I've ever been in a bar in my life."

"Not to worry, they won't force you to drink anything alcoholic," he told her, tongue-in-cheek. "And if they tried, I'd have to call local law and have them arrested. You're underage."

"Local law?"

"I'm not sanctioned to arrest people outside my own jurisdiction," he reminded her. "But you could make a citizen's arrest. Anybody can if they see a crime being committed. It's just that we don't advise it. Could get you killed, depending on the circumstances."

"I see what you mean."

He got out and opened her door, lifting her gently down from the truck by the waist. He held her just in front of him for a minute, smiling into her soft eyes. "You're as light as a feather," he commented softly. "And you smell pretty."

A shocked little laugh left her throat. "I smell pretty?"

"Yes. I remember my grandmother by her scent. She wore a light, flowery cologne. I recognize it if I smell it anywhere. She always smelled so good."

Her hands rested lightly on his broad shoulders. He was very strong. She loved his strength, his size. She smiled into his dark eyes. "You smell good, too. Spicy."

He nuzzled her nose with his. "Thanks."

She sighed and slid her arms around his neck. She tucked her face into his throat. "I feel so safe with you," she said softly. "Like nothing could ever hurt me."

"Now, Jake, that's not the sort of thing a man likes to hear."

She lifted her head, surprised. "Why?"

He pursed his lips. "We want to hear that we're dangerous and exciting, that we stir you up and make you nervous."

"You do?"

"It's a figure of speech."

She searched his eyes. "You don't want me to feel comfortable with you?" she faltered.

"You don't understand what I'm talking about, do you?" he wondered gently.

"No…not really. I'm sorry."

It was early days yet, he reminded himself. It was

disappointing that she wasn't shaky when he touched her. But, then, she kept secrets. There must be a reason why she was so icy inside herself.

He set her down but he didn't let her go. "Some things have to be learned," he said.

"Learned."

He framed her face with his big, warm hands. "Passion, for instance."

She blinked.

It was like describing ice to a desert nomad. He smiled wistfully. "You haven't ever been kissed in such a way that you'd die to have it happen again?"

She shook her head. Her eyes were wide and innocent, unknowing. She flushed a little and shifted restlessly.

"But you have been kissed in such a way that you'd rather undergo torture than have it happen again," he said suddenly.

She caught her breath. He couldn't know! He couldn't!

His black eyes narrowed on her face. "Something happened to you, Jake. Something bad. It made you lock yourself away from the world. And it wasn't your experience with the traveling auditor."

"You can't know…!"

"Of course not," he interrupted impatiently. "You know I don't pry. But I've been in law enforcement a long time, and I've learned to read people pretty good. You're afraid of me when I get too close to you."

She bit down hard on her lower lip. She drew blood.

"Stop that," he said in a tender tone, touching her lower lip where her teeth had savaged it. "I'm not going to try to browbeat you into telling me something you don't want to. But I wish you trusted me enough to talk to me about it. You know I'm not judgmental."

"It doesn't have anything to do with that."

He cocked his head. "Can't you tell me?"

She hesitated noticeably. She wanted to. She really wanted to. But…

He bent and kissed her eyelids shut. "Don't. We have all the time in the world. When you're ready to talk, I'll listen."

She drew in a long, labored breath and laid her forehead against his suit coat. "You're the nicest man I've ever known."

He smiled over her head. "Well, that's a start, I guess."

She smiled, too. "It's a start."

## *Chapter 4*

It was the liveliest place Jillian had ever been to. The dance band was on a platform at the end of a long, wide hall with a polished wooden floor. Around the floor were booths, not tables, and there was a bar in the next room with three bartenders, two of whom were female.

The music was incredible. It was Latin with a capital L, pulsing and narcotic. On the dance floor, people were moving to the rhythm. Some had on jeans and boots, others were wearing ensembles that would have done justice to a club in New York City. Still others, apparently too intimidated by the talent being displayed on the dance floor, were standing on the perimeter of the room, clapping and smiling.

"Wow," Jillian said, watching a particularly talented couple, a silver-haired lean and muscular man with a willowy blonde woman somewhat younger than he was.

They whirled and pivoted, laughing, with such easy grace and elegance that she couldn't take her eyes off them.

"That's Red Jernigan," he told her, indicating the silver-haired man, whose thick, long hair was in a ponytail down his back.

"He isn't redheaded," she pointed out.

He gave her an amused look. "It doesn't refer to his coloring," he told her. "They called him that because in any battle, he was the one most likely to come out bloody."

She gasped. "Oh."

"I have some odd friends." He shrugged, then smiled. "You'll get used to them."

He was saying something profound about their future. She was confused, but she returned his smile anyway.

The dance ended and Theodore tugged her along with him to the dance floor, where the silver-haired man and the blonde woman were catching their breath.

"Hey, Red," he greeted the other man, who grinned and gripped his hand. "Good to see you."

"About time you came up for a visit." Red's dark eyes slid to the small blonde woman beside the police chief. His eyebrows arched.

"This is Jillian," Theodore said gently. "And this is Red Jernigan."

"I'm Melody," the pretty blonde woman said, introducing herself. "Nice to meet you."

Red slid his arm around the woman and pulled her close. "Nice to see Ted going around with somebody," he observed. "It's painful to see a man come alone to a dance club and refuse to dance with anyone except the owner's wife."

"Well, I don't like most modern women." Theodore excused himself. He smiled down at a grinning Jillian. "I like Jake, here."

"Jake?" Red asked, blinking.

"He's always called me that," Jillian sighed. "I've known him a long time."

"She has," Theodore drawled, smiling. "She likes cattle."

"I don't," Melody laughed. "Smelly things."

"Oh, but they're not smelly if they're kept clean," Jillian protested at once. "Sammy is always neat."

"Her calf," Theodore explained.

"Is he a bull?" Red asked.

"She's a heifer," Jillian inserted. "A little black baldy."

Red and Melody were giving her odd looks.

"As an acquaintance of mine in Jacobsville, Texas, would say," Red told them, "if Johnny Cash could sing about a girl named Sue, a person can have a girl animal with a boy's name." He leaned closer. "He has a female border collie named Bob."

They burst out laughing.

"Well, don't stand over here with us old folks," Red told them. "Get out there with the younger generation and show them how to tango."

"You aren't old, Bud," Theodore told his friend with twinkling eyes. "You're just a hair slower than you used to be, but with the same skills."

"Which I hope I'm never called to use again," Red replied solemnly. "I'm still on reserve status."

"I know."

* * *

"Red was a bird colonel in spec ops," Theodore explained to Jillian later when they were sitting at a table sampling the club's exquisitely cooked seasoned steak and fancy baked sweet potatoes, which it was as famous as for its dance band.

"And he still is?" she asked.

He nodded. "He can do more with recruits than any man I ever knew, and without browbeating them. He just encourages. Of course, there are times when he has to get a little more creative, with the wilder sort."

"Creative?"

He grinned. "There was this giant of a kid from Milwaukee who was assigned to his unit in the field. Kid played video games and thought he knew more about strategy and tactics than Red did. So Red turns him loose on the enemy, but with covert backup."

"What happened?" she asked, all eyes.

"The kid walked right into an enemy squad and froze in his tracks. It's one thing to do that on a computer screen. Quite another to confront armed men in real life. They were aiming their weapons at him when Red led a squad in to recover him. Took about two minutes for them to eliminate the threat and get Commando Carl back to his own lines." He shook his head. "In the excitement, the kid had, shall we say, needed access to a restroom and didn't have one. So they hung a nickname on him that stuck."

"Tell me!"

He chuckled. "Let's just say that it suited him. He took it in his stride, sucked up his pride, learned to follow orders and became a real credit to the unit. He later became mayor of a small town somewhere up north, where he's still known, to a favored few, as 'Stinky.'"

She laughed out loud.

"Actually, he was in good company. I read in a book on World War II that one of our better known generals did the same thing when his convoy ran into a German attack. Poor guy. I'll bet Stinky cringed every time he saw that other general's book on a rack."

"I don't doubt it."

She sipped her iced tea and smiled. "This is really good food," she said. "I've never had a steak that was so tender, not even from beef my uncle raised."

"This is Kobe beef," he pointed out. "Red gets it from Japan. God knows how," he added.

"I read about those. Don't they actually massage the beef cattle?"

"Pamper them," he agreed. "You should try that sweet potato," he advised. "It's really a unique combination of spices they use."

She frowned, picking at it with her fork. "I've only ever had a couple of sweet potatoes, and they were mostly tasteless."

"Just try it."

She put the fork into it, lifted it dubiously to her lips and suddenly caught her breath when the taste hit her tongue like dynamite. "Wow!" she exclaimed. "What do they call this?"

"Red calls it 'the ultimate jalapeño-brown-sugar-sweet-potato delight.'"

"It's heavenly!"

He chuckled. "It is, isn't it? The jalapeño gives it a kick like a mule, but it's not so hot that even tenderfeet wouldn't eat it."

"I would never have thought of such a combination. And I thought I was a good cook."

"You are a good cook, Jake," he said. "The best I ever knew."

She blushed. "Thanks, Theodore."

He cocked his head. "I guess it would kill you to shorten that."

"Shorten what?"

"My name. Most people call me Ted."

She hesitated with the fork in midair. She searched his black eyes for a long time. "Ted," she said softly.

His jaw tautened. He hadn't expected it to have that effect on him. She had a soft, sweet, sexy voice when she let herself relax with him. She made his name sound different; special. New.

"I like the way you say it," he said, when she gave him a worried look. "It's—" he searched for a word that wouldn't intimidate her "—it's stimulating."

"Stimulating." She didn't understand.

He put down his fork with a long sigh. "Something happened to you," he said quietly. "You don't know me well enough to talk to me about it. Or maybe you're afraid that I might go after the man who did it."

She was astounded. She couldn't even manage words. She just stared at him, shocked.

"I'm in law enforcement," he reminded her. "After a few years, you read body language in a different way than most people do. Abused children have a look, a way of dressing and acting, one that's obvious to a cop."

She went white. She bit her lower lip and her fingers toyed with her fork as she stared at it, fighting tears.

His big hand curled around hers, gently. "I wish you could tell me. I think it would help you."

She looked up into quiet, patient eyes. "You wouldn't… think badly of me?"

"For God's sake," he groaned. "Are you nuts?"

She blinked.

He grimaced. "Sorry. I didn't mean to put it that way. Nothing I found out about you would change the way I feel. If that's why you're reluctant."

"You're sure?"

He glared at her.

She lowered her eyes and curled her small hand into his big one, a trusting gesture that touched him in a new and different way.

"When I was fifteen, Uncle John had this young man he got to do odd jobs around here. He was a drifter, very intelligent. He seemed like a nice, trustworthy person to have around the house. Then one day Uncle John felt bad and went to bed, left me with the hired man in the kitchen."

Her jaw clenched. "At first, he was real helpful. Wanted to put out the trash for me and sweep the floor. I thought it was so nice of him. Then all of a sudden, he asked what was my bra size and if I wore nylon panties."

Theodore's eyes began to flash.

She swallowed. "I was so shocked I didn't know what to do or say. I thought it was some sick joke. Until he tried to take my clothes off, mumbling all the time that I needed somebody to teach me about men and he was the perfect person, because he'd had so many virgins."

"Good God!"

"Uncle John was asleep. There was nobody to help me. But the Peales lived right down the road, and I knew a back way through the woods to their house. I hit him in a bad place and ran out the door as fast as

my legs could carry me. I was almost naked by then."
She closed her eyes, shivering with the memory of the
terror she'd felt, running and hearing him curse behind
her as he crashed through the undergrowth in pursuit,

"I didn't think what danger I might be placing Sassy
Peale and her mother and stepsister in, I just knew
they'd help me and I was terrified. I banged on the
door and Sassy came to it. When she saw how I looked,
she ran for the shotgun they kept in the hall closet. By
the time the hired man got on the porch, Sassy had the
shotgun loaded and aimed at his stomach. She told him
if he moved she'd blow him up."

She sipped tea while she calmed a little from the remembered fear. Her hand was shaking, but just a little.
Her free hand was still clasped gently in Theodore's.

"He tried to blame it on me, to say I'd flirted and
tried to seduce him, but Sassy knew better. She held
him at bay until her mother called the police. They took
him away." She drew in a breath. "There was a trial.
It was horrible, but at least it was in closed session, in
the judge's chambers. The hired man plea-bargained.
You see, he had priors, many of them. He drew a long
jail sentence, but it did at least spare me a public trial."
She sipped tea again. "His sister lived over in Wyoming.
She came to see me, after the trial." Her eyes closed.
"She said I was a slut who had no business putting a
sweet, nice guy like him behind bars for years." She
managed a smile. "Sassy was in the kitchen when the
woman came to the door. She marched into the living
room and gave that woman hell. She told her about her
innocent brother's priors and how many young girls had
suffered because of his inability to control his own desires. She was eloquent. The woman shut up and went

away. I never heard from her again." She looked over at him. "Sassy's been my friend ever since. Not a close one, I'm sorry to say. I was so embarrassed at having her know about it that it inhibited me with her and everyone else. Everyone would believe the man's sister, and that I'd asked for it."

His fingers curled closer into hers. "No young woman asks for such abuse," he said softly. "But abusers use that argument to defend themselves. It's a lie, like all their other lies."

"Sometimes," she said, to be fair, "women do lie, and men, innocent men, go to jail for things they didn't do."

"Yes," he agreed. "But more often than not, such lies are found out, and the women themselves are punished for it."

"I guess so."

"I wasn't here when that happened."

"No. You were doing that workshop at the FBI Academy. And I begged the judge not to tell you or anybody else. She was very kind to me."

He looked over her head, his eyes flashing cold and black as he thought what he might have done to the man if he'd been in town. He wasn't interested in Jillian as a woman back then, because she was still almost a child, but he'd always been fond of her. He would have wiped the floor with the man.

His expression made her feel warm inside. "You'd have knocked him up and down main street," she ventured.

He laughed, surprised, and met her eyes. "Worse than that, probably." He frowned. "First the hired man, then the accountant."

"The accountant was my fault," she confessed. "I

never told him how old I was, and I was infatuated with him. He was drinking when he tried to persuade me." She shook her head. "I can't believe I even did that."

He stared at her. "You were a kid, Jake. Kids aren't known for deep thought."

She smiled. "Thanks for not being judgmental."

He shrugged. "I'm such a nice man that I'm never judgmental."

Her eyebrows arched.

He grinned. "And I really can do the tango. Suppose I teach you?"

She studied his lean, handsome face. "It's a very, well, sensual sort of dance, they say."

"Very." He pursed his lips. "But I'm not an aggressive man. Not in any way that should frighten you."

She colored a little. "Really?"

"Really."

She drew in a long breath. "I guess every woman should dance the tango at least once."

"My thoughts exactly."

He wiped his mouth on the linen napkin, took a last sip of the excellent but cooling coffee and got to his feet.

"You have to watch your back on the dance floor, though," he told her as he led her toward it.

"Why is that?"

"When the other women see what a great dancer I am, they'll probably mob you and take me away from you," he teased.

She laughed. "Okay." She leaned toward him. "Are you packing?"

"Are you kidding?" he asked, indicating the automatic nestled at his waist on his belt. "I'm a cop. I'm always packing. And you keep your little hands off my gun," he added sternly. "I don't let women play with it, even if they ask nicely."

"Theodore, I'm scared of guns," she reminded him. "And you know it. That's why *you* come over and sit on the front porch and shoot bottles on stumps, just to irritate me."

"I'll try to reform," he promised.

"Lies."

He put his hand over his heart. "I only lie when I'm salving someone's feelings," he pointed out. "There are times when telling the truth is cruel."

"Oh, yeah? Name one."

He nodded covertly toward a woman against the wall. "Well, if I told that nice lady that her dress looks like she had it painted on at a carnival, she'd probably feel bad."

She bit her lip trying not to laugh. "She probably thinks it looks sexy."

"Oh, no. Sexy is a dress that covers almost everything, but leaves one little tantalizing place bare," he said. "That's why Japanese kimonos have that dip on the back of the neck, that just reveals the nape, when the rest of the woman is covered from head to toe. The Japanese think the nape of the neck is sexy."

"My goodness!" She stared up at him, impressed. "You've been so many places. I've only ever been out of Montana once, when I drove to Wyoming with Uncle John to a cattle convention. I've never been out of the country at all. You learn a lot about other people when you travel, don't you?"

He nodded. He smiled. "Other countries have different customs. But people are mostly the same everywhere. I've enjoyed the travel most of all, even when I had to do it on business."

"Like the time you flew to London with that detective from Scotland Yard. Imagine a British case that involved a small town like Hollister!" she exclaimed.

"The perpetrator was a murderer who came over here fishing to provide himself with an alibi while his wife committed the crime and blamed it on her absent husband. In the end, they both drew life sentences."

"Who did they kill?" she asked.

"Her cousin who was set to inherit the family estate and about ten million pounds," he said, shaking his head. "The things sensible people will do for money never ceases to amaze me. I mean, it isn't like you can take it with you when you die. And how many houses can you live in? How many cars can you drive?" He frowned. "I think of money the way the Crow and Cheyenne people do. The way most Native Americans do. The man in the tribe who is the most honored is always the poorest, because he gives away everything he has to people who need it more. They're not capitalists. They don't understand societies that equate prestige with money."

"And they share absolutely everything," she agreed. "They don't understand private property."

He laughed. "Neither do I. The woods and the rivers and the mountains are ageless. You can't own them."

"See? That's the Cheyenne in you talking."

He touched her blond hair. "Probably it is. We going to dance, or talk?"

"You're leading, aren't you?"

He tugged her onto the dance floor. "Apparently." He drew her gently to him and then hesitated. After what she'd told him, he didn't want to do anything that would make her uncomfortable. He said so.

"I don't…well, I don't feel uncomfortable, like that, with you," she faltered, looking up into his black eyes. She managed a shaky little smile. "I like being close to you." She flushed, afraid she'd been too bold. Or that he'd think she was being forward. Her expression was troubled.

He just smiled. "You can say anything to me," he said gently. "I won't think you're being shallow or vampish. Okay?"

She relaxed. "Okay. Is this going to be hard to learn?"

"Very."

She drew in a long breath. "Then I guess we should get started."

His eyes smiled down at her. "I guess we should."

He walked her around the dance floor, to her amusement, teaching her how the basic steps were done. It wasn't like those exotic tangos she'd seen in movies at first. It was like kindergarten was to education.

She followed his steps, hesitantly at first, then a little more confidently, until she was moving with some elegance.

"Now, this is where we get into the more exotic parts," he said. "It involves little kicks that go between the legs." He leaned to her ear. "I think we should have kids one day, so it's very important that you don't get overenthusiastic with the kicks. And you should also be very careful where you place them."

It took her a minute to understand what he meant, and then she burst out laughing instead of being embarrassed.

He grinned. "Just playing it safe," he told her. "Ready? This is how you do it."

It was fascinating, the complexity of the movements and the fluid flow of the steps as he paced the dance to the music.

"It doesn't look like this in most movies," she said as she followed his steps.

"That's because it's a stylized version of the tango," he told her. "Most people have no idea how it's supposed to be done. But there are a few movies that go into it in depth. One was made in black and white by a British woman. It's my favorite. Very comprehensive. Even about the danger of the kicks." He chuckled.

"It's Argentinian, isn't it? The dance, I mean."

"You'd have to ask my buddy about that, I'm not sure. I know there are plenty of dance clubs down there that specialize in tango. The thing is, you're supposed to do these dances with strangers. It's as much a social expression as it is a dance."

"Really?"

He nodded. He smiled. "Maybe we should get a bucket and put all our spare change into it. Then, when we're Red's age, we might have enough to buy tickets to Buenos Aires and go dancing."

She giggled. "Oh, I'm sure we'd have the ticket price in twenty or thirty years."

He sighed as he led. "Or forty." He shook his head. "I've always wanted to travel. I did a good bit of it in the service, but there are plenty of places I'd love to see. Like those ruins in Peru and the pyramids, and the Sonoran desert."

She frowned. "The Sonoran desert isn't exotic."

He smiled. "Sure it is. Do you know, those Saguaro

cacti can live for hundreds of years? And that if a limb falls on you, it can kill you because of the weight? You don't think about them being that heavy, but they have a woody spine and limbs to support the weight of the water they store."

"Gosh. How do you know all that?"

He grinned. "The *Science Channel,* the *Discovery Channel,* the *National Geographic Channel...*"

She laughed. "I like to watch those, too."

"I don't think I've missed a single nature special," he told her. He gave her a droll look. "Now that should tell you all you need to know about my social life." He grinned.

She laughed, too. "Well, my social life isn't much better. This is the first time I've been on a real date."

His black eyebrows arched.

She flushed. She shrugged. She averted her eyes.

He tilted her face up to his and smiled with a tenderness that made her knees weak. "I heartily approve," he said, "of the fact that you've been saving yourself for me, just like your uncle did," he added outrageously.

She almost bent over double laughing. "No fair."

"Just making the point." He slid his arm around her and pulled her against him. She caught her breath.

He hesitated, his dark eyes searching hers to see if he'd upset her.

"My...goodness," she said breathlessly.

He raised his eyebrows.

She averted her eyes and her cheeks took on a glow. She didn't know how to tell him that the sensations she was feeling were unsettling. She could feel the muscles of his chest pressed against her breasts, and it was stimulating, exciting. It was a whole new experience to be held close to a man's body, to feel its warm strength, to smell the elusive, spicy cologne he was wearing.

"You've danced with men before."

"Yes, of course," she confessed. She looked up at him with fascination. "But it didn't, well, it didn't… feel like this."

That made him arrogant. His chin lifted and he looked down at her with possession kindling in his eyes.

"Sorry," she said quickly, embarrassed. "I just blurt things out."

He bent his head, so that his mouth was right beside her ear as he eased her into the dance. "It's okay," he said softly.

She bit her lip and laughed nervously.

"Well, it's okay to feel like that with me," he corrected. "But you should know that it's very wrong for you to feel that way with any other man. So you should never dance with anybody but me for the rest of your life."

She burst out laughing again.

He chuckled. "You're a quick study, Jake," he noted as she followed his steps easily. "I think we may become famous locally for this dance once you get used to it."

"You think?" she teased.

He turned her back over his arm, pulled her up, and spun her around with skill. She laughed breathlessly. It was really fun.

"I haven't danced in years," he sighed. "I love to do it, but I'm not much of a party person."

"I'm not, either. I'm much more at home in a kitchen than I am in a club." She grimaced. "That's not very modern, either, for a woman. I always feel that I should be working my way up a corporate ladder somewhere or immersing myself in higher education."

"Would you like to be a corporate leader?"

She made a face. "Not really. Jobs like that are demanding, and you have to want them more than anything. I'm just not ambitious, I guess. Although," she mused, "I think I might like to take a college course."

"What sort?" he asked.

"Anthropology."

He stopped dancing and looked down at her, fascinated. "Why?"

"I like reading about ancient humans, and how archaeologists can learn so much from skeletal material. I go crazy over those National Geographic specials on Egypt."

He laughed. "So do I."

"I'd love to see the pyramids. All of them, even those in Mexico and Asia."

"There are pyramids here in the States," he reminded her. "Those huge earthen mounds that primitive people built were the equivalent of pyramids."

She stopped dancing. "Why do you think they built them?"

"I don't know. It's just a guess. But most of the earthen mounds are near rivers. I've always thought maybe they were where the village went to get out of the water when it flooded."

"It's as good a theory as any other," she agreed. "But what about in Egypt? I don't think they had a problem with flooding," she added, tongue-in-cheek.

"Now, see, there's another theory about that. Thousands of years ago, Egypt was green and almost tropical, with abundant sources of water. So who knows?"

"It was green?" she exclaimed.

He nodded. "There were forests."

"Where did you learn that?"

"I read, too. I think it was in Herodotus. They called him the father of history. He wrote about Egypt. He admitted that the information might not all be factual, but he wrote down exactly what the Egyptian priests told him about their country."

"I'd like to read what he said."

"You can borrow one of my books," he offered. "I have several copies of his Histories."

"Why?"

He grimaced. "Because I keep losing them."

She frowned. "How in the world do you lose a book?"

"You'll have to come home with me sometime and see why."

Her eyes sparkled. "Is that an invitation? You know, 'come up and see my books'?"

He chuckled. "No, it's not a pickup line. I really mean it."

"I'd like to."

"You would?" His arm contracted. "When? How about next Saturday? I'll show you my collection of maps, too."

"Maps?" she exclaimed.

He nodded. "I like topo maps, and relief maps, best of all. It helps me to understand where places are located."

She smiled secretively. "We could compare maps."

"What?"

She sighed. "I guess we do have a lot in common. I think I've got half the maps Rand McNally ever published!"

## Chapter 5

"Well, what do you know?" He laughed. "We're both closet map fanatics."

"And we love ancient history."

"And we love shooting targets from the front porch."

She glowered up at him.

He sighed. "I'll try to reform."

"You might miss and shoot Sammy," she replied.

"I'm a dead shot."

"Anybody can miss once," she pointed out.

"I guess so."

They'd stopped on the dance floor while the band got ready to start the next number. When they did, he whirled her around and they started all over again. Jillian thought she'd never enjoyed anything in her life so much.

\* \* \*

Ted walked her to the front door, smiling. "It was a nice first date."

"Yes, it was," she agreed, smiling back. "I've never had so much fun!"

He laughed. She made him feel warm inside. She was such an honest person. She wasn't coy or flirtatious. She just said what she felt. It wasn't a trait he was familiar with.

"What are you thinking?" she asked curiously.

"That I'm not used to people who tell the truth."

She blinked. "Why not?"

"Almost all the people I arrest are innocent," he ticked off. "They were set up by a friend, or it was a case of mistaken identity even when there were eyewitnesses. Oh, and, the police have it in for them and arrest them just to be mean. That's my personal favorite," he added facetiously.

She chuckled. "I guess they wish they were innocent."

"I guess."

She frowned. "There's been some talk about that man you arrested for the bank robbery getting paroled because of a technicality. Is it true?"

His face set in hard lines. "It might be. His attorney said that the judge made an error in his instructions to the jury that prejudiced the case. I've seen men get off in similar situations."

"Ted, he swore he'd kill you if he ever got out," she said worriedly.

He pursed his lips and his dark eyes twinkled. "Frightened for me?"

"Of course I am."

He sighed and pulled her close. "Now, that's exactly the sort of thing that makes a man feel good about himself, when some sweet little woman worries about him."

"I'm not little, I'm not sweet and I don't usually worry," she pointed out.

"It's okay if you worry about me," he teased. "As long as you don't do it excessively."

She toyed with the top button of his unbuttoned jacket. "There are lots of safer professions than being a police chief."

He frowned. "You're kidding, right?"

She grimaced. "Ted, Joe Brown's wife was one of my uncle's friends. She was married to that deputy sheriff who was shot to death a few years ago. She said that she spent their whole married lives sitting by the phone at night, almost shaking with worry every time he had to go out on a case, hoping and praying that he'd come home alive."

His hands on her slender waist had tightened unconsciously. "Anyone who marries someone in law enforcement has to live with that possibility," he said slowly.

She bit her lower lip. She was seeing herself sitting by the phone at night, pacing the floor. She was prone to worry anyway. She was very fond of Ted. She didn't want him to die. But right now, she wasn't in love. She had time to think about what she wanted to do with her life. She was sure she should give this a lot of thought before she dived headfirst into a relationship with him that might lead very quickly to marriage. She'd heard people talk about how it was when people became very physical with each other, that it was so addictive that they couldn't bear to be apart at all. Once that happened, she wouldn't have a chance to see things rationally.

Ted could almost see the thoughts in her mind. Slowly he released her and stepped back.

She felt the distance, and it was more than physical. He was drawing away in every sense.

She looked up at him. She drew in a long breath. "I'm not sure I'm ready, Ted."

"Ready for what?"

That stiffness in him was disturbing, but she had to be honest. "I'm not sure I'm ready to think about marriage."

His black eyes narrowed. "Jillian, if we don't get married, there's a California developer who's going to make this place into hot real estate with tourist impact, and Sammy could end up on a platter."

She felt those words like a body blow. Her eyes, tormented, met his. "But it's not fair, to rush into something without having time to think about it!" she exclaimed. "The wills didn't say we have to get married tomorrow! There's no real time limit!"

There was, but he wasn't going to push her. She had cold feet. She didn't know him that well, despite the years they'd been acquainted, and she wasn't ready for the physical side of marriage. She had hang-ups, and good reasons to have them.

"Okay," he said after a minute. "Suppose we just get to know each other and let the rest ride for a while?"

"You mean, go on dates and stuff?"

He pursed his lips. "Yes. Dates and stuff."

She noticed how handsome he was. In a crowd, he always stood out. He was a vivid sort of person, not like she was at all. But they did enjoy the same sorts of things and they got along, most of the time.

"I would like to see your place," she said.

"I'll come and get you Saturday morning," he said quietly.

He waited for her answer with bridled impatience. She could see that. He wasn't sure of her at all. She hated being so hesitant, but it was a rushed business. She would have to make a decision in the near future or watch Uncle John's ranch become a resort. It didn't bear thinking about. On the other hand, if she said yes to Ted, it would mean a relationship that she was certain she wasn't ready for.

"Stop gnawing your lip off and say yes," Ted told her. "We'll work out the details as we go along."

She sighed. "Okay, Ted," she said after a minute.

He hadn't realized that he'd been holding his breath. He smiled slowly. She was going to take the chance. It was a start.

"Okay." He frowned. "You don't have any low-cut blouses and jeans that look like you've been poured into them, do you?"

"Ted!"

"Well, I was just wondering," he said. "Because if you do, you can't wear them over at my place. We have a dress code."

"A dress code." She nodded. "So your cowboys have to wear dresses." She nodded again.

He burst out laughing. He bent and kissed her, hard, but impersonally, and walked down the steps. "I'll see you Saturday."

"You call that a kiss?" she yelled after him, and shocked herself with the impertinent remark that had jumped out of her so impulsively.

But he didn't react to it the way she expected. He just threw up his hand and kept walking.

* * *

They worked side by side in his kitchen making lunch. He was preparing an omelet while she made cinnamon toast and fried bacon.

"Breakfast for lunch," she scoffed.

"Hey, I very often have breakfast for supper, if I've been out on a case," he said indignantly. "There's no rule that says you have to have breakfast in the morning."

"I suppose not."

"See, you don't know how to break rules."

She gasped. "You're a police chief! You shouldn't be encouraging anybody to break rules."

"It's okay as long as it's only related to food," he replied.

She laughed, shaking her head.

"You going to turn that bacon anytime soon?" he asked, nodding toward it, "or do you really like it raw on one side and black on the other?"

"If you don't like it that way, you could fry it yourself."

"I do omelets," he pointed out. "I don't even eat bacon."

"What?"

"Pig meat," he muttered.

"I like bacon!"

"Good. Then you can eat it. I've got a nice country ham all carved up and cooked in the fridge. I'll have that with mine."

"Ham is pig meat, too!"

"I think of it as steak with a curly tail," he replied.

She burst out laughing. He was so different off the job. She'd seen him walking down the sidewalk in town, somber and dignified, almost unapproachable. Here, at home, he was a changed person.

"What are you brooding about?" he wondered.

"Was I? I was just thinking how different you are at home than at work."

"I should hope so," he sighed, as he took the omelet up onto a platter. "I mean, think of the damage to my image if I cooked omelets for the prisoners."

"Chief Barnes used to," she said. "I remember Uncle John talking about what a sweet man he was. He'd take the prisoners himself to funerals when they had family members die, and in those days, when the jail was down the hall from the police department, he'd cook for them, too."

"He was a kind man," Ted agreed solemnly.

"To think that it was one of the prisoners who killed him," she added quietly as she turned the bacon. "Of all the ironies."

"The man was drunk at the time," Ted said. "And, if you recall, he killed himself just a few weeks later while he was waiting for trial. He left a note saying he didn't want to put the chief's family through any more pain."

"Everybody thought that was so odd," she said. "But people forget that murderers are just like everybody else. They aren't born planning to kill people."

"That's true. Sometimes it's alcohol or drugs that make them do it. Other times it's an impulse they can't control. Although," he added, "there are people born without a conscience. They don't mind killing. I've seen them in the military. Not too many, thank goodness, but they come along occasionally."

"Your friend who was a sniper, was he like that?"

"Not at all," he said. "He was trained to think of it

as just a skill. It was only later, when it started to kill his soul, that he realized what was happening to him. That was when he got out."

"How in the world did he get into law enforcement, with such a background?" she wondered.

He chuckled. "Uncle Sam often doesn't know when his left hand is doing something different than his right one," he commented. "Government agencies have closed files."

"Oh. I get it. But those files aren't closed to everyone, are they?"

"They're only accessible to people with top-secret military clearance." He glanced at her amusedly. "Never knew a civilian, outside the executive branch, who even had one."

"That makes sense."

He pulled out her chair for her.

"Thank you," she said, with surprise in her tone.

"I'm impressing you with my good manners," he pointed out as he sat down across from her and put a napkin in his lap.

"I'm very impressed." She tasted the omelet, closed her eyes and sighed. "And not only with your manners. Ted, this is delicious!"

He grinned. "Thanks."

"What did you put in it?" she asked, trying to decide what combination of spices he'd used to produce such a taste.

"Trade secret."

"You can tell me," she coaxed. "After all, we're almost engaged."

"The 'almost' is why I'm not telling," he retorted. "If

things don't work out, you'll be using my secret spices in your own omelets for some other man."

"I could promise."

"You could, but I'm not telling."

She sighed. "Well, it's delicious, anyway."

He chuckled. "The bacon's not bad, either," he conceded, having forgone the country ham that would need warming. He was hungry.

"Thanks." She lifted a piece of toast and gave it a cold look. "Shame we can't say the same for the toast. Sorry. I was busy trying not to burn the bacon, so I burned the toast instead."

"I don't eat toast."

"I do, but I don't think I will this time." She pushed the toast aside.

After they ate, he walked her around the property. He only had a few beef steers in the pasture. He'd bought quite a few Angus cattle with his own uncle, and they were at the ranch that Jillian had shared with her uncle John. She was pensive as she strolled beside him, absently stripping a dead branch of leaves, thinking about the fate of Uncle John's prize beef if she didn't marry Ted sometime soon.

"Deep thoughts?" he asked, hands in the pockets of his jeans under his shepherd's coat.

She frowned. She was wearing her buckskin jacket. One of the pieces of fringe caught on a limb and she had to stop to disentangle it. "I was thinking about that resort," she confessed.

"Here. Let me." He stopped and removed the branch from the fringe. "Do you know why these jackets always had fringe?"

She looked up at him, aware of his height and

strength so close to her. He smelled of tobacco and coffee and fir trees. "Not really."

He smiled. "When the old-timers needed something to tie up a sack with, they just pulled off a piece of fringe and used that. Also, the fringe collects water and drips it away from the body."

"My goodness!"

"My grandmother was full of stories like that. Her grandfather was a fur trapper. He lived in the Canadian wilderness. He was French. He married a Blackfoot woman."

She smiled, surprised. "But you always talk about your Cheyenne heritage."

"That's because my other grandmother was Cheyenne. I have interesting bloodlines."

Her eyes sketched his high-cheekboned face, his black eyes and hair and olive complexion. "They combined to make a very handsome man."

"Me?" he asked, surprised.

She grinned. "And not a conceited bone in your body, either, Ted."

He smiled down at her. "Not much to be conceited about."

"Modest, too."

He shrugged. He touched her cheek with his fingertips. "You have beautiful skin."

Her eyebrows arched. "Thank you."

"You get that from your mother," he said gently. "I remember her very well. I was only a boy when she died, but she was well-known locally. She was the best cook in two counties. She was always the first to sit with anyone sick, or to take food when there was a funeral."

"I only know about her through my uncle," she replied. "My uncle loved her. She was his only sister, much older than he was. She and my father had me unexpectedly, late in life."

Which, he thought, had been something of a tragedy.

"And then they both died of the flu, when I was barely crawling," she sighed. "I never knew either of them." She looked up. "You did at least know your parents, didn't you?"

He nodded. "My mother died of a stroke in her early thirties," he said. "My father was overseas, working for an oil corporation as a roughneck, when there was a bombing at the installation and he died. My grandmother took me in, and my uncle moved in to help support us."

"Neither of us had much of a childhood," she said. "Not that our relatives didn't do all they could for us," she added quickly. "They loved us. Lots of orphaned kids have it a lot worse."

"Yes, they do," he agreed solemnly. "That's why we have organizations that provide for orphaned kids."

"If I ever get rich," she commented, "I'm going to donate to those."

He grinned. "I already do. To a couple, at least."

She leaned back against a tree and closed her eyes, drinking in the sights and sounds and smells of the woods. "I love winter. I know it isn't a popular season," she added. "It's cold and there's a lot of snow. But I enjoy it. I can smell the smoke from fireplaces and woodstoves. If I close my eyes, it reminds me of campfires. Uncle John used to take me camping with him when I was little, to hunt deer."

"Which you never shot."

She opened her eyes and made a face. "I'm not shooting Bambi."

"Bull."

"People shouldn't shoot animals."

"That attitude back in colonial times would have seen you starve to death," he pointed out. "It's not like those old-timers could go to a grocery store and buy meat and vegetables. They had to hunt and garden or die."

She frowned. "I didn't think about that."

"In fact," he added, "people who refused to work were turned out of the forts into the wilderness. Some stole food from the Indians and were killed for it. Others starved or froze to death. It was a hard life."

"Why did they do it?" she wondered aloud. "Why leave their families and their homes and get on rickety old ships and go to a country they'd never even seen?"

"A lot of them did it to escape debtor's prison," he said. "They had debts they couldn't pay. A few years over here working as an indentured servant and they could be free and have money to buy their own land. Or the people they worked for might give them an acre or two, if they were generous."

"What about when the weather took their crops and they had nothing to eat?"

"There are strings of graves over the eastern seaboard of pilgrims who starved," he replied. "A sad end to a hopeful beginning. This is a hostile land when it's stripped of supermarkets and shopping centers."

A silence fell between them, during which he stared at the small rapids in the stream nearby. "That freezes over in winter," he said. "It looks pretty."

"I'd like to see it then."

He turned. "I'll bring you over here."

She smiled. "Okay."

His black eyes looked long and deep into hers across the distance, until she felt as if something snapped inside her. She caught her breath and forced her eyes away.

Ted didn't say anything. He just smiled. And started walking again.

She loved it that he didn't pressure her into a more physical relationship. It gave her a breathing space that she desperately needed.

He took her to a play in Billings the following weekend, a modern parody of an old play about two murderous old women and their assorted crazy relatives.

She laughed until her sides ached. Later, as they were driving home, she realized that it had been a long time since she'd been so amused by anything.

"I'm so glad I never had relatives like that," she ventured.

He laughed. "Me, too. The murderous cousin with the spooky face was a real pain, wasn't he?"

"His associate was even crazier."

She sat back against the seat, her eyes closed, still smiling. "It was a great play. Thanks for asking me."

"I was at a loose end," he commented. "We have busy weekends and slow weekends. This was a very slow one, nothing my officers couldn't handle on their own."

That was a reminder, and not a very pleasant one, of what he did for a living. She frowned in the darkness of the cab, broken only by the blue light of the instrument panel. "Ted, haven't you ever thought about doing something else for a living?"

"Like what?" he asked. "Teaching chemistry to high school students?"

He made a joke of it, but she didn't laugh. "You're not likely to be killed doing that."

"I guess you don't keep up with current events," he remarked solemnly, and proceeded to remind her of several terrible school shootings.

She grimaced. "Yes, but those are rare incidents. You make enemies in your work. What if somebody you locked up gets out and tries to kill you?"

"It goes with the job," he said laconically. "So far, I've been lucky."

Lucky. But it might not last forever. Could she see herself sitting by the phone every night of her life, waiting for that horrible call?

"You're dwelling on anticipation of the worst," he said, glancing her way. "How in the world do you think people get by who have loved ones with chronic illness or life-threatening conditions?"

She looked at him in the darkness. "I've never thought about it."

"My grandmother had cancer," he reminded her. "Had it for years. If I'd spent that time sitting in a chair, brooding on it, what sort of life would it have been for her?"

She frowned. "Lonely."

"Exactly. I knew it could happen, anytime. But I lived from day to day, just like she did. After a while, I got used to the idea, like she did, and we went on with our lives. It was always there, in the background, but it was something we just—" he searched for the word "—lived with. That's how husbands and wives of people in law enforcement and the military deal with it."

It was a new concept for her, living with a terrifying reality and getting used to it.

"You're very young," he said heavily. "It would be harder for you."

It probably would. She didn't answer him. It was something new to think about.

He walked her up the steps to her front door. He looked good in a suit, she thought, smiling.

"What are you thinking?" he teased.

"That you look very elegant in a suit."

He shrugged. "It's a nice suit."

"It's a nice man wearing it."

"Thanks. I like your dress."

She grinned. "It's old, but I like the color. It's called Rose Dust."

He fingered the lacy collar. He wouldn't have told her, because it would hurt her feelings, but it looked like the sort of dress a high school girl would wear. It wasn't sophisticated, or even old enough for her now. But he just smiled.

"Nice color," he agreed.

She cocked her head, feeling reckless. "Going to kiss me?" she asked.

"I was thinking about it."

"And what did you decide?"

He stuck his hands in his pockets and just smiled down at her. "That would be rushing things a little too much," he said gently. "You want to date and get to know each other. I think that's a good idea. Plenty of time for the other, later."

"Well, my goodness!"

"Shocked by my patience, are you?" he asked with a grin. "Me, too."

"Very."

His eyes were old and wise. "When things get physical, there's a difference in the way two people are, together. There's no time to step back and look at how things really are."

She nodded. "You mean, like Sassy and her husband, John Callister, when they first got married. They couldn't stand to be apart, even for an hour or two. They still pretty much go everywhere together. And they're always standing close, or touching."

"That's what I mean."

She frowned. "I haven't ever felt like that," she said.

He smiled. "I noticed."

She flushed. "I'm sorry, I just blurt things out…"

"I don't mind that you're honest," he said. "It helps. A lot."

She bit her lower lip. "I'd give anything if Uncle John hadn't hired that man to come work for him."

"I'm sure your uncle felt the same way. I'm surprised that he never told me about it," he added curtly.

"I imagine he thought you'd hold him responsible for it. He blamed himself," she added softly. "He never stopped apologizing." She sighed. "It didn't help very much."

"Of course it didn't." He stepped closer and tilted her chin up. "You'll deal with it. If you don't think you can, there are some good psychologists. Our department works with two, who live in Billings."

She made a face. "I don't think I could talk about something like that to a total stranger."

He stared at her for a long time. "How about me?" he asked suddenly. "Could you talk about it to me?"

## Chapter 6

Jillian stared up at him with conflicting emotions. But after a minute she nodded. "I think I could," she replied finally.

He beamed. His black eyes were twinkling. "That's a major step forward."

"Think so?"

"I know so."

She moved a step closer. "I enjoyed tonight. Thank you."

He gave her a teasing look and moved a step away. "I did, too, and I'll thank you to keep your distance. I don't want to be an object of lust to a single woman who lives alone."

She gasped theatrically. "You do so!"

"I do?"

"Absolutely!" she agreed. She grinned. "But not right now. Right?"

He laughed. "Not right now." He bent and brushed a lazy kiss against her forehead. "Get some sleep. I'll call you Monday."

"You do that. Not early," she added, without telling him why. She had a secret, and she wasn't sharing it.

"Not early," he agreed. "Good night."

"Good night, Ted."

He bounded down the steps, jumped in his truck and sat there deliberately until she got the message. She went inside, locked the door and turned off the porch light. Only then did he drive away. It made her feel safe, that attitude of his. Probably it was instinctive, since he was in law enforcement, but she liked it. She liked it very much.

Snow came the next morning. Jillian loved it. She drove slowly, so that she didn't slip off the road. But there wasn't much traffic, and she lived close to town. It was easier than she expected to get in on the country roads.

When she left again, at noon, it was a different story. The snow had come fast and furiously, and she could barely crawl along the white highway. The road crews had been busy, spreading sand and gravel, but there were icy spots just the same.

She hesitated to go all the way back to the ranch when she couldn't see the road ahead for the blinding snow, so she pulled into the town's only restaurant and cut off the engine.

"Well," she said to herself, "I guess if worse comes to worst, they might let me sleep in a booth in the restaurant." She laughed at the imagery.

She grabbed her purse and got out, grateful for her

high-heeled cowboy boots that made it easier to get a foothold in the thick, wet snow. This was the kind that made good snowmen. She thought she might make one when she finally got home. A calf, perhaps, to look like Sammy. She laughed. Ted would howl at that, if she did it.

She opened the door of the restaurant and walked right into a nightmare. Davy Harris, the man who had almost raped her, was standing by the counter, paying his bill. He was still thin and nervous-looking, with straggly brown hair and pale eyes. He looked at her with mingled distaste and hatred.

"Well, well, I hoped I might run into you again," he said in a voice dripping with venom. "I don't guess you expected to see me, did you, Jillian? Not the man you put in prison for trying to kiss you!"

The owner of the restaurant knew Jillian, and liked her, but he was suddenly giving her a very odd look. There was another customer behind him, one who'd known Jillian's uncle. He gave her an odd look, too.

"There was more to it than that," Jillian said unsteadily.

"Yes, I wanted to marry you, I can't imagine why, you little prude," he said with contempt. "Put a man in prison for trying to teach you about life."

She flushed. She had a good comeback for that, but it was too embarrassing to talk about it in public, especially around men she didn't really know. She felt sick all over.

He came up to her, right up to her, and looked down at her flushed face. "I'm going to be in town for a while, Jillian," he said. "And don't get any ideas about having your boyfriend try to boot me out, or I'll tell him a few things he doesn't know about you."

With that shocking statement, he smiled at the owner, praised the food and walked out the door.

Jillian sat drinking coffee with cold, trembling hands. She felt the owner's eyes on her, and it wasn't in a way she liked. He seemed to be sizing her up with the new information his customer had given him about her.

People who didn't know you tended to accept even unsavory details with openhandedness, she thought miserably. After all, how well did you really know somebody who worked for you a few days a week? Jillian lived outside town and kept to herself. She wasn't a social person.

There would be gossip, she was afraid, started by the man who'd just gotten out of prison. And how had he gotten out? she wondered. He'd been sentenced to ten years.

When she finished her coffee, she paid for it and left a tip, and paused to speak to the owner. She didn't really know what to say. Her enemy had made an accusation about her, but how did she refute it?

"What he said," she stammered, "there's a lot more to it than it sounds like. I was…fifteen."

The owner wasn't a stupid man. He'd known Jillian since she was a child. "Listen," he said gently, "I don't pay any mind to gossip. I know Jack Haynes, the assistant circuit D.A. He'd never prosecute a man unless he was sure he could get a conviction."

She felt a little relieved. "Thanks, Mr. Chaney."

He smiled. "Don't worry about it. You might talk to Jack, though."

"Yes, I might." She hesitated. "You won't, well, fire me?"

"Don't be ridiculous. And you be careful out there in the snow. If it gets worse, stay home. I can get old Mrs. Barry to sub for you in the morning, okay?"

"Okay," she said. "Thanks."

"We don't want to lose you in an accident," he replied. She smiled back.

Jack Haynes had his office in the county courthouse, in Hollister. She walked in, hesitantly, and asked the clerk if he was there and could she see him.

"Sure," he said. "He's just going over case files." He grimaced. "Not a fun thing to do. Court's next week."

"I can imagine."

He announced her and she walked in. Jack Haynes smiled, shook hands with her and offered her a chair.

"Davy Harris is out of prison," she blurted out. "I walked right into him at the restaurant this morning."

He scowled. "Who's out?"

She repeated the man's name.

He pushed the intercom button. "Did we receive notification that they'd released Davy Harris in that attempted rape case?"

"Just a minute, sir, I'll check."

The prosecutor cursed under his breath. "I had no idea! You saw him?"

She nodded. "He told everybody in earshot that I had him put in prison for trying to kiss me." She flushed. "What a whitewash job!"

"Tell me about it."

The intercom blared. "Sir, they sent a notification, but it wasn't on the server. I'm sorry. I don't know how it got lost."

"Electronic mail," Haynes scoffed. "In my day, we went to the post office to get mail!"

"And even there it gets lost sometimes, sir," his clerk said soothingly. "Sorry."

"So am I. How did Harris get out?"

"On a technicality, pertaining to the judge's instructions to the jury being prejudicial to his case," came the reply. "He's only out until the retrial."

"Yes, well, that could take a year or two," Haynes said coldly.

"Yes," his clerk said quietly.

"Thanks, Chet," he replied, and closed the circuit.

He turned his attention back to Jillian. "That's the second piece of unsettling news I've had from the court system this week," he said curtly. "They've released Smitty Jones, the bank robber, who threatened our police chief, also on a technicality. He's out pending retrial, too." His face hardened. "It shouldn't come as a surprise that they have the same lawyer, some hotshot from Denver."

Jillian clenched her teeth. "He said he'd kill Ted."

Haynes smiled reassuringly. "Better men than him have tried to kill Ted," he pointed out. "He's got good instincts and he's a veteran law enforcement officer. He can take care of himself, believe me."

"I know that, but anybody can be ambushed. Look at Chief Barnes. He was a cautious, capable law enforcement officer, too."

He grimaced. "I knew him. He was such a good man. Shame, what happened."

"Yes."

He gave her a long look. "Jillian, we can't do anything about Harris while he's out on bond," he told her.

"But you can take precautions, and you should. Don't go anywhere alone."

"I live alone," she pointed out, worriedly.

He drew in a sharp breath. He'd seen cases like this before, where stalkers had vowed revenge and killed or raped their accusers when they were released from prison. He hated the thought of having something bad happen to this poor woman, who'd seen more than her share of the dark side of men.

"I'll tell Ted," she said after a minute.

His eyebrows arched.

She averted her eyes. "We're sort of in a situation, about the ranch. Our uncles left a clause that if we don't get married, the ranch has to be sold at public auction. Ted thinks we should get married very soon. But I've been hesitant," she said, and bit off the reason.

He knew, without being told by her. "You need to be in therapy," he said bluntly.

She grimaced. "I know. But I can't, I just can't talk about things like that to a stranger."

He had a daughter about her age. He thought how it would be for her in a similar circumstance. It made him sad.

"They're used to all sorts of terrible stories," he began.

"I can't talk about personal things to a stranger," she repeated.

He sighed. "It could ruin your whole life, lock you up in ways you don't even realize yet," he said gently. "I've seen cases where women were never able to marry because of it."

She nodded.

"Don't you want a husband and a family?"

"Very much," she said. She ground her teeth together. "But it seems just hopeless right now." She looked up. "That California developer is licking his lips over my ranch already. But I don't know if I can be a good wife. Ted thinks so, but it's a terrible gamble. I know I have hang-ups."

"They'll get worse," he said bluntly. "I speak from experience. I've tried many cases like yours over the years. I've seen the victims. I know the prognosis. It isn't pretty."

Her eyes were haunted and sad. "I don't understand why he did it," she began.

"It's a compulsion," he explained. "They know it's wrong, but they can't stop. It isn't a matter of will." He leaned forward. "It's like addiction. You know, when men try to give up alcohol, but there's something inside them that pushes them to start drinking again. It doesn't excuse it," he said immediately. "But I'm told that even when they try to live a normal life, it's very difficult. It's one day at a time."

He shook his head. "I see the results of addiction all the time. Alcohol, sex, cards, you name it. People destroy not only their own lives, but the lives of their families because they have a compulsion they can't control."

"It's a shame there isn't a drug you can give people to keep them from getting addicted," she said absently.

He burst out laughing. "Listen to you. A drug. Drugs are our biggest headache."

She flushed. "Sorry. Wasn't thinking."

He gave her a compassionate smile. "Talk to Ted," he said. "He'll look out for you until our unwanted visitor leaves. In fact, there's a vagrancy law on the books that could give him a reason to make the man leave. Tell him I said so."

She smiled. "I will. Thanks so much, Mr. Haynes."

She stood up. He did, too, and shook her hand.

"If you need help, and you can't find Ted, you can call me," he said unexpectedly. He pulled out a business card and handed it to her. "My Jessica is just your age," he added quietly. "Nothing like that ever happened to her. But if it had, I'd have a hard time remembering that my job is to uphold the law."

"Jessica is very nice."

"Why, thank you," he chuckled. "I think so, too."

They didn't discuss why he'd raised Jessica alone. Her mother had run off with a visiting public-relations man from Nevada and divorced Mr. Haynes. He'd been left with an infant daughter that his wife had no room for in her new and exciting life of travel and adventure. But he'd done very well raising her. Jessica was in medical school, studying to be a doctor. He was very proud of her.

"Don't forget," he told Jillian on the way out. "If you need me, you call."

She was very touched. "Thanks, Mr. Haynes."

He shrugged. "When I'm not working, which isn't often even after hours, my social life is playing World of Warcraft online." He smiled. "I don't get out much. You won't bother me if you call."

"I'll remember."

She went out and closed the door, smiling at the young clerk on her way outside.

She ran headlong into Ted, who had bounded up the steps, wearing an expression that would have stopped a charging bull.

"What did he say to you?" he demanded hotly. His black eyes were sparking with temper.

"What… Mr. Haynes?" she stammered, nodding toward the office she'd just left.

"Not him. That…" He used some language that lifted both her eyebrows. "Sorry," he said abruptly. "I heard what happened."

She let out a breath. "He announced in the diner that he got put in prison because he wanted to marry me and I didn't want him to kiss me," she said coldly. "He's out on bond because of a technicality, Mr. Haynes said."

"I know. I phoned the prison board."

She tried to smile. "Mr. Haynes says you can arrest him for vagrancy if he stays in town long enough."

He didn't smile back. "He got a job," he said angrily.

She had to lean against the wall for support. "What?"

"He got a damned job in town!" he snapped. "Old Harrington at the feed store hired him on as a day laborer, delivering supplies to ranchers."

She felt sick to her stomach. It meant that Davy Harris had no plans to leave soon. He was going to stay. He was going to live in her town, be around all the time, gossip about her to anybody who would listen. She felt hunted.

Ted saw that and grimaced. He drew her into his arms and held her gently, without passion. "I'll find a way to get him out of here," he said into her hair.

"You can't break the law," she said miserably. She closed her eyes and felt the strong beat of his heart under her ear. "It gets worse. Smitty Jones, that man you arrested for bank robbery, got out, too, didn't he?"

He hesitated. "Yes."

"I guess it's our day for bad news, Ted," she groaned.

He hugged her, hard, and then let her go. "I don't like the idea of your living alone out at the ranch," he said curtly. "It makes you a better target if he came here with plans for revenge. Which he might have."

She bit her lower lip. "I don't want to get married yet."

He let out an exasperated sigh. "I don't have funds that I could use to get you police protection," he said angrily. "And even if I did, the man hasn't made any threats. He's just here."

"I know," she said. "And he's got a job, you said."

He nodded. "I could have a word with the owner of the feed store, but that would be crossing the line, big time. I can't tell a merchant who to hire, as much as I'd like to," he added.

"I know that. He'd just find another job, anyway, if he's determined to stay here." She closed her eyes on a grimace. "He'll talk to everybody he meets, he'll say I had him put away for some frivolous reason." She opened her eyes. "Ted, he makes it all sound like I was just a prude that he shocked with a marriage proposal. He can tell a lie and make it believeable."

"Some people will believe anything they hear," he agreed. His black eyes were turbulent. "I don't like it."

"I don't, either." She felt sick all over. She'd thought things were bad before. Now, they were worse. "I could leave town."

"That would make it worse," he said flatly. "If you run, it will give him credibility."

"I guess so." She looked up at him worriedly. "Don't you let him convince you that I had him put away for trying to kiss me. It was a lot more than that."

He only smiled. "I'm not easy to sway. Besides, I've known you most of your life."

That was true. She didn't add that Ted hadn't known her really well until just recent times.

"There are other people he won't convince, including the prosecutor."

"Mr. Haynes said I could call him if I got in trouble and you weren't available," she said.

He smiled. "He'd come, too. He's a good guy."

"I can't understand why a woman would run away from her husband and a little baby," she said. "He's such a nice person."

"Some women don't want nice, they want dangerous or reckless or vagabond."

"Not me," she said. "I want to stay in Hollister my whole life."

"And have kids?"

She looked up at Ted worriedly. "I want kids a lot," she told him. "It's just…"

"It's just what you have to do to make them," he replied.

She blushed.

"Sorry," he said gently. "I didn't mean for it to come out like that."

"I'm a prude. I really am."

"You're not."

She was beginning to wonder. She didn't like recalling what had happened with the man in her past, but his accusations had disturbed her. Was she really so clueless that she'd sent him to prison for something that wasn't his fault? Had she overreacted? She had been at fault with the auditor; she'd gone with him to the motel and at first she'd let him kiss her. Then things got out of hand and she panicked, largely because of what Davy Harris had done to her.

Ted was looking at his watch. "Damn! I've got a meeting with a defense attorney in my office to take a deposition in a theft case. I'll have to go." He bent and kissed her cheek. "You stay clear of that coyote, and if he gives you any trouble, any at all, you tell me. I'll throw his butt in jail."

She smiled. "I will. Thanks, Ted."

"What are friends for?" he asked, and smiled back.

She watched him walk away with misgivings. She wanted to tell him that she wasn't confident about her actions in the past, tell him that maybe the man she'd accused wasn't as guilty as she thought. She wished she had somebody to talk to about it.

She sighed and got in her truck and drove to the ranch. It was going to be the biggest problem of her life, and she didn't know how she was going to solve it.

Things went from bad to worse very quickly. She went in to work the next morning and Davy Harris was sitting in a booth the minute the doors opened. She had to come out to arrange pies and cakes in the display case for the lunch crowd. She didn't work lunch, but she did much of the baking after she'd finished making breakfast for the customers.

Every time she came out to arrange the confections, the man was watching her. He sat as close to the counter as he could get, sipping coffee and giving her malicious looks. He made her very nervous.

"Sir, can I get you anything else?" the waitress, aware of Jillian's discomfort, asked the man in a polite but firm tone.

He lifted his eyebrows. "I'm finishing my coffee."

"Breakfast is no longer being served, sir. We're getting ready for the lunch crowd."

"I know. I'll be back for lunch," he assured her. "I'm almost done."

"Yes, sir." She produced the check and put it next to his plate, and went back to her other customer, the only other one left in the room.

"You always did cook sweets so well, Jilly," Harris told her with a long visual appraisal. "I loved the lemon cake you used to make for your uncle."

"Thanks," she muttered under her breath.

"You live all alone in that big ranch house, now, don't you?" he asked in a pleasant tone that was only surface. His eyes were full of hate. "Don't you get scared at night?"

"I have a shotgun," she blurted out.

He looked shocked. "Really!"

"Really," she replied with a cold glare. "It would be so unwise for anybody to try to break in at night."

He laughed coldly. "Why, Jilly, was that a threat?" he asked, raising his voice when the waitress came back to that side of the restaurant. "Were you threatening to shoot me?"

"I was saying that if anybody broke into my house, I would use my shotgun," she faltered.

"Are you accusing me of trying to break in on you?" he asked loudly.

She flushed. "I didn't say that."

"Are you sure? I mean, accusing people of crimes they haven't committed, isn't that a felony?" he persisted.

The waitress marched back to his table. "Are you

finished, sir?" she asked with a bite in her voice, because she was fond of Jillian. "We have to clear the tables now."

He sighed. "I guess I'm finished." He looked at the bill, pulled out his wallet, left the amount plus a ten-cent tip. He gave the waitress an amused smile. "Now, don't you spend that whole tip all in one place," he said with dripping sarcasm.

"I'll buy feed for my polo ponies with it," she quipped back.

He glared at her. He didn't like people one-upping him, and it showed. "I'll see you again, soon, Jilly," he purred, with a last glance.

He left. Jillian felt her muscles unlocking. But tears stung her eyes.

"Oh, Jill," the waitress, Sandra, groaned. She put her arms around Jillian and hugged her tight. "He'll go away," she said. "He'll have to, eventually. You mustn't cry!"

Jillian bawled. She hadn't known the waitress well at all, until now.

"There, there," Sandra said softly. "I know how it is. I was living with this guy, Carl, and he knocked me around every time he got drunk. Once, he hit me with a glass and it shattered and cut my face real bad. I loved him so much," she groaned. "But that woke me up, when that happened. I moved out. He made threats and even tried to set fire to my house. But when he finally realized I meant it, he gave up and found another girlfriend. Last I heard, she was making weekly trips to the emergency room up in Billings."

Jillian pulled back, wiping her eyes. "It wasn't like that," she whispered. "I was fifteen, and he tried to…"

*"Fifteen?"*

Jillian bit her lower lip. "My uncle hired him as a handy man."

"Good Lord! You should have had him arrested!"

"I did," Jillian said miserably. "But he got out, and now he's going to make my life hell."

"You poor kid! You tell Chief Graves," she said firmly. "He'll take care of it."

Jillian's eyes were misty. "You can't have somebody thrown out of town without good reason," she said. "He hasn't threatened me or done anything except show up here to eat all the time. And it's the only restaurant in town, Sandra," she added.

"Yes, but he was making some pretty thick accusations," she reminded the other girl.

"Words. Just words."

"They can hurt as bad as fists," Sandra said curtly. "I ought to know. My father never hesitated to tell me how ugly and stupid I was."

Jillian gasped. Nobody in her family had ever said such things to her.

"I guess you had nice people to live with, huh?" Sandra asked with a worldly smile. "That wasn't the case with me. My father hated me, because I wasn't his. My mother had an affair. People do it all the time these days. She came back, but he could never get over the fact that she had me by somebody else. She died and he made me pay for it."

"I'm so sorry."

"You're a nice kid," Sandra told her quietly. "That guy makes any trouble for you in here, he'll have to deal with me."

Jillian chuckled. "I've seen you handle unruly customers. You're good at it."

"I ought to be. I was in the army until two years ago," she added. "I worked as military police. Not much I don't know about hand-to-hand combat."

Jillian beamed. "My heroine!"

Sandra just laughed. "Anyway, you get those cakes arranged and go home. I'll deal with the visiting problem while you're away."

"Thanks. For everything."

"Always wished I had a kid sister," Sandra scoffed. She grinned. "So now I do. You tell people I'm your sister and we'll have some laughs."

That would have been funny, because Sandra's skin was a very dark copper, compared to Jillian's very pale skin. Sandra was, after all, full-blooded Lakota.

"Chief Graves is Cheyenne," she said aloud.

"Nothing wrong with the Cheyenne, now that we're not bashing each other's brains out like we did a century ago," came the amused reply. Sandra winked. "Better get cracking. The boss is giving us dark looks."

Jillian grinned. "Can't have that!" she laughed.

Jillian did feel better, and now she had an ally at work. But she was still worried. That man had obviously come to Hollister to pay her back for his jail sentence, and now she was doubting her own story that had cost him his freedom.

## Chapter 7

Jillian had never considered that she might become a victim of a stalker. And she wondered if it could even be called stalking. Davy Harris came into the restaurant every morning to eat. But it was the only diner in town. So was that stalking?

Ted thought so, but the law wasn't on the victim's side in this case. A man couldn't be arrested for stalking by eating in the only restaurant in town.

But he made Jillian uptight. She fumbled a cake onto the floor two mornings later, one that had taken a lot of trouble to bake, with cream filling. Harris laughed coldly.

"Why, Jilly, do I make you nervous?" he chided. "I'm only having breakfast here. I haven't tried to touch you or anything."

She cleaned the floor, flushed and unsettled. Sandra had called in sick that morning, so they had a substitute waitress, one who just did her job and didn't waste time on getting to know the other employees. She had no one to back her up, now.

"I only wanted to marry you," Harris said in a soft, quiet tone. "You were real young, but I thought you were mature enough to handle it. And you liked me. Remember when the little white kittens were born and they were going to have to be put down because you couldn't keep them all? I went around to almost every house in town until I found places for them to live."

She bit her lip. That was true. He'd been kind.

"And when your uncle John had that virus and was so sick that he couldn't keep the medicine down? I drove both of you to the hospital."

"Yes," she said reluctantly.

He laughed. "And you repaid my kindness by having me put in prison with murderers."

Her face was stricken as she stared at him.

He got to his feet, still smiling, but his eyes were like a cobra's. "Did you think I'd just go away and you'd never have to see me again?"

She got up, a little wobbly. "I didn't realize…"

"What, that I really would go to prison because you exaggerated what happened?" he interrupted. "What kind of woman does that to a man?"

She felt really sick. She knew her face was white.

"I just wanted to marry you and take care of you, and your uncle," he said. "I wouldn't have hurt you. Did I ever hurt you, Jilly?"

She was growing less confident by the second. Had she misjudged him? Was he in prison because she'd blown things out of proportion?

He put a five-dollar bill down beside his plate. "Why

don't you think about that?" he continued. "Think about what you did to me. You don't know what it's like in prison, Jilly. You don't know what men can do to other men, especially if they aren't strong and powerful." His face was taut with distaste. "You stupid little prude," he said harshly. "You landed me in hell!"

"I'm… I'm sorry," she stammered.

"Are you really?" he asked sarcastically. "Well, not sorry enough, not yet." He leaned toward her. "But you're going to be," he said in a voice that didn't carry. "You're going to wish you never heard my name when I'm through with you."

He stood back up again, smiling like a used car salesman. "It was a really good breakfast, Jilly," he said out loud. "You're still a great little cook. Have a nice day, now."

He walked out, while the owner of the restaurant and the cashier gave him a thoughtful look. Jillian could imagine how it would sound. Here was the poor, falsely accused man trying to be nice to the woman who'd put him away. Jillian wasn't going to come out smelling like roses, no matter what she said or did. And now she had her own doubts about the past. She didn't know what she was going to do.

Ted came by the next day. She heard his car at the front door of the ranch house and she went to the steps with a feeling of unease. She didn't think Ted would take the side of the other man, but Davy could be very convincing.

Ted came up the steps, looking somber. He paused when he saw her expression.

"What's happened?" he asked.

She blinked. "What do you mean?"

"You look like death warmed over."

"Do I? It must be the flour," she lied, and forced a laugh. "I've been making a cherry pie."

Once, he would have made a joke, because it was his favorite. But he was quiet and preoccupied as he followed her into the kitchen.

"Any coffee going?" he asked as he sailed his hat onto the counter.

"I can make some."

"Please."

She started a pot, aware of his keen and penetrating gaze, following her as she worked.

"What's going on with you and Harris?" he asked suddenly.

The question startled her so much that she dropped a pan she'd been putting under the counter. Her hands were shaking.

She turned back to him. "No...nothing," she stammered, but her cheeks had flushed.

His face hardened. "Nothing."

"He comes in the restaurant to have breakfast every day," she said.

"And you'd know this, how?"

She put the pan down gently on the counter and drew in a breath. "Because I've got a job there, cooking for the breakfast crowd."

He looked angry. "Since when?"

She hesitated. She hadn't realized how difficult it was going to be, telling him about her job, and explaining why she'd decided to keep it secret from him. It would look bad, as if she didn't trust him.

The guilt made him angrier.

She poured coffee into a mug and put it in front of him on the table. Her hands were unsteady. "I realize it must seem like I'm keeping secrets," she began.

"It sounds a lot like that."

"I was going to tell you," she protested.

"When?"

She hesitated.

"You said you didn't want to get married yet. Is that why?" he persisted. "You got a job so you could take care of your bills here, so that you could refuse to honor the terms of our uncles' wills?"

It was sounding worse than it was. He was mad. He couldn't even hide it.

He hadn't touched his coffee. He got to his feet. "You back away every time I come close to you. When I take you out, you dress like a teenager going to a dance in the gym. You get a job and don't tell me. You're being over-heard flirting with the man who supposedly assaulted you years ago." His eyes narrowed as she searched for ways to explain her behavior. "What other secrets are you keeping from me, Jillian?"

She didn't know what to say that wouldn't make things worse. Her face was a study in misery.

"I'm not flirting with him," she said.

"That isn't what one of the diners said," he returned.

She bit her lower lip. "I've been wondering," she began.

"Wondering what?"

She lifted one shoulder. "Maybe I made a mistake," she blurted out. "Maybe I did exaggerate what happened, because I was so naive." She swallowed hard. "Like with the auditor, when I went out with him and didn't tell him my age, and he got in trouble."

Ted's expression wasn't easily explained. He just stared at her with black eyes that didn't give any quarter at all.

"Davy Harris was kind to Uncle John," she had to admit. "And he was always doing things for him, and for me." She lowered her eyes to the floor, so miserable that she almost choked on her own words. "He said the other men did things to him in prison."

He still hadn't spoken.

She looked up, wincing at his expression. "He wasn't a mean sort of person. He never hurt me…"

He picked up his hat, slammed it over his eyes, and walked out the door.

She ran after him. "Ted!"

He kept walking. He went down the steps, got into his truck and drove off without a single word.

Jillian stared after him with a feeling of disaster.

Sandra gaped at her the next morning at work. "You told Ted Graves that you made a mistake?" she asked. "What in the world is the matter with you? You were so young, Jillian! What sort of man tries to get it on with a kid barely in high school?"

"He was just twenty-one," she protested.

"He should have known better. No jury in the world would have turned him loose for making advances to you."

"Yes, but he, well, while he was in prison, some of the men…" She hesitated, searching for the words to explain.

"I know what you mean," Sandra replied shortly. "But you're missing the whole point. A grown man tried to make you go to bed with him when you were young then. Isn't that what happened?"

Jillian drew in a long breath. "Yes. I guess so."

"Then why are you trying to take the blame for it? Did you lead him on? Did you wear suggestive clothing, flirt with him, try to get him to come into your room when your uncle wasn't around?"

"Good heavens, no!" Jillian protested.

Sandra's black eyes narrowed. "Then why is it your fault?"

"He went to prison on my testimony."

"Sounds to me like he deserved to," Sandra replied curtly.

"But he was a kind man," she said. "He was always doing things for other people. One week when Uncle John was real sick, he even did the grocery shopping for us."

"A few years back in a murder trial, a witness testified that the accused murderer helped her take her groceries into the house. Another told the jury that he tuned up her old car when it wouldn't start. What does that have to do with a man's guilt or innocence?"

Jillian blinked. "Excuse me?"

"Don't you think that a man can do kind things and still kill someone, given the motive?" she asked.

"I never thought of it like that."

"Even kind people can kill, Jillian," Sandra said bluntly. "I knew this guy on the reservation, Harry. He'd give you the shirt off his back. He drove old Mr. Hotchkiss to the doctor every month to get his checkup. But he killed another man in an argument and got sent to prison for it. Do you think they should have acquitted him because he did a couple of kind things for other people?"

"Well, no," she had to admit.

"We all have good and evil in us," the older woman replied. "Just because we're capable of good doesn't mean we can't do something evil."

"I guess I understand."

"You think about that. And stop trying to assume responsibility for something that wasn't your fault. You were just out of grade school when it happened. You weren't old enough or mature enough to permit any man liberties like that, at the time. You weren't old enough to know better, Jillian, but he was."

She felt a little better.

"Besides that, did you like it?"

"Are you kidding?" Jillian exclaimed. "No, I hated it!"

"Then that should tell you who's at fault, shouldn't it?"

Jillian began to relax. "You have a way with words."

"I should have been a writer," Sandra agreed. She grinned, showing perfect white teeth. "Now you stop spouting nonsense and start working on that bacon. We'll have customers ranting because breakfast isn't ready!"

Jillian laughed. "I guess we will. Thanks."

Sandra grinned. "You're welcome."

Jillian didn't go out front when the doors opened, not even to put out the cakes and pies. Sandra did that for her.

"Curious," she said when she came back into the kitchen.

"What is?"

"Your old friend Davy wasn't out there."

"Maybe he decided to leave," Jillian said hopefully.

"It would take somebody more gullible than me to believe that," the older woman replied.

"Yes, but I can hope."

"Know what the Arabs say?" Sandra asked. "They say, trust in Allah, but tie up your camel. Sound advice," she added, shaking a long finger at the other woman.

Jillian did hope for the best, anyway, and not only about Davy Harris leaving town. She hoped that Ted might come by to talk, or just smooth things over with her. But he didn't come to the restaurant, or to the ranch. And the next morning, Davy Harris was right back in the same booth, waiting for his breakfast.

"Did you miss me?" he teased Jillian, having surprised her as she was putting a pound cake in the display case.

"I didn't notice you were gone," she lied, flushing.

"We both know better than that, don't we?" He leaned back in the booth, his pale eyes so smug that it made her curious. "I've been talking to people about you."

She felt uneasy. "What people?"

"Just people."

She didn't know what to say. She got to her feet and went back into the kitchen. Her stomach was cutting somersaults all the way.

That afternoon, as she went out to get into her old vehicle to go home, she walked right into Davy.

She gasped and jumped back. He laughed.

"Do I make you nervous?" he chided. "I can't imagine why. You know, I never tried to hurt you. I never did. Did I?"

"N-no," she blurted out, embarrassed, because a few people standing outside the bank were listening, and watching them.

"I told your uncle I wanted to marry you," he said, without lowering his voice. He even smiled. "He said that he hoped I would, because he liked me and he knew I'd take care of you. But that was before you told those lies about me, wasn't it, Jilly? That was before you got me put in jail for trying to kiss you."

She was embarrassed because they were talking about something private in a very public location, and several people were listening.

"It wasn't…wasn't like that," she stammered, flushing.

"Yes, it was, you just don't like admitting that you made a mistake," he said, his voice a little louder now. "Isn't that the truth?"

She was fumbling for words. She couldn't get her mind to work at all.

"You lied about me," he continued, raising his voice. "You lied."

She should have disputed that. She should have said that it was no lie, that he'd tried to assault her in her own home. But she was too embarrassed. She turned and almost ran to her truck. Once inside, she locked the door with cold, trembling fingers.

Davy stood on the sidewalk, smiling. Just smiling. A man and woman came up to him and he turned and started talking to them as Jillian drove away. She wondered what they were saying. She hoped it wasn't about her.

\* \* \*

But in the next few days, she noticed a change in attitude, especially in customers who came to the restaurants. Her pretty cakes had been quickly bought before, but now they stayed in the case. Jill took most of them back home. When she went to the bank, the teller was polite, but not chatty and friendly as she usually was.

Even at the local convenience store where she bought gas, the clerk was reserved, all business, when she paid at the counter.

The next morning, at work, she began to understand why she was being treated to a cold shoulder from people she'd known most of her life.

"Everybody thinks you did a job on me, Jilly," Davy said under his breath when she was putting a cake on the counter—only one cake today, instead of the variety she usually produced, since they weren't selling.

She glared at him over the cake. "It wouldn't do to tell them the truth."

"What is the truth?" He leaned back in the booth, his eyes cold and accusing. "You had me sent to jail."

She stood up, tired of being harassed, tired of his unspoken accusations, tired of the way local people were treating her because of him.

"I was a freshman in high school and you tried to force me to have sex with you," she said shortly, aware of a shocked look from a male customer. "How hard is that to understand? It's called statutory rape, I believe…?"

Davy flushed. He got to his feet and towered over her. "I never raped you!"

"You had my clothes off and the only reason you stopped was because I slugged you and ran. If Sassy

Peale hadn't had a shotgun, you never would have stopped! You ran after me all the way to her house!"

He clenched his fists by his side. "I went to jail," he snapped. "You're going to pay for that. I'll make sure you pay for that!"

She took the cake, aimed it and threw it right in his face.

"I could have you arrested for assault!" he sputtered.

"Go ahead," she said, glaring at him. "I'll call the police for you, if you like!"

He took a quick step toward her, but the male customer stood up all at once and moved toward him. He backed away.

"You'll be sorry," he told Jillian. He glared at the other customer, and walked out, wiping away cake with a handkerchief.

Jillian was shaking, but she hadn't backed down. She took a shaky breath, fighting tears, and started picking up cake.

"You think he'll go away," the customer, a tall blond man with a patch over one eye, said quietly, in an accented tone, like a British accent, but with a hard accent on the consonants. She recalled hearing accents like that in one of the *Lethal Weapon* movies. "He won't."

She stopped picking up cake and got to her feet, staring at him.

He was tall and well built. His blond hair was in a ponytail. His face was lean, with faint scars, and he had one light brown eye visible. He looked like the sort of man who smiled a lot, but he wasn't smiling now. He had a dangerous look.

"You should talk to a lawyer," he said quietly.

She bit her lip. "And say what? He eats here every day, but this is the only restaurant in town."

"It's still harassment."

She sighed. "Yes. It is. But I can't make him leave."

"Talk to Ted Graves. He'll make him leave."

"Ted isn't speaking to me."

He lifted an eyebrow expressively.

"I ticked him off, too, by saying I might have made a mistake and overreacted to what Davy did to me," she said miserably. "Davy made it sound as if I did. And then he reminded me about all the kind things he did for my uncle and me…"

"Adolph Hitler had a dog. He petted it and took it for walks and threw sticks for it to chase," he said blandly.

She grimaced. She went back down and picked up more cake.

"If you were so young and it took a shotgun to deter him," the man continued, "it wasn't an innocent act."

"I'm just beginning to get that through my thick skull," she sighed.

"This sort of man doesn't quit," he continued, sticking his hands deep in the pockets of his jeans. His eye was narrow and thoughtful. "He's here for more than breakfast, if you get my drift. He wants revenge."

"I guess so."

"I hope you keep a gun."

She laughed. "I hate guns."

"So do I," he mused. "I much prefer knives."

He indicated a huge Bowie knife on one hip, in a fringed leather sheath.

She stared at it. "I don't guess you'd have to do much more than show that to somebody to make them back off."

"That's usually the case."

She finished cleaning up the cake. "They aren't selling well lately, but I thought this one might. Davy seems to have been spending all his spare time telling people what an evil woman I am. There's a distinct chill in the air wherever I go now."

"That's because he's telling his side of the story to anybody who'll listen," he replied. "And that's harassment, as well."

"I can see Ted arresting him for talking to someone," she said sarcastically.

"It depends on what he's saying. I heard what he said in here. If you need a witness, I'm available."

She frowned. "He didn't say much."

"He said enough," he replied.

She shrugged. "I like to handle my own problems."

"Ordinarily I'd say that's admirable. Not in this case. You're up against a man who's done hard time and came out with a grudge. He wants blood. If you're not very careful, he'll get it. He's doing a number on your character already. People tend to believe what they want to believe, and it isn't always the truth. Especially when a likeable young man who's apparently been railroaded by a nasty young girl tells the right kind of story."

She blinked. "I'd be the nasty young girl in this story?"

He nodded.

She put the remnants of her cake into the trash can behind the counter. She shrugged. "I never thought of myself as a bad person."

"It's his thoughts that you have to worry about. If he's mad enough, and I think he is if he came here expressly to torment you, he won't stop with gossip."

That thought had occurred to her, too. She looked up at the customer with wide, worried eyes. "Maybe I should get a job over in Billings."

"And run for it?" he asked. "Fat chance. He'd follow you."

She gasped. "No…!"

His face hardened. "I've seen this happen before, in a similar case," he said tersely. "In fact, I was acting as an unpaid bodyguard as a favor to a friend. The perp not only got out of jail, he went after the girl who testified against him and beat her up."

She glared. "I hope you hurt him."

"Several of us," he replied, "wanted to, but her boyfriend got to him first. He's back in jail. But if she'd been alone, there might not have been anybody to testify."

She felt sick to her stomach. "You're saying something, aren't you?"

"I'm saying that such men are unpredictable," he replied. "It's better to watch your back than to assume that everything will work itself out. In my experience, situations like this don't get better."

She put down the rag she'd been cleaning with, and looked up with worried eyes. "I wish Ted wasn't mad at me," she said quietly.

"Go make up with him," he advised. "And do it soon." He didn't add that he'd seen the expression on her assailant's face and he was certain the man would soon resort to violence to pay her back.

"I suppose I should," she said. She managed a smile. "Thanks, Mr.…?"

"Just call me Rourke," he said, and grinned. "Most people do."

"Are you visiting somebody local?"

His eyebrows arched. "Don't I look like a local?"

She shook her head, softening the noncomment with a smile.

He laughed. "Actually," he said, "I came by to see the police chief. And not on a case. Ted and I were in the military together. I brought a message from an old friend who works as a police chief down in Texas."

She cocked her head. "That wouldn't be the one who taught him to tango?"

He blinked his single eye. "He taught Ted to dance?"

She nodded. "He's pretty good, too."

Rourke chuckled. "Wonders never cease."

"That's what I say."

He smiled down at her. "Talk to Ted," he advised. "You're going to need somebody who can back you up, if that man gets violent."

"I'll do that," she said after a minute. "And thanks."

"You're welcome, but for what?"

"For making me see the light," she replied flatly. "I've been blaming myself for sending Davy to prison."

"You mark my words," he replied. "Very soon, Davy is going to prove to you that it was where he belonged."

She didn't reply. She just hoped it wasn't a prophecy. But she was going to see Ted, the minute she got off work.

# *Chapter 8*

Before Jillian could finish her chores and get out of the restaurant, Sassy Peale Callister came into the restaurant and dragged her to one side.

"I can't believe what I just heard," she said shortly. "Did you actually say that you might have been wrong to have Davy Harris put in jail?"

Jillian flushed to the roots of her hair. "How did you hear about that?" she stammered.

"Hollister is a very small town. You tell one person and everybody else knows," the other woman replied. "Come on, is it true?"

Jillian felt even more uncomfortable. "He was reminding me how much he helped me and Uncle John around the ranch. He was always kind to us. Once, when we were sick, he went to the store and pharmacy for us, and then nursed us until we were well again."

Sassy wasn't buying it. Her face was stony. "That

means he's capable of doing good deeds. It doesn't mean he can't do bad things."

"I know," Jillian said miserably. "It's just…well, he's been in here every day. He makes it sound like I over-reacted…"

"You listen to me, he's no heartsick would-be suitor," Sassy said firmly. "He's a card-carrying coyote with de-lusions of grandeur! I wasn't sure that he wasn't going to try to take the shotgun away from me, even if I'd pulled the trigger. He was furious! Don't you remem-ber what he said?"

Jillian glanced around her. The restaurant was empty, but the owner was nearby, at least within earshot.

"He said that he'd get both of us," Sassy replied. "John thinks he meant it and that he's here for revenge. He hired me a bodyguard, if you can believe that." She indicated the tall man with a long blond ponytail and a patch over one eye.

"That's Rourke," Jilly exclaimed.

Sassy blinked. "Excuse me?"

"That's Rourke. He was in here this morning, when I threw a cake at Davy." She ignored Sassy's gasp and kept going. "He said that I was nuts trying to make ex-cuses for the man, and that I should make up with Ted. He thinks Davy is dangerous."

"So do I," Sassy said quietly. "You should come and stay with us until this is over, one way or the other."

Jillian was tempted. But she thought of little Sammy and a means of revenge that might occur to a mind as twisted as Davy's. He might even burn the house down. She didn't dare leave it unattended.

"Thanks," she said gently, "but I can't do that. Any-way, I've got my uncle's shotgun."

"Which you've never touched," Sassy muttered. "I doubt it's been cleaned since he died."

Jillian stared at the floor. "Ted would clean it for me if I asked him to."

"Why don't you ask him to?" came the short reply. "And then tell him why you need it cleaned. I dare you."

"I don't think Davy would hurt me, really," she said slowly.

"He assaulted you."

"Maybe he just got, well, overstimulated, and..."

"He assaulted you," Sassy replied firmly.

Jillian sighed. "I hate unpleasantness."

"Who doesn't? But this isn't just a man who let a kiss go too far. This is a man who deliberately came to Hollister, got a job and devils you every day at your place of work," Sassy said quietly. "It's harassment. It's stalking. Maybe you can't prove it, but you should certainly talk to Ted about it."

"He'll think I'm overreacting."

"He's a policeman," Sassy reminded her. "He won't."

Jillian was weakening. She was beginning to feel even more afraid of Davy. If Sassy's husband thought there was a threat, and went so far as to hire his wife a bodyguard, he must be taking it seriously.

"John tried to have him arrested, but Ted reminded him that you can't put somebody behind bars for something he said years ago. He has to have concrete evidence."

That made things somehow even worse. Jillian's worried eyes met her friend's. "Davy does scare me."

Sassy moved closer. "I'm going to have Rourke keep an eye on you, too, when I'm safely home with John. We've got enough cowboys at the ranch who have federal backgrounds to keep me safe," she added with a chuckle. "One of them used to work for the godfather of John's sister-in-law. He was a mercenary with mob connections. He's got millions and he still comes to see her." She leaned forward, so that Rourke couldn't hear. "There was gossip once that Rourke was his son. Nobody knows and Rourke never talks about him."

"Wow," Jillian exclaimed. "That would be K.C. Kantor, wouldn't it?"

Sassy was impressed. "How did you know?"

"I wouldn't have, but your husband was talking about him at the restaurant one morning when you were on that shopping trip to Los Angeles and he had to eat in town."

"Eavesdropping, were you?" Sassy teased.

Jillian smiled. "Sorry. Sometimes a waitress can't help it."

"I don't mind." She drew in a breath. "I have to go. But if you need anything, you call. I'll lend Rourke to you."

"My ears work, even if I'm missing one eye," the tall blond man drawled.

Both women turned, surprised.

"And K.C. Kantor is not my father." He bit off every word. "That's malicious gossip, aimed at my dad, who was a military man in South Africa and made enemies because of his job."

"Sorry," Sassy said at once, and looked uneasy. Rourke rarely did anything except smile pleasantly and crack jokes, but his pale brown eye was glittering and he looked dangerous.

He saw the consternation his words had produced, and fell back into his easygoing persona with no visible effort. He grinned. "I eavesdrop shamelessly, too," he added. "I never know when some pretty young woman might be making nice remarks about me. Wouldn't want to miss it."

They both relaxed.

"Sorry," Sassy said again. "I wasn't saying it to be unkind."

He shrugged. "I know that. Kantor took me in when I was orphaned, because he and my dad were friends. It's a common misconception." He frowned. "You're right about Jillian. Living alone is dangerous when you've got an enemy with unknown intentions. Mrs. Callister is safe at night, unless she's going out without her husband. I could come over and sleep on your sofa, if you like."

"Yes, he could," Sassy seconded at once.

That made Jillian visibly uncomfortable. She averted her eyes. "That's very kind of you, thanks, but I'll manage."

Rourke lifted an eyebrow. "Is it my shaving lotion? I mean, it does sometimes put women off," he said blandly.

Sassy laughed. "No. It's convention."

"Excuse me?"

"She won't stay alone at night with a man in the house," Sassy said. "And before you say anything—" she stopped him when he opened his mouth to reply "—I would have felt exactly the same way when I was single. Women in small towns, brought up with certain attitudes, don't entertain single men at night."

He looked perplexed.

"You've never lived in a small town," Jillian ventured.

"I was born in Africa," he said, surprisingly. "I've lived in small villages all my life. But I don't know much about small American towns. I suppose there are similarities. Well, except for the bride price that still exists in some places."

"Bride price?" Jillian stared at him, waiting.

"A man who wants to marry a woman has to give her father a certain number of cattle."

She gaped at him.

"It's a centuries-old tradition," he explained. He pursed his lips and smiled at Jillian. "I'll bet your father would have asked a thousand head for you."

She glared at him. "My father would never have offered to sell me to you!" she exclaimed.

"Different places, different customs," he said easily. "I've lived in places, in ways, that you might never imagine."

"John said you were a gunrunner," Sassy mused.

He glared at her. "I was not," he said indignantly. Then he grinned. "I was an arms dealer."

"Semantics!" she shot back.

He shrugged again. "A man has to make a living when he's between jobs. At the time, there wasn't much action going on in my part of Africa for mercenaries."

"And now you work as a bodyguard?" Jillian asked.

He hesitated. "At times, when I'm on vacation. I actually work as an independent contractor these days. Legit," he added when they looked at him with open suspicion. "I don't do mercenary work anymore."

"So that case in Oklahoma where you helped free a kidnapping victim was legit, too?" Sassy asked.

"I was helping out a friend," he replied, chuckling. "He works for the same federal agency I work for these days."

"But you're an African citizen, aren't you?" Jillian asked. "I mean, if you were born there...?"

"I have American citizenship now," he said, and looked uncomfortable.

"When he went to work for Mr. Kantor, he had to have it," Sassy murmured. "I imagine he pulled some strings at the state department?"

Rourke just looked at her, without speaking.

She held out her hands, palms up. "Okay, I'm sorry, I won't pry. I'm just grateful you're around to look out for me." She glanced at Jillian. "But you still have a problem. What if Harris decides he wants to get even one dark night, and you can't get to that shotgun in time? The one that hasn't been cleaned since your uncle died?"

"I said I'd get Ted to clean it for me," the other woman protested.

"You and Ted aren't speaking."

"I'll come over and clean it for you," Rourke said quietly. "And teach you to shoot it."

Jillian looked hunted. "I hate guns," she burst out. "I hated it when Ted would come over and shoot targets from the front porch. I'll never get used to the sound of them. It's like dynamite going off in my ears!"

Rourke looked at her with shocked disdain. "Didn't anybody ever tell you about earplugs?"

"Earplugs?"

"Yes. You always wear them on the gun range," he explained, "unless you want to go deaf at an early age. Ear protectors are fine on the range, but earplugs can be inserted quickly if you're on a job and expecting trouble."

"How do you hear?"

"They let in sound. They just deaden certain frequencies of sound," he explained. He glanced at Sassy. "You won't need me tonight. I heard your husband say he's lined up a new werewolf movie to watch with you on pay-per-view."

She laughed. "Yes. It's the second in a vampire trilogy, actually. I love it!"

He didn't react. He glanced toward Jillian. "So I'll be free about six. I can come over and clean the shotgun and do a security sweep. If you need locks and silent sentries, I can install them."

She bit her lip, hard. She couldn't afford such things. She could barely pay the bills on what she made as a cook.

The owner of the restaurant, who had been blatantly eavesdropping, joined them. "You can have an advance on your salary anytime you need it," he told Jillian gently. "I'd bar Harris from coming on the premises, if I could, but he's the sort who'd file a lawsuit. I can't afford that," he added heavily.

"Thanks, Mr. Chaney," Jillian said quietly. "I thought you might fire me, because of all that's going on right now."

"Fat chance," he said amusedly. "You're the best cook I've ever had."

"He shouldn't be allowed to harass her while she's doing her job," Sassy said curtly.

"I agree," the restaurant owner said gently. "But this is a business and I can't bar people I dislike without proof they're causing problems. I've never heard him threaten Jillian or even be disrespectful to her."

"That's because he whispers things to me that he doesn't want anybody to overhear," she said miserably. "He made me believe that I had him locked up for no reason at all."

"I live in Hollister," he said quietly. "Even if it's not

in blaring headlines, most of us know what's going on here. I remember the case. My sister, if you recall, was the assistant prosecutor in the case. She helped Jack Haynes with the precedents."

"I do remember," Jillian said. She folded her arms over her slight breasts. "It's so scary. I never thought he'd get out."

"People get out all the time on technicalities," Rourke said. "A case in point is the bank robber your police chief put away. And a friend of mine in the FBI in Texas has a similar problem. A man he sent away for life just got out and is after him. My friend can't do much more than you're doing. The stalker doesn't do anything he could even be charged with."

"Life is hard," Sassy said.

"Then you die," Rourke quipped, and grinned. "Did you watch that British cop show, too? You're pretty young."

"Everything's on disc now, even those old shows. It's one of John's favorites," Sassy chuckled.

"Mine, too," Chaney added, laughing. "They were an odd mix, the female British cop and the American one, in a team."

"Pity it ended before we knew how things worked out between them," Rourke sighed. "I would have loved a big, romantic finale."

Both women and the restaurant owner stared at him.

"I'm a romantic," he said defensively.

The women stared pointedly at the pistol in the shoulder holster under his loose jacket.

"I can shoot people and still be romantic," he said belligerently. "Out there somewhere is a woman who can't wait to marry me and have my children!"

They stared more.

He moved uncomfortably. "Well, my profession isn't conducive to child-raising, I guess, but I could still get married to some nice lady who wanted to cook and darn my socks and take my clothes to the dry cleaner when I was home between jobs."

"That's not romantic, that's delusional," Sassy told him.

"And you're living in the wrong century," Jillian added.

He glared. "I'm not shacking up with some corporate raider in a pin-striped business suit."

"It's not called shacking up, it's called cohabiting," Sassy said drolly. "And I really can't see you with a corporate raider. I should think a Dallas Cowboy linebacker would be... Don't hit me, I'll tell John!" she said in mock fear when he glowered and took a step forward.

"A woman in a pin-striped suit," he qualified.

Sassy nodded. "A female mob hit-person."

He threw up his hands. "I can't talk to you."

"You could if you'd stop mixing metaphors and looking for women who lived in the dark ages." She frowned. "You don't get out much, do you?"

He looked out the window of the restaurant. "In this burg, it wouldn't matter if I did. I think there are two unmarried ladies who live in this town, and they're both in their sixties!"

"We could ask if anybody has pretty cousins or nieces who live out of town," Jillian offered.

He gave her a pursed-lip scrutiny. "You're not bad. You have your own ranch and you can cook."

"I don't want to get married," Jillian said curtly.

"That's true," Sassy said sadly. "I think Harris has put her off men for life. She won't even marry Ted, and that means she'll lose the ranch to a developer."

"Good grief," Rourke exclaimed. "Why?"

"It's in my uncle's will and his uncle's will that we have to marry each other or the ranch gets sold at public auction," Jillian said miserably. "There's a California developer licking his lips in the background, just waiting to turn my ranch into a resort."

Rourke was outraged. "Not that beautiful hunk of land!"

She nodded. "It will look like the West Coast when he gets through. He'll cut down all the trees, pave the land, and build expensive condominiums. I hear he even has plans for a strip mall in the middle. Oh, and an amusement park."

Rourke was unusually thoughtful. "Nice piece of land, that," he remarked.

"Very nice."

"But that doesn't solve your problem," Sassy replied.

"I can be over about six, if that's okay?" he told Jillian, with a questioning glance at Sassy.

"That will be fine with us," Sassy assured him. She glared at Jillian, who was hesitating. "If Ted won't talk to you, somebody has to clean the shotgun."

"I suppose so."

"Enthusiasm like that has launched colonies," Rourke drawled.

Jillian laughed self-consciously. "Sorry. I don't mean to sound reluctant. I just don't know what Ted will think. He's already mad because I said I might have overreacted to Davy Harris when I had him arrested."

"It wasn't overreaction," the restaurant owner, Mr. Chaney, inserted indignantly. "The man deserved what he got. I'm just sorry I can't keep him out of here. If he ever insults you or makes a threat, you tell me. I'll bar him even if I do get sued."

"Thanks, boss. Really," Jillian said.

"Least I could do." He glanced at the front door. "Excuse me. Customers." He left with a smile.

"He always greets people when they come in," Jillian explained with a smile, "and then he comes around to the tables and checks to make sure the service and the food are okay with them. He's a great boss."

"It's a good restaurant," Rourke agreed. "Good food." He grinned at Jillian.

"So. Six?" he added.

Jillian smiled. "Six. I'll even feed you."

"I'll bring the raw materials, shall I?" he asked with a twinkle in his eyes. "Steaks and salad?"

"Lovely!" Jillian exclaimed. "I haven't had a steak in a long time!"

"You've got all that beef over there and you don't eat steak?" he exclaimed. "What about that prime young calf, the little steer…?"

*"Sammy?"* Jillian gasped. "She's not eating beef!"

"She?" he asked.

"She's a cow. Or she will be one day."

"A cow named Sammy." He laughed. "Sounds like Cy Parks, down in Jacobsville, Texas. He's got a girl dog named Bob."

Everyone laughed.

"See?" Jillian said indignantly. "I'm not the only person who comes up with odd names for animals."

Sassy hugged her. "No, you aren't. I'm going home. You let Rourke clean that shotgun."

"Okay. Thanks," she added.

"My pleasure," Rourke said.

Sassy grinned. "And don't let him talk you into marrying him," she added firmly. "Ted will never speak to us again."

"No danger of that," Jillian sighed. "Sorry," she added to Rourke.

"Don't be so hasty, now," Rourke said. "I have many good qualities. I'll elaborate on them tonight. See you at six."

He left with Sassy. Jillian stared after them, grateful but uneasy. What was Ted going to think?

Rourke showed up promptly at six with a bag of groceries.

He put his purchases out on the table. Expensive steaks, lettuce, all the ingredients for salad plus a variety of dressings, and a cherry pie and a pint of vanilla ice cream.

"I know you cook pies and cakes very well," he explained, "but I thought you might like a taste of someone else's cooking. Mrs. Callister's new cook produced that. It's famous where she comes from, up in Billings, Montana."

"I'll love it. Cherry pie is one of my favorites."

"Mine, too."

He started the steaks and then used her gourmet knives to do a fantastic chopping of vegetables for the salad.

Jillian watched his mastery of knives with pure fascination. "It must have taken you a long time to learn to do that so effortlessly."

"It did. I practiced on many people."

She stared at him, uncertain how to react.

He saw that and burst out laughing. "I was joking,"

he explained. "Not that I've never used knives on people, when the occasion called for it."

"I suppose violence is a way of life to someone in your position."

He nodded. "I learned to handle an AK-47 when I was ten years old."

She gasped.

"Where I grew up, in Africa, there were always regional wars," he told her. "The musclemen tried to move in and take over what belonged to the local tribes. I didn't have family at that time, was living in an orphanage, so I went to fight with them." He laughed. "It was an introduction to mean living that I've never been able to get past. Violence is familiar."

"I suppose it would have to be."

"I learned tactics and strategy from a succession of local warlords," he told her. "Some of them were handed down from the time of Shaka Zulu himself."

"Who was that?"

"Shaka Zulu? The most famous of the Zulu warriors, a strategist of the finest kind. He revolutionized weaponry and fighting styles among his people and became a great warlord. He defeated the British, with their advanced weapons."

"Good grief! I never heard of him."

"There was a miniseries on television about his exploits," he said while he chopped celery and cucumbers into strips. "I have it. I watch it a lot."

"I saw *Out of Africa.*"

He smiled. "That's a beaut."

"It is. I loved the scenery." She laughed. "Imagine, playing Mozart for the local apes."

"Inventive." He stopped chopping, and his eye became dreamy. "I think Africa is the most beautiful place on earth. It's sad that the animals are losing habitat so quickly. Many of the larger ones will go extinct in my lifetime."

"There are lots of people trying to save them. They raise the little ones and then turn them back out onto the land."

"Where poachers are waiting to kill them," he said laconically. "You can still find ivory, and elephant feet used for footstools, and rhinoceros horn in clandestine shops all over the world. They do catch some of the perps, but not all of them. It's tragic to see a way of life going dead. Like the little Bushmen," he added quietly. "Their culture was totally destroyed, denigrated, ridiculed as worthless by European invaders. The end result is that they became displaced people, living in cities, in slums. Many are alcoholics."

"I could tell you the same is true here, where Native Americans received similar treatment," she told him.

He smiled. "It seems that the old cultures are so primitive that they're considered without value. Our greatest modern civilizations are less than two thousand years old, yet those of primitive peoples can measure in the hundreds of thousands. Did you know that the mighty civilizations of Middle America were based on agriculture? Ours are based on industry."

"Agriculture. Farming."

He nodded. "Cities grew up around irrigated lands where crops were planted and grew even in conditions of great drought. The Hohokam in Arizona had canals. The Mayan civilization had astronomy." He glanced at her. "The medical practitioners among the Incas knew how to do trepanning on skulls to relieve pressure in the brain. They used obsidian scalpels. It isn't well-known, but they're still in use today in scalpels for surgery."

"How did you learn all that?" she wondered.

"Traveling. It's one of the perks of my job. I get to see things and mix with people who are out in the vanguard of research and exploration. I once acted as bodyguard to one of the foremost archaeologists on earth in Egypt."

"Gosh!"

"Have you ever traveled?" he asked.

She thought about that. "Well, I did go to Oklahoma City, once," she said. "It was a long drive."

He was holding the knife in midair. "To Oklahoma City."

She flushed. "It's the only place outside Montana that I've ever been," she explained.

He was shocked. "Never to another country?"

"Oh, no," she replied. "There was never enough money for…" She stopped and glanced out the window. A pickup truck pulled up in the yard, very fast. The engine stopped, the door opened and was slammed with some fury.

Rourke's hand went involuntarily to the pistol under his arm.

"Oh, dear," Jillian said, biting her lip.

"Harris?" he asked curtly.

She sighed. "Worse. It's Ted."

## Chapter 9

There were quick, heavy footsteps coming up onto the porch. Jillian didn't have to ask if Ted was mad. When he wasn't, his tread was hardly audible at all, even in boots. Now, he was walking with a purpose, and she could hear it.

He knocked on the door. She opened it and stepped back.

His black eyes glittered at her. "I hear you have company," he said shortly.

Rourke came out of the kitchen. His jacket was off, so the .45 automatic he carried was plainly visible in its holster. "She does, indeed," he replied. He moved forward with easy grace and extended a hand. "Rourke," he introduced himself. "I'm on loan from the Callisters."

Ted shook the hand. "Theodore Graves. Chief of police," he added.

Rourke grinned. "I knew that. I came to town to try

to see you the other day, but you were out on a case. Cash Grier said to tell you hello."

Ted seemed surprised. "You know him?"

"We used to work together under, shall we say, unusual conditions, in Africa," came the reply.

Ted relaxed a little. "Rourke. I think he mentioned you."

He shrugged. "I get around. I really came over to clean her shotgun for her, but I'm cooking, too." He gave Ted an appraisal that didn't miss much, including the other man's jealousy. "I'm impressing her with my culinary skills, in hopes that she might want to marry me after supper."

Ted gaped at him. "What?"

"He's just kidding," Jillian said, flushing.

"I am?" Rourke asked, and raised both eyebrows.

Ted glared at the other man. "She's engaged to me."

"I am not!" Jillian told him emphatically.

Rourke backed up a step and held up a hand. "I think I'll go back into the kitchen. I don't like to get mixed up in family squabbles," he added with a grin.

"We are not a family, and we're not squabbling!" Jillian raged.

"We're going to be a family, and yes, we are," Ted said angrily.

Rourke discreetly moved into the kitchen.

"I could have cleaned the shotgun, if you'd just asked me," he said angrily.

"You stormed out of here in a snit and never said a word," she returned. "How was I supposed to ask you, mail a letter?"

"Email is quicker," came a droll voice from the kitchen.

"You can shut up, this is a private argument," Ted called back.

"Sorry," Rourke murmured. "Don't be too long now, cold steak is unappetizing."

"You're feeding him steak?" Ted exclaimed. "What did he do, carve up Sammy?"

"I don't eat ugly calves!" Rourke quipped.

"Sammy is not ugly, she's beautiful!" Jillian retorted.

"If you say so," Rourke said under his breath.

"There's nothing wrong with black baldies," she persisted.

"Unless you've never seen a Brahma calf," Rourke sighed. "Gorgeous little creatures."

"Brahmas are the ugliest cattle on earth," Ted muttered.

"They are not!" Rourke retorted. "I own some of them!"

Ted stopped. "You run cattle around here?" he asked.

Rourke came back into the room, holding a fork. "In Africa. My home is in Kenya."

Ted's eyes narrowed. "So that's how Cash met you."

"Yes. I was, shall we say, gainfully employed in helping oust a local warlord who was slaughtering children in his rush to power."

"Good for you," Ted replied.

"Now you're teaming up?" Jillian said, fuming.

"Only as far as cattle are concerned," Rourke assured her with a flash of white teeth. "I'm still a contender in the matrimonial sweepstakes," he added. "I can cook and clean and make apple strudel." He gave Ted a musing appraisal, as if to say, top that.

Ted was outdone. It was well-known that he couldn't boil water. He glared at the blond man. "I can knock pennies off bottles with my pistol," he said, searching for a skill to compare.

"I can do it with an Uzi," Rourke replied.

"Not in my town, you won't—that's an illegal weapon."

"Okay, but that's a sad way to cop out of a competition." He blinked. "I made a pun!"

"I'm not a cop, I'm a police chief."

"Semantics," Rourke said haughtily, borrowing Jillian's favorite word, and walked back to the kitchen.

Ted looked down at Jillian, who was struggling not to laugh. He was more worried than he wanted to admit about her assailant, who kept adding fuel to the fire in town with gossip about Jillian's past. He knew better, but some people wouldn't. He'd been irritable because he couldn't find a way to make the little weasel leave town. Jillian was pale and nervous. He hadn't helped by avoiding her. It was self-defense. She meant more to him than he'd realized. He didn't want her hurt, even if she couldn't deal with marrying him.

He rested his hand on the butt of the automatic holstered on his belt. "I heard about what happened in the restaurant. You should listen to Sassy. It's possible that Harris may try to get revenge on you here, where you're alone."

"She's not alone," Rourke chimed in. "I'm here."

"Not usually, and he'll know that," Ted said irritably. He didn't like the other man assuming what he thought of as his own responsibility.

"Mrs. Callister already asked her to come stay at the ranch, but she won't," came the reply.

Ted didn't like the idea of Jillian being closer to

Rourke, either. But he had to admit that it was the safest thing for her, if she wouldn't marry him.

"We could get married," he told her, lowering his voice.

"Can you cook?" Rourke asked. "Besides, I have all my own teeth."

Ted ignored him. He was worried, and it showed. He searched her eyes. "Harris bought a big Bowie at the hardward store yesterday."

"It's not illegal to own a knife," Rourke said.

"Technically it's not, although a Bowie certainly falls under the heading of an illegal weapon if he wears it in town. It has a blade longer than three-and-a-quarter inches. It's the implication of the purchase that concerns me," he added.

Rourke quickly became more somber. "He's making a statement of his intentions," he said.

"That's what I thought," Ted agreed. "And he knows there's not a damned thing I can do about it, unless he carries the weapon blatantly. He's not likely to do that."

Rourke didn't mention that he'd been wearing his own Bowie knife in town. "You could turn your back and I could have a talk with him," Rourke suggested, not completely facetiously.

"He'd have me arrest you, and he'd call his lawyer," was the reply.

"I suppose so."

"Maybe I could visit somebody out of state," Jillian said on a sigh.

"He'd just follow you, and pose a threat to anybody you stayed with," Ted said. "Besides that, you don't know anybody out of state."

"I was only joking," Jillian replied. "I'm not running," she added firmly.

The men looked at her with smiling admiration.

"Foolhardy," Rourke commented.

"Sensible," Ted replied. "Nobody's getting past me in my own town to do her harm."

"I'm not needed at the ranch at night," Rourke said. "I could stay over here."

Ted and Jillian both glared at him.

He threw up his hands. "You people have some incredible hang-ups for twenty-first century human beings!"

"We live in a small town," Jillian pointed out. "I don't want to be talked about. Any more than I already am, I mean," she said miserably. "I guess Harris has convinced half the people here that I'm a heartless flirt who had him arrested because he wanted to marry me."

"Good luck to anybody brain-damaged enough to believe a story like that," Rourke said. "Especially anybody who knows you at all."

"Thanks, Rourke," Jillian replied.

Ted shook his head. "There are people who will believe anything. I'd give real money if I could find a law on the books that I could use to make him leave town."

"Vagrancy would have been a good one until he got that job."

"I agree," Ted said.

"It's not right," Jillian blurted out. "I mean, that somebody can come here, harass me, make my life miserable and just get away with it."

Ted's expression was eloquent. His high cheekbones flushed with impotent bad temper.

"I'm not blaming you," Jillian said at once. "I'm not, Ted. I know there's nothing you can do about it."

"Oh, for the wild old days in Africa," Rourke sighed. "Where we made up the laws as we went along."

"Law is the foundation of any civilization," Ted said firmly.

"True. But law, like anything else, can be abused." Rourke pursed his lips. "Are you staying for supper? I actually brought three steaks."

Jillian frowned. "Three?"

He chuckled. "Let's say I anticipated that we might have company," he said with a wry glance at Ted.

Ted seemed to relax. He gave Jillian an appraising look. "After supper, we might sit on the front porch and do a little target shooting."

She glared at him.

"We could practice with her shotgun," Rourke agreed, adding fuel to the fire.

"I only have two shells," Jillian said curtly.

Rourke reached into a bag he'd placed on a nearby shelf. "I anticipated that, too." He handed the shells to Ted with a grin.

"Double ought buckshot," Ted mused. "We use that in our riot shotguns."

"I know."

"What does that mean?" Jillian wanted to know.

"It's a heavy load, used by law enforcement officers to ensure that criminals who fire on them pay dearly for the privilege," Ted said enigmatically.

"Tears big holes in things, love," Rourke translated.

Ted didn't like the endearment, and his black eyes glittered.

Rourke laughed. "I'll just go turn those steaks."

"Might be safer," Ted agreed.

Rourke left and Ted took Jillian's hand and led her into the living room. He closed the door.

"I don't like him being over here with you alone," he said flatly.

She gave him a hunted look. "Well, I wasn't exactly overflowing with people trying to protect me from Davy!"

He averted his eyes. "Sorry."

"Why did you get so angry?"

"You were making excuses for him," he said, his voice curt. "Letting him convince you that it was all a mistake. I got access to the court records, Jillian."

She realized what he was saying, and flushed to her hairline.

"Hey," he said softly. "It's not your fault."

"He said I wore suggestive things…"

"You never wore suggestive things in your life, and you were fifteen," he muttered. "How would you feel, at your age now, if a fifteen-year-old boy actually flirted with you?"

"I'd tell his mama," she returned.

"Exactly." He waited for that to register.

Her eyes narrowed. "You mean, I didn't have the judgment to involve myself with a man, even one just six years older than me."

"You didn't. And you never wore suggestive things."

"I wasn't allowed, even if I'd wanted to. My uncle was very conservative."

"Harris was a predator. He still is. But in his own mind, he didn't do anything wrong. That's why he's giving you the business. He really feels that he had every right to pursue you. He can't understand why he was arrested for it."

"But that's crazy!"

"No crazier than you second-guessing your own re-actions, when you actually had to run to a neighbor's house to save yourself from assault," he pointed out.

She gnawed her lower lip. "I was scared to death." She looked up at him. "Men are so strong," she said. "Even thin men like Davy. I almost didn't get away. And when I did, he went nuts. He was yelling threats all the way to the Peales' house. I really think he would have killed me if Sassy hadn't pulled that shotgun. He might have killed her, too, and it would have been my fault, for running over there for help. But it was the only house close enough."

"I'm sure Sassy never blamed you for that. She's a good person."

"So are you," she commented quietly. "I'm sorry I've been such a trial to you."

His face softened. His black eyes searched hers. "I should have been more understanding." He grimaced. "You don't get how it is, Jake, to go out with a woman you want and be apprehensive about even touching her."

She had a blank look on her face.

"You don't know what I'm talking about, do you?" he asked in a frustrated tone. He moved closer. "Maybe it's time you did."

He curled her into his body with a long, powerful arm and bent his head. He kissed her with soft persua-sion at first, then, when she relaxed, his mouth became invasive. He teased her lips apart and nibbled them. He felt her stiffen at first, but after a few seconds, she became more flexible. She stopped resisting and stood very still.

She hadn't known that she could feel such things. Up until now, Ted had been almost teasing when he kissed her. But this time, he wasn't holding anything back. His arm, at her back, arched her up against him. His big hand smoothed up from her waist and brushed lightly at the edges of her small, firm breast.

She really should protest, she told herself. She shouldn't let him do that. But as the kisses grew longer and hungrier, her body began to feel swollen and hot. She ached for more than she was getting, but she didn't understand what she wanted.

Ted felt those vague longings in her and knew how to satisfy them. His mouth ground down onto hers as his fingers began to smooth over the soft mound of flesh, barely touching, kindling hungers that Jillian had never known before.

She gasped when his fingers rubbed over the nipple and it became hard and incredibly sensitive. She tried to draw back, but not with any real enthusiasm.

"Scared?" he whispered against her mouth. "No need. We have a chaperone."

"The door...it's closed."

"Yes, thank goodness," he groaned, "because if it wasn't, I wouldn't dare do this."

"This" involved the sudden rise of her shirt and the bra up under her chin and the shocking, delicious, invasion of Ted's warm mouth over her breast.

She shuddered. It was the most intense pleasure she'd ever felt. Her short nails dug into his broad shoulders as she closed her eyes and arched backward to give him even better access to the soft, warm flesh that ached for his tender caress.

She felt his hand cupping her, lifting her, as his mouth opened over the nipple and he took it between his lips and tongue.

Her soft gasp was followed by a harsh, shivering little moan that cost him his control. Not only had it been a long, dry spell, but this woman was the most important person in his life and he wanted her with an obsessive hunger. He hadn't been able to sleep for thinking about how sweet it would be to make love to her. And now she was, despite her hang-ups, not only welcoming his touch, but enjoying it.

"You said you didn't want to marry me," he whispered roughly as his mouth became more demanding.

Her nails dug into his back. "I said a lot of things," she agreed. Her eyes closed as she savored the spicy smell of his cologne, the tenderness of his mouth on forbidden flesh. "I might have even…believed them, at the time."

He lifted his head and looked down at her. His expression tautened at the sight of her pretty, firm breasts, and his body clenched. "I took it personally. Like you thought there was something wrong with me."

"Ted, no!" she exclaimed.

He pulled back the hand that was tracing around her nipple.

She bit her lip. "I wasn't saying no to that," she said with hopeless shyness, averting her eyes. "I meant, I don't think there's anything wrong with you…!"

She gasped as he responded to the blatant invitation in her voice and teased the hard rise of flesh with his thumb and forefinger.

"You don't?" he whispered, and smiled at her in a way that he never had before.

"Of course not! I was just scared," she managed, because what he was doing was creating sensations in some very private places. "Scared of marriage, I mean."

"Marriage is supposed to be a feast of pleasure for two people who care about each other," he pointed out, watching with delight her fascination with what he was doing to her willing body. He drew in a long breath and bent his head. "I'm beginning to believe it."

He opened his mouth over her soft breast and drew it inside, suckling it with his lips and his tongue in a slow, easy caress that caused her whole body to clench and shiver. As his ardor increased, he felt with wonder the searching fingers on the buttons of his shirt. They hesitated.

"Men like to be touched, too," he whispered into her ear.

"Oh."

She finished opening the button, a little clumsily, and spread her hands over the thick, curling mass of hair that covered his chest. "Wow," she whispered when sensations rippled through her body and seemed to be echoed coming from his. "You like that?" she asked hesitantly.

"I love it," he gritted.

She smiled with the joy of discovery as she looked up at him, at his mussed hair, his sensuous mouth, his sparkling black eyes. It was new, this shared pleasure. And she'd been so certain that she'd never be able to feel it with him, with anyone.

He bent to her mouth and crushed his lips down over it as his body eased onto hers. She felt the press of his bare chest against her breasts and arched up to increase the contact. Her arms went around him tightly, holding on as the current of passion swept her along.

He eased one long, powerful leg between both of hers and moved against her in a rhythm that drew shudders and soft moans from her throat. She buried her teeth in his shoulder as the sensations began to rise and become obsessive. He must have felt something comparable, because he suddenly pushed down against her with a harsh groan as his control began to slip.

The soft knock on the door came again and again, until it was finally a hammering.

Ted lifted his head, his shocked eyes on Jillian's pretty pink breasts with visible passion marks, her face flushed and rigid with desire, her eyes turbulent as they met his.

"What?" Ted said aloud.

"Steak's ready! Don't let it get cold!" Rourke called, and there were audible footsteps going back down the hall.

With the passion slowly receding, Jillian was disturbed at letting Ted see her like this. Flushed, she fumbled her blouse and bra back on, wincing as the sensitive nipple was brushed by the fabric.

"Sorry," he whispered huskily. "I lost my head."

She managed a shaky smile. "It's okay. I lost mine, too." She looked at him with absolute wonder. "I didn't know it could feel like that," she stammered. "I mean, I never felt like that with anybody. Not that I ever let any man do that…!"

He put a long finger over her lips and smiled at her in a way he never had before. "It's okay, Jake."

She was still trying to catch her breath, and not doing a good job of it.

"I think you could say that we're compatible, in that way," he mused, enjoying her reaction to him more than he could find a way to express.

She laughed softly. "Yes, I think you could."

He smiled. "So, suppose we get married. And you can live with me, here on the ranch, and you'll never have to worry about Harris again."

She hesitated, but not for very long. She nodded, slowly. "Okay."

His high cheekbones went a ruddy color. It flattered him that she'd agree after a torrid passionate interlude, when he hadn't been able to persuade her with words.

"Don't get conceited," she said firmly, figuring out his thoughts.

His eyes twinkled. "Not possible."

She laughed. It was as if the world had changed completely in those few minutes. All her hang-ups had gone into eclipse the minute Ted turned the heat up.

"I wondered," he confessed, "if you'd be able to respond to a man after what happened to you."

"I did, too." She moved close to him and put her hands on his chest. "It was one reason I was afraid to let things go, well, very far. I didn't want to lead you on in any way and then pull away and run. I almost did that once."

"Yes," he said.

"If we get married, you'll give me a little time, won't you?" she asked worriedly. "I mean, I think I can do what you want me to. But it's just getting used to the idea."

Ted, who knew more than she did about women's re-actions when passion got really hot, only smiled. "No problem."

She grinned. "Okay, then. Do we get married in the justice of the peace's office…?"

"In a church," he interrupted. "And you have to have a white gown and carry a bouquet. I'll even wear my good suit." He smiled. "I'm only getting married once, you know. We have to do it right."

She loved that attitude. It was what she'd wanted, but she was sensitive about being pushy. "Okay," she said.

"You'll be beautiful in a wedding gown," he murmured, bending to kiss her tenderly. "Not that you aren't beautiful in blue jeans. You are."

"I'm not," she faltered.

"You are to me," he corrected. His black eyes searched hers and he thought about the future, about living with her, about loving her… He bent and kissed her hungrily, delighting when she returned the embrace fervently.

"The steak's going to be room temperature in about thirty seconds!" Rourke shouted down the hall.

Ted pulled back, laughing self-consciously. "I guess we could eat steak, since he's been nice enough to cook it," he told her. His eyes glittered. "We can tell him we're engaged before we even start eating."

"Rourke's not interested in me that way," she said easily, smiling. "He's a nice man, but he's just protective of women. It isn't even personal."

Ted had his doubts about that. Jillian underestimated her appeal to men.

"Come on," she said, and slid her little hand into his big one.

That knocked the argument right out of him. It was

the first physical move she'd made toward him. Well, not the first, but a big one, just the same. He slid his fingers between hers sensually, and smiled at her.

She smiled back. Her heart was hammering, her senses were alive and tumultuous. It was the beginning of a whole new life. She could hardly wait to marry Ted.

Rourke gave them a knowing smile when he noticed the telltale signs of what they'd been doing. He served up supper.

"This is really good," Ted exclaimed when he took the first bite of his steak.

"I'm a gourmet chef," Rourke replied, surprisingly. "In between dangerous jobs, I used to work in one of the better restaurants in Jo'burg," he said, giving Johannesburg it affectionate abbreviation.

"Wonders will never cease," Jillian said with a grin. "From steaks to combat."

"Oh, it was always combat first," Rourke said easily, "since I was born in Africa."

"Africa was always a rough venue, from what Cash told me," Ted said.

Rourke nodded. "We have plenty of factions, all trying to gain control of the disputed African states, although each is a sovereign nation in the Organization of African Unity, which contains fifty-four nations. The wars are always bloody. And there are millions upon millions of displaced persons, trying to survive with their children. A mercenary doesn't even have to look for work, it's all around him." His face hardened. "What's hardest is what they do to the kids."

"They must die very young there," Jillian commented sadly.

"No. They put automatic weapons in their hands when they're grammar school age, teach them to fire rocket launchers and set explosive charges. They have no sense of what childhood should actually be."

"Good heavens!" she exclaimed.

"You've never traveled, Jake," Ted said gently. "The world is a lot bigger than Hollister."

"I guess it is. But I never had the money, even if I'd had the inclination," she said.

"That's why I joined the army." Ted chuckled. "I knew it was the only way I'd get to travel."

"I wanted to see the world, too." Rourke nodded. "But most of what I've seen of it wouldn't be appropriate for any travel magazine."

"You have a ranch?" Ted asked.

He smiled. "Yes, I do. Luckily it's not in any of the contested areas, so I don't have to worry about politicians seizing power and taking over private land."

"And you run Brahmas," Ted said, shaking his head. "Ugly cattle."

"They're bred to endure the heat and sometimes drought conditions that we have in Africa," Rourke explained. "Our cattle have to be hearty. And some of your American ranchers use them as breeding stock for that very reason."

"I know. I've seen a lot of them down in Texas."

"They don't mind heat and drought, something you can't say for several other breed of cattle," Rourke added.

"I guess," Jillian said.

Rourke finished his steak and took a sip of the strong coffee he'd brewed. "Harris has been frustrated because

Jillian got one of the waitresses to start putting cakes out for her in the display case."

"They haven't been selling," Jillian said sadly. "They used to be very popular, and now hardly anybody wants slices of them. I guess Davy has convinced people that they shouldn't eat my cooking because I'm such a bad person."

"Oh, that's not true," Ted said at once. "Don't you know about the contest?"

She frowned. "What contest?"

"You don't read the local paper, do you?" Rourke chided her.

She shook her head. "We already know what's going on, we only read a paper to know who got caught. But I have him," she pointed at Ted, "to tell me that, so why do I need to spend money for a newspaper?"

They both laughed.

"The mayor challenged everyone in Hollister to give up sweets for two weeks. It's a competition between businesses and people who work for them. At the end of the two weeks, everybody gets weighed, and the business with the employees who lost the most weight gets a cash prize, put up by the businesses themselves. The employees get to decide how the money's spent, too, so they can use it for workplace improvements or cash bonuses."

Jillian perked up. "Then it isn't about me!"

"Of course not," Ted chuckled. "I've heard at least two men who eat in that restaurant complain because they couldn't eat those delicious cakes until the contest ended."

"I feel so much better," she said.

"I'm glad," Rourke told her. "But that still doesn't

solve your problem. Harris bought a Bowie knife and he doesn't hunt." He let the implication sink in. "He's facing at least ten to fifteen on the charges if he goes back to trial and is convicted again. He's been heard saying that he'll never go back to that hellhole voluntarily. So basically he's got nothing to lose." He glanced at Ted. "You know that already."

Ted nodded. "Yes, I do," he replied. He smiled at Jillian. "Which is why we're getting married Saturday."

She gasped. "Saturday? But there's not enough time…!"

"There is. We'll manage. Meanwhile," Ted said, "you're going to take Sassy's invitation seriously and stay out at her ranch until the ceremony. Right?"

She wanted to argue, but both males had set faces and determined expressions. So she sighed and said, "Right."

# Chapter 10

Not only did John and Sassy Callister welcome Jillian as a houseguest, Sassy threw herself into wedding preparations and refused to listen to Jillian's protests.

"I've never gotten to plan a wedding, not even my own," Sassy laughed. "John hired a professional to do it for us because so many important people came to the ceremony. So now I'm taking over preparations for yours."

"But I can't afford this store," the younger woman tried to complain. "They don't even put price tags on this stuff!"

Sassy gave her a smile. "John and I agreed that our wedding present to you is going to be the gown and accessories," she said. "So you can hand it down through your family. You might have a daughter who'd love to wear it at her own wedding."

Jillian hadn't thought about that. She became dreamy.

A child. A little girl that she could take on walks, cuddle and rock, read stories to. That was a part of marriage she'd never dwelled on before. Now, it was a delightful thought.

"So stop arguing," Sassy said gently, "and start making choices."

Jillian hugged her. "Thanks. For the gown and for letting me stay with you until the wedding."

"This is what friends are for. You'd do it for me in a heartbeat if our situations were reversed."

"Yes, but I could have gotten you killed that night by running to you for help," Jillian said. "It torments me."

"I was perfectly capable of handling Davy Harris. And now I've got John, who can handle anything."

"You're very lucky. He's a good man."

"Yes, he is," Sassy agreed with a smile.

"I've never seen anything as beautiful as these dresses," Jillian began.

"I hear you're getting married Saturday, Jilly," came a cold, taunting voice from behind her.

Both women turned. Davy Harris was watching them, a nasty look on his face.

"Yes, I'm getting married," Jillian told him.

"There was a time when I thought you'd marry me," he said. "I had it all planned, right down to what sort of dress you'd wear and where we'd live. I'd lined up a full-time job with a local rancher. Everything was set." His lips twisted. "Then you had to go and get outraged when I tried to show you how I felt."

"I'll show you how I feel," Sassy said pertly. "Where's my shotgun?"

"Terroristic threats and acts, Mrs. Callister," he shot

back. "Suppose I call the news media and tell them that you're threatening me?"

Jillian was horrified.

Sassy just smiled. "Well, wouldn't it be a shame if that same news media suddenly got access to the trial transcripts?" she asked pleasantly.

His face hardened. "You think you're so smart. Women are idiots. My father always said so. My mother was utterly worthless. She couldn't even cook without burning something!"

Jillian stared at him. "That doesn't make a woman worthless."

"She was always nervous," he went on, as if she hadn't spoken. "She called the police once, but my father made sure she never did it again. They put him in prison. I never understood why. She had him locked up. He was right to make her pay for it."

Sassy and Jillian exchanged disturbed looks.

Harris gave Jillian a chilling smile. "He died in prison. But I won't. I'm never going back." He shrugged. "You enjoy thinking about that wedding, Jilly. Because all you're going to get to do is think about it. Have a nice day, now."

He walked out.

The shopping trip was ruined for Jillian. Sassy insisted that they get the gown and the things that went with it, but Jillian was certain that Davy had meant what he said. He was going to try to kill her. Maybe he'd even kill himself, afterward. In his own mind, he was justified. There was no way to reason with such a person, a man who thought that his own mother deserved to die because she'd had his father arrested for apparently greatly abusing her.

"You know, there are scary people in the world," Jillian told Sassy in a subdued tone. "I'll bet if Uncle John had ever really talked to Davy, he'd never have let him in the front door in the first place. He's mentally disturbed, and it isn't apparent until he starts talking about himself."

"I noticed that," Sassy replied. She drew in a long breath. "I'm glad we have Rourke."

Jillian frowned. "Where is he?"

"Watching us. If Harris had made a threatening move, he'd already be in jail, probably after a trip to the emergency room. I've never seen Rourke mad, but John says it's something you don't want to experience."

"I got that impression." She laughed. "He cooked steaks for Ted and me."

"I heard about that," the other woman said in an amused tone. "Ted was jealous, was he?"

"Very. But after he realized that Rourke was just being friendly and protective, his attitude changed. Apparently he knows a police chief in Texas that Ted met at a workshop back east."

"Rourke does get around." She glanced at Jillian. "He acts like a perpetual clown, but if you see him when he thinks he's alone, it's all an act. He's a very somber, sad person. I think he's had some rough knocks."

"He doesn't talk about them much. Just about his ranch."

"He doesn't talk about K.C. Kantor, either," Sassy replied. "But there's some sound gossip about the fact that Rourke's mother was once very close to the man."

"From what everybody says about that Kantor man, he isn't the sort to have kids."

"That's what I thought. But a man can get into a

situation where he doesn't think with his mind," Sassy chuckled. "And when people get careless, they have kids."

"I'd be proud of Rourke, if I was his father."

"You're the wrong age and gender," Sassy said, tongue-in-cheek.

"Oh, you know what I mean. He's a good person."

"He is," Sassy said as she pulled up in front of the ranch house. "I'm glad John hired him. At least we don't have to worry about being assassinated on the way to town!"

"Amen," Jillian sighed.

John Callister was an easygoing, friendly man. He didn't seem at all like a millionaire, or at least, Jillian's vision of one. He treated her as he would a little sister, and was happy to have her around.

Jillian also liked Sassy's mother, who was in poor health, and her adopted sister, Selene, who was a whiz at math and science in grammar school. John took care of them, just as he took care of Sassy.

But the easygoing personality went into eclipse when he heard that Davy Harris had followed them into the dress shop in Billings.

"The man is dangerous," he said as they ate an early supper with Rourke.

"He is," Rourke agreed. "He shouldn't be walking around loose in the first place. What the hell is wrong with the criminal justice system in this country?"

John gave him a droll look. "It's better than the old vigilante system of the distant past," he pointed out. "And it usually works."

"Not with Harris," Rourke replied, his jaw set as he

munched on a chef's salad. "He can put on a good act for a while, but he can't keep it up. He starts talking, and you see the lunacy underneath the appearance of sanity."

"Disturbed people often don't know they're disturbed," Sassy said.

"That's usually the case, I'm sad to say," Rourke added. "People like Harris always think they're being persecuted."

"I knew a guy once who was sure the government sent invisible spies to watch him," John mused. "He could see them, but nobody else could. He worked for us one summer on the ranch back home. Gil and I put up with him because he was the best horse wrangler we'd ever had. But that was a mistake."

"How so?" Rourke asked.

"Well, he had this dog. It was vicious and he refused to get rid of it. One day it came right up on the porch and threatened Gil's little girls. Gil punched him and fired him. Then he started cutting fences and killing cattle. At the last, he tried to kill us. He ended up in prison, too."

"Good heavens!" Jillian said. "No wonder you hired a bodyguard for Sassy."

"Exactly," John replied tersely. He didn't mention that Sassy had been the victim of a predator herself, in the feed store where she was working when they met. That man was serving time now.

His eyes lingered on Sassy with warm affection. "Nobody's hurting my best girl. Or her best friend," he declared with a grin at Jillian.

"Not while I'm on the job," Rourke added, chuckling. "You could marry me, you know," he told Jillian.

"I really do have most of my own teeth left, and I can cook. Your fiancé can't boil water, I hear."

"That's true," Jillian said, smiling. "But I've known him most of my life, and we think the same way about most things. We'll have a good marriage." She was sure of that. Ted would be gentle, and patient, and he'd rid her of the distaste Davy had left in her about physical relationships. She'd never been more certain of anything.

"Well, it's a great shame," Rourke said with a theatrical sigh. "I'll have to go back home to my ugly cattle and live in squalor because nobody wants to take care of me."

"You'll find some lovely girl who will be happy living on a small farm in Africa," Jillian assured him.

John almost choked on his coffee.

Rourke gave him a cold glare.

"What is wrong with you?" Sassy asked her husband.

He wiped his mouth, still stifling laughter. "Private joke," he said, sharing a look with Rourke, who sighed and shrugged.

"But it had better be somebody who can dress bullet wounds," John added with a twinkle in his eyes as he glanced at the other man.

"I only get shot occasionally," Rourke assured him. "And I usually duck in time."

"That's true," John agreed, forking another piece of steak into his mouth. "He only has one head wound, and it doesn't seem to have affected his thinking processes." He didn't mention the lost eye, because Rourke was sensitive about it.

"That was a scalp wound," Rourke replied, touching a faint scar above his temple. He glared at the other man from a pale brown eye. "And not from a bullet. It was from a knife."

"Poor thing," Jillian murmured.

John choked on his steak.

"Will you stop?" Rourke muttered.

"Sorry." John coughed. He sipped coffee.

Jillian wished she knew what they were talking about. But it was really none of her business, and she had other worries.

The wedding gown was exquisite. She couldn't stop looking at it. She hung it on the door in the guest bedroom and sighed over it at every opportunity.

Ted came by to visit frequently and they took long walks in the woods, to talk and to indulge in a favorite of dating couples, the hot physical interludes that grew in intensity by the day.

He held her hand and walked with her down a long path through the snow, his fingers warm and strong in hers.

"I can't stand it if I go a whole day without seeing you," he said out of the blue.

She stopped walking and looked up at him with pure wonder. "Really?"

He pulled her into his arms. "Really." He bent and kissed her slowly, feeling her respond, feeling her warm lips open and move tenderly. She reached her arms up around his neck as if it was the most natural thing in the world. He smiled against her lips. It was a delightful surprise, her easy response to him.

"Maybe I can get used to Sammy following me around, and you can get used to me shooting targets off the front porch," he teased.

She grinned. "Maybe you can teach me to shoot, too."

He looked shocked. "I can?"

"We should share some interests," she said wisely. "You always go to that shooting range and practice. I could go with you sometimes."

He was surprised and couldn't hide it.

She toyed with a shirt button. "I don't like being away from you, either, Ted," she confessed and flushed a little. "It's so sweet…"

He pulled her close. One lean hand swept down her back, riveting her to his powerful body. "Sweeter than honey," he managed before he kissed her.

His hand pushed her hips against the sudden hardness of his own, eliciting a tiny sound from her throat. But it wasn't protest. If anything, she moved closer.

He groaned out loud and ground her hips into his.

"I can't wait until Saturday," he said in a husky tone, easing his hands under Jillian's blouse, under the bra to caress her soft breasts. "I'm dying!"

"So am I," she whispered shakily. "Oh, Ted!" she gasped when he pulled the garments out of his way and covered her breast with his mouth. It was so sweet. Too sweet for words!

He didn't realize what he was doing until they were lying on the cold ground, in the snow, while he kissed her until she was breathless.

She was shaking when he lifted his head, but not from cold or fear. Her eyes held the same frustrated desire that his held.

"I want to, so much!" she whispered.

"So do I," he replied.

For one long instant, they clung together on the hard

ground, with snow making damp splotches all down Jillian's back and legs, while they both fought for control.

Ted clenched his hands beside her head and closed his eyes as he rested his forehead against hers. He was rigid, helplessly aroused and unable to hide it.

She smoothed back his black hair and pressed soft, undemanding little kisses all over his taut face, finally against the closed eyelids and short thick black lashes.

"It's all right," she whispered. "It's all right."

He was amazed at the effect those words, and the caresses, had on him. They eased the torment. They calmed him, in the sweetest way he'd ever imagined. He smiled against her soft throat.

"Learning how to tame the beast, aren't you?" he whispered in a teasing tone.

She looked up at him with soft, loving eyes. "How to calm him down, anyway," she said with a little laugh. "I think marriage is going to be an adventure."

"So do I."

He stood and tugged her up, too, helping to rearrange her disheveled clothing. He grinned at her. "We both love maps and the tango. We'll go dancing every week."

Her eyes brightened. "I'd like that."

He enveloped her against him and stood holding her, quietly, in the silence of the snow-covered woods. "Heaven," he whispered, "must be very like this."

She smiled, hugging him. "I could die of happiness."

His heart jumped. "So could I, sweetheart."

The endearment made her own heart jump. She'd never been so happy in her life.

"Saturday can't come soon enough for me," he murmured.

"Or for me. Ted, Sassy bought me the most beauti-

ful wedding gown. I know you aren't supposed to see it
before the ceremony, but I just have to show it to you."

He drew back, smiling. "I'd like that."

They walked hand in hand back to the ranch house,
easy and content with each other in a way they'd never
been before. They looked as if they'd always been together, and always would be.

Sassy, busy in the kitchen with the cook, grinned at
them. "Staying for lunch, Ted? We're having chili and
Mexican corn bread."

"I'd love to, if you have enough to share."

"Plenty."

"Then, thanks, I will. Jillian wants me to see the
wedding gown."

"Bad luck," Sassy teased.

"We make our own luck, don't we, honey?" he asked
Jillian in a husky, loving tone.

She blushed at the second endearment in very few
minutes and squeezed his hand. "Yes, we do."

She opened her bedroom door and gasped, turning
pale. There, on the floor, were the remains of her wedding gown, her beautiful dress. It had been slashed to
pieces.

"Stop right there," Ted said curtly, his arm prevent-
ing Jillian from entering the room. "This is now a crime
scene. I'll get the sheriff's department's investigator out
here right now, and the state crime-lab techs. I know
who did this. I only want enough proof to have him arrested!"

Jillian wrapped her arms around her chest and shivered. Davy had come right into the house and nobody
knew. Not even Rourke. It was chilling. Sassy, arriving

late, took in the scene with a quick glance and hugged Jillian.

"It will be all right," she promised. But her own eyes were troubled. It was scary that he'd come into the house without being seen.

Rourke, when he realized what had happened, was livid. "That polecat!" he snarled. "Right under my bloody nose, and me like a raw recruit with no clue he was on the place! That won't happen again! I'm calling in markers. I'll have this place like a fortress before Saturday!"

Nobody argued with him. The situation had become a tragedy in the making. They'd all underestimated Davy Harris's wilderness skills, which were apparently quite formidable.

"He was a hunter," Jillian recalled. "He showed me how to track deer when he first started working with Uncle John, before he got to be a problem. He could walk so nobody heard a step. I'd forgotten that."

"I can ghost-walk myself," Rourke assured her.

"He used to set bear traps," Jillian blurted out, and reddened when everybody looked at her. "He said it was to catch a wolf that had been preying on the calves, but Uncle John said there was a dog caught in it…" She felt sick. "I'd forgotten that."

The men looked at each other. A bear trap could be used for many things, including catching unsuspecting people.

Jillian stared at Ted with horror. "Ted, he wouldn't use that on Sammy, would he?" she asked fearfully. Davy knew how much she loved her calf.

"No," he assured her with a comforting arm around her shoulders as he lied. "He wouldn't."

Rourke left the room for a few minutes. He came back, grim-faced. "We're going to have a lot of company very soon. All we need is proof that he was here, and he won't be a problem again."

Which would have been wonderful. Except that there wasn't a footprint in the dirt, a fingerprint, or any trace evidence whatsoever that Davy Harris had been near the Callister home. The technicians with all their tools couldn't find one speck of proof.

"So much for Locard's Exchange Principle," Ted said grimly, and then had to explain what it meant to Jillian. "A French criminalist named Edmond Locard noted that when a crime is committed, the perpetrator both carries away and leaves behind trace evidence."

"But Davy didn't," she said sadly.

"He's either very good or very lucky," Ted muttered. He slid a protective arm around Jillian. "And it won't save him. He's the only person in town who had a motive for doing this. It's just a matter of proving it."

She laughed hollowly. "Maybe you could check his new Bowie knife to see if it's got pieces of white lace sticking to it," she said, trying to make the best of a bad situation.

But he didn't laugh. He was thoughtful. "That might not be such a bad idea," he murmured. "All I'd need is probable cause, if I can convince a judge to issue a search warrant on the basis of it." He pursed his lips and narrowed his eyes, nodding to himself. "And that's just what I'm going to do. Stick close to the house today, okay?"

"Okay."

He kissed her and left.

But Ted came back a few hours later and stuck to her like glue. She noticed that he was suddenly visible near her, everywhere she went around the house and the barn. It was just after he'd received a phone call, to which nobody was privy.

"What's going on?" Jillian asked him bluntly.

He smiled, his usual easygoing self, as he walked beside her with his hands deep in the pockets of his khaki slacks. "What would be going on?"

"You're usually at work during the day, Ted," she murmured dryly.

He grinned at her. "Maybe I can't stay away from you, even on a workday," he teased.

She stopped and turned to him, frowning. "That's not an answer and you know…!"

She gasped as he suddenly whirled, pushing her to the ground as he drew his pistol and fired into a clump of snow-covered undergrowth near the house. Even as he fired, she felt a sting in her arm and then heard a sound like a high-pitched crack of thunder.

That sound was followed by the equally loud rapid fire of a .45 automatic above her. She heard the bullets as they connected with tree trunks in the distance.

"You okay?" he asked urgently.

"I think so."

He stopped firing, and eased up to his feet, standing very still with his head cocked, listening. Far in the distance was the sound of a vehicle door closing, then an engine starting. He whipped out his cell phone and made a call. He gave a quick explanation, a quicker description of the direction of travel of the vehicle and assurances that the intended victim was all right. He put up the cell phone and knelt beside a shaken Jillian.

There was blood on her arm. The sleeve of her gray sweatshirt was ripped. She looked at it with growing sensation. It stung.

"What in the world?" she stammered.

"You've been hit, sweetheart," he said curtly. "That's a gunshot wound. I didn't want to tell you, but one of my investigators learned that Harris bought a high-powered rifle with a telescopic sight this morning, after I had his rented room tossed for evidence."

"He's a convicted felon, nobody could have sold him a gun at all…!" she burst out.

"There are places in any town, even small ones, where people can buy weapons under the table." His face was hard as stone. "I don't know who sold it to him, but you'd better believe that I'm going to find out. And God help whoever did, when I catch up to him!"

She was still trying to wrap her mind around the fact that she'd been shot. Rourke, who'd been at the other end of the property, came screeching up in a ranch Jeep and jumped out, wincing when he saw the blood on Jillian's arm.

"I spotted him, I was tracking him, when I heard the gunshot. God, I'm sorry!" he exclaimed. "I should have been quicker. Do you think you hit him?" he asked Ted.

"I'm not sure. Maybe." He helped Jillian up. "I'll get you to a doctor." He glanced at Rourke. "I called the sheriff to bring his dogs and his best investigator out here," he added. "They may need some help. I told the sheriff you'd been on the case, working for the Callisters."

Rourke's pale brown eye narrowed. He looked far different from the man Jillian had come to know as her easygoing friend. "I let him get onto the property, and I'm sorry. But I can damned sure track him."

"None of us could have expected what happened here," Ted said reassuringly, and put a kindly hand on the other man's shoulder. "She'll be okay. Sheriff's department investigator is on his way out here. I gave the sheriff's investigator your cell phone number," Ted added.

Rourke nodded. He winced at Jillian's face. "I'm sorry," he said curtly.

She smiled, holding her arm. "It's okay, Rourke."

"I didn't realize he was on the place, either, until I heard the gunshots," Ted said.

"Not the first time you've been shot at, I gather?" she asked with black humor.

"Not at all. You usually feel the bullet before you hear the sound," he added solemnly.

"And that's a fact," Rourke added with faint humor.

"Let's go," Ted said gently.

She let him put her into the patrol car. She was feeling sick, and she was in some pain. "It didn't hurt at first," she said. "I didn't even realize I was shot. Oh, Ted, I'm sorry, you have to wait…!" She opened the door and threw up, then she cried with embarrassment.

He handed her a clean white handkerchief, put her back in the car, and broke speed limits getting her to the emergency room.

"It's never like that on television," she said drowsily, when she'd been treated and was in a semi-private room for the night. They'd given her something for pain, as well. It was making her sleepy.

"What isn't, sweetheart?"

She smiled at the endearment as he leaned over her, gently touching her face. "People getting shot. They don't throw up."

"That's not real life, either," he reminded her.

She was worried, but not only for herself.

"What is it?" he asked gently.

"Sammy," she murmured. "I know, it's stupid to be worried about a calf, but if he can't get to me, he might try to hurt something I love." She searched his eyes. "You watch out, too."

His dark eyes twinkled. "Because you love me?" he drawled.

She only nodded, her face solemn. "More than anyone in the world."

There was a flush on his high cheekbones. He cupped her head in his big hands and kissed her with blatant possession. "That goes double for me," he whispered against her lips.

She searched his eyes with fascination. "It does?"

"Why in the world do you think I'd want to marry you if I didn't love you?" he asked reasonably. "No parcel of land is worth that sort of sacrifice."

"You never said," she stammered.

"Neither did you," he pointed out, chuckling.

She laid her hand against his shoulder. "I didn't want to say it first."

He kissed her nose. "But you did."

She sighed and smiled. "Yes. I did."

For one long moment, they were silent together, savoring the newness of an emotion neither had realized was so intense.

Finally he lifted his head. "I don't want to leave you, but we've got a lot of work to do and not a lot of time to do it."

She nodded. "You be careful."

"I will."

"Ted, could you check on Sammy?" she asked worriedly.

"Yes. I'll make sure she's okay."

She smiled. "Thanks."

"No problem."

Sassy came and took her back to the Callister ranch as soon as the doctor released her.

"I still think they should have kept you overnight," Sassy muttered.

"They tried to, but I refused," Jillian said drowsily. "I don't like being in hospitals. Have you heard anything more?"

"About Harris?" Sassy shook her head. "I know they've got dogs in the woods, hunting him. But if he's a good woodsman, he'll know how to cover his trail."

"He talked about that once," Jillian recalled. "He said there were ways to cover up a scent trail so a dog couldn't track people. Funny, I never wondered why he'd know such a thing."

"I'm sorry he does," Sassy replied. "If he didn't have those skills, he'd be a lot easier to find."

"I guess so."

"I've got a surprise for you," Sassy said when they walked into the house. She smiled mysteriously as she led Jillian down the hall to the guest bedroom she'd been occupying.

"What is it?" Jillian asked.

Sassy opened the door. There, hanging on the closet door, was a duplicate of the beautiful wedding gown that Sassy had chosen, right down to the embroidery.

"They only had two of that model. The other was in a store in Los Angeles. I had them overnight it," Sassy chuckled. "Nothing is going to stop this wedding!"

Jillian burst into tears. She hugged Sassy, as close as her wounded arm would permit. "Thank you!"

"It's little enough to do. I'm sorry the other one was ruined. We're just lucky that there was a second one in your size."

Jillian fingered the exquisite lace. "It is the most beautiful gown I'd ever seen. I'll never be able to thank you enough, Sassy."

The other woman was solemn. "We don't talk about it, but I'm sure you know that I had a similar experience, with my former boss at the feed store where I worked just before I married John. I was older than you were, and it wasn't quite as traumatic as yours, but I know how it feels to be assaulted." She sighed. "Funny thing, I had no idea when you came running up to the door with Harris a step behind you that I'd ever face the same situation in my own life."

"I'm sorry."

"Yes, so am I. There are bad men in the world. But there are good ones, too," Sassy reminded her. "I'm married to one of them, and you're about to marry another one."

"If Davy doesn't find some horrible new way to stop it," Jillian said with real concern in her voice.

"He won't," Sassy said firmly. "There are too many people in uniforms running around here for him to take that sort of a chance."

She bit her lower lip. "Ted was going to see about Sammy. I don't know if Harris might try to hurt her, to get back at me."

"He won't have the chance," Sassy said. "John and two of our hands took a cattle trailer over to your house a few minutes before I left to pick you up at the hospital. They're bringing her over here, and she'll stay in our barn. We have a man full-time who does nothing but look after our prize bulls who live in it."

"You've done so much for me," Jillian said, fighting tears.

"You'd do it for me," was the other woman's warm reply. "Now stop worrying. You have two days to get well enough to walk down the aisle."

"Maybe we should postpone it," she began.

"Not a chance," Sassy replied. "We'll have you back on your feet by then if we have to fly in specialists!" And she meant it.

# *Chapter 11*

Jillian carried a small bouquet of white and pale pink roses as she walked down the aisle of the small country church toward Ted, who was waiting at the altar. Her arm was sore and throbbing a little, and she was still worried about whether or not Davy Harris might try to shoot one of them through the window. But none of her concerns showed in her radiant expression as she took her place beside Ted.

The minister read the marriage ceremony. Jillian repeated the words. Ted repeated them. He slid a plain gold band onto her finger. She slid one onto his. They looked at each other with wonder and finally shared a kiss so tender that she knew she'd remember it all her life.

They held hands walking back down the aisle, laughing, as they were showered with rose petals by two little girls who were the daughters of one of Ted's police officers.

"Okay, now, stand right here while we get the photos," Sassy said, stage-managing them in the reception hall where food and punch were spread out on pristine white linen tablecloths with crystal and china to contain the feast. She'd hired a professional photographer to record the event, over Jillian's protests, as part of the Callisters' wedding gift to them.

Jillian felt regal in her beautiful gown. The night before, she'd gone out to the barn with Ted to make sure little Sammy was settled in a stall. It was silly to be worried about an animal, but she'd been a big part of Jillian's life since she was first born, to a cow that was killed by a freak lightning strike the next day. Jillian had taken the tiny calf to the house and kept her on old blankets on the back porch and fed her around the clock to keep her alive.

That closeness had amused Ted, especially since the calf followed Jillian everywhere she went and even, on occasion, tried to go in the house with her. He supposed he was lucky that they didn't make calf diapers, he'd teased, or Jillian would give the animal a bedroom.

"Did anybody check to see if I left my jacket down that trail where I took Sammy for her walks?" Jillian asked suddenly. "The buckskin one, with the embroidery. It hasn't rained, but if it does, it will be soaked. I forgot all about it when I came to stay with Sassy."

"I'll look for it later," Ted told her, nuzzling her nose with his. "When we go home."

"Home." She sighed and closed her eyes. "I forgot. We'll live together now."

"Yes, we will." He touched her face. "Maybe not as closely as I'd like for a few more days," he teased deeply and chuckled when she flushed. "That arm is going to take some healing."

"I never realized that a flesh wound could cause so much trouble," she told him.

"At least it was just a flesh wound," he said grimly. "Damned if I can figure out why we can't find that polecat," he muttered, borrowing Rourke's favorite term. "We've had men scouring the countryside for him."

"Maybe he got scared and left town," she said hopefully.

"We found his truck deserted, about halfway between the Callisters' ranch and ours," he said. "Dogs lost his trail when it went off the road." He frowned. "One of our trackers said that his footprints changed from one side of the truck to the other, as if he was carrying something."

"Maybe a suitcase?" she wondered.

He shook his head. "We checked the bus station and we had the sheriff's department send cars all over the back roads. He just vanished into thin air."

"I'm not sorry," she said heavily. "But I'd like to know that he wasn't coming back."

"So would I." He bent and kissed her. "We'll manage," he added. "Whatever happens, we'll manage."

She smiled up at him warmly. "Yes. We will."

They settled down into married life. Ted had honestly hoped to wait a day or so until her arm was a little less sore.

But that night while they were watching a movie on television, he kissed her and she kissed him back. Then they got into a more comfortable position on the sofa. Very soon, pieces of clothing came off and were discarded on the floor. And then, skin against skin, they learned each other in ways they never had before.

Just for a minute, it was uncomfortable. He felt her stiffen and his mouth brushed tenderly over her closed eyelids. "Easy," he whispered. "Try to relax. Move with me. Move with me, sweetheart…yes!"

And then it was all heat and urgency and explosions of sensation like nothing she'd ever felt in her life. She dug her nails into his hips and moaned harshly as the hard, fierce thrust of his body lifted her to elevations of pleasure that built on each other until she was afraid that she might die trying to survive them.

"Yes," he groaned, and he bruised her thighs with his fingers as he strained to get even closer to her when the pleasure burst and shuddered into ecstacy.

She cried out. Her whole body felt on fire. She moved with him, her own hips arching up in one last surge of strength before the world dissolved into sweet madness.

She was throbbing all over, like her sore arm that she hadn't even noticed until now. She shivered under the weight of Ted's body.

"I was going to wait," he managed in a husky whisper.

"What in the world for?" she laughed. "It's just a sore arm." Her eyes met his with shy delight.

He lifted an eyebrow rakishly. "Is anything else sore?" he asked.

She grinned. "No."

He pursed his lips. "Well, in that case," he whispered, and began to move.

She clutched at him and gasped with pure delight.

He only laughed.


Much later, they curled up together in bed, exhausted and happy. They slept until late the next morning, missing church and a telephone call from the sheriff, Larry Kane.

"Better call me as soon as you get this," Larry said grimly on the message. "It's urgent."

Ted exchanged a concerned glance with Jillian as he picked up his cell phone and returned the call.

"Graves," he said into the phone. "What's up?"

There was a pause while he listened. He scowled. "What?" he exclaimed.

"What is it?" Jillian was mouthing at him.

He held up a hand and sighed heavily. "How long ago?"

He nodded. "Well, it's a pity, in a way. But it's ironic, you have to admit. Yes. Yes. I'll tell her. Thanks, Larry."

He snapped the phone shut. "They found Davy Harris this morning."

"Where is he?" she asked, gnawing her lip.

"They've taken him to the state crime lab."

She blinked. "I thought they only took dead people… Oh, dear. He's dead?"

He nodded. "They found him with his leg caught in a bear trap. He'd apparently been trying to set it on the ranch, down that trail where you always walk with Sammy, through the trees where it's hard to see the ground."

"Good Lord!" she exclaimed, and the possibilities created nightmares in her mind.

"He'd locked the trap into place with a log chain, around a tree, and padlocked it in place. Sheriff thinks he lost the key somewhere. He couldn't get the chain loose or free himself from the trap. He bled to death."

She felt sick all over. She pressed into Ted's arms and held on tight. "What a horrible way to go."

"Yes, well, just remember that it was how he planned for Sammy to go," he said, without mentioning that Harris may well have planned to catch Jillian in it.

"His sister will sue us all for wrongful death and say

we killed him," Jillian said miserably, remembering the woman's fury when her brother was first arrested.

"His sister died two years ago," he replied. "Of a drug overdose. A truly troubled family."

"When did you find that out?" she wondered.

"Yesterday," he said. "I didn't want to spend our wedding day talking about Harris, but I did wonder if he might run to his sister for protection. So I had an investigator try to find her."

"A sad end," she said.

"Yes. But fortunately, not yours," he replied. He held her close, glad that it was over, finally.

She sighed. "Not mine," she agreed.

Rourke left three days later to go back to Africa. He'd meant to leave sooner, but Sassy and John wanted to show him around Montana first, despite the thick snow that was falling in abundance now.

"I've taken movies of the snow to show back home," he mentioned as he said his farewells to Jillian and Ted while a ranch hand waited in the truck to drive him to the airport in Billings. "We don't get a lot of snow in Kenya," he added, tongue-in-cheek.

"Thanks for helping keep me alive," Jillian told him.

"My pleasure," he replied, and smiled.

Ted shook hands with him. "If you want to learn how to fish for trout, come back in the spring when the snows melt and we'll spend the day on the river."

"I might take you up on that," Rourke said.

They watched him drive away.

Jillian slid her arm around Ted's waist. "You coming home for lunch?" she asked as they walked to his patrol car.

"Thought I might." He gave her a wicked grin. "You going to fix food or are we going to spend my lunch hour in the usual way?"

She pursed her lips. "Oh, I could make sandwiches."

"You could pack them in a plastic bag," he added, "and I could take them back to work with me."

She flushed and laughed. "Of course. We wouldn't want to waste your lunch hour by eating."

He bent and kissed her with barely restrained hunger. "Absolutely not! See you about noon."

She kissed him back. "I'll be here."

He drove off, throwing up a hand as he went down the driveway. She watched him go and thought how far she'd come from the scared teenager that Davy Harris had intimidated so many years before. She had a good marriage and her life was happier than ever before. She still had her morning job at the local restaurant. She liked the little bit of independence it gave her, and they could use the extra money. Ted wasn't likely to get rich working as a police chief.

On the other hand, their lack of material wealth only brought them closer together and made their shared lives better.

She sighed as she turned back toward the house, her eyes full of dreams. Snow was just beginning to fall again, like a burst of glorious white feathers around her head. Winter was beautiful. Like her life.

\* \* \* \* \*

**Books by Brenda Jackson**

**Harlequin Desire**

*The Westmorelands*

*Texas Wild*
*One Winter's Night*
*Zane*
*Canyon*
*Stern*
*The Real Thing*
*The Secret Affair*
*The Rancher Returns*

**MIRA Books**

*The Grangers*

*A Brother's Honor*
*A Lover's Vow*
*A Man's Promise*

**HQN Books**

*The Protectors*

*Forged in Desire*

Visit the Author Profile page at Harlequin.com
for more titles.

# TEXAS WILD

## Brenda Jackson

To Gerald Jackson, Sr. My one and only.
My everything. Happy fortieth anniversary!

To my readers who asked for Rico Claiborne's story,
*Texas Wild* is especially for you!

To my Heavenly Father. How Great Thou Art.


Though your beginning was small,
yet your latter end would increase abundantly.
—*Job* 8:7

# *Prologue*

**"OMG**, who's the latecomer to the wedding?"

"Don't know, but I'm glad he made it to the reception."

"Look at that body."

"Look at that walk."

"He should come with a warning sign that says Extremely Hot."

Several ladies in the wedding party whispered among themselves, and all eyes were trained on the tall, ultrahandsome man who'd approached the group of Westmoreland male cousins across the room. The reception for Micah Westmoreland's wedding to Kalina Daniels was in full swing on the grounds of Micah Manor, but every female in attendance was looking at one particular male.

The man who'd just arrived.

"For crying out loud, will someone please tell me who he is?" Vickie Morrow, a good friend of Kalina's, pleaded in a low voice. She looked over at Megan Westmoreland. "Most of the good-looking men here are related to you in some way, so tell us. Is he another Westmoreland cousin?"

Megan was checking out the man just as thoroughly as all the other women were. "No, he's no kin of mine. I've never seen him before," she said. She hadn't seen the full view yet, either, just his profile, but even that was impressive—he had handsome features, a deep tan and silky straight hair that brushed against the collar of his suit. He was both well dressed and good-looking.

"Yes, he definitely is one fine specimen of a man and is probably some Hollywood friend of my cousins, since he seems to know them."

"Well, I want to be around when the introductions are made," Marla Ford, another friend of Kalina's, leaned over and whispered in Megan's ear. "Make that happen."

Megan laughed. "I'll see what I can do."

"Hey, don't look now, ladies, but he's turned this way and is looking over here," Marla said. "In fact, Megan, your brother Zane is pointing out one of us to him… and I hope it's me." Seconds later, Marla said in a disappointed voice, "It's *you,* Megan."

Marla had to be mistaken. Why would Zane point her out to that man?

"Yeah, look how the hottie is checking you out," Vickie whispered to Megan. "It's like the rest of us don't even exist. *Lordy, I do declare.* I wish some man would look at me that way."

Megan met the stranger's gaze. Everyone was right.

He was concentrated solely on her. And the moment their eyes connected, something happened. It was as if heat transmitted from his look was burning her skin, flaming her blood, scorching her all over. She'd never felt anything so powerful in her life.

*Instant attraction.*

Her heart pounded like crazy, and she shivered as everything and everyone around her seemed to fade into the background...everything except for the sound of the soft music from the orchestra that pulled her and this stranger into a cocoon. It was as if no one existed but the two of them.

Her hand, which was holding a glass of wine, suddenly felt moist, and something fired up within her that had never been lit before. Desire. As potent as it could get. How could a stranger affect her this way? For the first time in her adult life, at the age of twenty-seven, Megan knew what it meant to be attracted to someone in a way that affected all her vital signs.

And, as an anesthesiologist, she knew all about the workings of the human body. But up until now she'd never given much thought to her own body or how it would react to a man. At least, not to how it would react to this particular man...whomever he was. She found her own reaction as interesting as she found it disconcerting.

"That guy's hot for you, Megan."

Vickie's words reminded Megan that she had an audience. Breaking eye contact with the stranger, she glanced over at Vickie, swallowing deeply. "No, he's not. He doesn't know me, and I don't know him."

"Doesn't matter who knows who. What just happened between you two is called instant sexual attraction. I felt it. We all did. You would have to be dead not to have felt it. That was some kind of heat emitting between the two of you just now."

Megan drew in a deep breath when the other women around her nodded and agreed with what Vickie had said. She glanced back over at the stranger. He was still staring and held her gaze until her cousin Riley tapped him on the shoulder to claim his attention. And when Savannah and Jessica, who were married to Megan's cousins Durango and Chase, respectively, walked up to him, she saw how his face split in a smile before he pulled both women into his arms for a huge hug.

That's when it hit her just who the stranger was. He was Jessica and Savannah's brother, the private investigator who lived in Philadelphia, Rico Claiborne. The man Megan had hired a few months ago to probe into her great-grandfather's past.

Rico Claiborne was glad to see his sisters, but the woman Zane had pointed out to him, the same one who had hired him over the phone a few months ago, was still holding his attention, although he was pretending otherwise.

Dr. Megan Westmoreland.

She had gone back to talking to her friends, not looking his way. That was fine for now since he needed to get his bearings. What in the hell had that been all about? What had made him concentrate solely on her as if all those other women standing with her didn't exist? There was something about her that made her stand out, even before Zane had told him the one in the pastel pink was his sister Megan.

The woman was hot, and when she had looked at

him, every cell in his body had responded to that look. It wasn't one of those I'm-interested-in-you-too kind of looks. It was one of those looks that questioned the power of what was going on between them. It was quite obvious she was just as confused as he was. Never had he reacted so fiercely to a woman before. And the fact that she was the one who had hired him to research Raphel Westmoreland made things even more complicated.

That had been two months ago. He'd agreed to take the case, but had explained he couldn't begin until he'd wrapped up the other cases he was working on. She'd understood. Today, he'd figured he could kill two birds with one stone. He'd attend Micah's wedding and finally get to meet Micah's cousin Megan. But he hadn't counted on feeling such a strong attraction to her, one that still had heat thrumming all through him.

His sisters' husbands, as well as the newlyweds, walked up to join him. And as Rico listened to the conversations swirling around him, he couldn't help but steal glances over at Megan. He should have known it would be just a matter of time before one of his sisters noticed where his attention had strayed.

"You've met Megan, right? I know she hired you to investigate Raphel's history," Savannah said with a curious gleam in her eyes. He knew that look. If given the chance she would stick that pretty nose of hers where it didn't belong.

"No, Megan and I haven't officially met, although we've talked on the phone a number of times," he said, grabbing a drink off the tray of a passing waiter. He needed it to cool off. Megan Westmoreland was so freaking hot he could feel his toes beginning to burn.

"But I know which one she is. Zane pointed her out to me a few minutes ago," he added, hoping that would appease his sister's curiosity.

He saw it didn't when she smiled and said, "Then let me introduce you."

Rico took a quick sip of his drink. He started to tell Savannah that he would rather be introduced to Megan later, but then decided he might as well get it over with. "All right."

As his sister led him over to where the group of women stood, all staring at him with interest in their eyes, his gaze was locked on just one. And he knew she felt the strong attraction flowing between them as much as he did. There was no way she could not.

It was a good thing they wouldn't be working together closely. His job was just to make sure she received periodic updates on how the investigation was going, which was simple enough.

Yes, he decided, as he got closer to her, with the way his entire body was reacting to her, the more distance he put between himself and Megan the better.

# Chapter 1

*Three months later*

"Dr. Westmoreland, there's someone here to see you."

Megan Westmoreland's brow arched as she glanced at her watch. She was due in surgery in an hour and had hoped to grab a sandwich and a drink from the deli downstairs before then. "Who is it, Grace?" she asked, speaking into the intercom system on her desk. Grace Elsberry was a student in the college's work-study program and worked part-time as an administrative assistant for the anesthesiology department at the University of Colorado Hospital.

"He's hot. A Brad Cooper look-alike with a dark tan," Grace whispered into the phone.

Megan's breath caught and warm sensations oozed through her bloodstream. She had an idea who her visitor was and braced herself for Grace to confirm her suspicions. "Says his name is Rico Claiborne." Lowering her voice even more, Grace added, "But I prefer calling him Mr. Yummy…if you know what I mean."

Yes, she knew exactly what Grace meant. The man was so incredibly handsome he should be arrested for being a menace to society. "Please send Mr. Claiborne in."

"Send him in? Are you kidding? I will take the pleasure of *escorting* him into your office, Dr. Westmoreland."

Megan shook her head. She couldn't remember the last time Grace had taken the time to escort anyone into her office. The door opened, and Grace, wearing the biggest of grins, escorted Rico Claiborne in. He moved with a masculine grace that exerted power, strength and confidence, and he looked like a model, even while wearing jeans and a pullover sweater.

Megan moved from behind her desk to properly greet him. Rico was tall, probably a good six-four, with dark brown hair and a gorgeous pair of hazel eyes. They had talked on the phone a number of times, but they had only met once, three months ago, at her cousin Micah's wedding. He had made such an impact on her feminine senses that she'd found it hard to stop thinking about him ever since. Now that he had completed that case he'd been working on, hopefully he was ready to start work on hers.

"Rico, good seeing you again," Megan said, smiling, extending her hand to him. Grace was right, he did look like Brad Cooper, and his interracial features made his skin tone appear as if he'd gotten the perfect tan.

"Good seeing you again as well, Megan," he said, taking her hand in his.

The warm sensation Megan had felt earlier intensified with the touch of his hand on hers, but she fought to ignore it. "So, what brings you to Denver?"

He placed his hands in the pockets of his jeans. "I arrived this morning to appear in court on a case I handled last year, and figured since I was here I'd give you an update. I actually started work on your case a few weeks ago. I don't like just dropping in like this, but I tried calling you when I first got to town and couldn't reach you on your cell phone."

"She was in surgery all morning."

They both turned to note Grace was still in the room. She stood in the doorway smiling, eyeing Rico up and down with a look of pure female appreciation on her face. Megan wouldn't have been surprised if Grace started licking her lips.

"Thanks, and that will be all Grace," Megan said.

Grace actually looked disappointed. "You sure?"

"Yes, I'm positive. I'll call you if I need you," Megan said, forcing back a grin.

"Oh, all right."

It was only when Grace had closed the door behind her that Megan glanced back at Rico to find him staring at her. A shiver of nervousness slithered down her spine. She shouldn't feel uncomfortable around him. But she had discovered upon meeting Rico that she had a strong attraction to him, something she'd never had for a man before. For the past three months, out of sight had meant out of mind where he was concerned—on her good days. But with him standing in the middle of her office she was forced to remember why she'd been so taken with him at her cousin's wedding.

The man was hot.

"Would you like to take a seat? This sounds important," she said, returning to the chair behind her desk, eager to hear what he had to say and just as anxious to downplay the emotional reaction he was causing.

A few years ago, her family had learned that her great-grandfather, Raphel Stern Westmoreland, who they'd assumed was an only child, had actually had a twin brother, Reginald Scott Westmoreland. It all started when an older man living in Atlanta by the name of James Westmoreland—a grandson of Reginald— began genealogy research on his family. His research revealed a connection to the Westmorelands living in Denver—her family. Once that information had been uncovered, her family had begun to wonder what else they didn't know about their ancestor.

They had discovered that Raphel, at twenty-two, had become the black sheep of the family after running off with the preacher's wife, never to be heard from again. He had passed through various states, including Texas, Wyoming, Kansas and Nebraska, before settling down in Colorado. It was found that he had taken up with a number of women along the way. Everyone was curious about what happened to those women, since it appeared he had been married to each one of them at some point. If that was true, there were possibly even more Westmorelands out there that Megan and her family didn't know about. That was why her oldest cousin, Dillon, had taken it upon himself to investigate her great-grandfather's other wives.

Dillon's investigation had led him to Gamble, Wyoming, where he'd not only met his future wife, but he'd also found out the first two women connected with Raphel hadn't been the man's wives, but were women he had helped out in some way. Since that first investigation, Dillon had married and was the father of one child, with another on the way. With a growing family, he was too busy to chase information about Raphel's third and fourth wives. Megan had decided to resume the search, which was the reason she had hired Rico, who had, of course, come highly recommended by her brothers and cousins.

Megan watched Rico take a seat, thinking the man was way too sexy for words. She was used to being surrounded by good-looking men. Case in point, her five brothers and slew of cousins were all gorgeous. But there was something about Rico that pulled at her in a way she found most troublesome.

"I think it's important, and it's the first break I've had," he responded. "I was finally able to find something on Clarice Riggins."

A glimmer of hope spread through Megan. Clarice was rumored to have been her great-grandfather's third wife. Megan leaned forward in her chair. "How? Where?"

"I was able to trace what I've pieced together to a small town in Texas, on the other side of Austin, called Forbes."

"Forbes, Texas?"

"Yes. I plan to leave Thursday morning. I had thought of leaving later today, after this meeting, but your brothers and cousins talked me out of it. They want me to hang out with them for a couple of days."

Megan wasn't surprised. Although the West-

morelands were mostly divided among four states—
Colorado, Georgia, Montana and Texas—the males
in the family usually got together often, either to go
hunting, check on the various mutual business interests or just for a poker game getaway. Since Rico was
the brother-in-law to two of her cousins, he often joined
those trips.

"So you haven't been able to find out anything about
her?" she asked.

"No, not yet, but I did discover something interesting."

Megan lifted a brow. "What?"

"It's recorded that she gave birth to a child. We can't
say whether the baby was male or female, but it was a
live birth."

Megan couldn't stop the flow of excitement that
seeped into her veins. If Clarice had given birth, that
could mean more Westmoreland cousins out there somewhere. Anyone living in Denver knew how important
family was to the Westmorelands.

"That could be big. Really major," she said, thinking. "Have you mentioned it to anyone else?"

He shook his head, smiling. "No, you're the one who
hired me, so anything I discover I bring to you first."

She nodded. "Don't say anything just yet. I don't
want to get anyone's hopes up. You can say you're going
to Texas on a lead, but nothing else for now."

Presently, there were fifteen Denver Westmorelands.
Twelve males and three females. Megan's parents, as
well as her aunt and uncle, had been killed in a plane
crash years ago, leaving Dillon and her oldest brother,
Ramsey, in charge. It hadn't been easy, but now all of
the Westmorelands were self-supporting individuals.

All of them had graduated from college except for the two youngest—Bane and Bailey. Bane was in the U.S. Navy, and Bailey, who'd fought the idea of any education past high school, was now in college with less than a year to go to get her degree.

There had never been any doubt in Megan's mind that she would go to college to become an anesthesiologist. She loved her job. She had known this was the career she wanted ever since she'd had her tonsils removed at six and had met the nice man who put her to sleep. He had come by to check on her after the surgery. He'd visited with her, ate ice cream with her and told her all about his job. At the time, she couldn't even pronounce it, but she'd known that was her calling.

Yet everyone needed a break from their job every once in a while, and she was getting burned out. Budget cuts required doing more with less, and she'd known for a while that it was time she went somewhere to chill. Bailey had left that morning for Charlotte to visit their cousin Quade, his wife, Cheyenne, and their triplets. Megan had been tempted to go with her, since she had a lot of vacation time that she rarely used. She also thought about going to Montana, where other Westmorelands lived. One nice thing about having a large family so spread out was that you always had somewhere to go.

Suddenly, a thought popped into Megan's head, and she glanced over at Rico again to find him staring at her. Their gazes held for a moment longer than necessary before she broke eye contact and looked down at the calendar on her desk while releasing a slow breath. For some reason she had a feeling he was on the verge of finding out something major. She wanted to be there when he did. More than anything she wanted to be present when he found out about Clarice's child. If she was in Denver while he was in Texas, she would go nuts waiting for him to contact her with any information he discovered. Once she'd gotten her thoughts and plans together, she glanced back up at him.

"You're leaving for Texas in two days, right?"

He lifted a brow. "Yes. That's my plan."

Megan leaned back in her chair. "I've just made a decision about something."

"About what?"

Megan smiled. "I've decided to go with you."

Rico figured there were a lot of things in life he didn't know. But the one thing he did know was that there was no way Megan Westmoreland was going anywhere with him. Being alone with her in this office was bad enough. The thought of them sitting together on a plane or in a car was too close for comfort. It was arousing him just thinking about it.

He was attracted to her big-time and had been from the moment he'd seen her at Micah's wedding. He had arrived late because of a case he'd been handling and had shown up at the reception just moments before the bride and groom were to leave for their honeymoon. Megan had hired him a month earlier, even though they'd never met in person. Because of that, the first thing Rico did when he arrived at the reception was to ask Zane to point her out.

The moment his and Megan's gazes locked he had felt desire rush through him to a degree that had never happened before. It had shocked the hell out of him. His gaze had moved over her, taking in every single thing he saw, every inch of what he'd liked. And he'd liked it all. Way too much. From the abundance of dark curls on her head to the creamy smoothness of her mahogany skin, from the shapely body in a bridesmaid gown to the pair of silver stilettos on her feet. She had looked totally beautiful.

At the age of thirty-six, he'd figured he was way too old to be *that* attracted to any woman. After all, he'd dated quite a few women in his day. And by just looking at Megan, he could tell she was young, that she hadn't turned thirty yet. But her age hadn't stopped him from staring and staring and staring…until one of her cousins had reclaimed his attention. But still, he had thought about her more than he should have since then.

"Well, with that settled, I'll notify my superiors so they can find a replacement for me while I'm gone," she said, breaking into his thoughts. "There are only a few surgeries scheduled for tomorrow, and I figure we'll be back in a week or so."

Evidently she thought that since he hadn't said anything, he was okay with the idea of her accompanying him to Texas. Boy, was she wrong. "Sorry, Megan, there's no way I'll let you come with me. I have a rule about working alone."

He could tell by the mutinous expression on her face that he was in for a fight. That didn't bother him. He had two younger sisters to deal with so he knew well how to handle a stubborn female.

"Surely you can break that rule this one time."

He shook his head. "Sorry, I can't."

She crossed her arms over her chest. "Other than the fact that you prefer working alone, give me another reason I can't go with you."

He crossed his arms over his own chest. "I don't need another reason. Like I said, I work alone." He did have a reason, but he wouldn't be sharing it with her. All he had to do was recall what had almost happened the last time he'd worked a case with a woman.

"Why are you being difficult?"

"Why are you?" he countered.

"I'm not," she said, throwing her head back and gritting out her words. "This is my great-grandfather we're talking about."

"I'm fully aware of who he was. You and I talked extensively before I agreed to take on this case, and I recall telling you that I would get you the information you wanted…doing things my way."

He watched as she began nibbling on her bottom lip. Okay, so now she was remembering. Good. For some reason, he couldn't stop looking into her eyes, meeting her fiery gaze head on, thinking her eyes resembled two beautiful dark orbs.

"As the client, I demand that you take me," she said, sharply interrupting his thoughts.

He narrowed his gaze. "You can demand all you want, but you're not going to Texas with me."

"And why not?"

"I've told you my reasons, now can we move on to something else, please?"

She stood up. "No, we can't move on to something else."

He stood, as well. "Now you're acting like a spoiled child."

Megan's jaw dropped. "A spoiled child? I've never acted like a spoiled child in my entire life. And as for going to Texas, I will be going since there's no reason that I shouldn't."

He didn't say anything for a moment. "Okay, there is another reason I won't take you with me. One that you'd do well to consider," he said in a calm, barely controlled tone. She had pushed him, and he didn't like being pushed.

"Fine, let's hear it," she snapped furiously.

He placed his hands in the pockets of his jeans, stood with his legs braced apart and leveled his gaze on her when he spoke in a deep, husky voice. "I want you, Megan. Bad. And if you go anywhere with me, I'm going to have you."

He then turned and walked out of her office.

Shocked, Megan dropped back down in her chair. "Gracious!"

Three surgeries later, back in her office, Megan paced the floor. Although Rico's parting statement had taken her by surprise, she was still furious. Typical man. Why did they think everything began and ended in the bedroom? So, he was attracted to her. Big deal. Little did he know, but she was attracted to him as well, and she had no qualms about going to Texas with him. For crying out loud, hadn't he ever heard of self-control?

She was sister to Zane and Derringer and cousin to Riley and Canyon—three were womanizers to the core. And before marrying Lucia, Derringer had all but worn his penis on his sleeve and Zane, Lord help him, wore his anywhere there was a free spot on his body. She couldn't count the number of times she'd unexpectedly shown up at Zane's place at the wrong time or how many pairs of panties she'd discovered left behind at Riley's. And wasn't it just yesterday she'd seen a woman leave Canyon's place before dawn?

Besides that, Rico Claiborne honestly thought all he had to do was decide he wanted her and he would have her? Wouldn't she have some kind of say-so in the matter? Evidently he didn't think so, which meant he really didn't know whom he was dealing with. The doctors at the hospital, who thought she was cold and incapable of being seduced, called her "Iceberg Megan."

So, okay, Rico had thawed her out a little when she'd seen him at the wedding three months ago. And she would admit he'd made her heart flutter upon seeing him today. But he was definitely under a false assumption if he thought all he had to do was snap his fingers, strut that sexy walk and she would automatically fall into any bed with him.

She scowled. The more she thought about it, the madder she got. He should know from all the conversations they'd shared over the phone that this investigation was important to her. Family was everything to her, and if there were other Westmorelands out there, she wanted to know about them. She wanted to be in the thick of things when he uncovered the truth as to where those Westmorelands were and how quickly they could be reached.

Megan moved to the window and looked out. September clouds were settling in, and the forecasters had predicted the first snowfall of the year by the end of the week. But that was fine since she had no intention of being here in Denver when the snow started. Ignoring what Rico had said about her not going to Texas with him, she had cleared her calendar for not only the rest of the week, but also for the next month. She had the vacation time, and if she didn't use it by the end of the year she would end up losing it anyway.

First, she would go to Texas. And then, before returning to work, she would take off for Australia and spend time with her sister Gemma and her family. Megan enjoyed international travel and recalled the first time she'd left the country to visit her cousin Delaney in the Middle East. That had been quite an enjoyable experience.

But remembering the trip to visit her cousin couldn't keep her thoughts from shifting back to Rico, and she felt an unwelcoming jolt of desire as she recalled him standing in her office, right in this very spot, and saying what he'd said, without as much as blinking an eye.

If he, for one minute, thought he had the ability to tell her what to do, he had another thought coming. If he was *that* attracted to her then he needed to put a cap on it. They were adults and would act accordingly. The mere thought that once alone they would tear each other's clothes off in some sort of heated lust was total rubbish. Although she was attracted to him, she knew how to handle herself. It *was* going to be hard to keep her hands to herself.

But no matter what, she would.

"You sure I'm not putting you out, Riley? I can certainly get a room at the hotel in town."

"I won't hear of it," Riley Westmoreland said, smiling. "Hell, you're practically family."

Rico threw his luggage on the bed, thinking he certainly hadn't felt like family earlier when he'd been alone with Megan. He still couldn't get over her wanting to go to Texas with him. Surely she had felt the sexual tension that seemed to surround them whenever they were within a few feet of each other.

"So how are things going with that investigation you're doing for Megan?" Riley asked, breaking into Rico's thoughts.

"Fine. In fact, I'm on my way to Texas to poke around a new lead."

Riley's brow lifted. "Really? Does Megan know yet?"

"Yes. I met with her at the hospital earlier today."

Riley chuckled. "I bet she was happy about that. We're all interested in uncovering the truth about Poppa Raphel, but I honestly think Megan is obsessed with it and has been ever since Dillon and Pam shared those journals with her. Now that Dillon has made Megan the keeper of the journals she is determined to uncover everything. She's convinced we have more relatives out there somewhere."

Rico had read those journals and had found them quite interesting. The journals, written by Raphel himself, had documented his early life after splitting from his family.

"And it's dinner tonight over at the big house. Pam called earlier to make sure I brought you. I hope you're up for it. You know how testy pregnant women can get at times."

Rico chuckled. Yes, he knew. In fact, he had noted the number of pregnant women in the Westmoreland family. Enough to look like there was some sort of epidemic. In addition to Pam, Derringer's wife, Lucia, was expecting and so was Micah's wife, Kalina. There were a number of Atlanta Westmorelands expecting babies, as well.

Case in point, his own sisters. Jessica was pregnant

again, and Savannah had given birth to her second child earlier that year. They were both happily married, and he was happy for them. Even his mother had decided to make another go of marriage, which had surprised him after what she'd gone through with his father. But he liked Brad Richman, and Rico knew Brad truly loved his mother.

"Well, I'll let you unpack. We'll leave for Dillon's place in about an hour. I hope you're hungry because there will be plenty of food. The women are cooking, and we just show up hungry and ready to eat," Riley said, laughing.

A half hour later Rico had unpacked all the items he needed. Everything else would remain in his luggage since he would be leaving for Texas the day after tomorrow. Sighing, he rubbed a hand down his face, noting his stubble-roughened jaw. Before he went out anywhere, he definitely needed to shave. And yes, he was hungry since he hadn't eaten since that morning, but dinner at Dillon's meant most of the Denver Westmorelands who were in town would be there. That included Megan. Damn. He wasn't all that sure he was ready to see her again. He was known as a cool and in-control kind of guy. But those elements of his personality took a flying leap around Megan Westmoreland.

Why did he like the way she said his name? To pronounce it was simple enough, but there was something about the way she said it, in a sultry tone that soothed and aroused.

Getting aroused was the last thing he needed to think about. It had been way too long since he'd had bedroom time with a woman. So he was in far worse shape than he'd realized. Seeing Megan today hadn't helped matters. The woman was way too beautiful for her own good.

Grabbing his shaving bag off the bed, Rico went into the guest bath that was conveniently connected to his room. Moments later, after lathering his face with shaving cream, he stared into the mirror as he slowly swiped a razor across his face. The familiar actions allowed his mind to wander, right back to Megan.

The first thing he'd noticed when he'd walked into her office was that she'd cut her hair. She still had a lot of curls, but instead of flowing to her shoulders, her hair crowned her face like a cap. He liked the style on her. It gave her a sexier look…not that she needed it.

He could just imagine being wheeled into surgery only to discover she would be the doctor to administer the drug to knock you out. Counting backward while lying flat on your back and staring up into her face would guarantee plenty of hot dreams during whatever surgery you were having.

He jolted when he nicked himself. Damn. He needed to concentrate on shaving and rid his mind of Megan. At least he didn't have to worry about that foolishness of hers, about wanting to go with him to Texas. He felt certain, with the way her eyes had nearly popped out of the sockets and her jaw had dropped after what he'd said, that she had changed her mind.

He hadn't wanted to be so blatantly honest with her, but it couldn't be helped. Like he told her, he preferred working alone. The last time he had taken a woman with him on a case had almost cost him his life. He remembered it like it was yesterday. An FBI sting operation and his female partner had ended up being more hindrance than help. The woman blatantly refused to follow orders.

Granted, there was no real danger involved with Megan's case per se. In fact, the only danger he could think of was keeping his hands to himself where Megan was concerned. That was a risk he couldn't afford. And he had felt the need to be blunt and spell it out to her. Now that he had, he was convinced they had an understanding.

He would go to Texas, delve into whatever he could discover about Clarice Riggins and bring his report back to her. Megan was paying him a pretty hefty fee for his services, and he intended to deliver. But he would have to admit that her great-grandfather had covered his tracks well, which made Rico wonder what all the old man had gotten into during his younger days. It didn't matter, because Rico intended to uncover it all. And like he'd told Megan, Clarice Riggins had given birth, but there was nothing to indicate that she and Raphel had married. It had been a stroke of luck that he'd found anything at all on Clarice, since there had been various spellings of the woman's name.

He was walking out of the bathroom when his cell phone rang, and he pulled it off the clip. He checked and saw it was a New York number. He had several associates there and couldn't help wondering which one was calling.

"This is Rico."

There was a slight pause and then… "Hello, son. This is your father."

Rico flinched, drew in a sharp breath and fought for control of his anger, which had come quick…as soon as he'd recognized the voice. "You must have the wrong number because I don't have a father."

Without giving the man a chance to say anything else, he clicked off the phone. As far as he was concerned, Jeff Claiborne could go to hell. Why on earth would the man be calling Rico after all this time? What had it been? Eighteen years? Rico had been happy with his father being out of sight and out of mind.

To be quite honest, he wished he could wash the man's memory away completely. He could never forget the lives that man had damaged by his selfishness. No, Jeff Claiborne had no reason to call him. No reason at all.

# Chapter 2

Megan tried to downplay her nervousness as she continued to cut up the bell pepper and celery for the potato salad. According to Pam, Rico had been invited to dinner and would probably arrive any minute.

"Has Rico found anything out yet?"

Megan glanced over at her cousin-in-law. She liked Pam and thought she was perfect for Dillon. The two women were alone for now. Chloe and Bella had gone to check on the babies, and Lucia, who was in the dining room, was putting icing on the cake.

"Yes, there's a lead in Texas he'll follow up on when he leaves here," Megan said. She didn't want to mention anything about Clarice. The last thing she wanted to do was get anyone's hopes up.

"How exciting," Pam said as she fried the chicken, turning pieces over in the huge skillet every so often. "I'm sure you're happy about that."

Megan would be a lot happier if Rico would let her go to Texas with him, but, in a way, she had solved that problem and couldn't wait to see the expression on his face when he found out how. Chances were, he thought he'd had the last word.

She sighed, knowing if she lived to be a hundred years old she wouldn't be able to figure out men. Whenever they wanted a woman they assumed a woman would just naturally want them in return. How crazy was that bit of logic?

There was so much Megan didn't know when it came to men, although she had lived most of her life surrounded by them. Oh, she knew some things, but this man-woman stuff—when it came to wants and desires—just went over her head. Until she'd met Rico, there hadn't been a man who'd made her give him a second look. Of course, Idris Elba didn't count.

She lifted her gaze from the vegetables to look over at Pam. Megan knew Pam and Dillon had a pretty good marriage, a real close one. Pam, Chloe, Lucia and Bella were the older sisters she'd never had, and, at the moment, she needed some advice.

"Pam?"

"Hmm?"

"How would you react if a man told you he wanted you?"

Pam glanced her way and smiled. "It depends on who the man is. Had your brother told me that, I would have kicked my fiancé to the curb a lot sooner. The first thing I thought when I saw Dillon was that he was hot."

That was the same thing Megan had thought when she'd seen Rico. "So you would not have gotten upset had he said he wanted you?"

"Again, it depends on who the man is. If it's a man I had the hots for, then no, I wouldn't have gotten upset. Why would I have? That would mean we were of the same accord and could move on to the next phase."

Megan raised a brow. "The next phase?"

"Yes, the I-want-to-get-to-know-you-better phase." Pam looked over at her. "So tell me. Was this a hypothetical question or is there a man out there who told you he wants you?"

Megan nervously nibbled on her bottom lip. She must have taken too long to answer because Pam grinned and said, "I guess I got my answer."

Pam took the last of the chicken out of the skillet, turned off the stove and joined Megan at the table. "Like I said, Megan, the question you should ask yourself is…if he's someone you want, too. Forget about what he wants for the moment. The question is what do *you* want?"

Megan sighed. Rico was definitely a looker, a man any woman would want. But what did she really know about him, other than that he was Jessica and Savannah's older brother, and they thought the world of him?

"He doesn't want to mix business with pleasure, not that I would have, mind you. Besides, I never told him that I wanted him."

"Most women don't tell a man. What they do is send out vibes. Men can pick up on vibes real quick, and depending on what those vibes are, a man might take them as a signal."

Megan looked perplexed. "I don't think I sent out anything."

Pam laughed. "I hate to say this, but Jillian can probably size a man up better than you can. Your brothers

and cousins sheltered you too much from the harsh realities of life." Jillian was Pam's sister, who was a sophomore in college.

Megan shook her head. "It's not that they sheltered
me, I just never met anyone I was interested in."

"Until now?"

Megan lifted her chin. "I'm really not interested
in him, but I want us to work closer together, and he
doesn't…because he wants me."

"Well, I'm sure there will be times at the hospital
when the two of you will have no choice but to work
together."

Pam thought the person they were discussing was
another doctor. Megan wondered what Pam's reaction
would be if she found out the person they were talking
about was one of her dinner guests.

Megan heard loud male voices and recognized all of
them. One stood out, the sound a deep, husky timbre
she'd come to know.

Rico had arrived.


Rico paused in his conversation with Dillon and
Ramsey when Megan walked into the room to place a
huge bowl on the dining room table. She called out to
him. "Hello, Rico."

"Megan."

If his gaze was full of male appreciation, it couldn't
be helped. She had changed out of the scrubs he'd seen
her in earlier and into a cute V-neck blue pullover
sweater and a pair of hip-hugging jeans. She looked
both comfortable and beautiful. She had spoken, which
was a good indication that he hadn't offended her by
what he'd told her. He was a firm believer that the truth

never hurt, but he'd known more than one occasion when it had pissed people off.

"So, you're on your way to Texas, I hear." Dillon Westmoreland's question penetrated Rico's thoughts.

He looked at Dillon and saw the man's questioning gaze and knew he'd been caught ogling Megan. Rico's throat suddenly felt dry, and he took a sip of his wine before answering. "Yes. I might have a new lead. Don't want to say what it is just yet, until I'm certain it is one."

Dillon nodded. "I understand, trust me. When I took that time off to track down information on Raphel, it was like putting together pieces of a very complicated puzzle. But that woman," he said, inclining his head toward Pam when she entered the room, "made it all worthwhile."

Rico glanced over to where Pam was talking to Megan. He could see how Pam could have made Dillon feel that way. She was a beautiful woman. Rico had heard the story from his sisters, about how Dillon had met Pam while in Wyoming searching for leads on his great-grandfather's history. Pam had been engaged to marry a man who Dillon had exposed as nothing more than a lying, manipulating, arrogant SOB.

Rico couldn't help keeping his eye on Megan as her brother Ramsey and her cousins Dillon and Riley carried on conversations around him. Thoughts of her had haunted him ever since they'd met back in June. Even now, he lay awake with thoughts of her on his mind. How could one woman make such an impression on him, he would never know. But like he told her, he wanted her, so it was best that they keep their distance, considering his relationship with the Westmoreland family.

"So when are you leaving, Rico?"

He turned to meet Ramsey Westmoreland's inquisitive gaze. The man was sharp and, like Dillon, had probably caught Rico eyeing Megan. The hand holding Rico's wineglass tensed. He liked all the Westmorelands and appreciated how the guys included him in a number of their all-male get-togethers. The last thing he wanted was to lose their friendship because he couldn't keep his eyes off their sister and cousin.

"I'm leaving on Thursday. Why do you ask?"

Ramsey shrugged. "Just curious."

Rico couldn't shake the feeling that the man was more than just curious. He frowned and stared down at his drink. It was either that or risk the wrath of one of the Westmorelands if he continued to stare at Megan, who was busy setting the table.

Dillon spoke up and intruded into Rico's thoughts when he said, "Pam just gave me the nod that dinner is ready."

Everyone moved in the direction of the dining room. Rico turned to follow the others, but Ramsey touched his arm. "Wait for a minute."

Rico nodded. He wondered why Ramsey had detained him. Had Megan gone running to her brother and reported what Rico had said to her earlier? Or was Ramsey about to call him out on the carpet for the interest in Megan that he couldn't hide? In either of those scenarios, how could he explain his intense desire for Megan when he didn't understand it himself? He'd wanted women before, but never with this intensity.

When the two of them were left alone, Ramsey turned to him and Rico braced himself for whatever the man had to say. Rico was older brother to two sisters of his own so he knew how protective brothers could be. He hadn't liked either Chase or Durango in the beginning only because he'd known something was going on between them and his sisters.

Ramsey was silent for a moment, doing nothing more than slowly sipping his wine, so Rico decided to speak up. "Was there something you wanted to discuss with me, Ramsey?" There were a couple of years' difference in their ages, but at the moment Rico felt like it was a hell of a lot more than that.

"Yes," Ramsey replied. "It's about Megan."

Rico met Ramsey's gaze. "What about her?"

"Just a warning."

Rico tensed. "I think I know what you're going to say."

Ramsey shook his head, chuckling. "No. I don't think that you do."

Rico was confused at Ramsey's amusement. Hell, maybe he didn't know after all. "Then how about telling me. What's the warning regarding Megan?"

Ramsey took another sip of his drink and said, "She's strong-willed. She has self-control of steel and when she sets her mind to do something, she does it, often without thinking it through. And…if you tell her no, you might as well have said yes."

Rico was silent for a moment and then asked, "Is there a reason you're telling me this?"

Ramsey's mouth curved into a smile. "Yes, and you'll find out that reason soon enough. Now come on, they won't start dinner without us."

Megan tried drowning out all the conversation going on around her. As usual, whenever the Westmorelands got together, they had a lot to talk about.

She was grateful Pam hadn't figured out the identity of the man they'd been discussing and seated them beside each other. Instead, Rico was sitting at the other end of the table, across from Ramsey and next to Riley. If she had to look at him, it would be quite obvious she was doing so.

Riley said something and everyone chuckled. That gave her an excuse to look down the table. Rico was leaning back against the chair and holding a half-filled glass of wine in his hand, smiling at whatever the joke was about. Why did he have to look so darn irresistible when he smiled?

He must have felt her staring because he shifted his gaze to meet hers. For a moment she forgot to breathe. The intensity of his penetrating stare almost made her lips tremble. Something gripped her stomach in a tight squeeze and sent stirrings all through her nerve endings.

At that moment, one thought resonated through her mind. The same one Pam had reiterated earlier. *It doesn't matter if he wants you. The main question is whether or not you want him.*

Megan immediately broke eye contact and breathed in slowly, taking a sip of her wine. She fought to get her mind back on track and regain the senses she'd almost lost just now. She could control this. She had to. Desire and lust were things she didn't have time for. The only reason she wanted to go to Texas with Rico was to be there when he discovered the truth about Raphel.

Thinking it was time to make her announcement, she picked up her spoon and tapped it lightly against her glass, but loud enough to get everyone's attention. When all eyes swung her way she smiled and said, "I have an announcement to make. Most of you know I rarely take vacation time, but today I asked for an entire month off, starting tomorrow."

Surprised gazes stared back at her…except one. She saw a look of suspicion in Rico's eyes and noted the way his jaw tightened.

"What's wrong? You're missing Bailey already and plan to follow her to North Carolina?" her cousin Stern asked, grinning.

Megan returned his grin and shook her head. "Although I miss Bailey, I'm not going to North Carolina."

"Let me guess. You're either going to visit Gemma in Australia or Delaney in Tehran," Chloe said, smiling.

Again Megan shook her head. "Those are on my to-do list for later, but not now," she said.

When others joined in, trying to guess where she was headed, she held up her hand. "Please, it's not that big of a deal."

"It's a big deal if you're taking time off. You like working."

"I don't like working, but I like the job I do. There is a difference. And to appease everyone's curiosity, I talked to Clint and Alyssa today, and I'm visiting them in Texas for a while."

"Texas?"

She glanced down the table at Riley, which allowed her to look at Rico again, as well. He was staring at her, and it didn't take a rocket scientist to see he wasn't pleased with her announcement. Too bad, too glad. She couldn't force him to take her to Texas, but she could certainly go there on her own. "Yes, Riley, I'm going to Texas."

"When are you leaving?" her brother Zane asked. "I need to, ah, get that box from you before you leave."

She nodded, seeing the tense expression in Zane's features. She wondered about the reason for it. She was very much aware that he had a lock box in her hall closet. Although she'd been tempted, she'd never satisfied her curiosity by toying with the lock and looking inside. "That will be fine, Zane. I'm not leaving until Friday."

She took another quick glance at Rico before resuming dinner. He hadn't said anything, and it was just as well. There really wasn't anything he could say. Although they would end up in the same state and within mere miles from each other, they would not be together.

Since he didn't want her to accompany him, she would do a little investigating on her own.

## Chapter 3

The next morning Rico was still furious.

Now he knew what Ramsey's warning had been about. The little minx was going to Texas, pretty damn close to where he would be. He would have confronted her last night, but he'd been too upset to do so. Now here he was—at breakfast time—and instead of joining Zane, Riley, Canyon and Stern at one of the local cafés that boasted hotcakes to die for, he was parked outside Megan's home so he could try and talk some sense into her.

Did she not know what red-hot desire was about? Did she not understand how it was when a man really wanted a woman to the point where self-control took a backseat to longing and urges? Did she not comprehend there was temptation even when she tried acting cool and indifferent?

Just being around her last night had been hard

enough, and now she was placing herself in a position where they would be around each other in Texas without any family members as buffers. Oh, he knew the story she was telling her family, that she would be visiting Clint in Austin. Chances were, she would—for a minute. He was friends with Clint and Alyssa and had planned to visit them as well, during the same time she planned to be there. Since Forbes wasn't that far from Austin, Clint had offered Rico the use of one of their cabins on the Golden Glade Ranch as his headquarters, if needed.

But now Megan had interfered with his plans. She couldn't convince Rico that she didn't have ulterior motives and that she didn't intend to show up in Forbes. She intended to do some snooping, with or without him. So what the hell was she paying him for if she was going to do things her way? He got out of the car and glanced around, seeing her SUV parked at the side of her house. She had a real nice spread, and she'd kept most of it in its natural state. In the background, you could see rolling hills and meadows, mountains and the Whisper Creek Canyon. It was a beautiful view. And there was a lake named after her grandmother Gemma. Gemma Lake was huge and, according to Riley, the fish were biting all the time. If Megan hadn't been throwing him for a loop, Rico would have loved to find a fishing pole while he was here to see if the man's claim was true.

Megan's home was smaller than those owned by her brothers and male cousins. Their homes were two or three stories, but hers was a single story, modest in size, but eye-catching just the same. It reminded him of a vacation cabin with its cedar frame, wraparound porch and oversize windows. It had been built in the perfect location to take advantage of both lake and canyon.

He'd heard the story of how the main house and the three hundred acres on which it sat had been willed to Dillon, since he was the oldest cousin. The remaining Denver Westmorelands got a hundred acres each once they reached their twenty-fifth birthdays. They had come up with pet names for their particular spreads. There was Ramsey's Web, Derringer's Dungeon, Zane's Hideout and Gemma's Gem. Now, he was here at Megan's Meadows.

According to Riley, Megan's property was prime land, perfect for grazing. She had agreed to let a portion of her land be used by Ramsey for the raising of his sheep, and the other by Zane and Derringer for their horse training business.

If Riley suspected anything because of all the questions Rico had asked last night about Megan, he didn't let on. And it could have been that the man was too preoccupied to notice, since Riley had his little black book in front of him, checking off the numbers of women he intended to call.

It was early, and Rico wondered if Megan was up yet. He would find out soon enough. Regardless, he intended to have his say. She could pretend she hadn't recognized the strong attraction between them, that sexual chemistry that kept him awake at night, but he wasn't buying it. However, just in case she didn't have a clue, he intended to tell her. Again. There was no need for her to go to Texas, and to pretend she was going just to visit relatives was a crock.

The weather was cold. Tightening his leather jacket around him, he moved quickly, walking up onto the porch. Knocking on the door loudly, he waited a minute and then knocked again. When there was no answer, he was about to turn around, thinking that perhaps she'd gone up to the main house for breakfast, when suddenly the door was snatched open. His jaw almost dropped. The only thing he could say when he saw her, standing there wearing the cutest baby-doll gown, was *wow.*

Megan stared at Rico, surprised to see him. "What are you doing here?"

He leaned in the doorway. "I came to talk to you. And what are you doing coming to the door without first asking who it is?"

She rolled her eyes. "I thought you were one of my brothers. Usually they are the only ones who drop by without notice."

"Is that why you came to the door dressed like that?"

"Yes, what do you want to talk to me about? You're letting cold air in."

"Your trip to Texas."

Megan stared at him, her lips tight. "Fine," she said, taking a step back. "Come in and excuse me while I grab my robe."

He watched her walk away, thinking the woman looked pretty damn good in a nightgown. Her shapely backside filled it out quite nicely and showed what a gorgeous pair of legs she had.

Thinking that the last thing he needed to be thinking about was her legs, he removed his jacket and placed it on the coatrack by the door before moving into the living room. He glanced around. Her house was nice and cozy. Rustic. Quaint. The interior walls, as well as the ceiling and floors, were cedar like the outside.

The furniture was nice, appropriate for the setting and comfortable-looking. From where he stood, he could see an eat-in kitchen surrounded by floor-to-ceiling windows where you could dine and enjoy a view of the mountains and lake. He could even see the pier at her brother Micah's place that led to the lake and where the sailboat docked.

"Before we start talking about anything, I need my coffee."

Rico turned when she came back into the room, moving past him and heading toward the kitchen. He nodded, understanding. For him, it was basically the same, which was why he had drunk two cups already. "Fine. Take your time," he said. "I'm not going anywhere because I know what you're doing."

She didn't respond until she had the coffeemaker going. Then she turned and leaned back against a counter to ask, "And just what am I doing?"

"You're going to Texas for a reason."

"Yes, and I explained why. I need a break from work."

"Why Texas?"

She lifted her chin. "Why not Texas? It's a great state, and I haven't been there in a while. I missed that ball Clint, Cole and Casey do every year for their uncle. It will be good to see them, especially since Alyssa is expecting again."

"But that's not why you're going to Texas and you know it, Megan. Can you look me in the eyes and say you don't plan to set one foot in Forbes?"

She tilted her head to look at him. "No. I can't say that because I do."

"Why?"

Megan wondered how she could get him to understand. "Why not? These are my relatives."

"You are paying me to handle this investigation," he countered.

She tried not to notice how he filled the entrance to her kitchen. It suddenly looked small, as if there was barely any space. "Yes, and I asked to go to Forbes with you. It's important for me to be there when you find out if I have more relatives, but you have this stupid rule about working alone."

"Dammit, Megan, when you hired me you never told me you would get involved."

She crossed her arms over her chest. "I hadn't planned on getting involved. However, knowing I might have more kin out there changes everything. Why can't you understand that?"

Rico ran a frustrated hand down his face. In a way, he did. He would never forget that summer day when his mother had brought a fifteen-year-old girl into their home and introduced her as Jessica—their sister. Savannah had been sixteen, and he had been nineteen, a sophomore in college. It hadn't mattered to him that he hadn't known about Jessica before that time. Just the announcement that he had another sister had kicked his brotherly instincts into gear.

"I do understand, Megan," he said in a calm voice. "But still, there are things that I need to handle. Things I need to check out before anyone else can become involved."

She lifted a brow. "Things like what?"

Rico drew in a deep breath. Maybe he should have leveled with her yesterday, but there were things that had come up in his report on Raphel that he needed to confirm were fact or fiction. So far, everything negative about Raphel had turned out not to be true in Dillon's investigation. Rico wanted his final report to be as factual as possible, and he needed to do more research of the town's records.

She poured a cup of coffee for herself and one for him, as well. "What's wrong, Rico? Is there something you're not telling me?"

He saw the worry in her eyes as he accepted his coffee. "Look, this is my investigation. I told you that I was able to track down information on Clarice and the fact that she might have given birth to a child. That's all I know for now, Megan. Anything else is hearsay."

"Hearsay like what?"

"I'd rather not say."

After taking a sip of coffee, she said, "You're being evasive."

He narrowed his gaze. "I'm being thorough. If you want to go to Texas to visit Clint and Alyssa, then fine. But what I *don't* need is you turning up where you don't need to be."

"Where I don't need to be?" she growled.

"Yes. I have a job to do, and I won't be able to do it with you close by. I won't be able to concentrate."

"Men!" Megan said, stiffening her spine. "Do you all think it's all about you? I have brothers and male cousins, plenty of them. I know how you operate. You want one woman one day and another woman the next. Get over it already. Please."

Rico just stared at her. "And you think it's that simple?"

"*Yesss*. I'm Zane and Derringer's sister, Riley, Canyon and Stern's cousin. I see them. I watch them. I know their M.O. Derringer has been taken out of the mix by marrying Lucia, thank goodness. But the rest of them, and now the twins…oh, my God…are following in their footsteps.

"You see. You want. You do. But not me. *You,* Rico Claiborne, assume just because you want me that you're going to get me. What was your warning? If we go somewhere together alone, that you're going to *have* me. Who are you supposed to be? Don't I have a say-so in this matter? What if I told you that I *don't* want you?"

Rico just stared at her. "Then I would say you're lying to yourself. You want me. You might not realize it, but you want me. I see it every time you look at me. Damn, Megan, admit there's a strong attraction between us."

She rolled her eyes. "Okay, I find you attractive. But I find a lot of men attractive. No big deal."

"And are you sending out the same vibes to them that you're sending to me?" he asked in a deep, husky voice.

Megan recalled that Pam had said something about vibes. Was she sending them out to him without realizing she was doing so? No, she couldn't be. Because right now she wasn't feeling desire for him, she was feeling anger at him for standing there and making such an outlandish claim.

But still, she would have to admit that her heart was pounding furiously in her chest, and parts of her were quivering inside. So, could he be right about those vibes? Naw, she refused to believe it. Like she'd told him, she'd seen men in operation. Zane probably had a long list of women he wanted who he imagined were sending out vibes.

From the first, Rico had come across as a man who

knew how to control any given situation, which was why she figured he was the perfect person for the job she'd hired him to do. So what was his problem now? If he did want her, then surely the man could control his urges.

"Look, I assure you, I can handle myself, and I can handle you, Rico," she said, "All of my senses are intact, and you can be certain lust won't make me lose control. And nothing you or any man can say or do will place me in a position where I will lose my self-control." The men who thought so didn't call her "Iceberg Megan" for nothing.

"You don't think so?" Rico challenged her. "You aren't made of stone. You have feelings. I can tell that you're a very passionate woman, so consider your words carefully."

She chuckled as if what he'd said was a joke. "Passionate? Me?"

"Yes, you. When I first looked at you at the wedding reception and our gazes connected, the air between us was bristling with so much sexual energy I'm sure others felt it," he said silkily. "Are you going to stand there and claim you didn't feel it?"

Megan gazed down into her coffee and erased her smile. Oh, she remembered that day. Yes, she'd felt it. It had been like a surge of sexual, electrical currents that had consumed the space between them. It had happened again, too, every time she saw him looking at her. Until now, she'd assumed she had imagined it, but his words confirmed he had felt the connection, as well.

After that night at the wedding, she'd gone to bed thinking about him and had thought of him several nights after that. What she'd felt had bothered her, and she had talked to Gemma about it. Some of the things her married sister had shared with her she hadn't wanted to hear, mainly because Megan was a firm believer in self-control. Everybody had it, and everybody could manage it. Regardless of how attracted she was to Rico, she had self-control down pat. Hers was unshakable.

She'd had to learn self-control from the day she was told she would never see her parents again. She would never forget how Dillon and Ramsey had sat her down at the age of twelve and told her that not only her parents, but also her aunt and uncle, whom she'd adored, had been killed in a plane crash.

Dillon and Ramsey had assured her that they would keep the family together and take care of everyone, although the youngest—Bane and Bailey—were both under nine at the time. On that day, Ramsey had asked her to stay strong and in control. As the oldest girl in the Denver Westmoreland family, they had depended on her to help Gemma and Bailey through their grief. That didn't mean she'd needed to put her own grief aside, but it had meant that in spite of her grief, she'd had to be strong for the others. And she had. When the younger ones would come to her crying, she was the one who would comfort them, regardless of the circumstances or her emotions.

The ability to become emotionally detached, to stay in control, was how she'd known being an anesthesiologist was her calling. She went into surgery knowing some patients wouldn't make it through. Although she assured the patient of her skill in putting them to sleep, she never promised they would pull through. That decision was out of her hands. Some of the surgeons had lost patients and, in a way, she felt she'd lost them, as well. But no matter what, she remained in control.

Drawing in a deep breath, she eyed Rico. "You might have a problem with control, but I don't. I admit I find you desirable, but I can regulate my emotions. I can turn them on and off when I need to, Rico. Don't worry that I'll lose control one day and jump your bones, because it won't happen. There's not that much desire in the world."

Rico shook his head. "You honestly believe that, don't you?"

She placed her coffee cup on the counter. "Honestly believe what?"

"That you can control a desire as intense as ours."

"Yes, why wouldn't I?"

"I agree that certain desires can be controlled, Megan. But I'm trying to tell you, what you refuse to acknowledge or accept—desire as intense as ours can't always be controlled. What we have isn't normal."

She bunched her forehead. "Not normal? That's preposterous."

Rico knew then that she really didn't have a clue. This was no act. He could stand here until he was blue in the face and she still wouldn't understand. "What I'm trying to say, Megan," he said slowly, trying not to let frustration get the best of him, "is that I feel a degree of desire for you that I've never felt for any woman before."

She crossed her arms over her chest and glared at him. "Should I get excited or feel flattered about it?"

He gritted his teeth. "Look, Megan…"

"No, *you* look, Rico," she said, crossing the room to stand in front of him. "I don't know what to tell you. Honestly, I don't. I admitted that I'm attracted to you, as well. Okay, I'll admit it again. But on that same note, I'm also telling you I won't lose control over it. For crying out loud, there're more important things in life than sexual attraction, desire and passion. It's not about all of that."

"Isn't it?" He paused a moment, trying to keep his vexation in check. And it wasn't helping matters that she was there, standing right in front of him, with a stubborn expression on her face and looking as beautiful as any woman could. And he picked up her scent, which made him fight to keep a grip on his lust. The woman was driving him mad in so many ways.

"Let me ask you something, Megan," he said in a voice he was fighting to keep calm. "When was the last time you were with a man you desired?"

Rico's question surprised Megan, and she didn't say anything. Hell, she'd never been with a man she truly desired because she'd never been with a man period. She had dated guys in high school, college, and even doctors at the hospital. Unfortunately, they'd all had one thing in common. They had reminded her too much of her player-card-toting brothers and cousins, even hitting on her using some of the same lines she'd heard her family use. And a few bold ones had even had the nerve to issue ultimatums. She had retaliated by dropping those men like hot potatoes, just to show she really didn't give a royal damn. They said she was cold and couldn't be thawed and that's when they'd started calling her Iceberg Megan. Didn't bother her any because none of those men had gotten beyond the first boring kiss. She was who she was and no man—coming or going—would change it.

"I'm waiting on an answer," Rico said, interrupting her thoughts.

She gazed up at him and frowned. "Wait on. I don't intend to give you an answer because it's none of your business."

He nodded. "All right. You claim you can control the passion between us, right?"

"Yes."

"Then I want to see how you control this."

The next thing Megan knew, Rico had reached out, pulled her into his embrace and swooped his mouth down onto hers.

Desire that had been lingering on the edges was now producing talons that were digging deep into Megan's skin and sending heated lust all through her veins—and making her act totally out of control. He parted her lips with his tongue and instead of immediately going after her tongue, he rolled the tip around, as if on a tasting expedition. Then he gradually tasted more of it until he had captured it all. And when she became greedy, he pulled back and gave her just the tip again. Then they played the tongue game over and over again.

She felt something stir within her that had never stirred before while kissing a man. But then no man had ever kissed her like this. Or played mouth games with her this way.

He was electrifying her cells, muddling her brain as even more desire skittered up her spine. She tried steadying her emotions, regaining control when she felt heat flooding between her thighs, but she couldn't help but release a staggering moan.

Instead of unlocking their mouths, he intensified the

kiss, as his tongue, holding hers in a dominant grip, began exploring every part of her mouth with strokes so sensual her stomach began doing somersaults. She felt her senses tossed in a number of wild spins, and surprised herself when she wrapped her arms around his neck and began running her fingers through the softness of his hair, absently curling a strand around her finger.

She could taste the hunger in his kiss, the passion and the desire. Her emotions were smoldering, and blocking every single thought from her already chaotic mind. The man was lapping up her mouth, and each stroke was getting hotter and hotter, filling her with emotions she had pushed aside for years. Was he ever going to let go of her mouth? Apparently no time soon.

This kiss was making her want to do things she'd never done before. Touch a man, run her hands all over him, check out that huge erection pressing against her belly.

She felt his hands rest on her backside, urging her closer to his front. And she shifted her hips to accommodate what he wanted. She felt the nipples of her breasts harden and knew her robe was no barrier against the heat coming from his body.

No telling how long they would have stood in the middle of her kitchen engaged in one hell of a feverish kiss if his cell phone hadn't gone off. They broke apart, and she drew in a much needed breath and watched him get his phone out of the back pocket of his jeans.

She took note of the angry look on his face while he talked and heard him say to the caller, "I don't want you calling me." He then clicked off the line without giving the person a chance to respond.

She tensed at the thought that the person he'd just

given the brush-off was a woman. Megan lifted her chin. "Maybe you should have taken that call."

He glanced over at her while stuffing his phone back into the pocket of his jeans. She watched as his hazel eyes became a frosty green. "I will never take *that* call."

She released a slow, steady breath, feeling his anger as if it were a personal thing. She was glad it wasn't directed at her. She wondered what the woman had done to deserve such animosity from him. At the moment, Megan didn't care because she had her own problems. Rico Claiborne had made her lose control. He had kissed her, and she had kissed him back.

And rather enjoyed it.

Dread had her belly quaking and her throat tightening when she realized she wasn't an iceberg after all. Rico had effectively thawed her.

She drew in a deep breath, furious with herself for letting things get out of hand when she'd boasted and bragged about the control she had. All it had taken was one blazing kiss to make a liar out of her. It was a fluke, it had to be. He had caught her off guard. She didn't enjoy kissing him as much as she wanted to think she did.

Then why was she licking her lips and liking the taste he'd left behind? She glanced over and saw he'd been watching her and was following the movement of her tongue. Her fingers knotted into a fist at her side, and she narrowed her gaze. "I think you need to leave."

"No problem, now that I've proven my point. You're as passionate as you are beautiful, Megan. Nothing's changed. I still want you, and now that I've gotten a taste, I want you even more. So take my warning, don't come to Texas."

A part of Megan knew that if she was smart, she would take his warning. But the stubborn part of her refused to do so. "I'm going to Texas, Rico."

He didn't say anything for a long moment, just stood there and held her gaze. Finally, he said, "Then I guess I'll be seeing you at some point while you're there. Don't say I didn't warn you."

Rico strode away and, before opening the door to leave, he grabbed his jacket off the coatrack. He turned, smiled at her, winked and then opened the door and walked out.

Megan took a deep breath to calm her racing heart. She had a feeling that her life, as she'd always known it, would never, ever be the same. Heaven help her, she had tasted passion and already she was craving more.

# Chapter 4

Upon arriving at Megan's place early Friday morning, Ramsey glanced down at the two overpacked traveling bags that sat in the middle of her living room. "Hey, you're planning on coming back, aren't you?" he asked, chuckling.

Megan smiled and tapped a finger to her chin. "Umm, I guess I will eventually. And those bags aren't *that* bad."

"They aren't? I bet I'll strain my back carrying them out to the truck. And how much you want to bet they're both overweight and you'll pay plenty when you check them in at the airport."

"Probably, but that's fine. A lot of it is baby stuff I bought for Alyssa. She's having a girl and you know how I like buying all that frilly stuff." He would know since his two-year-old daughter, Susan, had been the first female born to the Denver Westmorelands since

Bailey. Megan simply adored her niece and would miss her while away in Texas.

She looked up at Ramsey, her oldest brother, the one she most admired along with her cousin Dillon. "Ram?"

He looked over at her after taking a sip of the coffee she'd handed him as soon he had walked through the door. "Yes?"

"I was a good kid while growing up, wasn't I? I didn't give you and Dillon any trouble, right?"

He grinned, reached out and pulled one of her curls. "No, sport, you didn't give us any trouble. You were easier to handle than Bailey, the twins and Bane. But everyone was easier than those four."

He paused a moment and added, "And unlike a lot of men with sisters, I never once had to worry about guys getting their way with the three of you. You, Gemma and Bail did a good job of keeping the men in line yourselves. If a guy became a nuisance, you three would make them haul ass the other way. Dillon and I got a chuckle out of it, each and every time. Especially you. I think you enjoyed giving the guys a hard time."

She playfully jabbed him in the ribs. "I did not."

He laughed. "Could have fooled us." He grabbed her close for a brotherly hug. "At one time we thought you were sweet on Charlie Bristol when you were a senior in high school. We knew for a fact he was sweet on you. But according to Riley, he was too scared to ask you out."

Megan smiled over at him as she led him to the kitchen. She remembered Charlie Bristol. He used to spend the summers with one of his aunts who lived nearby. "He was nice, and cute."

"But you wouldn't give him the time of day," he said, sitting down at the table.

Ramsey was right, she hadn't. She recalled having a crush on Charlie for a quick second but she'd been too busy helping out with Gemma and Bailey to think about boys.

"I'm going to miss you, sport," Ramsey said, breaking into her thoughts.

Megan smiled over at him as she joined him at the table. "And I'm going to miss you, as well. Other than being with Gemma during the time she was giving birth to CJ, and visiting Delaney those two weeks in Tehran, this is the first real vacation I've taken, and the longest. I'll be away from the hospital for a full month."

"How will they make it without you?" Ramsey teased.

"I'm sure they'll find a way." Even while attending college, she had stayed pretty close to home, not wanting to go too far away. For some reason, she'd felt she was needed. But then, she'd also felt helpless during Bailey's years of defiance. She had tried talking to her baby sister, but it hadn't done any good. She'd known that Bailey's, the twins' and Bane's acts of rebellion were their way of handling the grief of losing their parents. But still, at the time, she'd wished she could do more.

"Ram, can I ask you something?"

He chuckled. "Another question?" He faked a look of pain before saying, "Okay, I guess one more wouldn't hurt."

"Do you think having control of your emotions is a bad thing?" She swallowed tightly as she waited for his answer.

He smiled at her. "Having too much self-control isn't healthy, and it can lead to stress. Everyone needs to know how to let loose, release steam and let their hair down every once in a while."

Megan nodded. Releasing steam wasn't what she was dealing with. Letting go of a buildup of sexual energy was the problem. And that kiss the other day hadn't helped matters any.

She hadn't seen Rico since then, and she knew he'd already left for Texas. She'd been able to get that much out of Riley when he'd dropped by yesterday. "So it's okay to…"

"Get a little wild every once in a while?" He chuckled. "Yes, I think it is, as long as you're not hurting anyone."

He paused a second and then asked, "You're planning to enjoy yourself while you're in Texas, right?"

"Yes. But as you know, it won't be all fun, Ram." Ramsey and Dillon were the only ones she'd told the real reason why she was going to Texas. They also knew she had asked Rico to take her with him, and he'd refused. Of course, she hadn't told them what he'd told her as the reason behind his refusal. She'd only told them Rico claimed he preferred working alone and didn't need her help in the investigation. Neither Dillon nor Ramsey had given their opinions about anything, because she hadn't asked for them. The "don't ask—don't tell" rule was one Dillon and Ramsey implemented for the Westmorelands who were independent adults.

"You can do me a favor, though, sport," he said in a serious tone.

She lifted an eyebrow. "What?"

"Don't be too hard on Rico for not wanting to take

you along. You're paying him to do a job, and he wants to do it."

Megan rolled her eyes. "And he will. But I want to be there. I could help."

"Evidently he doesn't want your help."

*Yes, but he does want something else,* Megan thought. She could just imagine what her brother would think if he knew the real reason Rico didn't want her in Texas. But then, Ramsey was so laid-back it probably wouldn't faze him. He'd known for years how Callum had felt about Gemma. But he'd also known his sisters could handle their business without any interference from their big brother unless it became absolutely necessary.

"But what if there are other Westmorelands somewhere?" she implored. "I told you what Rico said about Clarice having a baby."

"Then Rico will find out information and give it to you to bring to us, Megan. Let him do his job. And another thing."

"Yes?"

"Rico is a good guy. I like him. So do the rest of the Westmorelands. I judge a man by a lot of things and one is how he treats his family. He evidently is doing something right because Jessica and Savannah think the world of their brother."

Megan leaned back in her chair and frowned. "Is there a reason you're telling me that?"

Ramsey was silent for a moment as he stared at her. Then a slow smile touched his lips. "I'll let you figure that one out, Megan."

She nodded and returned his smile. "Fair enough. And about that self-control we were discussing earlier?"

"Yes, what about it?" he asked.

"It *is* essential at times," she said.

"I agree, it is. At times."

"But I'm finding out I might not have as much as I thought. That's not a bad thing, right, Ram?"

Ramsey chuckled. "No, sport, it's just a part of being human."

Rico had just finished eating his dinner at one of the restaurants in Forbes when his cell phone vibrated. Standing, he pulled it out of his back pocket. "This is Rico."

"Our father called me."

Rico tensed when he heard Savannah's voice. He sat back down and leaned back in his chair. "He called me as well, but I didn't give him a chance to say anything," he said, trying to keep his anger in check.

"Same here. I wonder what he wants, and I hope he doesn't try contacting Jessica. How long has it been now? Close to eighteen years?"

"Just about. I couldn't reach Jessica today, but I did talk to Chase. He said Jess hadn't mentioned anything about getting a call from Jeff Claiborne, and I think if she had, she would have told him," said Rico.

"Well, I don't want him upsetting her. She's pregnant."

"And you have a lot on your hands with a new baby," he reminded her.

"Yes, but I can handle the likes of Jeff regardless. But, I'm not sure Jessica can, though. It wasn't our mother who committed suicide because of him."

"I agree."

"Where are you?" Savannah asked him.

"Forbes, Texas. Nice town."

"Are you on a work assignment?"

"Yes, for Megan," he replied, taking a sip of his beer.

"Is she there with you?"

Rico's eyebrows shot up. "No. Should she be?"

"Just asking. Well, I'll be talking with—"

"Savannah?" he said in that particular tone when he knew she was up to something. "Why would you think Megan was here with me? I don't work that way."

"Yes, but I know the two of you are attracted to each other."

He took another sip of his beer. "Are we?"

"Yes. I noticed at Micah's wedding. I think everyone did."

"Did they?"

"Yes, Rico, and you're being evasive."

He laughed. "And you're being nosy. Where's Durango?" he asked, changing the subject.

"Outside giving Sarah her riding lessons."

"Tell him I said hello and give my niece a hug."

"I will…and Rico?"

"Yes?"

"I like Megan. Jess does, too."

Rico didn't say anything for a long moment. He took another sip of his beer as he remembered the kiss they'd shared a couple of days ago. "Good to hear because I like her, too. Now, goodbye."

He clicked off the phone before his sister could grill him. Glancing around the restaurant, he saw it had gotten crowded. The hotel had recommended this place, and he was glad they had. They had served good Southern food, the tastiest. But nothing he ate, no matter how spicy, could eradicate Megan's taste from his tongue. And personally, he had no problem with that because what he'd said to Savannah was true. He liked Megan. A capricious smile touched his lips. Probably, too damn much.

He was about to signal the waitress for his check when his phone rang. He hoped it wasn't Savannah calling back being nosy. He sighed in relief when he saw it was Martin Felder, a friend who'd once worked with the FBI years ago but was now doing freelance detective work. He was an ace when it came to internet research. "Sorry, I meant to call you earlier, Rico, but I needed to sing Anna to sleep."

Rico nodded, understanding. Martin had become a single father last year when his wife, Marcia, had died from pancreatic cancer. He had pretty much taken early retirement from the Bureau to work from home. He had been the one to discover information about Clarice's pregnancy.

"No problem, and I can't tell you enough about what a great job you're doing with Anna."

"Thanks, Rico. I needed to hear that. She celebrated her third birthday last week, and I wished Marcia could have been here to see what a beautiful little girl we made together. She looks more and more like her mom every day."

Martin paused a minute and then said, "I was on the internet earlier today and picked up this story of a woman celebrating her one-hundredth birthday in Forbes. They were saying how sharp her memory was for someone her age."

"What's her name?" Rico asked, sitting up straight in his chair.

"Fanny Banks. She's someone you might want to talk to while in town to see if she remembers anything about Clarice Riggins. I'll send the info over to you."

"That's a good idea. Thanks." Rico hung up the phone and signaled for the waitress.

A few moments later, back in his rental car, he was reviewing the information Martin had sent to his iPhone. The woman's family was giving her a birthday party tomorrow so the earliest he would be able to talk to her would be Saturday.

His thoughts shifted to Megan and the look in her eyes when she'd tried explaining why it was so important for her to be there when he found out information on Raphel. Maybe he *was* being hard-nosed about not letting her help him. And he had given her fair warning about how much he wanted her. They'd kissed, and if she hadn't realized the intensity of their attraction before, that kiss should have cinched it and definitely opened her eyes.

It had definitely opened his, but that's not all it had done. If he'd thought he wanted her before then he was doubly certain of it now. He hadn't slept worth a damn since that kiss and sometimes he could swear her scent was in the air even when she wasn't around. He had this intense physical desire for her that he just couldn't kick. Now he had begun to crave her and that wasn't good. But it was something he just couldn't help. The woman was a full-blown addiction to his libido.

He put his phone away, thinking Megan should have arrived at Clint's place by now. It was too late to make a trip to Austin tonight, but he'd head that way early tomorrow…unless he could talk himself out of it overnight.

And he doubted that would happen.

# *Chapter 5*

"I can't eat a single thing more," Megan said, as she looked at all the food Alyssa had placed on the table for breakfast. It wouldn't be so bad if she hadn't arrived yesterday at dinnertime to a whopping spread by Chester, Clint's cook, housekeeper and all-around ranch hand.

Megan had met Chester the last time she'd been here, and every meal she'd eaten was to die for. But like she'd said, she couldn't eat a single thing more and would need to do some physical activities to burn off the calories.

Clint chuckled as helped his wife up from the table. Alyssa said the doctor claimed she wasn't having twins but Megan wasn't too sure.

"Is there anything you need me to do?" she asked Alyssa when Clint had gotten her settled in her favorite recliner in the living room.

Alyssa waved off Megan's offer. "I'm fine. Clint is doing great with Cain," she said of her three-year-old son, who was the spitting image of his father. "And Aunt Claudine will arrive this weekend."

"How long do you think your aunt will visit this time?" Megan asked as she took the love seat across from Alyssa.

"If I have anything to do with it, she won't be leaving," Chester hollered out as he cleared off the kitchen table.

Megan glanced over at Clint, and Alyssa only laughed. Then Clint said, "Chester is sweet on Aunt Claudine, but hasn't convinced her to stay here and not return to Waco."

"But I think he might have worn her down," Alyssa said, whispering so Chester wouldn't hear. "She mentioned she's decided to put her house up for sale. She told me not to tell Chester because she wants to surprise him."

Megan couldn't help but smile. She thought Chester and Alyssa's aunt Claudine, both in their sixties, would make a nice couple. She bet it was simply wonderful finding love at that age. It would be grand to do so at any age…if you were looking for it or interested in getting it. She wasn't.

"If it's okay, I'd like to go riding around the Golden Glade, especially the south ridge. I love it there."

Clint smiled. "Most people do." He looked lovingly at Alyssa. "We've discovered it's one of our most favorite places on the ranch."

Megan watched as Alyssa exchanged another loving look with Clint. She knew the two were sharing a private moment that involved the south ridge in some way.

They made a beautiful couple, she thought. Like all the other Westmoreland males, Clint was too handsome for his own good, and Alyssa, who was even more beautiful while pregnant, was his perfect mate.

Seeing the love radiating between the couple— the same she'd witnessed between her cousins and their wives, as well as between her brothers and their wives—made a warm feeling flow through Megan. It was one she'd never felt before. She drew in a deep breath, thinking that feeling such a thing was outright foolish, but she couldn't deny what she'd felt just now.

As if remembering Megan was in the room, Clint turned to her, smiled and said, "Just let Marty know that you want to go riding, and he'll have one of the men prepare a horse for you."

"Thanks." Megan decided it was best to give Clint and Alyssa some alone time. Cain was taking a nap, and Megan could make herself scarce real fast. "I'll change into something comfortable for riding."

After saying she would see them later, she quickly headed toward the guest room.

One part of Rico's mind was putting up one hell of an argument as to why he shouldn't be driving to Austin for Megan. Too bad the other part refused to listen. Right now, the only thing that particular part of his brain understood was his erection throbbing something fierce behind the zipper of his pants. Okay, he knew it shouldn't be just a sexual thing. He shouldn't be allowing all this lust to be eating away at him, practically nipping at his balls, but hell, he couldn't help it. He wanted her. Plain and simple.

Although there was really nothing plain and simple about it, anticipation made him drive faster than he should. *Slow down, Claiborne. Are you willing to get a speeding ticket just because you want to see her again?*

*Yes.*

He drew in a sharp breath, not understanding it. So he continued driving and when he finally saw Austin's city-limits marker, he felt a strong dose of adrenaline rush through his veins. It didn't matter that he still had a good twenty minutes to go before reaching the Golden Glade Ranch. Nor did it matter that Megan would be surprised to see him, and even more surprised that he would be taking her back with him to Forbes to be there when he talked to Fanny Banks.

But he would explain that taking her to meet Fanny would be all he'd let her do. He would return Megan to the Golden Glade while he finished up with the investigation. Nothing had changed on that front. Like he'd told her, he preferred working alone.

He checked the clock on the car's dashboard. Breakfast would be over by the time he reached the ranch. Alyssa might be resting, and if Clint wasn't around then he was probably out riding the range.

Rico glanced up at the sky. Clear, blue, and the sun was shining. It was a beautiful day in late September, and he planned to enjoy it. He pressed down on the accelerator. Although he probably didn't need to be in a hurry, he was in one anyway.

A short while later he released a sigh of anticipation when he saw the marker to the Golden Glade Ranch. Smiling, he made a turn down the long, winding driveway toward the huge ranch house.

Megan was convinced that the south-ridge pasture of the Golden Glade was the most beautiful land she'd ever seen. The Westmorelands owned beautiful property back in Denver, but this here was just too magnificent for words.

She dismounted her horse and, after tying him to a hitching post, she gazed down in the valley where it seemed as though thousands upon thousands of wild horses were running free.

The triplets, Clint, Cole and Casey, had lived on this land with their Uncle Sid while growing up. Sid Roberts had been a legend in his day. First as a rodeo star and then later as a renowned horse trainer. Megan even remembered studying about him in school. In their uncle's memory, the triplets had dedicated over three thousand acres of this land along the south ridge as a reserve. Hundreds of wild horses were saved from slaughter by being shipped here from Nevada. Some were left to roam free for the rest of their days, and others were shipped either to Montana, where Casey had followed in her uncle's footsteps as a horse trainer, or to Denver, where some of her cousins and brothers were partners in the operation.

Megan could recall when Zane, Derringer and Jason had decided to join the partnership that included Clint, their cousin Durango, Casey and her husband, McKinnon. All of the Westmorelands involved in the partnership loved horses and were experts in handling them.

Megan glanced across the way and saw a cabin nestled among the trees. She knew it hadn't been here the last time she'd visited. She smiled, thinking it was probably a lovers' hideaway for Clint and Alyssa and was probably the reason for the secretive smile they'd shared this morning.

Going back to the horse, she unhooked a blanket

she'd brought and the backpack that contained a book to read and a Ziploc bag filled with the fruit Chester had packed. It didn't take long to find the perfect spot to spread the blanket on the ground and stretch out. She looked up at the sky, thinking it was a gorgeous day and it was nice to be out in it. She enjoyed her job at the hospital, but there was nothing like being out under the wide-open sky.

She had finished one chapter of the suspense thriller that her cousin Stone Westmoreland, aka Rock Mason, had written. She was so engrossed in the book that it was a while before she heard the sound of another horse approaching. Thinking it was probably Clint or one of the ranch hands coming to check on her, to make sure she was okay, she'd gotten to her feet by the time a horse and rider came around the bend.

Suddenly she felt it—heat sizzling down her spine, fire stirring in her stomach. Her heart began thumping hard in her chest. She'd known that she would eventually run in to Rico, but she'd thought it would be when she made an appearance in Forbes. He had been so adamant about her not coming to Texas with him that she'd figured she would have to be the one to seek him out and not the other way around.

Her breasts began tingling, and she could feel her nipples harden against her cotton shirt when he brought his horse to a stop beside hers. Nothing, she thought, was more of a turn-on than seeing a man, especially this particular man, dismount from his horse…with such masculine ease and virile precision, and she wondered if he slid between a woman's legs the same way.

She could feel her cheeks redden with such brazen thoughts, and her throat tightened when he began walking toward her. Since it seemed he didn't have anything to say, she figured she would acknowledge his presence. "Rico."

He tilted his hat to her. She thought he looked good in his jeans, chambray shirt and the Stetson. "Megan."

She drew in a deep breath as he moved toward her. His advance was just as lethal, just as stealthy, as a hunter who'd cornered his prey. "Do you know why I'm here?" he asked her in a deep, husky voice.

Megan she shook her head. "No. You said you wanted to work alone."

He smiled, and she could tell it didn't quite reach his eyes. "But you're here, which means you didn't intend on letting me do that."

She lifted her chin. "Just pretend I'm not here, and when you see me in Forbes, you can pretend I'm not there."

"Not possible," he said throatily, coming to a stop in front of her. Up close, she could see smoldering desire in the depths of his eyes. That should have jarred some sense into her, but it didn't. Instead it had just the opposite effect.

Megan tilted her head back to look up at him and what she saw almost took her breath away again—hazel eyes that were roaming all over her, as if they were savoring her. There was no way she could miss the hunger that flared in their depths, making her breath come out in quick gulps.

"I think I need to get back to the ranch," she said.

A sexy smile touched his lips. "What's the rush?"

There was so much heat staring at her that she knew any minute she was bound to go up in flames. "I asked why you're here, Rico."

Instead of answering, he reached out and gently cradled her face between his hands and brought his mouth so close to hers that she couldn't keep her lips from quivering. "My answer is simple, Megan. I came for you."

He paused a moment and then added, "I haven't been able to forget that kiss and how our tongues tangled while I became enmeshed in your taste. Nothing has changed other than I think you've become an addiction, and I want you more than before."

And then he lowered his mouth to hers.

He knew the instant she began to lose control because she started kissing him back with a degree of hunger and intimacy that astounded him.

He wrapped his arms around her waist while they stood there, letting their tongues tangle in a way that was sending all kinds of sensual pulses through his veins. This is what had kept him up nights, had made him drive almost like a madman through several cities to get here. He had known this would be what awaited him. Never had a single kiss ignited so much sexual pressure within him, made him feel as if he was ready to explode at any moment.

She shifted her body closer, settling as intimately as a woman still wearing clothes could get, at the juncture of his legs. The moment she felt his hard erection pressing against her, she shifted her stance to cradle his engorged shaft between her thighs.

If he didn't slow her down, he would be hauling her off to that blanket she'd spread on the ground. Thoughts of making love to her here, in such a beautiful spot and under such a stunning blue sky, were going through his mind. But he knew she wasn't ready for that. She es-

pecially wasn't ready to take it to the level he wanted
to take it.

His thoughts were interrupted when he felt her hand
touch the sides of his belt, trying to ease his shirt out of
his pants. She wanted to touch some skin, and he had
no problems letting her do so. He shifted again, a deliberate move on his part to give her better access to
what she wanted, although what she wanted to do was
way too dangerous to his peace of mind. It wouldn't
take much to push him over the edge.

When he felt her tugging at his shirt, pulling it out
of his jeans, he deepened the kiss, plunging his tongue
farther into her mouth and then flicking it around with
masterful strokes. He wasn't a man who took advantage
of women, but then he was never one who took them
too seriously, either, even while maintaining a level of
respect for any female he was involved with.

But with Megan that respect went up more than a
notch. She was a Westmoreland. So were his sisters.
That was definitely a game changer. Although he
wanted Megan and intended to have her, he needed
to be careful how he handled her. He had to do things
decently and in the right order. As much as he could.

But doing anything decently and in the right order
was not on his mind as he continued to kiss her, as his
tongue explored inside her mouth with a hunger that
had his erection throbbing.

And when she inched her hand beneath his shirt to
touch his skin, he snatched his mouth from hers to draw
in a deep breath. He held her gaze, staring down at her
as the silence between them extended. Her touch had
nearly scorched him it had been so hot. He hadn't been
prepared for it. Nor had he expected such a reaction to it.

He might have reeled in his senses and moved away from her if she hadn't swiped her tongue across her lips. That movement was his downfall, and he felt fire roaring through his veins. He leaned in closer and began licking her mouth from corner to corner. And when she let out a breathless moan, he slid his tongue back inside to savor her some more.

Their tongues tangled and dueled and he held on to her, needing the taste as intense desire tore through him. He knew he had to end the kiss or it could go on forever. And when her hips began moving against him, rotating against his huge arousal, he knew where things might lead if he didn't end the kiss here and now.

He slowly pulled back and let out a breath as his gaze seized her moistened lips. He watched the eyes staring back at him darken to a degree that would have grown hair on his chest, if he didn't have any already.

"Rico?"

Heat was still simmering in his veins, and it didn't help him calm down when she said his name like that. "Yes?"

"You did it again."

He lifted a brow. "What did I do?"

"You kissed me."

He couldn't help but smile. "Yes, and you kissed me back."

She nodded and didn't deny it. "We're going to have to come to some kind of understanding. About what we can or cannot do when we're alone."

His smile deepened. *That would be interesting.* "Okay, you make out that list, and we can discuss it."

She tilted her head back to look at him. "I'm serious."

"So am I, and make sure it's a pretty detailed list

because if something's not on there, I'll be tempted to try it."

When she didn't say anything, he chuckled and told her she was being too serious. "You'll feel better after getting dinner. You missed lunch."

She shook her head as he led her over to the horses. "I wasn't hungry."

He licked his mouth, smiled and said, "Mmm, baby, you could have fooled me."

# Chapter 6

Once they had gotten back to the ranch and dismounted, Rico told the ranch hand who'd come to handle the horses not to bother, that he would take care of them.

"You're from Philadelphia, but you act as if you've been around horses all your life," she said, watching him remove the saddles from the animals' back.

He smiled over at her across the back of the horse she'd been riding. "In a way, I have. My maternal grandparents own horses, and they made sure Savannah and I took riding lessons and that we knew how to care for one."

She nodded. "What about Jessica?"

He didn't say anything for a minute and then said, "Jessica, Savannah and I share the same father. We didn't know about Jess until I was in college."

"Oh." Megan didn't know the full story, but it was obvious from Rico's and Savannah's interracial features that the three siblings shared the same father and not the same mother. She had met Rico and Savannah's mother at one of Jessica's baby showers and thought she was beautiful as well as kind. But then Megan had seen the interaction between the three siblings and could tell their relationship was a close one.

"You, Jessica and Savannah are close, I can tell. It's also obvious the three of you get along well."

He smiled. "Yes, we do, especially since I'm no longer trying to boss them around. Now I gladly leave them in the hands of Chase and Durango and have to admit your cousins seem to be doing a good job of keeping my sisters happy."

Megan would have to agree. But then she would say that all the Westmorelands had selected mates that complemented them, and they all seemed so happy together, so well connected. Even Gemma and Callum. She had visited her sister around the time Gemma's baby was due to be born and Megan had easily felt the love radiating between Gemma and her husband. And Megan knew Callum Junior, or CJ as everyone called him, was an extension of that love.

"We'll be leaving first thing in the morning, Megan."

She glanced back over at Rico, remembering what he'd said when he'd first arrived. He had come for her. "And just where are we supposed to be going?"

She couldn't help noticing how a beam of light that was shining in through the open barn door was hitting him at an angle that seemed to highlight his entire body. And as weird as it sounded, it seemed like there was a halo over his head. She knew it was a figment of her imagination because the man was no angel.

"I'm taking you back to Forbes with me," he said,

leading both horses to their stalls. "You did say you wanted to be included when I uncover information about Clarice."

She felt a sudden tingling of excitement in her stomach. Her face lit up. "Yes," she said, following him. "You found out something?"

"Nothing more than what I told you before. However, my man who's doing internet research came across a recent news article. There's a woman living in Forbes who'll be celebrating her one-hundredth birthday today. And she's lived in the same house for more than seventy of those years. Her address just happens to be within ten miles of the last known address we have for Clarice. We're hoping she might remember her."

Megan nodded. "But the key word is *remember*. How well do you think a one-hundred-year-old person will be able to remember?"

Rico smiled. "According to the article, she credits home remedies for her good health. I understand she still has a sharp memory."

"Then I can't wait for us to talk to her."

Rico closed the gate behind the horses and turned to face her. "Although I'm taking you along, Megan, I'm still the one handling this investigation."

"Of course," she said, looking away, trying her best not to get rattled by his insistence on being in charge. But upon remembering what Ramsey had said about letting Rico do his job without any interference from her, she decided not to make a big deal of it. The important thing was that Rico was including her.

He began walking toward the ranch house, and she fell in step beside him. "What made you change your mind about including me?" she asked as she tilted her head up.

He looked over at her. "You would have shown up in Forbes eventually, and I decided I'm going to like having you around."

Megan stopped walking and frowned up at him. "It's not going to be that kind of party, Rico."

She watched how his lips curved in a smile so sensuous that she had to remind herself to breathe. Her gaze was drawn to the muscular expanse of his chest and how the shirt looked covering it. She bet he would look even better shirtless.

Her frown deepened. She should not be thinking about Rico without a shirt. It was bad enough that she had shared two heated kisses with him.

"What kind of party do you think I'm having, Megan?"

She crossed her arms over her chest. "I don't know, you tell me."

He chuckled. "That's easy because I'm not having a party. You'll get your own hotel room, and I'll have mine. I said I wanted you. I also said eventually I'd have you if you came with me. But I'll let you decide when."

"It won't happen. Just because we shared two enjoyable kisses and—"

"So you did enjoy them, huh?"

She wished she could swipe that smirk off his face. She shrugged. "They were okay."

He threw his head back and laughed. "Just okay? Then I guess I better improve my technique the next time."

She nibbled on her bottom lip, thinking if he got any better she would be in big trouble.

"Don't do that."

She raised a brow. "Don't do what?"

"Nibble on your lip that way. Or else I'm tempted to improve my technique right here and now."

Megan swallowed, and as she stood there and stared up at him, she was reminded of how his kisses could send electrical currents racing through her with just a flick of his tongue.

"I like it when you do that."

"Do what?"

"Blush. I guess guys didn't ever talk to you that way, telling you what they wanted to do to you."

She figured she might as well be honest with him. "No."

"Then may I make a suggestion, Megan?"

She liked hearing the sound of her name from his lips. "What?"

"Get used to it."

Rico sat on a bar stool in the kitchen while talking to Clint. However, he was keeping Megan in his peripheral vision. When they'd gotten back to the house, Clint had been eager to show Rico a beauty of a new stallion he was about to send to his sister Casey to train, and Alyssa wanted to show Megan how she'd finished decorating the baby's room that morning.

Cain was awake, and, like most three-year-olds, he wanted to be the life of the party and hold everyone's attention. He was doing so without any problems. He spoke well for a child his age and was already riding a horse like a pro.

Rico had admired the time Clint had spent with his son and could see the bond between them. He thought about all the times he had wished his father could have been home more and hadn't been. Luckily, his grandfather had been there to fill the void when his father had been living a double life.

Megan had gone upstairs to take a nap, and by the time he'd seen her again it had been time for dinner. She had showered and changed, and the moment she had come down the stairs it had taken everything he had to keep from staring at her. She was dressed in a printed flowing skirt and a blouse that showed what a nice pair of shoulders she had. He thought she looked refreshed and simply breathtaking. And his reaction upon seeing her reminded him of how it had been the first time he'd seen her, that day three months ago.

"Rico?" Clint said, snapping his fingers in front of his face.

Rico blinked. "Sorry. My mind wandered there for a minute."

"Evidently," Clint said, grinning. "How about if we go outside where we can talk without your mind wandering so much?"

Rico chuckled, knowing Clint knew full well where his concentration had been. "Fine," he said, grabbing his beer off the counter.

Moments later, while sitting in rocking chairs on the wraparound porch, Clint had brought Rico up to date on the horse breeding and training business. Several of the horses would be running in the Kentucky Derby and Preakness in the coming year.

"So how are things going with the investigation?" Clint asked when there was a lull in conversation. "Megan mentioned to Alyssa something about an old lady in Forbes who might have known Clarice."

"Yes, I'm making plans to interview her in a few

days, and Megan wants to be there when I do." Rico spent the next few minutes telling Clint what the news article had said about the woman.

"Well, I hope things work out," Clint said. "I know how it is when you discover you have family you never knew about, and I guess Megan is feeling the same way. If it hadn't been for my mother's deathbed confession, Cole, Casey and I would not have known that our father was alive. Even now, I regret the years I missed by not knowing."

Clint stood and stretched. "Well, I'm off to bed now. Will you and Megan at least stay for breakfast before taking off tomorrow?"

Rico stood, as well. "Yes. Nothing like getting on the road with a full stomach, and I'm sure Chester is going to make certain we have that."

Clint chuckled. "Yes, I'm certain, as well. Good night."

By the time they went back into the house, it was quiet and dark, which meant Alyssa and Megan had gone to bed. Rico hadn't been aware that he and Clint had talked for so long. It was close to midnight.

Clint's ranch house was huge. What Rico liked most about it was that it had four wings jutting off from the living room—north, south, east and west. He noted that he and Megan had been given their own private wing—the west wing—and he couldn't help wondering if that had been intentional.

He slowed his pace when he walked past the guest room Megan was using. The door was closed but he could see light filtering out from the bottom, which meant she was still up. He stopped and started to knock and then decided against it. It was late, and he had no reason to want to seek her out at this hour.

"Of course I can think of several reasons," he muttered, smiling as he entered the guest room he was using. He wasn't feeling tired or sleepy so he decided to work awhile on his laptop.

Rico wasn't sure how long he had been sitting at the desk, going through several online sites, piecing together more information about Fanny Banks, when he heard the opening and closing of the door across the hall, in the room Megan was using. He figured she had gotten up to get a cup of milk or tea. But when moments passed and he didn't hear her return to her room, he decided to find out where she'd gone and what she was doing.

Deciding not to turn on any lights, he walked down the hall in darkness. When he reached the living room, he glanced around before heading for the kitchen. There, he found her standing in the dark and looking out the window. From the moonlight coming in through the glass, he could tell she was wearing a bathrobe.

Deciding he didn't want to startle her, he made his presence known. "Couldn't you sleep?"

She swung around. "What are you doing up?"

He leaned in the doorway with his shoulder propped against a wall. "I was basically asking you the same thing."

She paused a moment and didn't say anything and then said, "I tried sleeping but couldn't. I kept thinking about my dad."

His brows furrowed. "Your dad?"

"Yes. This Saturday would have been his birthday. And I'm proud to say I was a daddy's girl," she said, smiling.

"Were you?"

She grinned. "Yes. Big-time. I remember our last conversation. It was right before he and Mom got ready to leave for the airport. As usual, the plan was for Mrs. Jones to stay at the house and keep us until my parents returned. He asked that I make sure to help take care of Gemma, Bailey and the twins. Ramsey was away at college, Zane was about to leave for college and Derringer was in high school. I was twelve."

She moved away from the window to sit at the table. "The only thing was, they never returned, and I didn't do a good job of taking care of Bailey and the twins. Gemma was no problem."

Rico nodded. Since getting to know the Denver Westmorelands, he had heard the stories about what bad-asses Bailey, the twins and Bane were. And each time he heard those stories, his respect and admiration for Dillon and Ramsey went up a notch. He knew it could not have been easy to keep the family together the way they had. "I hope you're not blaming yourself for all that stupid stuff they did back then."

She shook her head. "No, but a part of me wishes I could have done more to help Ramsey with the younger ones."

Rico moved to join her at the table, figuring the best thing to do was to keep the conversation going. Otherwise, he would be tempted to pull her out of that chair and kiss her again. Electricity had begun popping the moment their gazes had connected. "You were only twelve, and you did what you could, I'm sure," he said, responding to what she'd said. "Everybody did. But people grieve in different ways. I couldn't imagine losing a parent that young."

"It wasn't easy."

"I bet, and then to lose an aunt and uncle at the same time. I have to admire all of you for being strong during that time, considering what all of you were going through."

"Yes, but think of how much easier it would have been had we known the Atlanta, Montana and Texas Westmorelands back then. There would have been others, and Dillon and Ramsey wouldn't have had to do it alone. Oh, they would have still fought to keep us together, but they would have had some kind of support system. You know what they say…it takes a village to raise a child."

Yes, he'd heard that.

"That's one of the reasons family is important to me, Rico. You never know when you will need the closeness and support a family gives to each other." Silence lingered between them for a minute and then she asked, "What about you? Were you close to your parents…your father…while growing up?"

He didn't say anything for a while. Instead, he got up and walked over to the refrigerator. To answer her question, he needed a beer. He opened the refrigerator and glanced over his shoulder. "I'm having a beer. Want one?"

"No, but I'll take a soda."

He nodded and grabbed a soda and a beer out of the refrigerator and then closed the door. Returning to the table, he turned the chair around and straddled it. "Yes. Although my father traveled a lot as a salesman, we were close, and I thought the world of him."

He popped the top on his beer, took a huge swig and then added, "But that was before I found out what a two-bit, lying con artist he was. He was married to my mother, who was living in Philly, while he was involved with another woman out in California, stringing both of them along and lying through his teeth. Making promises he knew he couldn't keep."

Rico took another swig of his beer. "Jessica's grandfather found out Jeff Claiborne was an imposter and told Jessica's mother and my mother. Hurt and humiliated that she'd given fifteen years to a man who'd lied to her, Jessica's mother committed suicide. My mother filed for a divorce. I was in my first year of college. He came to see me, tried to make me think it was all Mom's fault and said, as males, he and I needed to stick together, and that Mom wouldn't divorce him if I put in a good word for him."

Rico stared into his beer bottle, remembering that time, but more importantly, remembering that day. He glanced back at her. "That day he stopped being my hero and the man I admired most. It was bad enough that he'd done wrong and wouldn't admit to it, but to involve me and try to pit me against Mom was unacceptable."

Rico took another swig of his beer. A long one this time. He rarely talked about that time in his life. Most people who knew his family knew the story, and chances were that Megan knew it already since she was friends with both of his sisters.

She reached out and took his hand in hers, and he felt a deep stirring in his groin as they stared at each other, while the air surrounding them became charged with a sexual current that sent sparks of desire through his body. He knew she felt it, as well.

"I know that must have been a bad time for you, but that just goes to show how a bad situation can turn into a good one. That's what happened for you, Savannah and Jessica once the three of you found out about each other, right?"

Yes, that part of the situation had turned out well, because he couldn't imagine not having Jessica and Savannah in his life. But still, whenever he thought of how Jessica had lost her mother, he would get angry all over again. Yet he said, "Yes, you're right."

She smiled and released his hand. "I've been known to be right a few times."

For some reason, he felt at ease with her, more at ease than he'd felt with any other woman. Why they were sitting here in the dark he wasn't sure. In addition to the sexual current in the room, there was also a degree of intimacy to this conversation that was ramping up his libido, reminding him of how long it had been since he'd slept with a woman. And when she had reached out and touched his hand that hadn't helped matters.

He studied her while she sipped on her soda. Even with the sliver of light shining through the window from the outside, he could see the smooth skin of her face, a beautiful shade of mocha.

She glanced over at him, caught him staring, and he felt thrumming need escalate all through him. He'd kissed her twice now and could kiss her a dozen more times and be just as satisfied. But at some point he would want more. He intended to get more. She had been warned, and she hadn't heeded his warning. The attraction between them was too great.

He wouldn't make love to her here. But they would make love, that was a given.

However, he *would* take another kiss. One that would let her know what was to come.

She stood. "I think I'll go back to bed and try to sleep. You did say we were leaving early, right?" she asked, walking over to the garbage with her soda can.

"Yes, right after breakfast." He didn't say anything but his gaze couldn't help latching on to her backside. Even with her bathrobe on, he could tell her behind was a shapely one. He'd admired it in jeans earlier that day.

On impulse, he asked, "Do you want to go for a ride?"

She turned around. "A ride?"

"Yes. It's a beautiful night outside."

A frown tugged at her brow. "A ride where?"

"The south ridge. There's a full moon, and the last time I went there at night with Clint while rounding up horses under a full moon, the view of the canyon was breathtaking."

"And you want us to saddle horses and—"

"No," he chuckled. "We'll take my truck."

She stared at him like he couldn't be thinking clearly. "Do you know what time it is?"

He nodded slowly as he held her gaze. "Yes, a time when everyone else is sleeping, and we're probably the only two people still awake."

She tilted her head and her gaze narrowed. "Why do you want me to take a ride with you at this hour, Rico?"

He decided to be honest. "Because I want to take you someplace where I can kiss you all over."

# Chapter 7

The lower part of Megan's stomach quivered, and she released a slow breath. What he was asking her, and pretty darn blatantly, was to go riding with him to the south ridge where they could park and make out. They were too old for that sort of thing, weren't they? Evidently he didn't think so, and he was a lot older than she was.

And what had he said about kissing her all over? Did he truly know what he was asking of her? She needed to be sure. "Do you know what you're asking me when you ask me to go riding with you?"

A smile that was so sexy it could be patented touched his lips. "Yeah."

Well, she had gotten her answer. He had kissed her twice, and now wanted to move to the next level. What had she really expected from a man who'd told her he wanted her and intended to have her? In that case, she had news for him: two kisses didn't mean a thing. She had let her guard down and released a little of her emotional control, but that didn't mean she would release any more. Whenever he kissed her, she couldn't think straight, and she considered doing things that weren't like her.

She stood there and watched his hazel eyes travel all over her, roaming up and down. When his gaze moved upward and snagged hers, the very air between them crackled with an electrical charge that had certain parts of her tingling.

"Are you afraid of me, Megan?" he asked softly.

Their gazes held for one searing moment. No, she wasn't afraid of him per se, but she was afraid of the things he had the ability to make her feel, afraid of the desires he could stir in her, afraid of how she could lose control around him. How could she make him understand that being in control was a part of her that she wasn't ready to let go of yet?

She shook her head. "No, I'm not afraid of you, Rico. But you say things and do things I'm not used to. You once insinuated that my brothers and cousins might have sheltered me from the realities of life, and I didn't agree with you. I still don't, but I will say that I, of my own choosing, decided not to take part in a lot of things other girls were probably into. I like being my own person and not following the crowd."

He nodded, and she could tell he was trying to follow her so she wasn't surprised when he asked, "And?"

"And I've never gone parking with a guy before." There, she'd said it. Now he knew what he was up against. But when she saw the unmistakable look of deep hunger in his eyes, her heart began pounding, fast and furious.

Then he asked, "Are you saying no guy has ever taken you to lover's lane?"

Why did his question have to sound so seductive, and why did she feel like her nerve endings were being scorched? "Yes, that's what I'm saying, and it was my decision and not theirs."

He smiled. "I can believe that."

"I saw it as a waste of time." She broke eye contact with him to look at his feet. They were bare. She'd seen men's feet before, plenty of times. With as many cousins and brothers as she had she couldn't miss seeing them. But Rico's were different. They were beautiful but manly.

"Did you?"

She glanced back up at him. "Yes, it was a waste of time because I wasn't into that sort of thing."

"You weren't?"

She shook her head. "No. I'm too in control of my emotions."

"Yet you let go a little when we kissed," he reminded her.

And she wished she hadn't. "Yes, but I can't do that too often."

He got up from the table, and she swallowed deeply while watching him cross the floor and walk over to her on those beautiful but manly bare feet. He came to a stop in front of her, reached out and took her hand. She immediately felt that same sexual charge she'd felt when she'd taken his hand earlier.

"Yet you did let go with me."

Yes, and that's what worried her. Why with him and only him? Why not with Dr. Thad Miller, Dr. Otis Wells or any of the other doctors who'd been trying for years to engage her in serious—or not so serious—affairs?

"Megan?"

"Yes?"

"Would you believe me if I were to say I would never intentionally hurt you?"

"Yes." She could believe that.

"And would it help matters if I let you set the pace?" he asked huskily in a voice that stirred things inside of her.

"What do you mean?"

"You stay in control, and I'll only do what you allow me to do and nothing more."

She suddenly felt a bit disoriented. What he evidently didn't quite yet understand was that he was a threat to her self-imposed control. But then, hadn't Ramsey said that she should let loose, be wild, release steam and let her hair down every once in a while? But did that necessarily mean being reckless?

"Megan?"

She stared up at him, studying his well-defined features. Handsome, masculine. Refined. Strong. Controlled. But was he really controlled? His features were solid, unmovable. The idea that perhaps he shared something in common with her was a lot to think about. In the meantime…

Taking a ride with him couldn't hurt anything. She couldn't sleep, and perhaps getting out and letting the wind hit her face would do her some good. He did say he would let her be in control, and she believed him. Although he had a tendency to speak his mind, he didn't come across as the type of man who would force himself on any woman. Besides, he knew her brothers and cousins, and was friends with them. His sisters were married to Westmorelands, and he wouldn't dare do anything to jeopardize those relationships.

"Okay, I'll go riding with you, Rico. Give me a minute to change clothes."

Rico smiled the moment he and Megan stepped outside. He hadn't lied. It was a beautiful night. He'd always said if he ever relocated from Philadelphia, he would consider moving to Texas. It wasn't too hot and it wasn't too cold, most of the time. He had fallen in love with the Lone Star state that first time he'd gone hunting and fishing with his grandfather. His grandparents had never approved of his mother's marriage, but that hadn't stopped them from forging a relationship with their grandchildren.

"There's a full moon tonight," Megan said when he opened the SUV's door for her.

"Yes, and you know what they say about a full moon, don't you?"

She rolled her eyes. "If you're trying to scare me, please don't. I've been known to watch scary movies and then be too afraid to stay at my own place. I've crashed over at Ramsey's or Dillon's at times because I was afraid to go home."

He wanted to tell her that if she got scared tonight, she could knock on his bedroom door and join him there at any time, but he bit back the words. "Well, then I won't scare you," he said, grinning as he leaned over to buckle her seat belt. She had changed into a pretty dress that buttoned up the front. There were a lot of buttons, and his fingers itched to tackle every last one of them.

And he thought she smelled good. Something sweet

and sensual with an allure that had him wanting to do more than buckle her seat belt. He pulled back. "Is that too tight?"

"No, it's fine."

He heard the throatiness in her voice and wondered if she was trying to downplay the very thing he was trying to highlight. "All right." He closed the door and then moved around the front of the truck to get in the driver's side.

"If it wasn't for that full moon it would be pitch-black out here."

He smiled. "Yes, you won't be able to see much, but what I'm going to show you is beautiful. That's why Clint had that cabin built near there. It's a stunning view of the canyon at night, and whenever there's a full moon the glow reflects off certain boulders, which makes the canyon appear to light up."

"I can't wait to see it."

*And I can't wait to taste you again,* he thought, as he kept his hand firmly on the steering wheel or else he'd be tempted to reach across, lift the hem of her dress and stroke her thigh. When it came to women, his manners were usually impeccable. However, around Megan he was tempted to touch, feel and savor.

He glanced over at her when he steered the truck around a bend. She was gnawing on her bottom lip, which meant she was nervous. This was a good time to get her talking, about anything. So he decided to let the conversation be about work. Hers.

"So you think they can do without you for thirty days?"

She glanced over at him and smiled. "That's the same thing Ramsey asked. No one is irreplaceable, you know."

"What about all those doctors who're pining for you?"

She rolled her eyes. "Evidently you didn't believe me when I said I don't date much. Maybe I shouldn't tell you this, but they call me Iceberg Megan behind my back."

He jerked his eyes from the road to glance over at her. "Really?"

"Yes."

"Does it bother you?"

"Not really. They prefer a willing woman in their beds, and I'm not willing and their beds are the last places I'd want to be. I don't hesitate to let them know it."

"Ouch."

"Whatever," she said, waving her hand in the air. "I don't intend to get in any man's bed anytime soon."

He wondered if she was issuing a warning, and he decided to stay away from that topic. "Why did you decide to become an anesthesiologist?"

She leaned back in the seat, getting comfortable. He liked that. "When I got my tonsils out, this man came around to talk to me, saying he would be the one putting me to sleep. He told me all about the wonderful dreams I would have."

"And did you?"

She looked confused. "Did I what?"

"Have wonderful dreams?"

"Yes, if you consider dreaming about a promised trip to Disney World a wonderful dream."

He started to chuckle and then he felt the rumble in his stomach when he laughed. She was priceless. Wonderful company. Fun to have around. "Did you get that trip to Disney World?"

"Yes!" she said with excitement in her voice. "It was the best ever, and the first of many trips our family took together. There was the time…"

He continued driving, paying attention to both the rugged roads and to her. He liked the sound of her voice, and he noticed that more than anything else, she liked talking about her family. She had adored her parents, her uncle and aunt. And she thought the world of her brothers, cousins and sisters. There were already a lot of Westmorelands. Yet she was hoping there were still more.

His mother had been an only child, and he hadn't known anything about his father's family. Jeff Claiborne had claimed he didn't have any. Now Rico wondered if that had been a lie like everything else.

She gasped. He glanced over at her and followed her gaze through the windshield to look up at the sky. He brought the truck to a stop. "What?"

"A shooting star. I saw it."

"Did you?"

She nodded and continued to stare up at the sky. "Yes."

He shifted his gaze to stare back at her. "Hurry and make a wish."

She closed her eyes. A few minutes later she re-opened them and smiled over at him. "Done."

He turned the key in the ignition to start the truck back up. "I'm glad."

"Thanks for taking the time to let me do that. Most men would have thought it was silly and not even suggested a wish."

He grinned. "I'm not like most men."

"I'm beginning to see that, Mr. Claiborne."

He smiled as he kept driving, deciding not to tell her that if the truth be known, she hadn't seen anything yet.

# Chapter 8

"I think this is a good spot," Rico said, bringing the car to a stop.

Megan glanced around, not sure just what it was a good spot for, but decided not to ask. She looked over at him and watched as he unbuckled his seat belt and eased his seat back to accommodate his long legs. She decided to do the same—not that her legs were as long as his, mind you. He was probably six foot four to her five foot five.

When she felt his gaze on her, she suddenly felt heated. She rolled down her window and breathed in the deep scent of bluebonnets, poppies and, of all things, wild pumpkin. But there was another scent she couldn't ignore. The scent of man. Namely, the man sitting in the truck with her.

"Lean toward the dash and look out of the windshield."

Slowly, she shifted in her seat and did as he instructed. She leaned forward and looked down and what she saw almost took her breath away. The canyon appeared lit, and she could still see horses moving around. Herds of them. Beautiful stallions with their bands of mares. Since she and Rico were high up and had the help of moonlight, she saw a portion of the lake.

"So what do you think of this place, Megan?"

She glanced over at him. "It's beautiful. Quiet." *And secluded,* she thought, realizing just how alone they were.

"It didn't take you long to change clothes," he said.

She chuckled. "A habit you inherit when you have impatient brothers. Zane drove me, Gemma and Bailey to school every day when he was around. And when he wasn't, the duty fell on Derringer."

Rico seemed to be listening so she kept on talking, telling him bits and pieces about her family, fun times she'd encountered while growing up. She knew they were killing time and figured he was trying to make sure she was comfortable and not nervous with him. He wanted her to be at ease. For what, she wasn't sure, although he'd told her what he wanted to do and she'd come anyway. They had kissed twice so she knew what to expect, but he'd also said he would let her stay in control of the situation.

"You're hot?"

She figured he was asking because she'd rolled down the window. "I was, but the air is cooler outside than I thought," she said, rolling it back up. She took a deep, steadying breath and leaned forward again, trying to downplay the sexual energy seeping through her bones. He hadn't said much. He'd mainly let her talk and listened to what she'd said. But as she stared down at the canyon again she felt his presence in an intense way.

"Megan?"

Her pulse jumped when he said her name. With a deliberate slowness, she glanced over at him. "Yes?"

"I want you over here, closer to me."

She swallowed and then took note that she was sort of hugging the door. The truck had bench seats, and there was a lot of unused space separating them. Another body could sit between them comfortably. "I thought you'd want your space."

"I don't. What I want is you."

It was what he said as well as how he'd said it that sent all kinds of sensations oozing through her. His voice had a deep, drugging timbre that made her feel as if her skin were being caressed.

Without saying anything, she slid across the seat toward him, and he curved his arms across the back of the seat. "A little closer won't hurt," he said huskily.

She glanced up at him. "If I get any closer, I'll end up in your lap."

"That's the idea."

Megan's brows furrowed. He wanted her in his lap? He had to be joking, right? She studied his gaze and saw he was dead serious. Her stomach quivered as they stared at each other. The intensity in the hazel eyes that held her within their scope flooded her with all kinds of feelings, and she was breathless again.

"Do you recall the first time we kissed, Megan?"

She nodded. "Yes." How on earth could she forget it?

"Afterward, I lay awake at night remembering how it had been."

She was surprised a man would do that. She thought

since kisses came by the dozen, they didn't remember one from the next. "You did?"

"Yes. You tasted good."

She swallowed and felt her bottom lips began to tremble. "Did I?"

He reached out and traced a fingertip across her trembling lips. "Yes. And do you know what else I remembered?"

"No, what?"

"How your body felt pressed against mine, even with clothes on. And of course that made me think of you without any clothes on."

Desire filtered through her body. If he was saying these things to weaken her, break down her defenses, corrode her self-control, it was working. "Do you say this to all the girls?" she asked—a part of her wanted to know. Needed to know.

He frowned. "No. And in a way, that's what bothers me."

She knew she shouldn't ask but couldn't stop herself from doing so. "Bothers you how?"

He hesitated for a moment, broke eye contact with her to look straight ahead, out the window. Slowly, methodically, he returned his gaze back to her. "I usually don't let women get next to me. But for some reason I'm allowing you to be the exception."

He didn't sound too happy about it, either, she concluded. But then, wasn't she doing the same thing? She had let him kiss her twice, where most men hadn't made it as far as the first. And then she was here at two in the morning, sitting in a parked truck with him in Texas. If that wasn't wild, she didn't know what was.

"You have such warm lips."

He could say some of the most overwhelming words…
or maybe to her they were overwhelming because no
other man had said them to her before. "Thanks."

"You don't have to thank me for compliments. Everything I say is true. I will never lie to you, Megan."

For some reason, she believed him. But if she wasn't
supposed to thank him, what was she supposed to say?
She tilted her head back to look at him and wished she
hadn't. The intense look in his gaze had deepened, and
she felt a stirring inside of her, making her want things
she'd never had before.

He must have seen something in her eyes, because he
whispered, "Come here." And then he lifted her into his
arms, twisted his body to stretch his legs out on the seat
and sat her in his lap. Immediately, she felt the thick,
hard erection outlined against his zipper and pressed
into her backside. That set off a barrage of sensations
escalating through her, but nothing was as intense as
the sensual strokes she felt at the juncture of her thighs.

And then, before she could take her next breath, he
leaned down and captured her lips in his.

Rico wasn't sure just what there was about Megan
that made him want to do this over and over again—
mate his mouth with hers in a way that was sending him
over the edge, creating more memories that would keep
him awake at night. All he knew was that he needed to
taste her again like he needed to breathe.

In the most primal way, blood was surging through
his veins and desire was slamming through him, scorching his senses and filling him with needs that only she
could satisfy. He couldn't help but feel his erection
pressing against her and wishing he could be skin-to-

skin with her, but he knew this wasn't the time or the place. But kissing her here, now, was essential.

His tongue continued to explore her mouth with an intensity that had her trembling in his arms. But he wouldn't let up. It couldn't be helped. There was something between them that he couldn't explain. It was wild and, for him, unprecedented. First there had been that instant attraction, then the crackling of sexual chemistry. Then, later, after their first kiss, that greedy addiction that had him in a parked truck, kissing her senseless at two in the morning.

He slowly released her mouth to stare down at her and saw the glazed look in her eyes. Then he slowly began unbuttoning her shirt dress. The first sign of her bra had him drawing in a deep breath of air—which only pulled her scent into his nostrils, a sensuous blend of jasmine and lavender.

Her bra had a front clasp and as soon as his fingers released it, her breasts sprang free. Seeing them made him throb. As he stared down at them, he saw the nipples harden before his eyes, making hunger take over his senses. Releasing a guttural moan, he leaned down and swooped a nipple between his lips and began sucking on it. Earnestly.

Megan gasped at the contact of his wet mouth on her breast, but then, when the sucking motion of his mouth made her sex clench, she threw her head back and moaned. His tongue was doing the same things to her breasts that it had done inside her mouth, and she wasn't sure she could take it. The strokes were so keen and strong, she could actually feel them between her legs.

She reached out and grabbed at his shoulder and

when she couldn't get a firm grip there, she went for his hair, wrapping some of the silky strands around her finger as his mouth continued to work her breasts, sending exquisite sensations ramming through her.

But what really pushed her over the edge was when his hand slid underneath her dress to touch her thigh. No man had ever placed his hand underneath her dress. Such a thing could get one killed. If not by her, then surely by her brothers. But her brothers weren't here. She was a grown woman.

And when Rico slid his hands higher, touching her in places she'd never been touched, his fingertips making their way to her center, she shamelessly lifted her hips and shifted her legs wider to give him better access. Where was her self-control? It had taken a freaking hike the moment he had touched his mouth to hers.

Then he was kissing her mouth again, but she was fully aware of his hand easing up her thigh, easing inside the crotch of her panties to touch her.

She almost shot out of his lap at the contact, but he held her tight and continued kissing her as his fingers stroked her, inching toward her pulsating core.

He broke off the kiss and whispered, "You feel good here. Hot. Wet. I like my fingers here, touching you this way."

She bit down on her lips to keep from saying that she liked his fingers touching her that way, as well. Whether intentional or not, he was tormenting her, driving her over the edge with every stroke. She was feeling lightheaded, sensually intoxicated. He was inciting her to lose control, and she couldn't resist. The really sad thing was that a part of her didn't want to resist.

"And do you know what's better than touching you here?" he asked.

She couldn't imagine. Already she had been reduced to a trembling mess as he continued to stroke her. She gripped his hair tighter and hoped she wasn't causing him any pain. "No, I can't imagine," she whispered, struggling to get the words out. Forcing anything from her lungs was complicated at the moment.

"Then let me show you, baby."

Her mind had been so focused on his term of endearment that she hadn't realized he had quickly shifted their bodies so her head was away from him, closer to the passenger door. The next thing she knew he had pushed the rest of her dress aside, eased off her panties and lifted her hips to place her thighs over his shoulders.

He met her gaze once, but it was enough for her to see the smoldering heat in his eyes just seconds before he lowered his head between her legs. Shock made her realize what he was about to do, and she called out his name. "Rico!"

But the sound was lost and became irrelevant the moment his mouth touched her core and his tongue slid between the folds. And when he began stroking her, tasting her, she couldn't help but cry out his name again. "Rico."

He didn't let up as firm hands held her hips steady and a determined mouth licked her like she was a meal he just had to have. She continued to moan as blood gushed through her veins. His mouth was devouring her, driving her over the edge, kicking what self-control remained right out the window. The raw hunger he was exhibiting was sending her senses scurrying in all directions. She closed her eyes as moan after moan after moan tore from her lips. The feelings were intense. Their magnitude was resplendent and stunning. Pleasure coiled within her then slowly spread open as desire sharpened its claws on her. Making her feel things she had never felt before. Sensations she hadn't known were possible. And the feel of his stubble-roughened jaw on her skin wasn't helping her regain control.

"Rico," she whispered. "I—I need…" She couldn't finish her thought because she didn't have a clue what she needed. She'd never been with a man like this before, and neither had Gemma before Callum. All her sister had told Megan was that it was something well worth the wait. But if this was the prologue, the wait just might kill her.

And then he did something, she wasn't sure what, with his tongue. Some kind of wiggly formation followed by a fierce jab that allowed his mouth to actually lock down on her.

Sensations blasted through her, and she flung back her head and let out a high-pitched scream. But he wouldn't let go. He continued to taste and savor her as if she was not only his flavor of the day, but also his flavor of all time. She pushed the foolish thought from her mind as she continued to be bombarded with feelings that were ripping her apart.

She gasped for breath before screaming again when her entire body spiraled into another orgasm. She whimpered through it and held tight to his hair as she clutched his shoulders. He kept his mouth locked on her until the very last moan had flowed from her lips. She collapsed back on the car seat, feeling totally drained.

Only then did he pull back, adjusting their bodies to bring her up to him. He tightened his hold when she collapsed weakly against his chest. Then he lowered his head and kissed her, their lips locked together intensely. At that moment, she was craving this contact, this closeness, this very intimate connection. Moments later, when he released her mouth, he pulled her closer to him, tucking her head beneath his jaw, and whispered, "This is only the beginning, baby. Only the beginning."

# Chapter 9

The next morning, Rico and Megan left the Golden Glade Ranch after breakfast to head out to Forbes. He had been driving now for a little more than a half hour and his GPS indicated they had less than a hundred miles to go. He glanced up at the skies, saw the gray clouds and was certain it would rain before they reached their destination.

Rico then glanced over at Megan and saw she was still sleeping soundly and had been since he'd hit the interstate. Good. He had a feeling she hadn't gotten much sleep last night.

She had pretty much remained quiet on the drive back to the ranch from the south ridge, and once there, she quickly said good-night and rushed off to her room, closing the door behind her. And then this morning at breakfast, she hadn't been very talkative. Several times he had caught her barely able to keep her eyes open. If Clint and Alyssa had found her drowsiness strange, neither had commented on it.

Rico remembered every single thing about last night, and, if truth be told, he hadn't thought of much of anything else since. Megan Westmoreland had more passion in her little finger than most women had in their entire bodies. And just the thought that no other man had tempted her to release all that passion was simply mind-boggling to him.

Ramsey had warned him that she was strong-willed. However, even the most strong-willed person couldn't fight a well-orchestrated seduction. But then, being overcome with passion wasn't a surrender. He saw it as her acceptance that nothing was wrong with enjoying her healthy sexuality.

*I like being my own person and not following the crowd.* Those were the words she had spoken last night. He remembered them and had both admired and respected her for taking that stance. His sisters had basically been the same and had handled their own business. Even when Savannah had gotten pregnant by Durango, she had been prepared to go at it alone had he not wanted to claim the child as his. And knowing his sister, marriage had not been on her mind when she'd gone out to Montana to tell Durango he was going to be a father. Thanks to Jeff Claiborne, a bad taste had been left in Savannah's mouth where marriage was concerned. That same bad taste had been left in Rico's, as well.

But Savannah had married Durango and was happy and so were Jess and Chase. Rico was happy for them, and with them married off, he had turned his time and attention to other things. His investigation business mainly. And now, he thought, glancing over at Megan again, to her. She was the first woman in years who had garnered any real attention from him.

What he'd told her last night was true. What they'd started was just the beginning. She hadn't responded to what he'd said one way or the other, but he hadn't really expected her to. He had been tempted to ask if she'd wanted to talk about last night but she had dozed off before he could do so.

But before he had a conversation with her about anything, it would be wise to have one with himself. When it came to her, he was still in a quandary as to why he was as attracted to her as he was. What was there about her that he wanted to claim?

He would let her sleep, and when she woke up, they would talk.

The sound of rain and thunder woke Megan. She first glanced out the windshield and saw how hard it was raining, before looking over at Rico as he maneuvered the truck through the downpour. His concentration was on his driving, and she decided to allow her concentration to be on him.

Her gaze moved to the hands that gripped the steering wheel. They were big and strong. Masculine hands. Even down to his fingertips. They were hands that had touched her in places no other man would have dared. But he had. And what had happened as a result still had certain parts of her body tingling.

She started to shift in her seat but then decided to stay put. She wasn't ready for him to know she was awake. She needed time to think. To ponder. To pull herself together. She was still a little rattled from last night when she had literally come unglued. Ramsey had said that everyone needed to let loose and let her hair down every once in a while, and she had definitely taken her brother's suggestion.

She didn't have any regrets, as much as she wished she did. The experience had been simply amazing. With Rico's hands, mouth and tongue, she had felt things she had never felt before. He had deliberately pushed her over the edge, given her pleasure in a way she'd never received it before and wouldn't again.

*This is only the beginning.*

He had said that. She remembered his words clearly. She hadn't quite recovered from the barrage of pleasurable sensations that had overtaken her, not once but twice, when he had whispered that very statement to her. Even now she couldn't believe she had let him do all those things to her, touch her all over, touch her in all those places.

He'd said he would let her stay in control, but she had forgotten all about control from the first moment he had kissed her. Instead, her thoughts had been on something else altogether. Like taking every single thing he was giving, with a greed and a hunger that astounded her.

"You're awake."

She blinked and moved her gaze from his hands to his face. He'd shaven, but she could clearly remember the feel of his unshaven jaw between her legs. She felt a tingling sensation in that very spot. Maybe, on second thought, she should forget it.

She pulled up in her seat and stared straight ahead. "Yes, I'm awake."

Before she realized what he was doing, he had pulled the car over to the shoulder of the road, unleashed his seat belt and leaned over. His mouth took hers in a deep, languid and provocative kiss that whooshed the very air from her lungs. It was way too passionate and too roastingly raw to be a morning kiss, one taken on the side of the road amidst rush-hour traffic. But he was doing so, boldly, and with a deliberate ease that stirred everything within her. She was reminded of last night and how easily she had succumbed to the passion he'd stirred, the lust he had provoked.

He released her mouth, but not before one final swipe of his tongue from corner to corner. Her nipples hardened in response and pressed tightly against her blouse. Her mouth suddenly felt hot. Taken. Devoured.

"Hello, Megan," he said, against her lips.

"Hello." If this was how he would wake her up after a nap, then she would be tempted to doze off on him anytime.

"Did you get a good nap?"

"Yes, if you want to call it that."

He chuckled and straightened in his seat and resnapped his seat belt. "I would. You've been sleeping for over an hour."

She glanced back at him. "An hour?"

"Yes, I stopped for gas, and you slept through it."

She stretched her shoulders. "I was tired."

"I understand."

*Yes, he would,* she thought, refusing to look over at him as he moved back into traffic. She licked her lips and could still taste him there. Her senses felt short-circuited. Overwhelmed. She had been forewarned, but she hadn't taken heed.

"You feel like talking?"

Suddenly her senses were on full alert. She did look at him then. "What about?"

"Last night."

She didn't say anything. Was that the protocol with a man and a woman? To use the morning after to discuss the night before? She didn't know. "Is that how things are done?"

He lifted a brow. "What things?"

"The morning-after party where you rehash things. Say what you regret, what you wished never happened, and make promises it won't happen again."

She saw the crinkling of a smile touch the corners of his lips. "Not on my watch. Besides, I told you it will happen again. Last night was just the beginning."

"And do I have a say in the matter?"

"Yes." He glanced over at her. "All you have to say is that you don't want my hands on you, and I'll keep them to myself. I've never forced myself on any woman, Megan."

She could believe that. In fact, she could very well imagine women forcing themselves on him. She began nibbling at her bottom lip. She wished it could be that simple, just tell him to keep his hands to himself, but the truth of the matter was…she liked his hands on her. And she had thoroughly enjoyed his mouth and tongue on her, as well. Maybe a little too much.

Looking over at him, she said. "And if I *don't* tell you to keep your hands to yourself?"

"Then the outcome is inevitable," he said quietly, with a calmness that stirred her insides. She knew he meant it. From the beginning, he had given her fair warning.

"Okay, let's talk," she said softly.

He pulled to the side of the road again, which had her wondering if they would ever reach their destination. He unfastened his seat belt and turned to her. "It's like this, Megan. I want you. I've made no secret of that. The degree of my attraction to you is one that I can't figure out. Not that I find the thought annoying, just confusing, because I've never been attracted to a woman to this magnitude before."

*Welcome to the club,* she thought. She hadn't ever been this attracted to a man before, either.

"This should be a business trip, one to find the answers about your family's history. Now that you're here, it has turned into more."

She lifted a brow. "What has it turned into now?"

"A fact-finding mission regarding us. Maybe constantly being around you will help me understand why you've gotten so deeply under my skin."

Megan's heart beat wildly in her chest. He wanted to explore the reason why they were so intensely attracted to each other? Did there need to be any other reason than that he was man and she was woman? With his looks, any woman in her right mind would be attracted to him, no matter the age. He had certainly done a number on Grace, without even trying. But Megan had been around good-looking men before and hadn't reacted the way she had with him.

"I won't crowd you, and when we get to Forbes you will have your own hotel room if you want."

He paused a moment and then added, "I'm not going to assume anything in this relationship, Megan. But you best believe I plan to seduce the hell out of you. I'm not like those other guys who never made it to first base. I plan on getting in the game and hitting a home run."

*You are definitely in the game already, Rico Claiborne.* She broke eye contact with him to gaze out the window. If nothing else, last night should have solidified the knowledge that her resistance was at an all-time low around him. Her self-control had taken a direct hit, and since he was on a fact-finding mission, maybe she needed to be on one, as well. Why was she willing to let him go further than any man had before?

"If you think I'm going to sit here and say I regret anything about last night, then you don't have anything to worry about, Rico."

He lifted a brow. "I don't?"

"No."

She wouldn't tell him that he had opened her eyes about a few things. That didn't mean she regretted not engaging in any sort of sexual activity before, because she didn't. What it meant was that there was a reason Rico was the man who'd given her her first orgasm. She just didn't know what that reason was yet, which was why she wanted to find out. She needed to know why he and he alone had been able to make her act in a way no other man before him had been capable of making her act.

"So we have an understanding?" he asked.

"Sort of."

He raised a brow. "Sort of?" He started the ignition and rejoined traffic again. It had stopped raining, and the sun was peeking out from beneath the clouds.

"Yes, there's still a lot about you that I don't know."

He nodded. "Okay, then ask away. Anything you want."

"Anything?"

A corner of his mouth eased into a smile. "Yes, anything, as long I don't think it's private and privileged information."

"That's fair." She considered the best way to ask her first question, then decided to just come out with it. "Have you ever been in love?"

He chuckled softly. "Not since Mrs. Tolbert."

"Mrs. Tolbert?"

"Yes, my third-grade teacher."

"You've got to be kidding me."

He glanced over at her and laughed at her surprised expression. "Kidding you about what? Being in love with Mrs. Tolbert or that she was my third-grade teacher?"

"Neither. You want me to believe that other than Mrs. Tolbert, no other woman has interested you?"

"I didn't say that. I'm a man, so women interest me. You asked if I've ever been in love, and I told you yes, with Mrs. Tolbert. Why are you questioning my answer?"

"No reason. So you're like Zane and Riley," she said.

"Maybe you need to explain that."

"Zane and Riley like women. Both claim they have never been in love and neither wants their names associated with the word."

"Then I'm not like Zane and Riley in that respect. Like I said, women interest me. I am a man with certain needs on occasion. However, falling in love doesn't scare me and it's not out of the realm of possibility. But I haven't been in a serious relationship since college."

She was tempted to ask him about that phone call he'd refused to take at her place the other day. Apparently, some woman was serious even if he wasn't. "But you have been in a serious relationship before?"

"Yes."

Her brow arched. "But you weren't in love?"

"No."

"Then why were you in the relationship?"

He didn't say anything for a minute. "My maternal grandparents are from old money and thought that as their grandson the woman I marry should be connected to old money, as well. They introduced me to Roselyn. We dated during my first year of college. She was nice, at least I thought she was, until she tried making me choose between her and Jessica."

Megan's eyes widened. "Your sister?"

"Yes. Roselyn said she could accept me as being interracial since it wasn't quite as obvious, but there was no way she could accept Jessica as my sister."

Megan felt her anger boiling. "Boy, she had some nerve."

"Yes, she did. I had just met Jessica for the first time a month before and she felt that since Jessica and I didn't have a bond yet, she could make such an ultimatum. But she failed to realize something."

"What?"

"Jessica was my sister, whether Roselyn liked it or not, and I was not going to turn my back on Jessica or deny her just because Roselyn had a problem with it. So I broke things off."

*Good for you,* Megan thought. "How did your grandparents feel about you ending things?"

"They weren't happy about it, at least until I told them why. They weren't willing to make the same mistake twice. They were pretty damn vocal against my mother marrying my father, and they almost lost her when Mom stopped speaking to them for nearly two years. There was no way they would risk losing me with that same foolishness."

"You're close to your grandparents?"

"Yes, very close."

"And your father? I take it the two of you are no longer close."

She saw how his jaw tightened and knew the answer before he spoke a single word. "That's right. What he did was unforgivable, and neither Jess, Savannah or I have seen him in almost eighteen years."

"That's sad."

"Yes, it is," he said quietly.

Megan wondered if the separation had been his father's decision or his but decided not to pry. However, there was another question—a very pressing one—that she needed answered right away. "Uh, do you plan to stop again anytime soon?" She recalled he'd said he had stopped for gas while she was asleep. Now she was awake, and she had needs to take care of.

He chuckled. "You have to go to the little girl's room, do you?"

She grinned. "Yes, you can say that."

"No problem, I'll get off at the next exit."

"Thanks."

He smiled over at her, and she immediately felt her pulse thud and the area between her thighs clench. The man was too irresistible, too darn sexy, for his own good. Maybe she should have taken heed of his warning and not come to Texas. She had a feeling things were going to get pretty darn wild now that they were alone together. Real wild.

# *Chapter 10*

Rico stopped in front of Megan and handed her the key. "This is for your room. Mine is right next door if you need me for anything. No matter how late it is, just knock on the connecting door. Anytime you want."

She grinned at his not-so-subtle, seductive-as-sin hint as she took the key from him. "Thanks, I'll keep that in mind."

She glanced around. Forbes, Texas, wasn't what she'd imagined. It was really a nice place. Upon arriving to town, Rico had taken her to one of the restaurants for lunch. It was owned by a Mexican family. In fact, most of the townspeople were Mexican, descended from the settlers who had founded the town back in the early 1800s. She had been tempted to throw Raphel's name out there to see if any of them had ever heard of him but had decided not to. She had promised Rico she would let him handle the investigation, and she intended to keep her word.

"You can rest up while I make a few calls. I want to contact Fanny Banks's family to see if we can visit in a day or so."

"That would be nice," she said as they stepped on the elevator together. The lady at the front desk had told them the original interior of the hotel had caught fire ten years ago and had been rebuilt, which was why everything inside was pretty modern, including the elevator. From the outside, it looked like a historical hotel.

They were the only ones on the elevator, and Rico stood against the panel wall and stared over at her. "Hey, come over here for a minute."

She swallowed, and her nipples pressed hard against her shirt. "Why?"

"Come over here and find out."

He looked good standing over there, and the slow, lazy smile curving his mouth had her feeling hot all over. "Come here, Megan. I promise I won't bite."

She wasn't worried about him taking a bite out of her, but there were other things he could do that were just as lethal and they both knew it. She decided two could play his game. "No, you come over here."

"No problem."

When he made a move toward her, she retreated and stopped when her back touched the wall. "I was just kidding."

"But I kid you not," he said, reaching her and caging her with hands braced against the wall on either side of her. "Open up for me."

"B-but, what if this elevator stops to let more people on? We'll be on our floor any minute."

He reached out and pushed the elevator stop button. "Now we won't." Then he leaned in and plied her mouth with a deep and possessively passionate kiss.

She did as he'd asked. She opened up for him, letting him slide his tongue inside her mouth. He settled the middle of himself against her, in a way that let her feel his solid erection right in the juncture of her thighs. The sensations that swamped her were unreal, and she returned his kiss with just as much hunger as he was showing.

Then, just as quickly as he'd begun, he pulled his mouth away. Drawing in a deep breath, she angled her head back to gaze up at him. "What was that for?"

"No reason other than I want you."

"You told me. Several times," she murmured, trying to get her heart to stop racing and her body to cease tingling. She glanced up at him—the elevator wasn't that big and he was filling it, looking tall, dark and handsome as ever. He was looking her up and down, letting his gaze stroke over her as if it wouldn't take much to strip her naked then and there.

"And I intend to tell you several more times. I plan to keep reminding you every chance I get."

"Why?" Was it some power game he wanted to play? She was certain he had figured out that her experience with men was limited. She had all but told him it was, so what was he trying to prove? Was this just one of the ways he intended to carry out his fact-finding mission? If that was the case, then she might have to come up with a few techniques of her own.

He pushed the button to restart the elevator, and she couldn't help wondering just where her self-control was when she needed it.

\* \* \*

Rico entered his hotel room alone and tossed his keys on the desk. Never before had he mixed business with pleasure, but he was doing so now without much thought. He shook his head. No, that wasn't true, because he was giving it a lot of thought. And still none of it made much sense.

He was about to pull off his jacket when his phone rang. He pulled his cell out of his jeans pocket and frowned when he recognized the number. Jeff Claiborne. Couldn't the man understand plain English? He started to let the call go to voice mail but impulsively decided not to.

Rico clicked on the phone. "What part of *do not call me back* did you not understand?"

"I need your help, Ricardo."

Rico gritted his teeth. "My help? The last thing you'll get from me is my help."

"But if I don't get it, I could die. They've threatened to kill me."

Rico heard the desperation in his father's voice. "Who are they?"

"A guy I owe a gambling debt. Morris Cotton."

Rico released an expletive. His grandfather had told Rico a few years ago that he'd heard Jeff Claiborne was into some pretty shady stuff. "Sounds like you have a problem. And I give a damn, why? And please don't say because you're my father."

There was a pause. "Because I'm a human being who needs help."

Rico tilted his head back and stared up at the ceiling. "You say you're in trouble? Your life is threatened?"

"Yes."

"Then go to the police."

"Don't you understand? I can't go to the police. They will kill me unless…"

"Unless what?"

"I come up with one hundred thousand dollars."

Rico's blood boiled with rage. "And you thought you could call the son and daughter you hadn't talked to in close to eighteen years to bail you out? Trust me, there's no love lost here."

"You can't say I wasn't a good father!"

"You honestly think that I can't? You were an imposter, living two lives, and in the end an innocent woman took her life because of you."

"I didn't force her to take those pills."

Rico couldn't believe that even after all this time his father was still making excuses and refusing to take ownership of his actions. "Let me say this once again. You won't get a penny out of me, Jessica or Savannah. We don't owe you a penny. You need money, work for it."

"Work? How am I supposed to work for that much money?"

"You used to be a salesman, so I'm sure you'll think of something."

"I'll call your mother. I heard she remarried, and the man is loaded. Maybe she—"

"I wouldn't advise you to do that," Rico interrupted to warn him. "She's not the woman you made a fool of years ago."

"She was my only wife."

"Yes, but what about Jessica's mother and the lies you told to her? What about how she ended her life because of you?"

There was a pause and then… "I loved them both."

Not for the first time, Rico thought his father was truly pitiful. "No, you were greedy as hell and used them both. They were good women, and they suffered because of you."

There was another pause. "Think about helping me, Ricardo."

"There's nothing to think about. Don't call me back." Rico clicked off the phone and released a deep breath. He then called a friend who happened to be a high-ranking detective in the NYPD.

"Stuart Dunn."

"Stuart, this is Rico. I want you to check out something for me."

A short while later Rico had showered and re-dressed, putting on khakis instead of jeans and a Western-style shirt he had picked up during his first day in Forbes. He knew one surefire way to get information from shop owners was to be a buying customer. Most of the people he'd talked to in town had been too young to remember Clarice. But he had gone over to the *Forbes Daily Times* to do a little research, since the town hadn't yet digitally archived their oldest records.

Unfortunately, the day he'd gone to the paper's office, he'd been told he would have to get the permission of the paper's owner before he could view any documents from the year he wanted. He'd found that odd, but hadn't put up an argument. His mind had been too centered on heading to Austin to get Megan.

Now that he had her—and right next door—he could think of a number of things he wanted to do with her, and, as far as he was concerned, every one of them was fair game. But would acting on those things be a smart move? After all, she was cousin-in-law to his sisters. But he *had* warned her, not once but several times. However, just to clear his mind of any guilt, he would try rattling her to the point where she might decide to leave. He would give her one last chance.

And if that didn't work, he would have no regrets, no guilty conscience and no being a nice, keep-your-hands-to-yourself kind of guy. He would look forward to putting his hands—his mouth, tongue, whatever he desired—all over her. And he desired plenty. He would mix work with pleasure in a way it had never been done before.

Suddenly, his nostrils flared as he picked up her scent. Seconds later, there was a knock at his hotel room door. Amazing that he had actually smelled her through that hard oak. He'd discovered that Megan had an incredible scent that was exclusively hers.

He crossed the room and opened the door. There she was, looking so beautiful he felt the reaction in his groin. She had showered and changed clothes, as well. Now she was wearing a pair of jeans and a pullover sweater. She looked spectacular.

"I'm ready to go snooping."

He lifted a brow. "Snooping?"

"Yes, I'm anxious to find out about Raphel, and you mentioned you were going back to the town's newspaper office."

Yes, he had said that in way of conversation during their drive. He figured they had needed to switch their topic back to business or else he would have been tempted to pull to the side of the road and tear away at her mouth again.

"I'm ready," he said, stepping out into the hall and

closing his hotel room door behind him. "I thought you would be taking a nap while I checked out things myself."

"I'm too excited to rest. Besides, I slept a lot in the car. Now I'm raring to go."

He saw she was. Her eyes were bright, and he could see excitement written all over her face. "Just keep in mind that this is my investigation. If I come across something I think is of interest I might mention it or I might not."

She frowned up at him as they made their way toward the elevator. "Why wouldn't you share anything you find with me?"

Yes, why wouldn't he? There was still that article Martin Felder had come across. Rico had been barely able to read it from the scan Martin had found on the internet, but what he'd read had made Rico come to Forbes himself to check out things.

"That's just the way I work, Megan. Take it or leave it. I don't have to explain the way I operate to you as long as the results are what you paid me to get."

"I know, but—"

"No buts." He stopped walking, causing her to stop, as well. He placed a stern look on his face. "We either do things my way or you can stay here until I get back." He could tell by the fire that lit her eyes at that moment that he'd succeeded in rattling her.

She crossed her arms over her chest and tilted her head back to glare up at him. "Fine, but your final report better be good."

He bent slowly and brushed a kiss across her lips. "Haven't you figured out yet that everything about me is good?" he whispered huskily.

"Arrogant ass."

He chuckled as he continued brushing kisses across her lips. "Hmm, I like it when you have a foul mouth."

She angrily pushed him away. "I think I'll take the stairs."

He smiled. "And I think I'll take you. Later."

She stormed off toward the door that led to the stairwell. He stared after her. "You're really going to take the stairs?"

"Watch me." She threw the words over her shoulder.

"I am watching you, and I'm rather enjoying the sight of that cute backside of yours right now."

She turned and stalked back over to him. The indignant look on her face indicated he might have pushed her too far. She came to a stop right in front of him and placed her hands on her hips. "You think you're the only one who can do this?"

He intentionally looked innocent. "Do what?"

"Annoy the hell out of someone. Trust me, Rico. You don't want to be around me when I am truly annoyed."

He had a feeling that he really wouldn't. "Why are you getting annoyed about anything? I meant what I said about making love to you later."

She looked up at the ceiling and slowly counted to ten before returning her gaze back to him. "And you think that decision is all yours to make?"

"No, it will be ours. By the time I finish with you, you'll want it as much as I do. I guarantee it."

She shook her head, held up her hand and looked as if she was about to say something that would probably blister his ears. But she seemed to think better of wasting her time doing so, because she tightened her lips together and slowly backed up as if she was trying to retain her control. "I'll meet you downstairs." She'd all but snarled out the words.

He watched her leave, taking the stairs.

Rico rubbed his hand over his jaw. Megan had had a particular look in her eyes that set him on edge. She had every reason to be ticked off with him since he had intentionally pushed her buttons. And now he had a feeling she would make him pay.

*The nerve of the man,* Megan thought as she took the stairs down to the lobby. When she had decided to take this route she had forgotten that they were on the eighth floor. If she needed to blow off steam, this was certainly one way to do it.

Rico had deliberately been a jerk, and he had never acted that way before. If she didn't know better she would think it had been intentional. Her eyes narrowed suspiciously, and she suddenly slowed her pace. Had it been intentional? Did he assume that if he was rude to her she would pack up and go running back to Denver?

Well, if that's what he thought, she had news for him. It wouldn't happen. Now that she was here in Forbes, she intended to stay, and he would find out that two could play his game.

Not surprisingly, he was waiting for her in the lobby when she finally made it down. Deciding to have it out with him, here and now, she walked over and stared up at him. "I'm ready to take you on, Rico Claiborne."

He smiled. "Think you can?"

"I'm going to try." She continued to hold his gaze, refusing to back down. She felt the hot, explosive chemistry igniting between them and knew he felt it, too.

"I don't think you know what you're asking for, Megan."

Oh, she knew, and if the other night was a sample, she was ready to let loose and let her hair down again. "Trust me, I know."

His smile was replaced with a frown. "Fine. Let's go."

They were on their way out the revolving doors when his cell phone rang. They stopped and he checked his caller ID, hoping it wasn't Jeff Claiborne again, and answered it quickly when he saw it was Fanny Banks's granddaughter returning his call. Moments later, after ending the call, he said to Megan, "Change in plans. We'll go to the newspaper office later. That was Dorothy Banks, and her grandmother can see us now."

# Chapter 11

"Yes, may I help you?"

"Yes, I'm Rico Claiborne and this is Megan Westmoreland. You were expecting us."

The woman, who appeared to be in her early fifties, smiled. "Yes, I'm Dorothy Banks, the one you spoke to on the phone. Please come in."

Rico stepped aside to let Megan enter before him and followed her over the threshold, admiring the huge home. "Nice place you have here."

If the house wasn't a historical landmark of some sort then it should be. He figured it had to have been built in the early 1900s. The huge two-story Victorian sat on what appeared to be ten acres of land. The structure of the house included two huge columns, a wraparound porch with spindles, and leaded glass windows. More windows than he thought it needed, but if you were a person who liked seeing what was happening outside, then it would definitely work. The inside was just as impressive. The house seemed to have retained the original hardwood floors and inside walls. The furniture seemed to have been selected to complement the original era of the house. Because of all the windows, the room had a lot of light from the afternoon sunshine.

"You mentioned something about Ms. Westmoreland being a descendant of Raphel Westmoreland?" the woman asked.

"Yes. I'm helping her trace her family roots, and in our research, the name Clarice Riggins came up. The research indicated she was a close friend of Raphel. Since Ms. Banks was living in the area at the time, around the early nineteen hundreds, we thought that maybe we could question her to see if she recalls anyone by that name."

Dorothy smiled. "Well, I can tell you that, and the answer is yes. Clarice Riggins and my grandmother were childhood friends. Although Clarice died way before I was born, I remember Gramma Fanny speaking of her from time to time when she would share fond memories with us."

Megan had reached out and touched his hand. Rico could tell she had gotten excited at the thought that the Bankses knew something about Clarice.

"But my grandmother is the one you should talk to," Dorothy added.

"We would love to," Megan said excitedly. "Are you sure we won't be disturbing her?

The woman stood and waved her hand. "I'm positive. My grandmother likes talking about the past." She chuckled. "I've heard most of it more times than I can count. I think she would really appreciate a new set of ears. Excuse me while I go get her. She's sitting on the back porch. The highlight of her day is watching the sun go down."

"And you're sure we won't be disrupting her day?" Megan asked.

"I'm positive. Although I've heard the name Clarice, I don't recall hearing the name of Raphel Westmoreland before. Gramma Fanny will have to tell you if she has."

Megan turned enthusiastic eyes to Rico. "We might be finding out something at last."

"Possibly. But don't get your hopes up, okay?"

"Okay." She glanced around. "This is a nice place. Big and spacious. I bet it's the family home and has been around since the early nineteen hundreds."

"Those were my thoughts."

"It reminds me of our family home and—"

Megan stopped talking when Dorothy returned, walking with an older woman using a cane. Both Megan and Rico stood. Fanny Banks was old, but she didn't look a year past eighty. To think the woman had just celebrated her one-hundredth birthday was amazing.

Introductions were made. Megan thought she might have been mistaken, but she swore she'd seen a hint of distress in Fanny's gaze. Why? In an attempt to assure the woman, Megan took her hand and gently tightened her hold and said, "It's an honor to meet you. Happy belated birthday. I can't believe you're a hundred. You are beautiful, Mrs. Banks."

Happiness beamed in Fanny Banks's eyes. "Thank you. I understand you have questions for me. And call me Ms. Fanny. Mrs. Banks makes me feel old."

"All right," Megan said, laughing at the teasing. She

looked over at Rico and knew he would do a better job of explaining things than she would. The last thing she wanted was for him to think she was trying to take over his job.

They continued to stand until Dorothy got Ms. Fanny settled into an old rocking chair. Understandably, she moved at a slow pace.

"Okay, now what do you want to ask me about Clarice?" Ms. Fanny asked in a quiet tone.

"The person we really want information about is Raphel Westmoreland, who we believe was an acquaintance of Clarice's."

Megan saw that sudden flash of distress again, which let her know she hadn't imagined it earlier. Ms. Fanny nodded slowly as she looked over at Megan. "And Raphel Westmoreland was your grandfather?"

Megan shook her head. "No, he was my great-grandfather, and a few years ago we discovered he had a twin brother we hadn't known anything about."

She then told Ms. Fanny about the Denver Westmorelands and how they had lost Raphel's only two grandsons and their wives in a plane crash, leaving fifteen of them without parents. She then told Fanny how, a few years ago, they discovered Raphel had a twin named Reginald, and how they had begun a quest to determine if there were more Westmorelands they didn't know about, which had brought them here.

Ms. Fanny looked down at her feeble hands as if studying them...or trying to make up her mind about something. She then lifted her gaze and zeroed in on Megan with her old eyes. She then said, "I'm so sorry to find out about your loss. That must have been a difficult time for everyone."

She then looked down at her hands again. Moments later, she looked up and glanced back and forth between Rico and Megan. "The two of you are forcing me to break a promise I made several years ago, but I think you deserve to know the truth."

Nervous tension flowed through Megan. She glanced over at Rico, who gazed back at her before he turned his attention back to Ms. Fanny and asked, "And what truth is that?"

The woman looked over at her granddaughter, who only nodded for her to continue. She then looked at Megan. "The man your family knew as Raphel Westmoreland was an imposter. The real Raphel Westmoreland died in a fire."

Megan gasped. "No." And then she turned and collapsed in Rico's arms.

"Megan," Rico whispered softly as he stroked the side of her face with his fingertips. She'd fainted, and poor Ms. Fanny had become nervous that she'd done the wrong thing, while her granddaughter had rushed off to get a warm facecloth, which he was using to try to bring Megan back around.

He watched as she slowly opened her eyes and looked at him. He recognized what he saw in her gaze. A mixture of fear and confusion. "She's wrong, Rico. She has to be. There's no way my great-grandfather was not who he said he was."

Rico was tempted to ask why was she so certain but didn't want to upset her any more than she already was. "Then come on, sit up so we can listen to her tell the rest of it and see, shall we?"

Megan nodded and pulled herself up to find she was

still on the sofa. There was no doubt in her mind that both Ms. Fanny and Dorothy had heard what she'd just said. Manners prompted her to apologize. "I'm sorry, but what you said, Ms. Fanny, is overwhelming. My great-grandfather died before I was born so I never knew him, but all those who knew him said he was a good and honest person."

Ms. Fanny nodded. "I didn't say that he wasn't, dear. What I said is that he wasn't the real Raphel."

Tightening his hand on Megan's, Rico asked, "If he wasn't Raphel, then who was he?"

Ms. Fanny met Rico's gaze. "An ex-convict by the name of Stephen Mitchelson."

"An ex-convict!" Megan exclaimed, louder than she'd intended to.

"Yes."

Megan was confused. "B-but how? Why?"

It took Ms. Fanny a while before she answered then she said, "It's a long story."

"We have time to listen," Rico said, glancing over at Megan. He was beginning to worry about her. Finding out upsetting news like this was one of the reasons he hadn't wanted her here, yet he had gone and brought her anyway.

"According to Clarice, she met Raphel when she was visiting an aunt in Wyoming. He was a drifter moving from place to place. She told him about her home here and told him if he ever needed steady work to come here and her father would hire him to work on their ranch."

She paused a moment and then said, "While in Wyoming, she met another drifter who was an ex-con by the name of Stephen Mitchelson. She and Stephen became involved, and she became pregnant. But she knew her family would never accept him, and she thought she would never see him again."

Ms. Fanny took a sip of water from the glass her granddaughter handed her. "Only the man who showed up later, here in Texas, wasn't Raphel but Stephen. He told her Raphel had died in a fire. To get a fresh start, he was going to take Raphel's identity and start a new life elsewhere. And she let him go, without even telling him she was pregnant with his child. She loved him that much. She wanted to give him a new beginning."

Ms. Fanny was quiet for a moment. "I was there the day she made that decision. I was there when he drove away and never looked back. I was also there when she gave birth to their child. Alone."

The room was silent and then Megan spoke softly. "What happened to her and the baby?"

"She left here by train to go stay with extended family in Virginia. Her father couldn't accept she had a baby out of wedlock. But she never made it to her destination. The train she was riding on derailed, killing her and the baby."

"My God," Megan said, covering her hands with her face. "How awful," she said. A woman who had given up so much had suffered such a tragic ending.

She drew in a deep breath and wondered how on earth she was going to return home to Denver and tell her family that they weren't Westmorelands after all.

Several hours later, back in his hotel room, Rico sat on the love seat and watched as Megan paced the floor. After leaving the Bankses' house, they had gone to the local newspaper office, and the newspaper articles they'd read hadn't helped matters, nor had their visit to the courthouse. The newspapers had verified the train wreck and that Clarice and her child had been killed. There was also a mention of the fire in Wyoming and that several men had been burned beyond recognition.

There were a lot of unanswered questions zigzagging through Rico's mind but he pushed them aside to concentrate on Megan. At the moment, she was his main concern. He leaned forward and rested his arms on his thighs. "If you're trying to walk a hole in the floor, you're doing a good job of it."

She stopped, and when he saw the sheen of tears in her eyes, he was out of his seat in a flash. He was unsure of what he would say, but he knew he had to say something. "Hey, none of that," he whispered quietly, pulling her into his arms. "We're going to figure this out, Megan."

She shook her head and pushed away from him. "This is all my fault. In my eagerness to find out everything about Raphel, I may have caused the family more harm than good. You heard Fanny Banks. The man everyone thought was Raphel was some ex-convict named Stephen Mitchelson. What am I going home to say? We're not really Westmorelands, we're Mitchelsons?"

He could tell by the sound of her voice she was really torn up over what Fanny Banks had said. "But there might be more to what she said, Megan."

"But Fanny Banks was there, Rico," she countered. "I always said there was a lot about my great-grandfather that we didn't know. He went to his grave without telling anyone anything about having a twin brother or if he had family somewhere. Now I know why. He probably didn't know any of Raphel's history. He could never claim anyone. I don't know how the fourth

woman named Isabelle fits in, but I do know Raphel—
Stephen—finally settled down with my great-grandmother Gemma. From the diary she left behind, the one
that Dillon let me read, I know they had a good marriage, and she always said he was a kind-hearted man.
He certainly didn't sound like the kind who would have
been an ex-con. The only thing I ever heard about Raphel was that he was a kind, loving and honorable man."

"That still might be the case, Megan."

As if she hadn't heard him, she said, "I have to face
the possibility that the man my father and uncle idol-
ized, the man they thought was the best grandfather in
the entire world, was nothing but a convict who wasn't
Raphel Westmoreland and—"

"Shh, Megan," he whispered, breaking in and pulling her closer into his arms. "Until we find out everything, I don't want you getting upset or thinking the
worst. We'll go to the courthouse tomorrow and dig
around some more."

Sighing deeply, she pulled away from him, swiped at
more tears and tilted her head back to look up at him. "I
need to be alone for a while so I'm going to my room.
Thanks for the shoulder to cry on."

Rico shoved his hands into the pockets of his khakis. "What about dinner?"

"I'm not hungry. I'll order room service later."

"You sure?"

She shrugged. "Right now, Rico, I'm not sure about
anything. That's why I need to take a shower and relax."

He nodded. "Are you going to call Dillon or Ramsey
and tell them the latest developments?"

She shook her head. "Not yet. It's something I
wouldn't be able to tell them over the phone anyway."

She headed for the door. "Good night. I'll see you in the morning."

"Try to get some sleep," he called out to her. She nodded but kept walking and didn't look back. She opened the connecting door and then closed it behind her.

Rico rubbed his hand down his face, feeling frustration and anger all rolled into one. He glanced at his watch and pulled his cell phone out of his back pocket. A few moments later a voice came on the line. "Hello."

"This is Rico. A few things came up that I want you to check out." He spent the next twenty minutes bringing Martin up to date on what they'd found out from Fanny Banks.

"And you're actually questioning the honesty of a one-hundred-year-old woman?"

"Yes."

Martin moaned. "Ah, man, she's one hundred."

"I know."

"All right. In that case, I'll get on it right away. If the man was an imposter then I'll find out," Martin said. "But we are looking back during a time when people took on new identities all the time."

That's the last thing Rico wanted to hear.

After hanging up the phone he stared across the room at the door separating him from Megan. Deciding to do something with his time, before he opened the connecting door, he grabbed his jacket and left to get something to eat.

An hour later, Megan had showered, slipped into a pair of pajamas and was lounging across her bed when she heard the sound of Rico returning next door. When she'd knocked on the connecting door earlier and hadn't gotten a response, she figured he had gone to get something to eat. She had ordered room service and had wanted to know if he wanted to share since the hotel had brought her plenty.

Now she felt fed and relaxed and more in control of her emotions. And what she appreciated more than anything was that when she had needed him the most, Rico had been there. Even while in the basement of the newspaper office, going through microfilm of old newspapers and toiling over all those books to locate the information they wanted, he had been there, ready to give her a shoulder to cry on if she needed one. And when she had needed one, after everything had gotten too emotional for her, she'd taken him up on his offer.

He had been in his room for no more than ten minutes when she heard a soft knock on the connecting door. "Come in."

He slowly opened the door, and when he appeared in her room the force of his presence was so powerful she had to snatch her gaze away from his and train it back on the television screen.

"I was letting you know I had returned," he said.

"I heard you moving around," she said, her fingers tightening around the remote.

"You've had dinner?" he asked her.

From out of the corner of her eye, she could see him leaning in the doorway, nearly filling it completely. "Yes, and it was good."

"What did you have?"

"A grilled chicken salad. It was huge." *Just like you,* she thought and immediately felt the blush spread into her features.

"Why are you blushing?"

Did the man not miss anything? "No reason."

"Then why aren't you looking at me?"

Yes, why wasn't she looking at him? Forcing herself to look away from the television, she slid her eyes over to his and immediately their gazes clung. That was the moment she knew why it had been so easy to let her guard down around him, why it had been so effortless to lose her control and why, even now, she was filled with a deep longing and the kind of desire a woman had for the man she loved.

*She had fallen in love with Rico.*

A part of her trembled inside with that admission. She hadn't known something like this could happen this way, so quickly, completely and deeply. He had gotten to her in ways no other man had. Around him she had let go of her control and had been willing to let emotions flow. Her love hadn't allowed her to hold anything back. And when she had needed his strength, he'd given it. Unselfishly. He had an honorable and loyal spirit that had touched her in ways she'd never been touched before. Yes, she loved him, with every part of her being.

She sucked in a deep breath because she also knew that what she saw in his eyes was nothing more than pent-up sexual energy that needed to be released. And as she continued to watch him, his lips curved into a smile.

Now it was her time to ask all the questions. "Why are you smiling?"

"I don't think you want to know," he said, doing away with his Eastern accent and replacing it with a deep Texas drawl.

"Trust me, I do." Tonight she needed to think about something other than her grandfather's guilt or innocence, something other than how, in trying to find out about him, she might have exposed her family to the risk of losing everything.

"Since you really want to know," he said, straightening his stance and slowly coming toward her. "I was thinking of all the things I'd just love to do to you."

His words made her nipples harden into peaks, and she felt them press hard against her pajama top. "Why just think about it, Rico?"

He stopped at the edge of the bed. "Don't tempt me, Megan."

She tilted her head to gaze up at him. "And don't tempt me, Rico."

"What do you know about temptation?"

She became caught up by the deep, sensuous look in his eyes. In one instant, she felt the need to look away, and then, in another instant, she felt the need to be the object of his stare. She decided to answer him the best way she knew how. "I know it's something I've just recently been introduced to," she said, remembering the first time she'd felt this powerful attraction, at Micah's wedding.

"And I know just how strong it was the first time I saw you. Something new for me. Then I remember our first kiss, and how the temptation to explore more was the reason I hadn't wanted it to end," she whispered softly.

"But I really discovered what temptation was the night you used your mouth on me," she said, not believing they were having this sort of conversation or that she was actually saying these things. "I've never known that kind of pleasure before, or the kind of satisfaction I experienced when you were finished, and it tempted me to do some things to you, to touch you and taste you."

She saw the darkening of his eyes, and the very air became heated, sensuously so. He reached out, extending his hand to hers, and she took it. He gently pulled her up off the bed. The feel of the hard, masculine body pressed against hers, especially the outline of his arousal through his khakis, made her shiver with desire. When his hand began roaming all over her, she drew in a deep breath.

"I want to make love to you, Megan," he said, lowering his head to whisper in her ear. "I've never wanted a woman as much as I want you."

For some reason she believed him. Maybe it was because she wanted to believe. Or it could be that she wanted the feeling of being in his arms. The feeling of him inside her while making love. She wanted to be the woman who could satisfy him as much as he could satisfy her.

He tilted her chin up so their gazes could meet again. She was getting caught up in every sexy thing about him, even his chin, which looked like it needed a shave, and his hair, which seemed to have grown an inch and touched his shoulders. And then he leaned down and captured her mouth in one long, drugging kiss. Pleasure shot to all parts of her body, and her nerve endings were bombarded with all sorts of sensations while he feasted on her mouth like it was the last morsel he would ever taste.

At that moment, she knew what she wanted. She wanted to lose control in a way she'd never lost it before. She wanted to get downright wild with it.

She pulled back from the kiss and immediately went

for his shirt, nearly tearing off the buttons in her haste. "Easy, baby. What are you doing?"

"I need to touch you," she said softly.

"Then here, let me help," he said, easing his shirt from his shoulders. A breathless moan slipped from her throat. The man was so perfectly made she could feel her womb convulsing, clinching with a need she was beginning to understand.

Her hand went to his belt buckle and within seconds she had slid it out of the loops to toss it on the floor. On instinct, she practically licked her lips as she eased down his zipper. Never had she been this bold with a man, never this brazen. But something was driving her to touch him, to taste him, the same way he had done to her last night.

All she could register in her mind was that this scenario was one she had played out several times in her dreams. The only thing was, all the other times she would wake up. But this was reality at its best.

"Let me help you with this, as well," he whispered.

And then she watched as he eased his jeans and briefs down his legs and revealed an engorged erection. He was huge, and on instinct, her hand reached out and her fingers curled around the head. She heard how his breathing changed. How he was forcing air into his lungs.

When she began moving her fingers, getting to know this part of him, she felt rippling muscles on every inch of him. The thick length of his aroused shaft filled her hand and then some. This was definitely a fine work of art. Perfect in every way. Thick. Hard. With large veins running along the side.

"Do you have what you want?" he asked in a deep, husky tone.

"Almost." And that was the last word she spoke before easing down to her knees and taking him into her mouth.

A breathless groan escaped from between Rico's lips. He gripped the curls on Megan's head and threw his head back as her mouth did a number on him. He felt his muscles rippling as her tongue tortured him in ways he didn't know were possible. Her head, resting against his belly, shifted each time her mouth moved and sent pleasurable quivers all through him.

He felt his brain shutting down as she licked him from one end to the other, but before it did, he had to know something. "Who taught you this?"

The words were wrenched from his throat, and he had to breathe hard. She paused a moment to look up at him. "I'll tell you later."

She then returned to what she was doing, killing him softly and thoroughly. What was she trying to do? Lick him dry and swallow him whole? Damn, it felt like it. Every lick of her tongue was causing him to inhale, and every long powerful suck was forcing him to exhale. Over and over again. He felt on the edge of exploding, but forced himself not to. He wanted it to be just like in his dreams. He wanted to spill inside of her.

"Megan." He gently tugged on a section of her hair, while backing up to pull out of her mouth.

And before she could say anything, he had whipped her from her knees and placed her on the bed, while removing her pajama top and bottoms in the process. He wanted her, and he wanted her now.

Picking up his jeans off the floor, he retrieved a condom packet from his wallet and didn't waste any time while putting it on. He glanced at her, saw her watching and saw how her gaze roamed over his entire body. "Got another question for you, Megan, and you can't put off the answer until later. I need to know now."

She shifted her gaze from below his waist up to face. "All right. What's your question?"

"How is your energy level?"

She lifted a brow. "My energy level?"

"Yes."

"Why do you want to know?"

"Because," he said, slowly moving toward the bed. "I plan to make love to you all night."

# Chapter 12

*A*ll night?

Before Megan had time to digest Rico's proclamation, he had crawled on the bed with her and proceeded to pull her into his arms and seize her mouth. They needed to talk. There were other things he needed to know besides her energy level; things she wanted to tell him. She wanted to share with him what was in her heart but considering what they were sharing was only temporary, it wouldn't be a good idea. The last thing she wanted was for him to feel guilty about not reciprocating her feelings. And then there was the issue of her virginity. He didn't have a clue right now, but pretty soon he would, she thought as he slid his tongue between her lips.

His skin, pressed next to hers, felt warm, intoxicating, and he was kissing her with a passion and greed that surpassed anything she'd ever known. There was no time for talking. Just time to absorb this, take it all in and enjoy. A shiver ran through her when he released her mouth and lowered his head to aim for her breasts, sucking a nipple.

He really thought they could survive an all-nighter? she asked herself. No way. And when he reached down to slide his fingers between her legs and stroked her there, she moaned out his name. "Rico."

He paid her no mind, but continued to let his mouth lick her hardened nipple, while his hand massaged her clit, arousing her to the point where jolts of pleasure were running through her body.

She knew from his earlier question that he assumed she was experienced with this sort of thing. Little did he know she was as green as a cucumber. Again she thought, he needed to be told, but not now. Instead, she reached out to grip his shoulders as his fingers circled inside of her, teasing her mercilessly and spreading her scent in the air.

Then he leaned up, leaving her breasts. Grabbing a lock of her hair with his free hand, he tugged, pulling her face to his and kissing her hard on the mouth, sending her passion skyrocketing while shock waves of pleasure rammed through her.

He pulled his mouth from hers and whispered against her moist lips. "You're ready for me now. You're so wet I can't wait any longer," he said, nibbling on her earlobe and running his tongue around the rim of her ear, so close that she could feel his hot breath.

He moved to slide between her legs and straddle her thighs, looked down at her and whispered, "I'm going to make it good for you, baby. The best you've ever had."

She opened her mouth to tell him not only would it be the best, but that it would also be the first she ever had when his tongue again slid between her lips. That's when she felt him pressing hard against her, trying to make an entry into her.

"You're tight, baby. Relax," he whispered against her cheek as he reached down and grabbed his penis, guiding it into her. He let the head stroke back and forth along her folds. She started moaning and couldn't stop. "There, you're letting go. Now I can get inside you," he whispered huskily.

"It's not going to be easy," she whispered back.

He glanced down at her. "Why do you say that?" he asked as he continued to stroke her gently, sliding back and forth through her wetness.

Megan knew he deserved an answer. "I'm tight down there for a reason, Rico."

"What reason is that?"

"Because I've never made love with a man before."

His hand went still. "Are you saying—"

"Yes, that's what I'm saying. But I've never wanted any man before." *Never loved one before you,* she wanted to say, but didn't. "Don't let that stop you from making love to me tonight, Rico."

He leaned in and gently kissed her lips. "Nothing can stop me from making love to you, sweetheart. I couldn't stop making love to you tonight even if my life depended on it."

And then he was kissing her again, this time with a furor that had her trembling. Using his knees, he spread her legs wider, and she felt the soft fabric against her skin when he grabbed a pillow to ease under her backside. He pulled back from the kiss. "I wish I could tell you it's not going to hurt. But…"

"Don't worry about it. Just do it."

He looked down at her. "Just do it?"

"Yes, and please do it now. I can't wait any longer. I've waited twenty-seven years for this, Rico." *And for you.*

She looked dead center into his eyes. She felt the head of him right there at her mound. He reached out and gently stroked the side of her face and whispered, "I want to be looking at you when I go inside of you."

Their gazes locked. She felt the pressure of him entering her and then he grabbed her hips, whispered for her to hold on and pushed deeper with a powerful thrust.

"Rico!" she cried out, but he was there, lowering his head and taking her mouth while he pushed even farther inside her, not stopping until he was buried deep. And then, as if on instinct, her inner muscles began clenching him hard.

He threw his head back and released a guttural moan. "What are you doing to me?"

*He would ask her that.* "I don't know. It just feels right" was the only reply she could give him. In response, he kissed her again while his lower body began moving. Slowly at first, as if giving her body time to adjust. And then he changed the rhythm, while leaning down to suck on her tongue.

Megan thought she was going to go out of her mind. Never had she thought, assumed, believed—until now. He was moving at a vigorous pace, and she cried out, not in pain but in sensations so pleasurable they made her respond out loud.

Her insides quivered, and she went after his tongue

with speed and hunger. She cried out, screamed, just like she'd done that night at the south ridge. That only made him thrust harder and penetrate deeper. Then they both ignited in one hell of an explosion that sent sparks flying all through her body, and especially to the area where their bodies were joined.

He shook, she shook and the bed shook almost off the hinges as he continued to pound into her…making her first time a time she would always remember. It seemed as if it took forever for them to come down off their orgasmic high. When they did, he shifted his weight off hers and pulled her to him.

"We'll rest up a bit," he said silkily. "How do you feel?"

She knew her eyes were filled with wonderment at what they'd done. "I feel good." And she meant it.

Her heart was beating fast, and her pulse was off the charts. She had totally and completely lost control. But all that was fine because she had gotten the one thing she'd wanted. A piece of Rico Claiborne.

Rico pulled her closer to him, tucked her body into the curve of his while he stroked a finger across her cheek. He'd only left the bed to dispose of the condom and get another. Now he was back and needed the feel of her in his arms. She had slept for a while, but now she was awake and he had questions.

"I think it's time to tell me how someone who can work their mouth on a man the way you do has managed to remain a virgin. I can think of one possibility, but I want to hear it from you."

She smiled up at him. "What? That I prefer oral sex to the real thing?" She shook her head. "That's not it, and just to set the record straight, I've never gone down on a man until you."

He leaned back and lifted a brow. "Are you saying that—"

"Yes. What I did to you tonight was another first for me."

He chuckled. "Hell, you could have fooled me."

Excitement danced in her eyes. "Really? I was that good?"

"Yeah," he said, running a finger across her cheek again. "Baby, you were that good. So, if I was your first, how did you know what to do?"

She snuggled closer to him. "I was snooping over at Zane's place one day, looking for a pair of shoes I figured I'd left there, and came across this box under his bed. I was curious enough to look inside and discovered a bunch of DVDs marked with *X*s. So of course I had to see what was on them."

Rico chuckled again. "Is that the box he mentioned he would get from you after dinner the other night?"

She smiled. "No, that's another box altogether, a lock box. So he would know if I had tampered with it. Those videos were in a shoe box, and to this day I've never told Zane about it. I was only seventeen at the time, but I found watching them pretty darn fascinating. I was curious about how a woman could give a man pleasure that way, with her mouth."

"But not curious enough to try it on anyone until now?"

There was amusement in his voice, but to her it wasn't amusing, not even a little bit, because what he'd said was true. She hadn't had any desire to try it out on any other man but him. "Yes."

"I'm glad. I'm also surprised you've never been curious enough to sleep with anyone."

"I couldn't see myself sharing a bed with a man just for the sake of curiosity. Had I been in a serious relationship things might have been different, but most of my life has been filled with either going to school or working. I never had time for serious relationships. And the few times that a man wanted to make it serious, I just wasn't feeling it."

But she hadn't had a problem feeling him. She had wanted him. Had wanted to taste him the way he had tasted her. Had wanted to put her mouth on him the same way he'd put his on her. And she didn't regret doing so.

But nothing had prepared her for when he had shed his pants and briefs and shown his body to her. He was so magnificently made, with a masculine torso and rippling muscles. What had captured her attention more than anything else was the engorged erection he had revealed. Seeing it had aroused her senses and escalated her desires.

But for her, last night had been about more than just sex. She loved him. She wasn't certain just how she felt being in a one-sided love affair, but she wouldn't worry about it for now. She had let her hair down and was enjoying the situation tremendously. She had been in control of her emotions for so long, and she'd thought that was the best way to be, but now she was seeing a more positive side of being out of control. She knew what it felt like to be filled with a need that only one man could take care of. She knew how it felt to be wild.

And she wanted to experience more of it.

She pulled away from Rico and shifted her body to straddle his.

"Hey, what do you think you're doing?" he asked, trying to pull her back into his arms.

She shook her head. "Taking care of this," she whispered. "You said I can have control so I'm claiming ownership. You also told me you wanted me, and you told me what would happen if we were together. It did happen, and now I want to show you how much I want you."

"But you're sore."

She chuckled. "And I'll probably be sore for a long time. You aren't a small man, you know. But I can handle it, and I can handle you. I want to handle you, Rico, so let me."

He held her gaze, and the heat radiating between them filled the room with desire. His hands lifted and stroked her face, touched her lips that had covered his shaft, and she understood the degree of hunger reflected in his eyes. There was no fighting the intense passion they seemed to generate. No fighting it, and no excusing it.

"Then you are going to handle it, baby. You are the only woman who can," she heard him whisper.

Pleased by what he said, she lowered her head, and he snagged her mouth by nibbling at her lips, stroking them with his tongue. She gripped his shoulders, and his erection stood straight up, aimed right for her womanly core like it had a mind of its own and knew what it wanted.

The need to play around with his mouth drove her to allow his tongue inside her lips. And then she toyed with his tongue, sucked on it and explored every aspect of his mouth. The way his hand was digging into her scalp made her tongue lash out even more, and she felt him tremble beneath her. The thought that she could make him feel this way, give him this much pleasure, sent her blood rushing through her veins.

She eased the lower part of her body down but deliberately did it in a way that had his penis under her and not inside of her. Then she moved her thighs to grind herself against his pubic bone.

"Oh, hell." The words rushed from his lips, and she closed her eyes, liking the feel of giving him such an intimate massage. Moving back and forth, around in circular motions, christening his flesh with her feminine essence.

"I need you now, Megan. I can't take any more." His voice was filled with torment. Deciding to put him out of his misery, she leaned up and positioned her body so he could slide inside of her.

Megan shuddered when she felt the head of his shaft pierce through her wetness, pushing all the way until it could go no more. She held his gaze as she began to ride him. She'd always heard that she was good at riding a horse, and she figured riding a man couldn't be much different. So she rode him. Easing lower then easing back up, she repeated the steps until they became a sensual cycle. She heard his growl of pleasure, and the sound drove her to ride him hard.

Grabbing her hips, he lifted his own off the bed to push deeper inside of her. "Aw, hell, you feel so damn good, Megan." His shaft got even larger inside of her, burying deeper.

His words triggered a need within her, a need that was followed by satisfaction when her body exploded.

She screamed and continued coming apart until she felt his body explode, as well. Pleasure was ripping through her, making it hard to breathe. He was rock-solid, engorged, even after releasing inside of her. He wouldn't go down. It was as if he wasn't through with her yet.

He shifted their bodies, pulling her beneath him with her back to him. "Let me get inside you this way, baby. I want to ride you from behind."

Pulling in as much energy as she could, she eased up on all fours, and no sooner had she done so than she felt the head of his erection slide into her. And then he began moving, slowly at first, taking long, leisurely strokes. Each one sent bristles of pleasure brushing over her. But then he increased the rhythm and made the strokes deeper, harder, a lot more provocative as he rode her from the back. She moved her hips against him, felt his stomach on the cheeks of her backside while his hand caressed her breasts.

She glanced over her shoulder, their gazes connected, and she saw the heated look in his eyes. It fueled even more desire within her, making her moan and groan his name aloud.

"Rico."

"That sounds good, baby. Now I want to hear you say 'Ricardo.'"

As spasms of pleasure ripped through her, she whispered in a low, sultry voice. "Ricardo."

Hearing her say his birth name made something savage inside of Rico snap. He grabbed her hips as unadulterated pleasure rammed through him, making him ride her harder, his testicles beating against her backside. The sound of flesh against flesh echoed loudly through the room and mingled with their moans and groans.

And then it happened. The moment he felt her inner muscles clamp down on him, felt her come all over him, he exploded. He wouldn't be surprised if the damn condom didn't break from the load. But, at that moment, the only thing he wanted to do was fill her with his essence. Only her. No other woman.

He continued to shudder, locked tight inside of her. He threw his head back and let out a fierce, primal growl. The same sound a male animal made when he found his true mate. As pleasure continued to rip through him, he knew, without a shadow of a doubt, that he had found his.

He lowered his head and slipped his tongue inside her mouth, needing the connection as waves of pleasure continued to pound into him. It seemed to take forever before the last spasm left his body. But he couldn't move. Didn't want to. He just wanted to lie there and stay intimately connected to her.

But he knew being on all fours probably wasn't a comfortable position for her, so he eased their bodies down in a way that spooned his body against hers but kept him locked inside of her. He needed this moment of just lying with her, being inside of her while holding her in his arms.

She was so damn perfect. What they'd just shared had been so out-of-this-world right. He felt fulfilled in a way he had never felt before, in a way he hadn't thought he was capable of feeling.

"Anything else you think I ought to know?" he asked, wrapping his arms around her, liking the feel of her snuggled tightly to him.

"There is this thing about you using a condom."

"Mmm, what about it?"

"You can make it optional if you want. I take birth control injections, to stay regulated, so I'm good."

He had news for her. She was better than good. "Thanks for telling me."

"And I'm healthy so I'm safe that way, as well," she added.

"So am I," he assured her softly, gently rubbing her stomach, liking the knowledge that the next time they made love they could be skin-to-skin.

"Rico."

He looked down at her. She had tilted her head back to see him.

"Yes?"

"I like letting go with you. I like getting wild."

He lowered his head to brush a kiss across her lips. "And I like letting go and getting wild with you, too."

And he meant it in a way he wasn't ready to explain quite yet. Right now, he wanted to do the job she had hired him to do. He hadn't accepted everything Ms. Fanny and her daughter had said, although the newspapers and those documents somewhat supported their claims, especially the details of the fire and the train wreck. There was still a gut feeling that just wouldn't go away.

Something wasn't adding up, but he couldn't pinpoint what it was. He had been too concerned about the impact of their words on Megan to take the time to dissect everything. He hadn't been on top of his A-game, which is one of the reasons he hadn't wanted her here. He tended to focus more on her than on what he was supposed to be doing.

But now, as he replayed everything that had transpired over the past fourteen hours in his mind, a lot of questions were beginning to form. In the morning, he would talk to Megan over breakfast. Right now, he just wanted to hold her in his arms for a while, catch a little sleep and then make love to her again.

If he had thought he was addicted to her before, he knew he was even more so now.

## Chapter 13

"I think Fanny Banks's story isn't true."

Megan peered across the breakfast table at Rico. It took a few seconds for his words to fully sink in. "You do?"

"Yes. Someone is trying to hide something."

Serious doubt appeared in her gaze. "I don't know, Rico. What could they be trying to hide? Besides, we saw the articles in the newspapers, which substantiated what she said."

"Did they?"

Megan placed her fork down and leaned back in her chair. "Look, I admit I was upset by what I learned, and I wish more than anything that Fanny Banks might have gotten her information wrong or that at one hundred years old she couldn't possible remember anything. But her memory is still sharp."

"Too sharp."

Megan leaned forward, wondering why he suddenly had a doubtful attitude. "Okay, why the change of heart? You seemed ready to accept what she said."

"Yes, I was too ready. I was too quick to believe it because, like you, I thought it made sense, especially after reading those newspaper articles. But last night while you slept, I lay there and put things together in my mind and there's one thing that you and I can't deny that we didn't give much thought to."

She lifted a brow. "And what is that?"

"It's no coincidence that the Westmorelands of Atlanta and the Denver Westmorelands favor. And I don't mean a little bit. If you put them in a room with a hundred other people and asked someone to pick out family members, I'd bet ninety-eight percent of all the Westmorelands in the room would get grouped together."

Megan opened her mouth to say something and then decided there was nothing she could say because he was right. The first time the two groups had gotten together, and Dare Westmoreland—one of the Atlanta Westmorelands who was a sheriff in the metro area— had walked into the room, every member of the Denver Westmorelands' jaws had dropped. He and Dillon favored so much it was uncanny.

"And that level of similarity in looks can only come from the same genes," Rico added. "If push comes to shove, I'll have DNA testing done."

She picked up her fork. "You still haven't given me a reason for Ms. Banks to make up such a story."

Rico tossed down his napkin. "I don't have a reason, Megan, just a gut feeling."

He reached across the table and took her hand in

his. "I saw yesterday that what she said took a toll on you and that became my main concern. I got caught up in your hurt and pain. I felt it, and I didn't want that for you."

She understood what he meant. Last night, making love to him had been an eye opener. She had felt connected to him in a way she'd never been connected to a man. She was in tune to her emotions and a part of her felt in tune to his, as well. Their time together had been so special that even now the memories gave her pause. "If your theory is true, how do we prove it?" she asked him.

"We don't. We visit them again and ask questions we didn't ask yesterday when our minds were too numb to do so."

He gently tightened his hold on her hand. "I need you to trust me on this. Will you do that?"

She nodded. "Yes, I will trust you."

After making a call to the Banks ladies after breakfast, they discovered they would have to put their visit on hold for a while. Dorothy Banks's daughter advised them that her mother and great-grandmother weren't at home and had gone on a day trip to Brownwood and wouldn't be returning until that evening.

So Rico and Megan went back to their hotel. The moment they walked into the room he gently grabbed her wrist and tugged her to him. "You okay? How is the soreness?"

He found it odd to ask her that since he'd never asked a woman that question before. But then he couldn't recall ever being any woman's first.

She rested her palms on his chest and smiled up at

him. "My body is fine. Remember, I do own a horse that I ride every day, and I think that might have helped some." She paused and then asked, "What about you?"

He raised a brow. "Me?"

"Yes," she said, smiling. "I rode you pretty darn hard."

Yes, she had. The memory of her doing so made his erection thicken against her. "Yes, but making love with you was amazing," he said, already feeling the air crackling with sexual energy. "Simply incredible. I enjoyed it tremendously."

Her smile widened, as if she was pleased. "Did you?"

"Yes. I can't really put it into words."

She leaned closer and ran the tip of her tongue alongside his lips. Tempting him. Seducing him, slowly and deliberately. "Then show me, Rico. Show me how much you enjoyed it. Let's get wild again."

He was already moving into action, tugging off his shirt and bending down to remove his shoes and socks. She wanted wild, he would give her wild. Texas wild. Following his lead, she began stripping off her clothes. He lowered his jeans and briefs while watching her ease her own jeans down her thighs. He discovered last night that she wore the cutest panties. Colorful. Sexy. No thongs or bikinis. They were hip-huggers, and she had the shapely hips for them. They looked great on her. Even better off her.

He stood there totally nude while she eased her panties down. She was about to toss them aside when he said, "Give them to me."

She lifted a brow as she tossed them over to him. He caught them with one hand and then raised them to his nose. He inhaled her womanly scent. His erection throbbed and his mouth watered, making him groan.

He tossed her panties aside and looked at her, watching her nipples harden before his eyes.

He lowered his gaze to her sex. She kept things simple, natural. Some men liked bikini or Brazilian, but he preferred natural. She was beautiful there, her womanly core covered with dark curls.

His tongue felt thick in his mouth, and he knew where he wanted it to be. He moved across the room and dropped to his knees in front of her. Grabbing her thighs he rested his head against her stomach and inhaled before he began kissing around her belly button and along her inner and outer thighs. He tasted her skin, licking it all over and branding it as his. And then he came face-to-face with the core of her and saw her glistening folds. With the tip of his tongue, he began lapping her up.

She grabbed hold of his shoulders, dug her fingernails into the blades, but he didn't feel any pain. He felt only pleasure as he continued to feast on her. Savoring every inch of her.

"Rico."

He heard her whimper his name, but instead of letting up, he penetrated her with his tongue, tightened his hold on her hips and consumed her.

He liked having his tongue in her sex, tasting her honeyed juices, sucking her and pushing her into the kind of pleasure only he had ever given her. Only him.

"Rico!"

She called out his name a little more forcefully this time, and he knew why. She removed her hands from his shoulders to dig into his hair as she released another high-pitched scream that almost shook the room. If hotel security came to investigate, it would be all her fault.

Moments later, she finished off her orgasm with an intense moan and would have collapsed to the floor had he not been holding her thighs. He stood. "That was just an appetizer, baby. Now for the meal."

Picking her up in his arms he carried her to the bedroom, but instead of placing her on the bed, he grabbed one of the pillows and moved toward the huge chair. He sat and positioned her in his lap, facing him. Easing up he placed the pillows under his knees.

"Now, this is going to work nicely. You want wild, I'm about to give you wild," he whispered, adjusting her body so that she was straddling him with her legs raised all the way to his shoulders. He lifted her hips just enough so he could ease into her, liking the feel of being skin-to-skin with her. The wetness that welcomed him as he eased inside made him throb even more, and he knew he must be leaking already, mingling with her wetness.

"You feel so good," he said in a guttural tone. They were almost on eye level, and he saw the deep desire in the depths of her gaze. She moved, gyrating her hips in his lap. Her movement caused him to moan, and then he began moving, setting the rhythm, rocking in place, grasping her hips tightly to receive his upward thrusts. And she met his demands, tilting her hips and pushing forward to meet him.

He could feel heat building between them, sensations overtaking them so intensely that he rocked harder, faster. His thrusts were longer, deeper, even more intense as they worked the chair and each other.

He knew the moment she came. He felt it gush all around him, triggering his own orgasm. He shuddered uncontrollably, as his body did one hell of a blast inside of her. She stared into his face and the look in her eyes told him she had felt his hot release shooting inside of her. And he knew that was another new experience for her. The thought was arousing, and he could only groan raggedly. "Oh, baby, I love coming inside of you. It feels so good."

"You feel good," she countered. And then she was kissing him with a passion that was like nothing he'd ever experienced before. No woman had ever put this much into her kiss. It was raw, but there was something else, something he couldn't define at the moment. It was more than just tongues tangling and mating aggressively. There were emotions beneath their actions. He felt them in every part of his body.

He would have given it further thought if she hadn't moved her mouth away to scream out another orgasm. As she sobbed his name, he felt his body explode again, as well. He cried out her name over and over as he came, increasing the rocking of the chair until he was convinced it would collapse beneath them.

But it didn't. It held up. Probably better than they did, he thought, as they fought for air and the power to breathe again. Megan's head fell to his chest and he rubbed her back gently. Passion had his vision so blurred he could barely see. But he could feel, and what he was feeling went beyond satisfying his lust for her. It was much deeper than that. With her naked body connected so tightly to his, he knew why they had been so in tune with each other from the first. He understood why the attraction had been so powerful that he hadn't been able to sleep a single night since without dreaming of her.

He loved her.

There was no other way to explain what he was feeling, no other way to explain why spending the rest of his life without her was something he couldn't do. He pulled in a deep breath before kissing her shoulder blades. When he felt her shiver, his erection began hardening inside of her all over again.

She felt it and lifted her head to stare at him with languid eyes, raising both brows. "You're kidding, right? You've just got to be."

He smiled and combed his hands through the thick curls on her head. "You said you wanted wild," he murmured softly.

She smiled and wrapped her hands around his neck, touching her own legs, which were still on his shoulders. "I did say that, didn't I?" she purred, beginning to rotate her hips in his lap.

He eased out of the chair with their bodies still locked together. "Yes, and now I'm going to take you against the wall."

"Hey, you awake over there?" Rico asked when he came to a traffic light. He glanced across the truck seat at Megan. She lifted her head and sighed. Never had she felt so satiated in her life. For a minute, she'd thought he would have to carry her out of the hotel room and down to the truck.

They had made love a couple more times after the chair episode. First against the wall like he'd said, and then later, after their nap, they'd made out in the shower. Both times had indeed been wild, and such rewarding experiences. Now she was bone-tired. She knew she would have to perk up before they got to the Bankses' place.

"I'm awake, but barely."

"You wanted it wild," he reminded her.

She smiled drowsily. "Yes, and you definitely know how to deliver."

He chuckled. "Thanks. And that's Texas wild. Wait until I make love to you in Denver and show you Colorado wild."

She wondered if he realized what he'd insinuated. It sounded pretty much like he had every intention of continuing their affair. And since he didn't live in Denver did that mean he planned to come visit her at some point for pleasure rather than business?

Before she could ask him about what he'd said, his cell phone rang. After he checked the ID, Megan heard him let out a low curse. "I thought I told you not to call me."

"You didn't say you would sic the cops on me," Jeffery Claiborne accused.

"I didn't sic the cops on you. I wanted to check out your story. I have, and you lied. You need money for other things, and I'm not buying." He then clicked off the phone.

Megan had listened to the conversation. That was the second time he'd received a similar phone call in her presence. The thought that he was still connected to some woman in some way, even if he didn't want to be bothered, annoyed her. She tried pushing it from her mind and discovered she couldn't. A believer in speaking her mind, she said, "Evidently someone didn't understand your rule about not getting serious."

He glanced over at her. His gaze penetrated hers. "What are you talking about?"

"That call. That's the second time she's called while I was with you."

"She?"

"Yes, I assume it's a female," she said, knowing she really didn't have any right to assume anything.

He said nothing for a minute and then, "No, that wasn't a female. That was the man who used to be my father."

She turned around in her seat. "Your father?" she asked, confirming what he'd said.

"Yes. He's called several times trying to borrow money from me. He's even called Savannah. Claims his life is in jeopardy because he owes a gambling debt. But I found out differently. Seems he has a drug problem, and he was fired from his last job a few months ago because of it."

Now it was her time to pause. Then she said, "So what are you going to do?"

He raised his brow and looked over at her. "What am I going to do?"

"Yes."

"Nothing. That man hurt my mother and because of him Jess lost hers."

Megan swallowed tightly, telling herself it wasn't any of her business, but she couldn't help interfering. "But he's your father, Rico."

"And a piss-poor one at that. I could never understand why he wasn't around for all the times that were important to me while growing up. His excuse was always that as a traveling salesman he had to be away. It never dawned on me, until later, that he really wasn't contributing to the household since we were mostly living off my mother's trust fund."

He stopped at another traffic light and said, "It was only later that we found out why he spent so much time in California. He was living another life with another family. He's never apologized for the pain he caused all of us, and he places the blame on everyone but himself. So, as far as me doing anything for him, the answer is I don't plan on doing a single thing, and I meant what I just told him. I don't want him to call me."

Megan bit down on her lips to keep from saying anything else. It seemed his mind was pretty made up.

"Megan?"

She glanced over at him. "Yes?"

"I know family means a lot to you, and, believe it or not, it means a lot to me, too. But some things you learn to do without…especially if they are no good. Jeff Claiborne is bad news."

"Sounds like he needs help, like drug rehab or something."

"Yes, but it won't be my money paying for it."

His statement sounded final, and Megan had a problem with it. It was just her luck to fall in love with a man who had serious issues with his father. What had the man done to make Rico feel this way? Should she ask him about it? She immediately decided not to. She had enough brothers and male cousins to know when to butt out of their business…until it was a safe time to bring it back up again. And she would.

# Chapter 14

"Mr. Claiborne, Ms. Westmoreland," Dorothy said, reluctantly opening the door to let them in. "My daughter told me you called. We've told you everything, and I'm not sure it will be good on my grandmother to have to talk about it again."

Rico stared at her. "Just the other day you were saying you thought it would be good for her to talk about it."

"Yes, but that was before I saw what discussing it did to her," she said. "Please have a seat."

"Thanks," he said, and he and Megan sat down on the sofa. "If your grandmother isn't available then perhaps you won't mind answering a few questions for us."

"I really don't know anything other than what Gramma Fanny told me over the years," she said, taking the chair across from them. "But I'll try my best because my grandmother hasn't been herself since your visit. She had trouble sleeping last night and that's not like her. I guess breaking a vow to keep a promise is weighing heavily on her conscience."

For some reason Rico felt it went deeper than that. "Thanks for agreeing to talk to us." He and Megan had decided that he would be the one asking the questions. "Everybody says your grandmother's memory is sharp as a tack. Is there any reason she would intentionally get certain facts confused?"

The woman seemed taken back. "What are you trying to say, Mr. Claiborne?"

Rico sighed deeply. He hadn't told Megan everything yet, especially about the recent report he'd gotten from Martin while she'd been sleeping. "Stephen Mitchelson was not the one who survived that fire, and I'd like to know why your grandmother would want us to think that he was."

The woman look surprised. "I don't know, but you seem absolutely certain my grandmother was wrong."

He wasn't absolutely certain, but he was sure enough, thanks to the information Martin had dug up on Mitchelson, especially the man's prison photo, which looked nothing like the photographs of Raphel that the Westmorelands had hanging on their wall at the main house in Denver.

He knew Megan was just as surprised by his assertion as Ms. Banks's granddaughter. But there was that gut feeling that wouldn't go away. "It could be that Clarice lied to her about everything," he suggested, although he knew that probably wasn't the case.

"Possibly."

"But that isn't the case, and you know it, don't you, Mr. Claiborne?"

Rico turned when he heard Fanny Banks's frail voice. She was standing in the doorway with her cane.

"Gramma Fanny, I thought you were still sleeping," Dorothy said, rushing over to assist her grandmother.

"I heard the doorbell."

"Well, Mr. Claiborne and Ms. Westmoreland are back to ask you more questions. They think that perhaps you were confused about a few things," Dorothy said, leading her grandmother over to a chair.

"I wasn't confused," the older woman said, settling in her chair. "Just desperate, child."

Confusion settled on Dorothy's face. "I don't understand."

Fanny Banks didn't say anything for a minute. She then looked over at Rico and Megan. "I'm glad you came back. The other day, I thought it would be easier to tell another lie, but I'm tired of lying. I want to tell the truth…no matter who it hurts."

Rico nodded. "And what is the truth, Ms. Fanny?"

"That it was me and not Clarice who went to Wyoming that year and got pregnant. And Clarice, bless her soul, wanted to help me out of my predicament. She came up with this plan. Both she and I were single women, but she had a nice aunt in the East who wanted children, so we were going to pretend to go there for a visit for six months, and I would have the baby there and give my baby to her aunt and uncle. It was the perfect plan."

She paused for a minute. "But a few weeks before we were to leave, Raphel showed up to deliver the news that Stephen had died in a fire, and Raphel wanted me to have the belongings that Stephen left behind. While he was here, he saw Clarice. I could see that they were instantly attracted to each other."

Rico glanced over at Megan. They knew firsthand just how that instant-attraction stuff worked. "Please go on, Ms. Fanny."

"I panicked. I could see Clarice was starting something with Raphel, which could result in her changing our plans about going out East. Especially when Raphel was hired on by Clarice's father to do odds and ends around their place. And when she confided in me that she had fallen in love with Raphel, I knew I had to do something. So I told her that Raphel was really my Stephen, basically the same story I told the two of you. She believed it and was upset with me for not telling him about the baby and for allowing him to just walk away and start a new life elsewhere. She had no idea I'd lied. Not telling him what she knew, she convinced her father Raphel was not safe to have around their place. Her father fired him."

She paused and rubbed her feeble hands together nervously. "My selfishness cost my best friend her happiness with Raphel. He never understood why she began rebuffing his advances, or why she had him fired. The day we caught the train for Virginia is the day he left Forbes. Standing upstairs in my bedroom packing, we watched him get in his old truck and drive off. I denied my best friend the one happiness she could have had."

Rico drew in a deep breath when he saw the tears fall from the woman's eyes. "What about the baby? Did Clarice have a baby?"

Ms. Fanny nodded. "Yes. I didn't find out until we reached her aunt and uncle's place that Clarice had gotten pregnant."

Megan gasped. "From Raphel?"

"Yes. She thought she'd betrayed me and that we were having babies from the same man. Even then I never told her the truth. She believed her parents would accept her child out of wedlock and intended to keep it. She had returned to Texas after giving birth only to find out differently. Her parents didn't accept her, and she was returning to Virginia to make a life for her and her baby when the train derailed."

"So it's true, both her and the baby died," Megan said sadly.

"No."

"No?" Rico, Megan and Dorothy asked simultaneously.

"Clarice didn't die immediately, and her son was able to survive with minor cuts and bruises."

"Son?" Megan whispered softly.

"Yes, she'd given birth to a son, a child Raphel never knew about…because of me. The baby survived because Clarice used her body as a shield during the accident."

Fanny didn't say anything for a minute. "We got to the hospital before she died, and she told us about a woman she'd met on the train, a woman who had lost her baby a year earlier…and now the woman had lost her husband in the train wreck. He was killed immediately, although the woman was able to walk away with only a few scratches."

Dorothy passed her grandmother a tissue so she could wipe away her tears. Through those tears, she added, "Clarice, my best friend, who was always willing to make sacrifices for others, who knew she would not live to see the next day, made yet another sacrifice by giving her child to that woman." Ms. Fanny's aged voice trembled as she fought back more tears. "Because she believed my lie, she wasn't certain she could leave her baby with me to raise because I would be constantly reminded of his father's betrayal. And her aunt couldn't afford to take on another child after she'd taken on mine. So Clarice made sure she found her baby a good home before she died."

Megan wiped tears away from her own eyes, looked over at Rico and said softly, "So there might be more Westmorelands out there somewhere after all."

Rico nodded and took her hand and entwined their fingers. "Yes, and if there are, I'm sure they will be found."

Rico glanced back at Fanny, who was crying profusely, and he knew the woman had carried the guilt of what she'd done for years. Now, maybe she would be able to move on with what life she had left.

Standing, Rico extended his hand to Megan. "We have our answers, now it's time for us to go."

Megan nodded and then hugged the older woman. "Thanks for telling us the truth. I think it's time for you to forgive yourself, and my prayer is that you will."

Rico knew then that he loved Megan as deeply as any man could love a woman. Even now, through her own pain, she was able to forgive the woman who had betrayed not only her great-grandfather, but also the woman who'd given birth to his child…a child he hadn't known about.

Taking Megan's hand in his, he bid both Banks women goodbye and together he and Megan walked out the door.

Rico pulled Megan into his arms the moment the hotel room door closed behind them, taking her mouth with a hunger and greed she felt in every portion of his body. The kiss was long, deep and possessive. In response, she wrapped her arms around his neck and returned the kiss with just as much vigor as he was putting into it. Never had she been kissed with so much punch, so much vitality, want and need. She couldn't do anything but melt in his arms.

"I want you, Megan." He pulled back from the kiss to whisper across her lips, his hot breath making her shudder with need.

"And I want you, too," she whispered back, then outlined his lips with the tip of her tongue. She saw the flame that had ignited in his eyes, felt his hard erection pressed against her and knew this man who had captured her heart would have her love forever.

Megan wanted to forget about Ms. Fanny's deceit, her betrayal of Clarice, a woman who would have done anything for her. She didn't want to think about the child Clarice gave up before she died, the child her great-grandfather had never known about. And she didn't want to think of her great-grandfather and how confused he must have been when the woman he had fallen in love with—at first sight—had suddenly not wanted anything to do with him.

She felt herself being lifted up in Rico's arms and carried into the bedroom, where he placed her on the bed. He leaned down and kissed her again, and she couldn't help but moan deeply. When he released her mouth, she whispered, "Let's get wild again."

They reached for each other at the same time, tearing at each other's clothes as desire, as keen as it could get, rammed through her from every direction. They kissed intermittently while undressing, and when all their clothes lay scattered, Rico lifted her in his arms. Instinctively, she wrapped her legs around him. The thickness of him pressed against her, letting her know he was willing, ready and able, and she was eager for the feel of him inside of her.

He leaned forward and took her mouth again. His tongue tasted her as if he intended to savor her until the end of time.

He continued to kiss her, to stimulate her to sensual madness as he walked with her over to the sofa. Once there, he broke off the kiss and stood her up on the sofa, facing him. Sliding his hands between her legs, he spread her thighs wide.

"You still want wild, I'm going to give you wild," he whispered against her lips. "Squat a little for me, baby. I want to make sure I can slide inside you just right."

She bent her knees as he reached out and grabbed her hips. His arousal was hard, firm and aimed right at her, as if it knew just where it should go. To prove that point, his erection unerringly slid between her wet folds.

"Mercy," he said. He inched closer, and their pelvises fused. He leaned forward, drew in a deep breath and touched his forehead to hers. "Don't move," he murmured huskily, holding her hips as he continued to ease inside of her, going deep, feeling how her inner muscles clenched him, trying to pull everything out of him. "I wish our bodies could stay locked together like this forever," he whispered.

She chuckled softly, feeling how deeply inside of her he was, how closely they were connected. "Don't know how housekeeping is going to handle it when they come in our room tomorrow to clean and find us in this position."

She felt his forehead move when he chuckled. His feet were planted firmly on the floor, and she was standing on the sofa. But their bodies were joined in a way that had tingling sensations moving all over her naked skin.

He then pulled his forehead back to look at her. "Ready?"

She nodded. "Yes, I'm ready."

"Okay, then let's rock."

With his hands holding her hips and her arms holding firm to his shoulders, they began moving, rocking their bodies together to a rhythm they both understood. Her nipples felt hard as they caressed his chest, and the way he was stroking her insides made her groan out loud.

"Feel that?" he asked, hitting her at an angle that touched her G-spot and caused all kinds of extraordinary sensations to rip through her. She released a shuddering moan.

"Yes, I feel it."

"Mmm, what about this?" he asked, tilting her hips a little to stroke her from another angle.

"Oh, yes." More sensations cascaded through her.

"And now what about this?" He tightened his hold on her hips, widened her legs even more and began thrusting hard within her. She watched his features and saw how they contorted with pleasure. His eyes glistened with a need and hunger that she intended to satisfy.

As he continued to rock into her, she continued to rock with him. He penetrated her with long, deep strokes. His mouth was busy at her breasts, sucking the nipples into his mouth, nipping them between his teeth. And then he did something below—she wasn't sure what—but he touched something inside of her that made her release a deep scream. He immediately silenced her by covering her mouth with his, still thrusting inside of her and gripping her hips tight. This was definitely wild.

She felt him. Hot molten liquid shot inside of her, and she let out another scream as she was thrown into another intense orgasm. She closed her eyes as the explosion took its toll.

"Wrap your legs around me now, baby."

She did so, and he began walking them toward the bed, where they collapsed together. He pulled her into his arms and gazed down at her. "I love you," he whispered softly.

She sucked in a deep breath and reached out to cup his jaw in her hand. "And I love you, too. I think I fell in love with you the moment you looked at me at the wedding reception."

He chuckled, pulling her closer. "Same here. Besides wanting you extremely badly, another reason I didn't want you to come to Texas with me was because I knew how much finding out about Clarice and Raphel meant to you. I didn't want to disappoint you."

"You could never disappoint me, but you will have to admit that we make a good team."

Rico leaned down and kissed her lips. "We most certainly do. I think it's time to take the Rico and Megan show on the road, don't you?"

She lifted a brow. "On the road?"

"Yes, make it permanent." When she still had a confused look on her face, he smiled and said, "You know. Marriage. That's what two people do when they discover they love each other, right?"

Joy spread through Megan, and she fought back her tears. "Yes."

"So is that a yes, that you will marry me?"

"Did you ask?"

He untangled their limbs to ease off the bed to get down on his knees. He reached out for her hand. "Megan Westmoreland, will you be my wife so I can have the right to love you forever?"

"Can we get wild anytime we want?"

"Yes, anytime we want."

"Then yes, Ricardo Claiborne, I will marry you."

"We can set a date later, but I intend to put an engagement ring on your finger before leaving Texas."

"Oh, Rico. I love you."

"And I love you, too. I'm not perfect, Megan, but I'll always try to be the man you need." He eased back in bed with a huge masculine smile on his face. "We're going to have a good life together. And one day I believe those other Westmorelands will be found. It's just so sad Fanny Banks has lived with that guilt for so many years."

"Yes, and she wasn't planning on telling us the truth until we confronted her again. Why was that?" Megan asked.

"Who knows? Maybe she was prepared to take her secret to the grave. I only regret Raphel never knew about his child. And there's still that fourth woman linked to his name. Isabelle Connors."

"Once I get back to Denver and tell the family everything, I'm sure someone will be interested in finding out about Isabelle as well as finding out what happened to Clarice and Raphel's child."

"You're anxious to find out as well, right?"

"Yes. But I've learned to let go. Finding out if there are any more Westmorelands is still important to me, but it isn't the most important thing in my life anymore. You are."

Megan sighed as she snuggled more deeply into Rico's arms. She had gotten the answers she sought, but there were more pieces to the puzzle that needed to be found. And eventually they would be. At the moment, she didn't have to be the one to find them. She felt cherished and loved.

But there were a couple of things she needed to discuss with Rico. "Rico?"

"Yes, baby?"

"Where will we live? Philly or Denver?"

He reached out and caressed the side of her face gently. "Wherever you want to live. My home, my life is with you. Modern technology makes it possible for me to work from practically anywhere."

She nodded, knowing her home and life was with him as well and she would go wherever he was. "And do you want children?"

He chuckled. "Most certainly. I intend to be a good father."

She smiled. "You'll be the best. There are good fathers and there are some who could do better...who should have done better. But they are fathers nonetheless."

She pulled back and looked up at him. "Like your father. At some point you're going to have to find it in your heart to forgive him, Rico."

"And why do you figure that?" She could tell from the tone of his voice and the expression on his face that he definitely didn't think so.

"Because," she said, leaning close and brushing a kiss across his lips. "Your father is the only grandfather our children will have."

"Not true. My mother has remarried, and he's a good man."

She could tell Rico wanted to be stubborn. "I'm sure he is, so in that case our children will have two grandfathers. And you know how important family is to me, and to you, as well. No matter what, Jeff Claiborne deserves a second chance. Will you promise me that you'll give him one?"

He held her gaze. "I'll think about it."

She knew when not to push. "Good. Because it would make me very happy. And although I've never met your dad, I believe he can't be all bad."

Rico lifted a brow. "How do you figure that?"

"Because you're from his seed, and you, Rico, are all good. I am honored to be the woman you want as your wife."

She could tell her words touched him, and he pulled her back down to him and kissed her deeply, thoroughly and passionately. "Megan Westmoreland Claiborne," Rico said huskily, finally releasing her lips. "I like the sound of that."

She smiled up at him. "I like the sound of that, as well."

Then she kissed him, deciding it was time to get wild again.

*Two weeks later, New York*

Rico looked around at the less than desirable apartment complex, knowing the only reason he was here was for closure. He might as well get it over with. The door was opened on the third knock and there stood the one man Rico had grown up loving and admiring—until he'd learned the truth.

He saw his father study Rico's features until recognition set in. Rico was glad his father recognized him because he wasn't sure if he would have recognized his father if he'd passed the old man in the street. It was obvious that drugs and alcohol had taken their toll. Jeff looked ten years older than what Rico knew his age to be. And the man who'd always taken pride in how he looked and dressed appeared as if he was all but homeless.

"Ricardo. It's been a while."

Instead of answering, Rico walked past his father to stand in the middle of the small, cramped apartment. When his father closed the door behind him, Rico decided to get to the point of his visit.

He shoved his hands into his pockets and said, "I'm getting married in a few months to a wonderful woman who believes family is important. She also believes everyone should have the ability to forgive and give others a second chance."

Rico paused a moment and then added, "I talked to Jessica and Savannah and we're willing to do that…to help you. But you have to be willing to help yourself. Together, we're prepared to get you into rehab and pay all the expenses to get you straightened out. But that's as far as our help will go. You have to be willing to get off the drugs and the alcohol. Are you?"

Jeff Claiborne dropped down in a chair that looked like it had seen better days and held his head in his hands. "I know I made a mess of things with you, Jessica and Savannah. And I know how much I hurt your mom…and when I think of what I drove Janice to do…" He drew in a deep breath. "I know what I did, and I know you don't believe me, but I loved them both—in different ways. And I lost them both."

Rico really didn't want to hear all of that, at least not now. He believed a man could and should love only one woman, anything else was just being greedy and without morals. "Are you willing to get help?"

"Are the three of you able to forgive me?"

Rico didn't say anything for a long moment and then said, "I can't speak for Jessica and Savannah, but with me it'll take time."

Jeff nodded. "Is it time you're willing to put in?"

Rico thought long and hard about his father's question. "Only if you're willing to move forward and get yourself straightened out. Calling your children and begging for money to feed your drug habit is unacceptable. Just so you know, Jess and Savannah are married to good men. Chase and Durango are protective of their wives and won't hesitate to kick your ass—father or no father—if you attempt to hurt my sisters."

"I just want to be a part of their lives. I have grandkids I haven't seen," Jeff mumbled.

"And you won't be seeing them if you don't get yourself together. So back to my earlier question, are you willing to go to rehab to get straightened out?"

Jeff Claiborne stood slowly. "Yes, I'm willing."

Rico nodded as he recalled the man his father had been once and the pitiful man he had become. "I'll be back in two days. Be packed and ready to go."

"All right, son."

Rico tried not to cringe when his father referred to him

as "son," but the bottom line, which Megan had refused to let him deny, was that he was Jeff Claiborne's son.

Then the old man did something Rico didn't expect. He held his hand out. "I hope you'll be able to forgive me one day, Ricardo."

Rico paused a moment and then he took his father's hand, inhaling deeply. "I hope so, too."

# *Epilogue*

"Beautiful lady, may I have this dance?"

"Of course, handsome sir."

Rico led Megan out to the dance floor and pulled her into his arms. It was their engagement party, and she was filled with so much happiness being surrounded by family and friends. It seemed no one was surprised when they returned from Texas and announced they were engaged. Rico had taken her to a jeweler in Austin to pick out her engagement ring, a three-carat solitaire.

They had decided on a June wedding and were looking forward to the day they would become man and wife. This was the first of several engagement parties for them. Another was planned in Philly and would be given by Rico's grandparents. Megan had met them a few weeks ago, and they had welcomed her to the family. They thought it was time their only grandson decided to settle down.

He pulled her closer and dropped his arms past her waist as their bodies moved in sensual sync with the music. Rico leaned in and hummed the words to the song in her ear. There was no doubt in either of their minds that anyone seeing them could feel the heat between them…and the love.

Rico tightened his arms around her and gazed down at her. "Enjoying yourself?"

"Yes, what about you?"

He chuckled. "Yes." He glanced around. "There are a lot of people here tonight."

"And they are here to celebrate the beginning of our future." She looked over his shoulder and chuckled.

Rico lifted a brow. "What's so funny?"

"Riley. Earlier today, he and Canyon pulled straws to see who would be in charge of Blue Ridge Management's fortieth anniversary Christmas party this year, and I heard he got the short end and isn't happy about it. We have close to a thousand employees at the family's firm and making sure the holiday festivities are top-notch is important…and a lot of work. I guess he figures doing the project will somehow interfere with his playtime, if you know what I mean."

Rico laughed. "Yes, knowing Riley as I do, I have a good idea what you mean."

The music stopped, and Rico took her hand and led her out the French doors and onto the balcony. It was the first week in November, and it had already snowed twice. According to forecasters, it would be snowing again this weekend.

They had made Denver their primary home. However, they planned to make periodic trips to Philly to visit Rico's grandparents, mother and stepfather. They would make occasional trips to New York as well to check on Rico's father, who was still in rehab. Megan had met him and knew it would be a while before he recovered, but at least he was trying.

"You better have a good reason for bringing me out here," she said, shivering. "It's cold, and, as you can see, I'm not wearing much of anything."

He'd noticed. She had gorgeous legs and her dress showed them off. "I'll warm you."

He wrapped his arms around her, pulled her to him and kissed her deeply. He was right; he was warming her. Immediately, he had fired her blood. She melted a little with every stroke of his tongue, which stirred a hunger that could still astound her.

Rico slowly released her mouth and smiled down at her glistening lips. Megan was his key to happiness, and he intended to be hers. She was everything he could possibly want and then some. His goal in life was to make her happy. Always.

\* \* \* \* \*

We hope you enjoyed reading
**WILL OF STEEL**
by *New York Times* bestselling author
**DIANA PALMER**
and
**TEXAS WILD**
by *New York Times* bestselling author
**BRENDA JACKSON**

Both were originally **Harlequin® Desire** stories!

**Harlequin Desire** stories feature sexy, romantic heroes who have it all: wealth, status, incredible good looks… everything but the right woman. Add some secrets, maybe a scandal, and start turning pages!

**Powerful heroes…scandalous secrets…burning desires.**

Look for six *new* romances every month
from **Harlequin Desire!**

Available wherever books are sold.

NYTHRS0317

## SPECIAL EXCERPT FROM

*Their weekend in Milan led to a child, but after an accident, rich jeweler Jaeger Ballantyne can't remember any of it! Now Piper Mills is back in his life, asking for his help, and once again he can't resist her...*

Read on for a sneak peek at
*HIS EX'S WELL-KEPT SECRET,*
the first in Joss Wood's
**BALLANTYNE BILLIONAIRES** series!

She had to calm down.

She was going to see Jaeger again. Her onetime lover, the father of her child, the man she'd spent the past eighteen months fantasizing about. In Milan she hadn't been able to look at him without wanting to kiss him, without wanting to get naked with him as soon as humanly possible.

Jaeger, the same man who'd blocked her from his life.

She had to pull herself together! She was not a gauche girl about to meet her first crush. She had sapphires to sell, her house to save, a child to raise.

Piper turned when male voices drifted toward her, and she immediately recognized Jaeger's deep timbre. Her skin prickled and burned and her heart flew out of her chest.

"Miss Mills?"

His hair was slightly shorter, she noticed, his stubble a little heavier. His eyes were still the same arresting blue, but his shoulders seemed broader, his arms under the sleeves of the black oxford shirt more defined. A soft leather belt was threaded through the loops of black chinos.

HDEXP0317

The corner of his mouth tipped up, the same way it had the first time they'd met, and like before, the butterflies in her stomach crashed into one another. She couldn't, wouldn't throw herself into his arms and tell him that her mouth had missed his, that her body still craved his.

He held out his hand. "I'm Jaeger Ballantyne."

*Yes, I know. We did several things to each other that, when I remember Milan, still make me blush.*

What had she said in Italy? *When we meet again, we'll pretend we never saw each other naked.*

Was he really going to take her statement literally?

Jaeger shoved his hand into the pocket of his pants and rocked on his heels, his expression wary. "Okay, skipping the pleasantries. I understand you have some sapphires you'd like me to see?"

His words instantly reminded her of her mission. She'd spent one night with the Playboy of Park Avenue and he'd unknowingly given her the best gift of her life, but that wasn't why she was here. She needed him to buy the gems so she could keep her house.

Piper nodded. "Right. Yes, I have sapphires."

"I only deal in exceptional stones, Ms. Mills."

Piper reached into the side pocket of her tote bag and hauled out a knuckle-size cut sapphire. "This exceptional enough for you, Ballantyne?"

*Don't miss*
*HIS EX'S WELL KEPT SECRET by Joss Wood,*
*available April 2017 wherever*
*Harlequin® Desire books and ebooks are sold.*

*And follow the rest of the Ballantynes with*
*REUNITED…AND PREGNANT, available June 2017,*
*Linc's story, available August 2017,*
*and Sage's story, available January 2018.*

www.Harlequin.com

# HARLEQUIN™ *Desire*

### Powerful heroes…scandalous secrets…burning desires.

THE TEN-DAY
BABY TAKEOVER

KAREN BOOTH

## Save **$1.00**

### on the purchase of ANY Harlequin® Desire book.

Available wherever books are sold, including most bookstores, supermarkets, drugstores and discount stores.

---

# Save $1.00

### on the purchase of any Harlequin® Desire book.

Coupon valid until May 31, 2017.
Redeemable at participating outlets in the U.S. and Canada only.
Not redeemable at Barnes & Noble stores. Limit one coupon per customer.

52614659

**Canadian Retailers:** Harlequin Enterprises Limited will pay the face value of this coupon plus 10.25¢ if submitted by customer for this product only. Any other use constitutes fraud. Coupon is nonassignable. Void if taxed, prohibited or restricted by law. Consumer must pay any government taxes. Void if copied. Inmar Promotional Services ("IPS") customers submit coupons and proof of sales to Harlequin Enterprises Limited, P.O. Box 3000, Saint John, NB E2L 4L3, Canada. Non-IPS retailer—for reimbursement submit coupons and proof of sales directly to Harlequin Enterprises Limited, Retail Marketing Department, 225 Duncan Mill Rd., Don Mills, ON M3B 3K9, Canada.

5 65373 00076 2 (8100)0 12259

**U.S. Retailers:** Harlequin Enterprises Limited will pay the face value of this coupon plus 8¢ if submitted by customer for this product only. Any other use constitutes fraud. Coupon is nonassignable. Void if taxed, prohibited or restricted by law. Consumer must pay any government taxes. Void if copied. For reimbursement submit coupons and proof of sales directly to Harlequin Enterprises, Ltd 482, NCH Marketing Services, P.O. Box 880001, El Paso, TX 88588-0001, U.S.A. Cash value 1/100 cents.

® and ™ are trademarks owned and used by the trademark owner and/or its licensee.

© 2017 Harlequin Enterprises Limited

NYTCOUP0317R

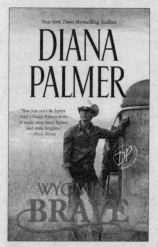